"I'm not going to kiss you."

Bud would kill him. Yes, think about that. A slow and painful death, not her full, soft lips. *Damnit.*

"Oh, you are going to kiss me." She walked right up to him and stood on tiptoe with her body pressed to his. His hands remained at his sides, wrapped around the edge of the desk. She ran her hands up his arms to his shoulders. "Kiss me, Blake. I want you to."

The devil inside him leaped. He cupped her face in his hands and stared down into her beautiful hazel eyes. *Be gentle. Give her that much.* "I've wanted to do this since the moment I saw you."

His lips touched hers, soft, tender. Just that one light meeting of lips and mingling of breath and she wanted more. More than she'd ever wanted for herself. For the first time in her life, she wanted to love this man and be loved by him. She had a thousand dreams run through her mind, and all of them were filled with Blake.

By Jennifer Ryan

WHEN IT'S RIGHT
AT WOLF RANCH
DYLAN'S REDEMPTION
FALLING FOR OWEN
THE RETURN OF BRODY MCBRIDE
CHASING MORGAN
THE RIGHT BRIDE
LUCKY LIKE US
SAVED BY THE RANCHER

Short Stories
CAN'T WAIT
(appears in ALL I WANT FOR CHRISTMAS IS A COWBOY)
WAITING FOR YOU
(appears in CONFESSIONS OF A SECRET ADMIRER)

WHEN
IT'S
RIGHT

A MONTANA MEN NOVEL

JENNIFER RYAN

AVONBOOKS

An Imprint of HarperCollinsPublishers

AVON BOOKS
An Imprint of HarperCollins*Publishers*
195 Broadway
New York, New York 10007

Copyright © 2015 by Jennifer Ryan
Excerpt from *Her Lucky Cowboy* copyright © 2015 by Jennifer Ryan
ISBN 978-0-06-233493-0
www.avonromance.com

First Avon Books mass market printing: April 2015

Avon Trademark Reg. U.S. Pat. Off. and in Other Countries, Marca Registrada, Hecho en U.S.A.
HarperCollins® is a registered trademark of HarperCollins Publishers.

Printed in the U.S.A.

10 9 8 7 6 5 4 3

For my mom. I love you.

For Aunt Jean, who loves her boys, including her very own Justin. Thank you for all your love and support.

For all the mothers out there, loving and caring for the children in your lives, whether they are yours or not.

WHEN

IT'S

RIGHT

CHAPTER 1

San Francisco, California

"**H**elp me!"

Home late from her shift washing dishes at the Jade Palace, Gillian pounded up the two flights of stairs as fast as her legs allowed. She hit the landing and turned right, racing down the hallway past her apartment's open door to Mrs. Wicks's unit at the end of the hall. She'd heard the screams from outside. Not the first time she'd answered that call, but so help her God, if her father touched one hair on Justin's head, she'd kill him.

"I'm calling the police," the babysitter, Mrs. Wicks, threatened loud enough for her voice to carry down the hall.

"Damnit, woman, he's my blood," Gillian's father bellowed.

Gillian rushed into the apartment and spotted Justin with his arm cradled in his hand and pressed to his chest, tears shimmering in his eyes but otherwise appearing unharmed. She looked her father up and down, assessing the situation in a glance and the odds on talking him down from whatever ludicrous idea had taken root in his shadowed mind. Dressed in the same clothes he'd left in four days ago, his hair an oily mass hanging lank to his shoulders, he reeked of whiskey, cigarette and pot smoke, and acrid body odor. The wild look in his bloodshot eyes told her he hadn't slept in a good long while. Riding a meth high, he'd probably binged for days. Soon he'd lose all sense of reality and need more of the drug, which wouldn't give him the high he needed, since he'd overloaded his system. He'd crash, his body shutting down and putting him into a deep sleep for a day, or two, or three before he woke up miserable, needing more of what put him in this psychotic state in the first place.

Frustrated and angry, but resigned to this same worn-out routine, she shored up her resolve to get through this night, like she'd done too many times in the past, trapped raising a child with little money and even fewer choices. None of them good.

Her father paced, his movements jerky. He scratched at his arm, his legs, the back of his neck with his grime-filled nails. He slapped at his thigh, then bit at the tips of his fingers. A hint at how far he'd fallen down the rabbit hole. Not good.

"Dad, come on. Let's go home. I'll make you something to eat," she coaxed, keeping her voice calm.

A powder keg of roiling rage, he could blow any second. You never knew what would set him off.

Justin cowered in the corner of the couch, his eyes wide and watchful. He didn't move, afraid of drawing her father's attention. Even at six, he knew the rules of this twisted game.

Mrs. Wicks moved into the kitchen, leaving Gillian to handle getting her father out of there and back to their place. She'd done it before. Usually, he'd come looking for her, but she'd been held up at work, and he'd found little Justin alone. Gillian never left Justin with him if she could help it, especially over the last year, when her father spent more time strung out and paranoid on meth than comfortably numb with booze and pot, like he'd been every day of her life.

The last two weeks had been hell. Gillian's patience had worn thin days ago. If she could hold on, get her father out of Mrs. Wicks's apartment and into theirs, she could take Justin and crash somewhere else for a few days until her father came down and leveled off.

Then, joy, they could start this whole thing over again.

I wish Justin and I were anywhere else.

Inside, the pressure built. How good it would feel to open her mouth and unleash a string of curses, insults, and blame for what her father put her and Justin through day in and day out. She hated him for spending his life drowning in a bottle and doing drugs, his life going up in smoke. Her life went up with it. Justin's too. She wanted it to end. One way or another, just end.

Her father swatted at some imaginary bird, or butterfly, or dragon for all she knew. Only he saw the tormenting hallucinations. If he was this far gone, he was even more volatile and dangerous than usual.

"Dad, come on. I'll make you a burger and get you a beer."

"We have to go." His words came out rushed. He swatted at the air again, this time spinning around to the right before he stopped and turned the other way again, tracking his imaginary flying devils, waving his arms over his head to swat them away.

She shook her head, frustrated and tired of dealing with him. This. Everything. She wanted to run away, but where would she go? It was all she could do now to keep a roof over Justin's head and food in his belly with the diminishing help her father supplied. Out on the streets, or in a shelter, they'd be vulnerable to even more horrors. What kind of life would that be for Justin? Better than this one? Maybe. Maybe not. Still, she needed to find a way to give Justin better than she'd had growing up with a volatile drunk who could barely keep a bartending job and supplemented his income selling drugs to support his own habits.

"We have to go. We have to go. We have to go," her father chanted, getting agitated, hitting the side of his head with one hand and scratching at his leg and the imaginary bugs crawling under his skin with the other.

Fed up, she stepped toward him to grab his arm and lead him back to their place. He jumped out of her reach and laughed. The sound held no humor but a touch of hysteria in the odd shriek. Her father pointed at her, shaking his head side to side. "No. No. No. No. No." Again, his ominous giggle sent a chill up her spine.

Her father grabbed Justin's arm and yanked him off the couch. She stood her ground in front of him. No way her father left here with Justin.

"Let him go. He needs to finish his homework." She made up the excuse, hoping her father released Justin and she got the boy out of there.

"He's mine. He'll keep them away. He's got the light that turns them away."

Paranoid, delusional asshole.

She sighed, knowing just where this was going and not liking it one bit. Soon her father would spiral into a psychotic delusion no one could talk him out of.

Please, just pass out already.

Not that lucky, she tensed and waited to see what came next. Her father pulled Justin in front of him, held him by both arms, and turned him this way and that, a shield against an enemy only he could see.

"Ow!" Justin cried out when her father's fingers dug into his thin arms.

"Keep them back." Her father tugged on Justin again. Hurt and scared, Justin planted his feet and pulled away, trying to get free. Her father held tighter and spun Justin around to face him. When Justin fell to the floor, tears spilling from his eyes, Gillian couldn't take the ache in her heart. Her anger exploded.

"Keep them back." Her father shook Justin again.

Gillian lost it. "I warned you, if you ever touched him . . ." She lunged for her father, striking him in the arm, breaking his hold on Justin. She shoved her father two steps back, and Justin ran for Mrs. Wicks in the kitchen. She rattled off the building address to the police on the phone. Not the first time someone called the cops on Gillian's father, and it probably wouldn't be the last. No way they got here in time to stop him now. Whatever happened next, Gillian would sure as hell make sure her father never got anywhere near Justin again.

Her father came after her in a drug-hazed rage that gave him strength and sent him into a mindless attack. All other thoughts disappeared behind the fury filling his mind. Her father only knew how to hurt. She'd been through this too many times to count and braced for the impact when his fist came at her, straight into her eye. Pain exploded in her head. She shoved him in the chest, but he came back with a slap to her jaw that stung something fierce. She kicked him in the shin and shoved him again. He fell back two steps, his hand coming up from behind his back. Momentarily stunned, she didn't move, but stared down the gun's black barrel in disbelief that he'd actually pulled a weapon on her. She didn't know where he'd gotten it, only that this added a whole other level to what had seemed like just another rotten night in her life.

Her father held the gun steady, even when he swatted the imaginary devils pestering him. His eyes narrowed on her, and in that moment she joined him in the madness she saw swirling in his gaze.

You or me?

One of them wasn't leaving that room alive.

Justin needs me.

You.

She rushed him, grabbed the gun, and spun her back into his chest, the gun in both their hands pointed to the window. He tried to wrench it free, punching her in the ribs with his free hand. She jerked on the gun again and again and scratched his hand to get him to release it, until he finally let go and the gun thumped onto the floor and skittered across the scarred hardwood. He shoved her from behind. She stumbled forward, scooped the gun off the floor, and turned to face him.

Never turn your back on a psycho.

He leaned forward and charged her like a wounded beast, murder in his eyes and a guttural yell that made the hairs on the back of her neck stand on end.

She swung the gun up and fired. Once. Twice.

Mrs. Wicks screamed.

Blood bloomed on his chest. Still he kept coming. His hands fisted in her T-shirt. He lifted her off her feet and shoved her backward into the window. Her back and head hit the glass with a crack a split second before it shattered. Glass tore and bit into her skin, but she didn't feel the pain past the one thought in her head. *It's done.*

Justin screamed, "Gillian, no!"

I'm sorry.

She flew through the window.

Her father's dark form stood in the opening, highlighted by the lights behind him. He literally dropped to the floor out of her sight.

Be safe, Justin. Be happy.

Her body slammed into the roof of a car with a sickening thud. Everything went black.

CHAPTER 2

Three Peaks Ranch, Montana

Blake Bowden tossed a flake of mixed grass into Bingo's feed holder. He pet the Thoroughbred on the neck and walked out of the stall.

Dee rushed down the aisle, ignoring the horses sticking their heads out to greet her. Her brow creased into worry lines. She kept her steady gaze locked on him. "You have to do something. I've never seen him like this. He's on his third shot of whiskey."

Blake caught the urgent tone, and his insides knotted with tension. Something terrible must have happened to get his old friend drinking the hard stuff. The man barely had more than a beer or two in a given week.

"He's in his office. He won't speak to me." Dee's eyes filled with fear and worry. She twisted the dish towel in her hands. Blake had never seen her this out of sorts.

He touched his hand to hers to reassure her. "Okay now, I'll go up and see what I can do."

Blake rushed up to the house, Dee hot on his trail. She stopped in the living room and held her hand out to indicate her husband, sitting in his study, his head bowed. Blake walked in and stood in front of Bud's desk. Bud didn't look up but continued to stare at the newspaper. A bottle of whiskey sat on the desk by his elbow, next to a half-filled tumbler. The desolate vibes coming off him filled the room and nearly stole Blake's breath. He'd known Bud since he was a kid, long before Bud made him a partner in Three Peaks Ranch. He'd never seen the man this miserable in his life.

"Bud, what happened?"

Several long moments passed, but finally Bud's gruff voice broke the eerie silence. "He's dead."

"Who?"

"Ron."

Dee gasped behind Blake. He turned and met her watery gaze. Her hand pressed to her open mouth.

Blake knew all about Ron, the man who convinced Bud's only daughter to run off with him when she was just eighteen. Wild and unruly, they spent years moving from town to town, from one dead-end job to the next, drinking and doing drugs. Bud lost track of them years ago, until one day he received a letter from the coroner's office asking him to claim his daughter's body. Bud hadn't caught up to her, but the drugs had. By the time Bud picked up Erin's ashes, Ron had split town with their daughter. No forwarding address as usual.

"What happened?" Blake figured he'd finally up and died from an overdose.

"She shot him."

"What? Who?"

"My granddaughter. Gillian. Twice. In the chest."

"Back up. How did you find out? Did she contact you?"

Bud shook his head, but he never took his eyes off the paper. "I had some time to kill at the airport in Denver, so I went into the bar and ordered a beer and a burger, thinking I'd pass the time before my flight watching a ball game on TV. Guy sitting next to me

swore and said, 'Some people deserve to get shot.' "
Bud smoothed his hand over the paper and the photo
Blake couldn't really see. "He got up and left, but didn't
take the paper. I slid it over to see what he'd been talking about." Bud sucked in a deep breath and traced his
finger over the photo.

Blake stepped closer to the desk. Bud spun the *San
Francisco Chronicle* and scooted it toward Blake. The
photo showed firefighters and police kneeling on top of
a car, helping someone who'd obviously fallen onto the
roof. Blake read the caption under the photo. " 'After an
altercation with her father, Gillian Tucker was thrown
through a second-story window. She survived. Her
father, Ron, died at the scene from gunshot wounds to
the chest.' "

Fate's a tricky beast.

It could bring you something you most desired or
dump you on your ass. Bud had been handed his ass
on a platter.

The picture was black and white, an up close view
of the gruesome scene. The only part of Gillian Blake
she could see was her feet. She'd been wearing a pair
of well-worn canvas shoes with a hole near the toe. Two
firemen, paramedics, and a police officer blocked the
rest of her, swallowed by the now-concave roof. Blake
couldn't take his eyes off her tiny feet hanging from the
top of the car.

The image transposed with the nightmare in his
mind of another woman's feet tangled in the limbs of a
felled tree. But that was the past. Maybe the confusion
in his mind between the past and the present explained
his surging need to help that poor girl. Not that it would
make up for what he'd done.

Bud's voice rang out like a gunshot exploding into

the silent room. He spoke in his normal tone, but the room, the house, seemed so empty, as empty as the man sitting behind the desk. "I called the San Francisco Police Department. I wanted to be sure it was him. I had to be sure it was her. She shot him after he beat her. She fired twice into his chest. Completely out of his mind on drugs, he still had the strength to grab her and shove her through the window before he died."

"Did they arrest and charge her with murder?"

Bud took a sip of the whiskey and continued to stare into nothing. "They're still investigating, but it looks like a clear case of self-defense. The neighbors in the building confirmed this wasn't the first time he'd hit her."

Bud downed the last of his drink. "I changed my flight and went to San Francisco last night. She refused to see me. I never even got a look at her. I tried again this morning, but she didn't change her mind. The doctor said she needed her rest. She'd be there several more days, so I came home. What the hell could I do?" He slammed his fist on the desk. "He nearly killed her."

"What did the doctor say?"

"Nothing specific. Her injuries are extensive, but she'll survive. I wonder, Blake—how much has she survived already that she had to shoot her own father to stop him from killing her?"

Blake wondered the same thing. "The point is, Bud, she did survive. What are you going to do now?"

"Anything I have to in order to get her here. Since she refused to talk to me, the doctor will speak to her on my behalf. I'm waiting for him to call me back." Bud fell silent again, staring at the wall, waiting for the phone to ring.

Blake eventually left to find Dee in the kitchen. She turned the pieces of fried chicken in a cast-iron skillet. Cooking to cope. She and Bud married long after Erin left with Ron and several years after Bud's first wife passed. Dee's sympathy was for Bud, not the man who spent the last years making Bud's life a misery of worry, regret, and hope that one day the guy would clean up his act and bring his granddaughter home. "How long's it been since Bud heard from Ron?"

"Years. He hasn't seen Gillian since she was a toddler. Since I married Bud, long before then, actually, Ron's never called or come back to town." Dee set the metal tongs on the counter and turned to face him. "He blames himself."

"Bud had nothing to do with this. Erin and Ron made their choices."

"Yes, and that poor girl paid the price." Sadness infused Dee's words and filled her eyes with concern.

"We don't know everything that happened. The article is very brief. Yes, he hit her, and she shot him, but beyond that we don't know anything about what her life with him has been like," Blake pointed out.

"Bud tried to find her years ago now. He never felt right leaving her with Ron. What if she doesn't want to come? What if he never gets a chance to make this right?"

"She shot her father. Maybe she needs time to recover and come to terms with what she's done."

"Do you think she did it on purpose?" Dee's eyes filled with worry and uncertainty.

"If someone hit me in the past and hit me again, and I had a gun in my hand, I'd sure as hell shoot the bastard." The anger roiled in Blake's gut for the man who pushed his daughter too far.

Dee pressed her lips together and nodded, silently agreeing with him.

Blake didn't feel bad for speaking his mind. Ron turned out to be the worst sort of man. You do not hit girls. You certainly never beat your child. The drugs had warped Ron's mind, or maybe he was just rotten to the core. Either way, Blake hated him for treating Gillian so poorly.

"Well, I guess we'll get the whole story when she gets here."

Blake headed back out to the stables and his beloved horses, haunted by thoughts of the woman with the tiny feet lying atop the car's smashed roof. He hoped she was okay, because he knew after a fall, whether from a window or a horse, everything changes.

CHAPTER 3

Gillian shifted in the bed, trying to get comfortable. Nothing worked. Everything ached, from her pounding head to her throbbing ankles. She could barely move, with her leg in a brace, one arm in a cast, the other wrapped in a bandage, and nearly her entire back and part of her head stitched. No high-tech safety glass in her eighty-year-old building. The brittle window broke into sharp pieces and sliced her to ribbons.

Last night, she'd stood in the bathroom with her back to the mirror and tried to count how many cuts crisscrossed her back. She'd closed her eyes, unable to bear the sight of all those cuts sewn together over the hours the doctors had worked on her. The overwhelming fear she'd felt the night she'd shot her father choked her. She tried to breathe but ended up hyperventilating. She'd never had a panic attack, but she imagined that's what it felt like.

This morning, she surfed the channels, trying to find something to distract her from the fact that Justin had been placed in protective custody with CPS. Damnit, she needed to get him out of that foster home and back in her arms.

Too much time to sit and think in this hospital bed. Her mind conjured those final moments with her father. The gruesome cycle of one snapshot after another played nonstop in her mind, like one of those View-Master toys that came with a disc of pictures that told a story. His fist inches from her face, right before he punched her. Her father pointing the gun at her. The flash and smoke exploding from the gun barrel when she shot her father. The blood in full bloom on his chest. His face contorted when he rushed her and pushed her out the window. His ominous black figure standing in the window as she fell.

"Gillian." The doctor said her name like he'd already tried to get her attention.

"What? Yes."

"How are you feeling today?" he asked, full of false cheer.

"Fine."

He frowned. She said the same thing every time he asked. He'd tried to get her to open up about what happened, the days, weeks, and years leading up to the shooting. She'd given him the gist of life with her father. Moving from one place to the next. Scrounging for money to pay the rent and buy food. Living on just this side of starvation and homelessness when she was too young to understand that others had a place to call home all the time and a refrigerator full of food that didn't come from a drive-thru or discount store.

She knew that life, and she'd tried so hard to make sure she and Justin didn't end up on the streets. As it was, they lived one paycheck away from that devastating life.

She'd given the same watered-down version to the police the other day, though they'd insisted on more details. To get out of trouble, she'd reluctantly supplied them with enough information to condemn her father and keep herself out of jail. Not that she wasn't justified in killing him. He came after her. Not the first time either. She'd suffered the slaps, the punches, and the beatings too many times to count. She'd feared him, probably from the day she was born, but nothing like the other night. She'd seen death in his eyes and known it was her or him.

Her own father made her make that choice.

He also freed her. She no longer had to fear him taking Justin away if she didn't stay and help with the bills, keeping him from ending up in the gutter, where he belonged. As much as he'd hurt her, he'd had an obsessive need to keep his children close. He'd sworn that if she ever took Justin, he'd find them, and she'd never see Justin again. When she was eighteen, he found her stash of money and clothes, along with her map and checklist for running away to give Justin a better life. He'd made sure she never tried to do that again. She felt the agony of that beating in her bones even now.

She'd tried to give Justin a good life, within the boundaries of the leash of threats her father kept tight around her neck. Every time she'd pulled, gotten just a little further in trying to take Justin away, he'd pulled that leash tight. Thoughts of what he could do to her and Justin made her fear actually leaving. The one threat she could never let happen—her father taking Justin and eventually losing him to the broken foster care system—made her give in every time. No way would she have allowed Justin to be left in a system where at best he'd have been ignored by strangers, or, worse, hurt and abused. She'd met other kids in the system and heard their awful stories. What if she'd tried to get him back and they'd deemed her unfit? She couldn't take that chance. Justin was better off with her loving him despite her father's erratic and hurtful behavior.

Her sweet baby. The only person who ever loved her. Her saving grace when everything seemed hopeless. Her eye of the storm when hurricane Ron blew in and turned her life upside down again and again. She'd do anything, everything, to protect him.

"Do you need any more pain meds?"

"I'm fine."

"You've been through a major trauma. Your injuries are severe. It's understandable if you need something to take the edge off."

"No more drugs. I need to go home to Justin."

"I just finished my interview with your social worker. She'll be in to see you in a moment."

"What did you tell her?"

"That while your injuries are severe and will make it difficult for you to care for Justin for a few weeks, they will not prevent you from doing so."

"I can take care of him," she assured the doctor, staring him down to make sure he knew she meant every word.

"I'm sure you can, but you'll need help."

"I don't need any help. I don't need anyone."

The doctor unclipped a fat envelope from his clipboard and handed it to her. "Your grandfather sent you this. Sometimes, Gillian, the only thing you can do is pick the best option available to you even if you don't like any of them." With that, the doctor stepped out as the social worker walked in. Great, they were tag-teaming her.

Above the doctor's name and the hospital's address, her grandfather had neatly printed her name. She opened the envelope and gaped at the stack of money inside. She pulled out the small piece of paper with her name on it and unfolded it. A man of few words, her grandfather had written only, *Please come home.*

Those simple words tore at her aching heart. She fought back the tears threatening to spill from her eyes. She'd never had a home. Not one that looked like those happy places on TV sitcoms. Not one like other kids had, with a mom and dad and dinner on the table every night. A home was supposed to be a safe place. She'd never had one of those.

"Gillian, I spoke to your grandfather this morning." The social worker broke into her thoughts.

Yeah, because she'd refused to talk to him herself. Like a petulant child. She deserved a little hostility, given the situation. She didn't know him, had never met him, and figured he was either dead or indifferent. Either way, it didn't matter much to her. Why should she care if he didn't? The call was too little, too late. Why did he all of a sudden care? What did he want?

She eyed Mrs. Carr, the social worker, who put up her hand to stop Gillian from yelling at her. "Don't worry. I didn't say anything about Justin."

Gillian didn't want her grandfather to know about Justin and try to gain custody because he thought her unfit to care for her little boy.

"He's very concerned about you. He wants you to come to Montana. He's willing to come and get you himself if that's what you want. There's a flight schedule in there, including enough cash for the plane ticket and extra for anything you might need to make the trip."

"Who says I'm going anywhere?"

"Your rent is two months past due. You're about to lose your apartment unless you can come up with the money immediately. In your condition, you will not be able to work for weeks. You don't have the money to support yourself and Justin until your injuries heal, when you can work again and earn a paycheck."

"I can work. Maybe not at all the jobs I do, but I can earn enough to take care of us."

"Gillian, Justin is in a safe home at this time, where he will be cared for and fed. While the doctor assures me it isn't beyond your ability to care for Justin, it will be extremely difficult for you to do so without a place to live and money to buy food. If you want to keep Justin, I'd take the money and go to Montana. Your grandfather is offering you a place to stay for free. You need someplace to rest and heal and decide what you want to do next."

Montana? That was a long way away. Still, maybe that's what Justin needed—to escape this waking nightmare.

"If you want Justin out of foster care when you leave this hospital, I need to know you're taking him to your family in Montana. Otherwise, he'll remain in foster care until you can prove that you are back to work, have a place to stay, and can afford to feed and care for him."

Unacceptable. She'd never leave Justin with strangers. After what happened, he needed her even more. As far as she was concerned, the only family she had left was Justin. She wouldn't let them take him from her. No way. She'd do anything to keep him.

"I can always call your grandfather back, tell him about Justin, and send him to Montana without you. But I don't want to do that. It's your choice."

"Not really a choice at all, is it?"

"Not everyone is out to hurt you and make your life a misery, Gillian. Your grandfather sounds like a good man. Give him a chance. Who knows, you might find exactly what you're looking for in Montana."

The only thing she wanted was a safe place for Justin to grow up happy and healthy. A place where he could run wild and be a little boy for as long as possible. A place where he'd learn to smile again. And maybe, if they were lucky, a place with kind and decent people to show him how to be a real man.

CHAPTER 4

The sky was so bright the blue of it hurt her eyes. Gillian stopped the truck two miles from the ranch to take a minute to gather her courage. Mid-March, she looked out across the two-lane road at the rolling green hills running toward the trees and up to the mountains that surrounded the more-green-than-brown valley as the grass rose up, breaking free of winter's icy hold. She'd never seen anything so beautiful in her life. She hadn't realized places like this existed. Oh, she'd seen pictures in books, but they'd seemed like a fairy tale compared to the cramped apartments in whatever low-rent town or city she'd existed in until two weeks ago. She hadn't known that grass could be three shades of green as it waved in the wind, or that trees could be so tightly packed you couldn't see through them.

She'd never seen dark the way she did out here. Last night, she and Justin slept in the truck along a dirt road just off the main highway. She hadn't wanted to waste any more of their money on a motel. The stars had shined so brightly, and by the millions that she couldn't conceive that she'd lived her whole life in one city or another and missed out on seeing such a spectacular celestial show.

Despite her terrible circumstances, she'd always loved San Francisco. One day soon she'd miss the smell of the ocean on the breeze and the way the fog rolled in like a wall of mist. Or how it sometimes snuck up on you like a ghost.

She'd miss the people from all walks of life and just about every country in the world. She'd miss China-town and getting chow mein and eating it on the wharf. She'd miss the bark of the sea lions and the scream of the gulls. But not today. Today she had a clear blue sky, clean air, and enough open space that she felt like spreading her arms wide and just taking it all in.

The mountains stood tall and foreboding. They made her think the land had risen up and warned, *Stay back,* like the walls she'd erected around herself.

She shifted on the bench seat and tried to avoid hitting the cuts on the backs of her legs. She hadn't seen another car in more than twenty miles, and there was nothing out her window but the land. Strangely, she felt that for the first time in her life she could breathe. She wanted to open the window and take in the cool mountain air. Justin slept quietly beside her, so she kept the window closed and the cold out. She thought about waking him before they reached the ranch. He'd love the meadow and tall moun-tains. She decided to let him rest. He'd earned it.

A hawk lifted off from the trees in the distance, soaring higher and higher into the air, a graceful flight that left her feeling sad. She wondered if she'd ever have that kind of feeling of soaring, flying, freedom.

The only feelings she could remember were fear and desperation. A constant in her life for so long, in the end she'd simply turned everything off inside herself. Each day was survival. Each day was work to earn enough money to feed herself and Justin. Each day was hoping for something, anything, that would whisk her away from the life she'd been living. That day had finally come.

All it took was a gun and a fall from a second-story window.

She hoped today would be the start of her new life after the fall. After the death of *that* life.

She pulled on her father's old quilted flannel jacket she'd had to bring with her for the cold weather. It wasn't adequate to keep the bite of the wind away, but it was all she'd been able to find among their meager belongings that would provide any kind of warmth. She hated wearing his things, because of the gruesome memories the smell and sight pulled from her mind. Cigarettes, pot, sweat, stale beer, and whiskey scents clung to the jacket and made her want to gag. She swallowed hard, holding back the bile rising in her throat. No amount of washing would ever eradicate those smells from the material. But she'd had no choice. Her limited wardrobe consisted mostly of jeans, T-shirts, and a couple of hoodies. Her meager funds weren't enough for the trip, food, and a new coat.

She looked back up at the towering mountains and felt their isolation to her soul.

"You can't sit here all day. You've come this far. Get your ass moving."

She wondered what her pride was going to taste like. In order to make this work, she'd have to swallow a lot of it. She was willing to gorge on it for Justin's sake. He was the only reason she'd accepted her grandfather's invitation to come live at his ranch. No way Justin stayed in foster care. No way they'd send him to a stranger's house alone, even if it was a relative. He deserved better than the life they'd been living. She'd make sure he got it.

She turned the key, and the engine came alive with a rumble. Pain shot up her arm, and she winced and breathed through it. Nothing else she could do. Pain had become her constant companion. Like every other day of her life, she wanted to be left alone. The pain didn't care. It had settled into her bones and muscles for a long stay.

She checked the rearview before she pulled back onto the road. She caught sight of her gruesome appearance in the mirror and turned away quickly. She controlled her emotions and grabbed the sunglasses off the dash. She put them on to hide some of the damage, then tucked her long mane of blonde hair into the collar of the jacket and zipped it up. Not exactly her best look, but beggars couldn't be choosers. The jacket covered the major portion of the damage done to her body, and the glasses hid part of her black-and-blue face, giving her a chance to conceal her expression when she met her grandfather. Cowardly, but she wasn't strong enough right now to take any criticism or pity. Pity would be worse.

The pounding in her head started hours ago. She needed a hot shower, a hot meal, and a pain pill. Not particularly in that order. She'd settle for whatever her grandfather was willing to give, since she didn't have enough money to get back to San Francisco. She could probably get to the next town. Careful with her money, she had to be. She'd made sure Justin had a new warm coat and plenty of food. He was her first, last, her every priority.

She pulled back onto the road and checked the map again. The grocery store clerk had written down the directions for her and even drawn her a crude map of the area. According to him, in another half mile, she'd see the fences for the ranch.

"You can't miss the place," he'd said.

She'd had a lot of time to think about what she'd find at the end of this journey. She wondered what kind of ranch her grandfather owned. Cattle, horses, some other kind of livestock? She wondered if it was some run-down shack on a dirt hill, or something grand. Either way, she'd make it work. She had to make it work.

Please, let it be someplace good for Justin.

If she'd gotten over her stubbornness and actually spoken to her grandfather on the phone, she could have asked him for details. The doctor had assured her that her grandfather meant to help. She wasn't as ready to give the benefit of the doubt. Her grandfather was going to have to prove it and earn her trust. She wouldn't put Justin's life on the line. Not anymore. Not again.

She needed to see her grandfather and look him in the eye. Then she'd know if he was going to help or hurt her.

So help her God, if he laid one hand on her or Justin, she'd kill him, too. *Never again*, she swore, clenching the steering wheel with her mostly good hand.

Never again.

Dark brown fences corralled the horses inside. She felt the tug of a smile on her lips when one of them ran across the field. She didn't think she'd ever seen anything quite so beautiful. His brown coat gleamed in the sun, and his black tail and mane blew out behind him in the wind. What a magnificent sight.

She imagined that when the snow lay heavy on the ground, the dark fences and bare trees would be a stark contrast to that blanket of white. She'd never seen snow. Not up close. She wanted to see it falling like wisps of light from a darkened sky. Justin would love it. They could build a snowman.

You're dreaming of impossible things again, she chided herself. *You've got no idea what's waiting for you up ahead.*

The thought tightened her stomach into a ball of nerves.

The turnoff for the ranch appeared, and she took it reluctantly. When she saw the two large pillars of stone holding the big black sign announcing Three Peaks Ranch, she felt an unexpected sense of homecoming. She'd never felt like she belonged anywhere, but for some odd reason, this wild land called to her. That horse running in the pasture called to her.

Three Peaks Ranch. Here I am. Now what?

Sure enough, the property sat below three towering peaks. She went through the open gate and headed down the drive. The road curved and headed down a soft slope. Taken aback by the sight in front of her, she stifled the urge to slam on the brakes and just stare.

The house sat to the left, a huge, two-story gray stone structure with decks on both levels. She'd never seen a grander house in her life. The front had a small lawn edged in pretty flowers. Spring had sprung in this piece of paradise. Flowers grew everywhere in so many vibrant colors that they were startling to see. Another large structure stood off to the right. Probably some kind of stable or barn for the horses. She imagined there could be at least fifty of them in the massive building. It had a stone base topped by white wood. The trim was done in a dark blue to match the house. Several horses stood outside open barn doors in fenced areas.

This place was perfect for Justin. A little boy could run wild on a spread like this. He could learn to ride the horses. Even have a dog or a cat. Justin could learn how to be a real man here.

That is, if her grandfather wasn't like her father.

She needed to find that out before she and Justin got too comfortable.

When she pulled up and stopped near the house, she spotted a horse in the closest corral. She wanted to kill whoever had hurt that poor animal. Half starved, his ribs and bones were clearly visible beneath his spotty brown coat. He looked like a mangy dog, only much larger and much more sad, because his eyes had the look of a lost child. She recognized that look, the one she often saw in the mirror when she just couldn't hide it or fake it anymore.

She didn't know anything about horses, but she knew a lot about neglect and abuse. She fought the urge to turn the truck around and leave. She didn't want to be here if this was how her grandfather treated the animals on this ranch.

All the other horses looked healthy. That was the only thing that gave her hope.

Two men stepped out of the house and stood on the porch, staring at her. She studied the older man, guessing he was her grandfather. Graying brown hair and mustache, taller than she expected, her grandfather probably topped out at six feet. The old man stood tall and proud. She liked that about him. He wore worn jeans and brown cowboy boots. She should have known. *Ranch and all.* His chambray shirt was neatly pressed, and he wore a black down vest to ward off the chill.

The other man's rugged good looks sparked something deep inside her. A bit taller than her grandfather and much younger—not quite thirty if she guessed right. His face was as tan as her grandfather's. He wore pretty much the same attire: jeans, shirt, black boots, and a heavy, shearling-lined denim jacket. His hair was mostly brown, though the sun brightened the dark mass with gold streaks that made the color shift and change with the waning light.

Something about him pulled at her. Yes, he was probably the most gorgeous man she'd ever laid eyes on, but that isn't what drew her in. No, it was the way he leaned against the porch post with such casual ease and patience, like he'd wait all day for her to come to him. Funny, she felt like doing just that, laying her head on his broad chest and snuggling into the comfort and warmth she saw in his dark eyes.

Stupid. You're here to give Justin a good life, not fall for a cowboy.

CHAPTER 5

Blake stepped out the front door and stood beside Bud on the porch. He surveyed the red '57 Chevy stepside truck in the driveway. He liked her taste in trucks. Old and scarred, but it had good tires. The engine purred before Gillian cut it. Definitely a good sign. She took care of her truck. With a little work and some money, she could have a killer classic.

Gillian got out of the truck, slowly, cautiously, and limped to the walkway leading to the porch. A brace covered her leg from her ankle up to her hip. A hinge on the metal bars along the sides kept her knee in a permanent slight bend that made her walk unevenly. She tried to walk on her toes, but she couldn't seem to put her weight on them, which made her hobble even more.

A little bit of a thing. What he could see of her, that is. Honey blonde hair disappeared into the back of the oversized man's jacket that engulfed her slight frame. The aviator sunglasses covered her eyes but didn't hide all of the bluish-green bruises on her cheek and along her jaw on the left side of her face. The bastard. Look what that asshole's fist had done to her beautiful face. Every drop of sadness wrung from his soul settled in the pit of his stomach for this waif of a woman. So much so that the sorrow engulfed him in a wave that rocked him and nearly sent him to his knees.

The first glimpse of her made everything inside Blake come to attention. The damage to her face sent a flash of fury through his veins that surprised him. He banked the rage quickly enough and felt his heart warm with something he'd never felt. The damn thing wanted to jump out of his chest and drop at her small feet. What the hell was wrong with him?

His parents had been married for more than thirty-five years, and he always thought of them as a one-in-a-million kind of couple. They were happy together. The kind of happy that had his father whistling in the barn early in the morning and his mother smiling over the dirty dishes as she cleaned his plate. It was the kind of love that had them snuggling on the couch, catching a movie, and his father stealing a kiss. Over and over he'd heard them tell the story of how they'd met at a Fourth of July picnic. Love at first sight. Blake had always rolled his eyes. *Yeah, right.*

His father had told him once that when he found the right woman, she'd stop him in his tracks. Yeah, well, he couldn't move now. He couldn't stop staring at her. Looking at Gillian, with her beaten face, the defensive edge to her posture, and the distance she kept between them, he didn't know how to begin to get her to trust him. But he already knew he'd work damn hard at it, because the compulsion to protect her overwhelmed him.

This other stuff swirling in his chest and gut, he didn't know what to make of it.

He wondered if this was how his big brother, Gabe, felt the first time he met his girl, Ella. She'd been in bad shape too, but that hadn't stopped Gabe from protecting and falling in love with her. In fact, it sparked everything.

Maybe that's all this was, his inner need to protect someone who needed protecting.

Against who? Her father is dead. You just want her.

Yep. That simple and that complicated. Because wanting her meant putting his personal and professional life with Bud and the ranch on the line. Not an option.

Gillian kept her distance from the porch, sucked in a deep breath, and mustered up her courage. A flash of pure rage lit the younger man's eyes when she stepped closer, making them narrow on her. A split second later, his eyes went soft with something she didn't recognize but made her want to take a closer look into his tawny eyes. She'd never seen someone look at her that way. Difficult to read, she'd keep her guard up around this man.

The guy and her grandfather shared a look, then turned back to stare at her. Her grandfather wasn't smiling. He seemed to expect her to come to him.

Beyond tired, she hurt everywhere. Driving for three days had really taken the life out of her. The doctor had warned her that she needed plenty of rest and time to heal. What she needed was a fresh start.

This is your chance, Gillian. Don't mess it up.

"Hello."

"Gillian, where have you been?" The question came out gruff and filled with rage, tinged with sympathy. She didn't know how to decipher the opposing emotions, which increased her anxiety.

Gillian opened her mouth to answer her grandfather, but for the life of her, she didn't know what to call him.

She didn't know this man. She didn't remember ever meeting him. "Grandfather" seemed appropriate, because he seemed to be larger than life and had an air of confidence that could wear a title like that. Still, not her style. "Grandpa" seemed too familiar. At a complete loss, she kept her mouth shut.

Since she wasn't inclined to speak, he took the lead.

"Why didn't you fly? I told the doctor I'd pick you up at the airport. Didn't you get the money I sent?"

She raised her chin defiantly. "I got it. I can work here at the ranch, or in town. I'll make the money back and pay you as soon as I can."

"I don't want you to pay me back. I want to know where you've been for the last six days."

She didn't like the gruff tone and took a step back, putting more distance between them. It only made him frown more. "Um, I had to get my things from the apartment building. The money you sent . . ." She took a deep breath. *Tell the truth and get it over with.* "The money you sent, plus what I had saved, I used to pay the back rent on the apartment. The apartment that the, ah, incident happened in had some damage, and I had to pay that person for the repairs. The rest I used for gas and food to get here."

"Do you have any left?"

"Eighty-seven dollars and nineteen cents. It's in my purse in the truck. I'll get it for you." She turned to fetch her purse but stopped at his command.

"No!"

She turned back and cocked her head, trying to figure out the reason for his hostility. If this is how he spoke and acted all the time, she'd leave. She couldn't spend another minute of her life constantly on guard, watching every word she said and everything she did.

"Sorry. You don't need to give me the money. I sent it for you to get here. I guess you managed that and taking care of your business back home.

"I have to say, I'm at a complete loss at your appearance. I mean, I knew he hurt you, but I never expected it to be this bad. Are you okay?"

"No," she answered honestly.

"Why'd you kill him?" her grandfather asked.

Might as well get everything out in the open. Maybe then they could move on.

Gillian thought about the answer to that loaded question. She could give him the simple answer. Her father had been a bastard. He'd hit her. He'd come at her with a gun, crazed on methamphetamines. Instead of going with the simple, she gave him the cold, hard truth.

"When I was five, I used to think he'd come into my room and kill me one night in a drunken, doped-up rage. By the time I was ten, there were a lot of days and nights that I thought if he hit my mother or me one more time I might just kill him. When I was fourteen, I knew I'd lay down my life if he ever crossed the line.

"He knew the line, and he crossed it. He brought the gun, not me. I did what I had to do. He had a choice. He didn't give me one.

"That man needed killing."

She watched his face as she spoke the harsh truth. His healthy glow withered, and he aged at least twenty years in the blink of an eye. Stress and fatigue took over his features, and his eyes and jaw softened. Looking closer, dark circles marred the underside of his eyes. He hadn't been sleeping well. Worry and concern filled his eyes, but she wasn't sure why.

Did he hate her for what she'd done?

Her words rang in Bud's mind. The way she said

them surprised him. No anger or fury. Just a cold, honest truth that shot through him. He hadn't known what to expect. This woman standing in front of him with strength of mind and pride enough for ten people surprised him even more. She wasn't just any girl. She was a survivor and wouldn't suffer fools or bullies. She wasn't the little girl he'd expected. Maybe somewhere under the bravado was the soft and sweet child he'd hoped to see. On second thought, anything soft and sweet in her had probably been squashed and decimated by Ron's harsh words and mighty fists.

"I killed my father, my own flesh and blood. I understand if you don't want me here."

He took a step toward the edge of the porch and called out to stop her from walking back to her truck and leaving. "I just wanted to know. I needed to hear the truth from you. Your mother, Erin . . ."

He hadn't said her name in years. The pain of all he'd lost, the regrets he carried like a stone in his gut, the dreams he'd had for his little girl that had left him brokenhearted when she'd thrown her life away on drugs washed through him.

"Erin had a wild streak no one could tame. She harbored unrealistic dreams of leaving this place and living a glamorous life. In high school, when her mother was ill and fighting the cancer, Erin found trouble around every turn with drinking and drugs and messing with boys. She barely managed to graduate. When she turned eighteen, it didn't take much coaxing from Ron for her to run off to the bright L.A. city lights. She left as fast as she could and never looked back. She didn't want any part of this ranch or me. She couldn't stand to watch her mother wither away and die. She wasn't strong enough to stay for her mother.

"I heard from her a handful of times that first year. Then, nothing. Ron controlled her. He didn't want me to find them and made sure I didn't the few times I tried to track them down. I didn't know about you until you were three. I tried to get in touch with you after your mother died, but Ron had already taken you away again. I didn't know your situation," he said miserably.

"How could you? My father was a master at working people and the system. He hated Montana. He always said that living on a ranch was too much work. That man did as little as possible as often as he could. He spent his life for the last twenty years tending bar in seedy dives and selling drugs. Within a month of them arriving in L.A., she was pregnant with me. They worked their way up the state and landed in the Bay Area. We moved around San Francisco and the surrounding areas. She was a drunk, a drug addict, and sometimes a whore. He didn't seem to mind any of those things so long as he got his cut. If he didn't, he made sure she didn't forget to pay up." She shrugged. What more was there to say?

Her grandfather's eyes filled with sorrow. Numb to her own feelings about her parents, she forgot that her grandfather remembered her mother as someone different. Maybe a happier, friendlier, the-world-is-full-of-possibilities-for-her kind of person. The someone she must have been at one time for him to show such grief.

"You must have had so many hopes and dreams for her." The way she did for Justin's future. "I'm sorry to be so callous. I never meant to . . ."

"You spoke your mind and the truth of your life and hers."

Gillian let the dead rest and started to tell him about herself. "I spent a lot of time at school and in the library." *Better to come home late, lessen the opportunity for someone to notice you. A better chance they'd be passed out drunk and stoned.* She kept that to herself. Better to stick to herself than her parents' fucked-up lives. "I made good grades and graduated top of my class in high school. I've worked all kinds of jobs. I'm good with my hands. I learn things quickly. If you show me what you want me to do around here, I'll work hard and earn my keep."

"Will you stay? Please."

"That depends. Are you responsible for that animal?" She cocked her head toward the sick and hurt horse in the nearest corral and tried to fight the clench in her heart every time she looked at him.

"He's mine," Bud answered.

Gillian cast them both a disgusted look and turned her back on them, but hesitated to walk back to her truck and leave. If her grandfather had hurt that horse, she needed a plan to get the hell out of here, now, but she didn't have anywhere else to go. With little more than eighty dollars, she'd never make it more than a few days. She'd never even get out of the state. Too damn cold to sleep in the truck again. She'd need to find a shelter.

Blake caught her hesitation and indecision and knew exactly where this conversation derailed. "He didn't hurt that horse. He saved him from the son of a bitch who neglected and hurt him. Bud wouldn't hurt a horse. No one on this ranch would hurt them. I'm trying to nurse him back to health."

He spoke to her back, but she listened, even if her gaze remained on Boots. Blake knew how she felt. Seeing that poor thing broke his heart, too. He imagined she saw herself in the horse.

"She thinks I hurt that horse," Bud whispered, disbelief in his words.

"She just wants to know if she's going to be safe here," Blake whispered back. "If she thinks you hurt that horse, it isn't a far leap for her to think you'd treat her the same. Give her a minute to work it out. I don't imagine she's ever felt safe. Anywhere."

And that stabbed him in the heart and made him ache. He tried to swallow his emotions. Something about Gillian had his feelings rising to the surface, when he'd had them buried for a good long time. A very new sensation. He wasn't sure he liked this turn of events.

"She'll damn well be safe here. I won't have her thinking otherwise."

"Telling her that and making her believe it are two very different things. She's been taught not to trust and not to let her guard down."

They both jumped at the sound of soft crying coming from the truck. Gillian took off and hobbled around the truck just as a small, brown-haired boy popped up into view.

Bud paled and stared at the pair, his eyes filled with disbelief.

Blake tried to think rationally, despite the blaze of shock racing through his veins, making his heart drop to his stomach. Could the boy be hers? She was only twenty. She'd have been a child herself when she had him. He wanted to ask her and didn't know how, or what to say. Bud saved him from having to speak the words.

"Is he yours?" Bud called out. She hadn't gotten the boy out of the truck yet.

Gillian looked over at her grandfather and wanted to throttle him. What kind of person did he think she was? She wasn't like her mother.

Keep your head. He doesn't know you. Give him the benefit of the doubt.

Still, she couldn't help her annoyance.

"He is now." Let him chew on that for a minute.

She opened the truck door. Justin launched himself into her arms. She bit back an oath as pain shot through her whole body. She wrapped her arms around him and kissed the side of his head. His crying stopped when he landed in her arms. She hadn't meant for him to wake up alone.

"Justin, we're here. You remember what I told you."

"Yes. I'll stay with you and do what you say."

"I talked to him. He seems nice. I think we'll be okay here. If not, I promise I'll take you away. We'll find our own place. Okay?"

"Okay." He pressed his face into her neck and held her tight. He believed her. She'd keep him safe. She always had. She always would.

CHAPTER 6

"**I**s that a horse?" Justin asked, his voice timid and afraid.

Gillian turned to look at the poor creature standing by the fence. "It is a horse. He's not feeling well."

"Did he do that to him?"

"He said he didn't." She made her way over to the fence with Justin still in her arms, his legs wrapped around her waist. It was killing her to carry him, but she didn't set him down. Not yet. He needed the cuddles and love. He'd only ever gotten them from her. She wouldn't tell him or let him see how much she hurt. "He took this horse away from someone who was mean to him. He's trying to make him better. I think that's a very good sign."

"Is he going to make you better?"

She hugged him tighter even though it cost her. Pain radiated up her back and down her leg, but she ignored it. She stood by the fence and looked at the sad animal, her own sadness mirrored in the horse's soulful brown eyes.

She didn't know how to answer Justin's question. She hoped that their grandfather would take them in and give them a roof over their heads and food to eat. Anything else was more than she could hope for or expect.

"He says he wants us to stay. We'll see."

Blake and Bud stood on the porch staring, completely dumbfounded by this new development. The screen door slammed, startling them.

"Well, what's taking you guys so long?" Dee looked out across the yard. "Who's that?"

Bud recovered enough to answer. "She says he's hers. I think she's still deciding if she's coming in."

"Well it's no wonder she hasn't come up the steps with you two standing here like sentries guarding the gate. The poor girl wouldn't step within twenty feet of two huge men after what her father did to her. With your size and strength, she knows she couldn't defend herself against the two of you. Didn't you think to move out of her way?"

Blake swore under his breath. He'd wondered why she hadn't come up on the porch with them to talk. Sure enough, she'd kept what had felt to him like an awkwardly long distance between them, but comfortable and safe for her. In fact, she'd made sure to keep enough distance that she could get to the truck before they overtook her.

"That girl is about five-foot-nothing and weighs as much as a fairy. In her condition, she couldn't defend herself against a fly. The two of you standing up here towering over her must have looked like a lot of muscle to get through. She doesn't know you, and you stood up here like giants waiting to eat her up. Go over there and invite her in. Give her space, but get her in the door. She's got to be tired, hungry, and hurting. For God's sake, I swear you two don't use the brains God gave you."

It was just the kick in the butt they needed. Dee had a way of getting them to do things, and it was usually her voice that rang with reason. Blake decided that if he was going to get Gillian to stay so that he could decipher the strange new pulse in his chest, he'd better go and introduce himself.

He'd tamed timid wild horses. Something about him calmed them. Maybe it would work with her.

Yeah, right. Like she'd trust him if he coaxed her into the house with a soft tone and soothing words. He cocked his head and studied her. *Worth a try.*

"Let me go get her," he suggested. "I'll be the mediary, just like the doctor."

Dee gave him a knowing smile, her eyes going soft on him. In all the time she'd known him, he'd never dated anyone special. Never more than a couple months before it fizzled out. He never brought a woman to the ranch. Lately, he spent all his time with his beloved horses. He got them. Women, not so much.

But he wanted to understand Gillian.

He crossed the yard and came to the fence about ten feet from her. *Give her space. Don't get too close, or you'll spook her.* Just like he'd approach the horse standing several feet from the fence.

"Gillian." At the sound of his voice, the boy clenched his arms tighter to her and buried his face in her neck. Blake hadn't even gotten a good look at him. "I'm Blake Bowden. I'm part owner, head trainer, and manager here at the ranch."

Her wary eyes remained on him. She leaned back to take a step away, but stopped herself at the last second. If she felt she needed more space, he'd give it to her. For now.

He took a step back and waited.

"It's nice to meet you." Her words came out soft and tentative. "This is Justin. He's not feeling well." She rubbed her cheek on the top of Justin's head. She pressed her hand to the boy's forehead, checking for a fever. If the boy was sick, they should get him into the house.

"Dee has supper ready. Why don't you come inside for dinner?" He kept his voice soft and low. Her tense body, ready to flee, relaxed. Just a fraction, but he'd take it.

"I should get our things from the truck. Will we be staying there?" She tilted her head to indicate the building off to the right of the stables.

"That's the bunkhouse where some of the guys stay. You'll stay in the main house with your grandfather and Dee."

"Who's Dee?"

"His wife. Dee has been married to your grandfather for about five, six years. She's nice. You'll like her. She keeps Bud and me in line. She's the best cook around, but don't tell my mom I said that." He smiled, but it fell away when she swayed. "You want me to take him? He must be heavy, and you look worn out."

"No!" Justin held on tighter.

Gillian took three steps back. "Stay away. I've got him."

Blake held up his hand, letting her know he had no intention of touching her or the boy. "He's all yours. You go on up to the house. Get settled. I'll bring in your stuff."

"I can get it."

"I know you can. My mother raised me right. No way I let you carry the bags. I'll take care of your luggage, you take care of him."

With a deep breath and a resigned look in her eyes, she admitted, "I'd appreciate the help. There's only my purse, a couple of boxes, and two bags. Um, and an envelope from the doctor. Medical records," she explained, as if her appearance wasn't sufficient.

"I'll get them and meet you inside."

"You'll probably beat me," she said with a self-deprecating tilt to her lips.

"Can you make it?" He didn't think she could, but he'd let her try. If she faltered again, he'd help her whether she liked it or not. He hated seeing anything hurt. The horses were the worst, but she broke his heart. Everything in him knew he'd see only pain if she took off those sunglasses. Tense, she held herself together with the last shreds of her energy. The longer this took, the paler she became, making the bruises on her face stand out even more vividly. What the hell was she hiding under that oversized coat? He didn't want to know, because whatever it was, it couldn't be good.

"I've made it this far." She limped away toward the house, where her grandfather and Dee stood, but she remained sideways to keep Blake in view, too. No sneaking up on her. It'd be hard to get past her guard, but he aimed to try. And keep trying until she trusted him.

The sky that had seemed so vivid blue when she arrived faded to a soft, dusky lavender gray as the sun sank closer to the mountaintops. Soon it would be dark. She couldn't stand out here all day.

Sure enough, by the time Gillian reached the porch steps, Blake was right behind her. It annoyed and unsettled her. Having him close made her nervous. Not in the same way her father had made her nervous. She didn't think Blake would hurt her. Something about the way he anticipated her, gave her space, waited her out drew her in and made her anxious. She couldn't quite figure him out.

She looked up the steps at Dee and thought that if ever there was a woman who was a born mother, she was it. The essence of nurture was stamped all over her. Pleasantly plump, Dee's nice round cheeks were flushed from the cool wind blowing. Her hair was a soft caramel color, her eyes dark as chocolate. If she'd been wearing a shirtdress and apron and standing with a tray of cookies, she couldn't have looked more perfect. She held a dish towel in her hands, which made her look domestic, but the caring, kind look on her face drew Gillian in. It was nothing like the indifference she saw in her mother's eyes every day before she died.

"Hi. I'm Gillian. This is Justin."

"Your son?" Dee asked, since Gillian had been vague enough with her grandfather that Dee needed to ask.

Both men avidly awaited her response.

"No. My brother."

Her grandfather's whole face lit up. "I have a grandson." He hugged Dee to his side. "I have two grandchildren." His excitement and happiness were another good sign.

"My mother got pregnant with him when I was fourteen. The first time in my life I'd ever seen the woman somewhat sober, and basically clean. When Justin was about two weeks old, she gave him to me to watch while she and Dad went out partying. She overdosed that night and never came back. I've raised him since then. On my own."

"Fourteen," her grandfather said in disbelief.

"Yes. That's when I knew that if he ever raised a hand to Justin, I'd do anything and everything to protect him."

She'd asked the doctor and police to leave Justin out of their reports. The social worker took some convincing, but once Gillian agreed to bring Justin here to live, she backed off. The nerves danced inside her, but she tamped them down. No way she let these people take

Justin from her. If they even hinted at gaining custody of him, she'd bolt with him.

She stood staring at her grandfather. He'd truly had no idea about Justin. Now he knew. He knew it all. She'd done what she'd had to do to protect Justin. The guilt over killing her father gnawed at her, but the anger muddied up the shame, because she'd had to do it.

He opened his mouth to say something but closed it again. In the end, he gave her words back to her. "The man needed killing."

Stunned he felt that way, she nodded and figured they'd come to an understanding.

"Social services agreed to let me keep him because you offered us a place to stay. But if you think you can take him from me, you're wrong."

"I would never take the boy from the only mother he's ever known. That's a promise."

Gillian believed him. His eyes, his words held the truth without a hint of deception.

"Would you like to come inside now?" he asked.

"Yes," Dee said. "Come inside. Get warm, and we'll have dinner."

Justin heard that and sat back on Gillian's good arm. "I'm hungry," he announced.

"Now why doesn't that surprise me?" she teased. His smile warmed her heart. "I have to put you down. I can't make it up the steps with you."

"Am I hurting you?"

She brushed her nose to his to wipe away the sad face. "No, baby. You could never hurt me."

"Is he going to hurt you?"

"No," she said firmly.

"Cause if he does, you'll shoot him."

That her brother thought that a reasonable solution

thwacked her in the gut. Life with her vile father had reduced them to this. Her six-year-old brother thought it okay to kill someone if they hurt you. Well, hadn't she taught him that lesson? Wouldn't she do the same thing if her grandfather harmed him? What kind of person did that make her? She didn't know, but keeping Justin safe would always be her first and last priority.

"That's right." She gave her grandfather a hard look to let him know she meant it.

"Justin, I promise you. You're safe here. No one is going to hurt you or your sister. If they do, they'll answer to me," her grandfather promised.

She appreciated her grandfather's attempt to reassure him, but he still had to prove it.

"Me, too," Blake said from behind them. "There are a lot of men who work on this ranch. They all work for your grandfather and me. If someone does or says something to either of you, we'll take care of it immediately. Is that going to be a problem for you, Gillian? The men on the ranch?"

She didn't know how to answer that question. She assumed the men who worked on a ranch were probably some rough and rowdy guys. She didn't know how she'd react if one of them got too close. She didn't like people too close. Since she didn't know how to answer him, she shrugged, then wished she hadn't moved at all. Pain shot through her, and she almost lost her grip on Justin. She set him on his feet and used her hands on her legs to push herself back up to standing. Everyone around her took a few steps closer, wanting to help. She held up her hand to ward them off and stood slowly.

"I'm fine. Let's go in. Justin's been fighting a bug. He shouldn't be out in the cold. He's running a fever. I don't want him to get worse."

Dee and her grandfather walked into the house and left the door open for them to follow. Justin stood at the top of the steps, waiting for her to hobble her way up the five stairs. Blake stood behind her. She was doing the best she could and resented his sticking close to make sure she didn't stumble on the stairs. Then again, she hated that she might falter in her condition. She couldn't win. Story of her life.

When she reached the top step, Justin wrapped his arm around her thigh and clung to her as they walked into the house. Man, if she thought the outside was nice, the inside was twice as good. She stepped into a wide room with a fireplace to the left. A huge blaze warmed the room. The smooth stones made the room look and feel homey. Muted cream walls complemented the dark, chunky wood mantel. A soft sage carpet covered the hardwood floor. The brown leather sofa looked comfortable, as did the matching chairs. A television dominated the corner. Justin would appreciate having one to watch. It wasn't something he'd had often enough for his liking.

Straight ahead, a wide set of stairs led up to the bedrooms. On the left of the stairs, a set of double doors opened into what looked like a library. Bookshelves lined the wall behind the desk. She wondered what kind of books her grandfather preferred. She loved to read. Maybe her grandfather would let her borrow his books. To the right of the stairs, the dining room led to an archway into the bright kitchen. The smell of chili and chocolate chip cookies filled the air. Her stomach couldn't decide if it wanted to grumble for food or turn over altogether. She hoped she could keep the food down so she could take her meds. She needed them. Bad.

Her grandfather and Dee stood near the entrance to

the dining room. Dee, with her sweet voice and smiling face, broke the tension of everyone watching them.

"I thought we could eat first. Then I'll take you up to your rooms. Justin, there's a room next to your sister's with a door between. You can keep it open so you can see her if you like."

Gillian got a nod even though he was still plastered to her thigh.

"Then let's take our coats off and sit down for a good meal." Dee and Bud headed into the kitchen and left everyone else to follow.

Gillian helped Justin off with his coat. She smoothed back his hair and leaned down. "Fever check." She pressed her lips to his forehead. He put his hands up and held her face as she kissed him. "You're hot. I think you need more medicine after you eat something."

Blake thought his heart had already taken a beating, but seeing her kiss Justin to check his temperature made it flip over again.

"You smell like him," Justin said. A tear slid from his big round eyes.

Gillian stood and wiped away the tears with her thumbs. She pulled the jacket off. "I know. I don't like it either, but I couldn't buy a new jacket. I tried to wash it, but there isn't enough soap and water in the world to get the smell out. I'll burn this thing as soon as I can afford my own."

Blake ripped the offending coat from her grasp, walked to the fireplace, and tossed it in to burn. He turned from the fire and saw her for the first time. Her mouth hung open in surprise, but the rest of her held his attention. About five-foot-three. Dee was right, she couldn't weigh more than a fairy. Her jeans, which she should have filled out nicely, hung on her hips. The simple white T-shirt didn't hide her soft curves. A bandage wrapped around her upper right arm peeked out from her sleeve.

Annoyed, she pulled off her glasses, revealing one eye nearly swollen shut and as darkly bruised as her cheek and jaw. His only thought was that she'd been right. The man had needed killing.

The jacket had hidden her hair, but now it hung halfway down her back. More blonde than brown, though the dancing flames highlighted the red and gold and brown throughout. It had been pulled back tight around her head, but now that it was loose, it seemed to take on a life of its own. It literally bounced up and filled out with soft waves.

They waited for him to explain his behavior, but words failed him. She literally took his breath away. Justin watched him with guarded eyes, standing half hidden behind his sister.

"There you go, little one," he said to Justin, then looked at Gillian. "I don't like seeing children cry or women hurt." He grabbed his jacket from the back of the sofa, walked toward her, and held it out at arm's length, saying, "Until I get you a new one." He stood as far away from her as he could while still giving her the chance to take the jacket.

"I can't take your coat."

"Sure you can. You don't want to be cooped up in the house. Besides, if you decide to run—not that anyone here will give you a reason to do so—you'll need the coat."

Gillian's eyes narrowed. She wasn't stupid. She'd need a coat here. Still, she didn't want to outright admit he was right about her plans if this didn't work out. She snatched the coat from his hand and took another step away.

He hated she felt the need and wished he had a quick solution to put her at ease.

She held the jacket to her chest, tilted her head, and smelled it.

So, not so indifferent and afraid of him. He hid a smile. It was a start, but it was still a long way from what he wanted.

Embarrassed she'd been caught, her eyes went soft and her steady gaze fell away for a second.

Trying to keep things casual, he said, "Let's eat, I'm starving."

He grabbed their bags and moved past a stunned and bewildered Gillian to set them by the stairs. He looked up the long staircase. "How are you going to get up those on your own? You barely made it up the porch steps."

"I'll manage."

He turned back to her and stared. "Is that your real hair color?"

"Is that yours?" she countered.

"I was born with brown, and the sun took care of the rest."

"My mother used to say that all my indecision is in my hair."

His gaze swept over her, taking in the cast on one arm that went up to her elbow, the bandage wrapped around her wrist on the other, the line of stitches that started at her hairline behind her ear and went down her neck and under the collar of her shirt. Blake thought about that picture of her lying on top of the car after going through a window and wondered just how bad the glass had sliced her up.

"How much damage is hiding under your shirt?" He imagined there was a lot she was still hiding.

"Enough," she said to his softly asked question.

"She looks like a sewn-up rag doll." Justin went around the back of her and pulled up her shirt. "See." His mouth turned down into a sad frown. "You're bleeding again."

Gillian grabbed the edge of her shirt and pulled it down. Not fast enough though. Blake got a glimpse of the bruising on her side that went up to her ribs.

"Bruises like that. Hurts to breathe, right? Let me have a look at the cuts."

"No."

"But you're bleeding." He tried to take a step toward her, and she took two back. He stopped. "I won't hurt you."

"Let's go eat. Justin needs to take his medicine and get some rest. It's been a long few days." Her words came out with a deliberate calm that did not match the wariness in her eyes.

"And what about what you need?" he asked.

"I need to be left alone."

Frustrated she wouldn't let him help her, he held his hand out wide and indicated the kitchen. "After you." She shook her head no. Stubborn, mistrustful woman. He let her have her way and walked ahead of her. He'd get a look at her back if he had to sneak up on her to do it.

He'd need more patience than he had at the moment to earn her trust. The reckless boy inside him wanted to push, but he'd done that in the past without thinking of the consequences, and others had paid the price. Never again. He rustled up some calm. If he pushed too hard and upset her, or, God help him, she decided to leave, Bud would have his head. And quite possibly kick him off his land.

CHAPTER 7

Gillian walked into the kitchen with Justin securely wrapped around her leg. Another spectacular, too-pretty-to-touch room. Windows dominated two sides, while the third was engulfed in cabinets and the cooking area, which contained a large stainless steel refrigerator and cooktop, a breakfast bar with a white marble countertop, and wrought-iron stools with tan suede seat cushions. Beautiful. Clean. Nothing like she was used to.

Her grandfather sat at the head of the long farmhouse table, drinking a mug of coffee. Dee bustled about, putting dishes and bowls on the table. Blake moved to the table and took his seat at the other end, like he'd done it every night of his life. He'd probably been eating in this kitchen for years. It struck her how much he belonged here. She didn't, and it was another blow to her heart that she couldn't ever remember feeling like she belonged anywhere.

"I hope you're all hungry. There's lots. We've even got fresh baked cookies for dessert." Dee smiled down at Justin as she put another bowl on the table.

Justin looked up at Gillian. She read the question in his eyes. "It's chili."

"I don't like chili."

"You can try it, at least." Tired to the bone, she didn't want to deal with a tantrum tonight. She wanted to sit down or fall down. At the moment, falling down raced toward the lead.

"You don't like chili?" her grandfather asked Justin. "Well now, I think my Dee could find something you do like. She's got the best-stocked kitchen in the whole state."

Justin peeked out around her leg at the big man. His smile was nice, not mean. Sometimes their father smiled so mean it scared you. Gillian patted Justin's back to reassure him.

"That I do, honey. What would you like? How about a nice grilled cheese sandwich? I have some leftover bacon from this morning we could put inside," Dee suggested.

Blake objected from the table. "Hey, you said there wasn't any more bacon this morning."

"You should be thanking me for that. I was saving your heart."

Blake fake pouted, and Dee gave him a placating smile. They seemed so easy with each other. Like a family should be. Yep, he fit, and she didn't, because she had no idea how to do that *thing* that came so easy to them.

Justin looked up at her. "Speak up," Gillian said. "She's willing to go out of her way to make you something. If you want it, then say so."

He nodded his head yes at Dee.

"Excuse me, I didn't hear you," Gillian reprimanded.

"I would like the sandwich."

"And what do you say?" Gillian coaxed him even more, trying her best to teach him the manners their father never used. Treating others with respect and kindness was important. She hoped the lessons she taught him now lasted far into his adulthood.

"Please."

Tears threatened in Dee's eyes. "Grilled cheese with bacon." Her words came out around a lump in her throat. "I've got some soda and milk in the fridge. I was expecting that might be what you wanted, Gillian. I'll get some juice for you, Justin, tomorrow. What kind do you like?"

Again he looked up at Gillian. Here was some of that pride she was going to have to swallow. Sure enough, it tasted sour. She needed her grandfather's help to feed Justin until she could work again. Until then, they were depending on the roof over their heads and the food her grandfather provided.

"Orange juice," she suggested.

"I don't like orange juice."

"Then I suggest you tell her what you do like." Gillian pulled him off her thigh and kneeled on her good knee in front of him, her braced leg out to her side. "I'm here with you, Justin. I promise you that I won't let anyone hurt you. But you have to learn to speak for yourself. What did I tell you before we came?"

"What you always say?"

"And what is that?" She put her hands on his little chest, and he put his hands on her shoulders.

"We have to try. If it doesn't work, at least we tried. Then we'll find a better way."

"That's right. If we don't try, we don't know if we can."

"Amen to that," Blake interjected from the table. As if she needed the reminder he was there, listening to every word, staring at her.

"Try doesn't mean one way, it means all the ways," Justin recited.

She kissed him on the head. "You're so smart."

"Fruit punch and grape juice," he said to Dee.

Uncomfortable with everyone staring at her, Gillian glanced at her grandfather. "I brought his school records. I need to enroll him in kindergarten here."

"There's a school bus. We'll get him registered and on the route. They'll pick him up out front at the road and drop him off. You'll like the school. They remodeled a few years back. They've got a great play-yard and nice teachers," he added.

"Monday, buddy. You're off to school."

"Oh man."

"No 'oh mans.' Please go take your seat at the table."

Her heart fluttered when he bounced over to the table and looked at the two seats between his grandfather and Blake. She waited to see what he'd do. He took the seat next to his grandfather and kicked his feet back and forth under the table. He wasn't afraid of the men. Her grandfather smiled. Justin actually smiled back, and she relaxed, pleased with his first courageous step into their new life here.

Still kneeling on the floor on one knee, she wondered how stupid she was to have gotten herself stuck in this position. Of course Blake noticed. The man hadn't stopped staring at her. Why? He liked her? He didn't? He thought she was here to take advantage of her grandparents? What? At least he kept his distance.

She rolled back on her heel and used her thigh muscles to lift herself up. When she was back on her feet, she swayed, and put her hand to her head. Blake popped up out of his chair so fast and came toward her that she barely had time to back up three steps before he got to her.

"I'm fine. I just stood up too fast."

"You aren't fine. Everyone in this room can see you aren't fine. Sit down before you fall down," Blake ordered.

"After you."

After a tense stare-down, he went back to the table and took his seat.

"Stubborn." Just to rile her, he used his foot to push out the chair between him and Justin. She might have wanted him to back off, but she was still going to have to sit next to him.

She took the seat. She wanted to lean back and rest, but she couldn't because of her back. She put her forearms on the armrests and slouched her back to relieve some of the tension and pain.

"Don't you have any pain meds to take?" Blake asked.

"I did."

"Where are they? I'll get them."

"They burned in the fireplace along with the jacket." She continued to stare at her plate and breathe as evenly as she could without hurting her ribs.

Blake sat back. He put both hands over his face and ran them through his hair. "Shit. I'm sorry, Gillian. I never meant . . ."

Justin looked at his hands in his lap. "He swore. That's bad."

Gillian put her hand over Justin's, trying to reassure him that Blake's swearing wasn't the same as their father going into a rage. "It's fine. Don't worry about it."

"You have to eat two helpings of vegetables," Justin said, staring at Blake.

Blake didn't say a word but piled two big helpings of salad on his plate. He speared a tomato and a bunch of lettuce with his fork, dragged it through some ranch dressing, and stuffed it in his mouth. Justin smiled and relaxed beside her.

Stunned that Blake would go along with her rule for

herself and Justin, she glanced at Blake, thinking she should say something to thank him for putting Justin at ease, but for the life of her, no words came to mind. She stared, trying to figure him out. The whole time, he took one bite after another of his salad, doing his penance for swearing without a word or outward sign he resented it. In fact, he cocked up one side of his mouth in amusement when she stared at him too long, so she quickly looked away.

Dee set the sandwich in front of Justin.

Gillian nudged his arm when he tried to pick it up. "What do you say?"

"Thank you."

Dee smiled across the table. "You're welcome. Please, everyone. Eat."

All the food got passed around the table, from her grandfather to Dee to Blake, who served Gillian up a huge bowl of chili, cornbread, and a large plate of salad with dressing. "Eat. All of it."

She shut her mouth with a hard click of her teeth so she wouldn't cuss him out for ordering her around in front of Justin.

She took the first bite and sighed. So good. "Thank you, Dee. This is amazing."

"You're welcome. I'm glad you like it."

Gillian did, so she ate her fill, ignoring the crackle of awareness with the too-gorgeous-for-his-own-good man beside her.

CHAPTER 8

Gillian tried to help Dee clean up the kitchen. The only thing Dee let her do was wrap up the last few pieces of cornbread. In hog heaven, Justin sat at the table devouring a bowl of vanilla bean ice cream and a cookie. Given half a chance, Dee would spoil him rotten. Gillian kind of liked the idea. Justin deserved to be spoiled after all he'd been through.

"So, if you're my grandfather, how come you never came to see us?" Justin held his spoon of ice cream halfway to his mouth.

Gillian waited for the answer despite Justin's rude question. She'd always thought her extended family, whoever they were, didn't care about her. That didn't exactly sync with what she thought of her grandfather now.

"I tried to keep in touch with your mom before she died and your dad after that, but they moved a lot. Ron didn't particularly want to see me," her grandfather answered.

"Why? Are you mean, too?"

"Justin," Gillian warned. "Mind your manners."

"No, Gillian. He wants to know, and I think that's a fair question under the circumstances."

All for honesty, she waited for his answer.

He turned to Justin and sat forward so that he was close and at Justin's level. "I don't believe in hurting people or animals. When your dad was young, I remember him as a nice boy. When he grew up and was a little bit younger than your sister is now, he got in with some bad people. He started taking drugs, and they changed him. That's why I didn't like him seeing my Erin. She didn't see that he wasn't good for her."

"Gillian says that drugs are bad. They killed my mom."

Bud glanced over at Gillian as she sat silently staring out the dark window. No doubt she listened to every word, despite not looking at him and Justin. He couldn't imagine what she'd been through living with Ron and Erin, watching them destroy their lives so recklessly. He couldn't imagine how she must have felt losing her mother to an overdose, and then having to raise her brother on her own.

No doubt Ron hadn't had a hand in raising the boy, who looked to Gillian for everything. When Justin finally felt full with dinner, he'd asked her for permission to be finished. He asked her for more milk. Every time, she made sure he minded his manners and sat up straight at the table. Not for show but to raise him right.

Bud glanced at Dee, who watched from the kitchen. She smiled her encouragement.

"I'm real sorry about your mom. I wish she'd let me help her."

"That's okay. I got Gillian. She's a good mom, even if she is my sister."

"Your sister's the best mom. You're a lucky kid to have her for a sister." Blake barely knew her, but she'd earned his admiration. He wanted to reach out, cover her hands, give her some kind of comfort to ease the pain etched into her too-pale face.

Tears slid down Gillian's cheeks. She didn't brush them away, just let them fall one by one and drop onto her folded arms on the table.

Justin looked at Blake warily. He didn't see his sister crying, but he leaned over and grabbed her shoulder to pull her down to him.

Gillian winced, but she didn't let him see that it hurt her. Blake got it. She didn't want Justin to ever think that he hurt her in any way. Discreetly, she brushed the last of the tears from her cheeks and listened to Justin whisper in her ear.

"We'll talk about that when we've settled in here and you're back in school. I haven't decided if you're ready to take care of one on your own. It's a big responsibility."

"But you'll think about it?"

"Yes. I told you I would. You could ask if there's already one here. It's a big place, and maybe they have one that you could practice with before I decide."

Blake leaned forward. He glanced at Bud and Dee, both as interested as he was in what the boy wanted.

Justin looked at his grandfather with all seriousness and eager eyes. "Do you have a dog?"

Justin had been through hell the last week—through most of his life—and he wanted a dog. A friend. Blake wanted to laugh at the pure anticipation in the boy's eyes. He wished at that moment that instead of sixty plus horses on the ranch he had a hundred dogs to give the boy.

Bud chuckled and sighed with a shake of his head and a soft smile. "I'm sorry, son. We don't have a dog. We have horses. Lots and lots of them. You can pet them if you want. I could take you over to where we have some of the foals, and you could pet them."

"What's a foal?"

"What's a foal? Well now, son, we have to educate you

on the family business. A foal is a baby horse. They're small and soft. Just the right size for you to pet."

"I want to see them." Justin jumped up to stand on his chair.

"Sit down, please," Gillian said firmly. "Justin, we need to talk about living here. You can't run off whenever you want to see the horses. They're big, and I'm sure your grandfather has some rules that you need to follow. The first one is that you don't go near the horses without an adult."

If any kid could pick a mom, they'd pick Gillian. Blake wondered if she wanted to have kids of her own. He imagined her with a dark-haired bundle in her arms, pressed to her heart. He'd never thought about having kids, but the idea started when he discovered that his brother Caleb and his wife, Summer, were expecting. Another generation of Bowdens would start with them. Gabe and Ella were getting married in May. Soon they'd start a family, too. The more Blake thought about his brothers, how happy they were with the women in their lives, the more he wanted something like that for himself. He'd never envied his brothers. Competed with them, yes. Nature of having siblings. Still, he envied them the women sharing their lives, the love and happiness they'd found. He wanted the same. He'd just never realized how much until now.

He turned his mind back to the conversation about the horses and having a six-year-old running around the ranch. Could be a dangerous situation for a boy who hadn't grown up around horses.

"Bud, how about I take them on a tour of the ranch tomorrow and go over the rules for young Justin." Blake looked at the boy. "Your sister is right about the first rule. You don't go near any of the horses without an adult. Most of the horses are nice, and you can pet them. They'll love it. But they're very big, and they could step on you and hurt you. Some of them bite, just like dogs. Okay?"

Justin spooned another mouthful of ice cream into his mouth. A dollop dripped down his chin, but he nodded to Blake.

"I think that's a great idea," Dee said. "We'll all take a tour tomorrow morning. It'll be a nice thing to do. Will you be able to walk around, Gillian?"

"I'll be fine. I want Justin to know his limits. If he breaks the rules, there will be consequences. Right, Justin?"

"Yes," he said, exasperated. Then he yawned so big his eyes squinted shut.

"Temperature check." Gillian leaned into Justin and kissed his forehead. "You're burning up, little one. Let's get some medicine into you, and then you can have a bath and go to bed." She looked to her grandfather and Dee, who was sitting beside him. "Would that be all right?" Another dose of bitter pride slid down her throat. She'd never had to answer to anyone before. Here, she did.

"Make yourself at home, Gillian, because that's where you are." Her grandfather smiled to make her feel more comfortable.

It seemed genuine. Maybe he was happy to have her and Justin here. Things had never gone this smoothly for her, so she waited for the other shoe to drop, dread a constant in her gut as anticipation stretched with every passing minute.

"Absolutely," Dee confirmed. "I'll go up with you and show you your rooms. I put extra towels in the bathroom for the both of you." Her gaze fell to Gillian's arms. "If you'd like some help, I can wash your hair in the sink if it'll be easier. I'll get you a plastic bag to go over your cast, and you can soak in a hot tub."

Gillian bit her lip and continued to stare out the window. Her eyes shined with unshed tears. No one had ever wanted to help so much.

"Accept the help, Gillian. I know it goes against everything in you, but we aren't going to stop offering." Blake raised his hand to place it over hers, but he set it back in his lap at the last second.

What would she do if he touched her? Flinch away, like she'd been taught by a man who never touched her in kindness? Get up and leave altogether? Or allow the sweet contact and fall apart right here in front of everyone?

Her raw emotions rose to the surface faster than she could squash them down. If she let herself feel one thing, she'd feel everything. Better to remain numb.

She hated that everything about her told him not to touch her, when a flicker of something in her heart begged for him to hold her and make all the bad go away.

Blake was bigger than her father, but nothing about him scared her. In fact, everything about him pulled at her, like he had his own gravity and she couldn't help but get sucked in.

Unable to look at him, she stared at her reflection in the black windows. He'd spoken so softly and with so much truth. It did go against everything in her to accept help. She'd done for herself or done without for so long that she didn't know how to ask for or accept help.

Justin. His name came to mind, and she knew that she had to do it for him. She had to try. It's what she'd been trying to teach him. She needed to do it herself.

"I can't take a bath with the stitches, but a quick shower would be nice. If you don't mind doing my hair in the morning, I'd appreciate the help. I just don't have it in me to bend over the sink while you do it tonight."

She couldn't sit still in her chair because she was in so much pain that she needed to keep moving to get comfortable. If Blake hadn't thrown the jacket with her medication into the fire, she'd have had her meds. She didn't blame him. He'd done it to make Justin, and her, feel better. A sweet gesture, she admitted, but one that cost her dearly. The frown and the apology in his eyes every time he caught her squirming made it easy to forgive him. He cared. That thought made her uncomfortable. She didn't know what to do with a man who actually cared about her feelings, so she ignored it.

She put her head down and held her throbbing temples between her two hands.

Justin put his hand on her shoulder. "You can cry if you want. I won't tell anyone."

Pull it together, Gillian. Don't lose it now. You're just tired. Don't let Justin see you break down.

She turned, took his face in her hands, and kissed him smack on the mouth. "I love you, baby. I'm not crying. I'm just really tired. Let's go get your bath done. I'll give you some medicine to make *you* feel better, and it's off to bed. We could both use some sleep." She stood and almost lost her balance again.

Blake didn't touch her, but grabbed her cast to hold her up straight. "Easy now. Come on, Gillian. I'll walk behind you up the stairs. That way, if you fall, I can catch you."

"Nobody needs to catch me. I'm fine."

"Yeah, you look it." His irritation came out in his voice. "Stubborn," he said under his breath, but she heard him.

"Yep." This time, she met his gaze, and they shared

an intense stare-down. He wanted her to give in. Not her style, but wouldn't it be nice to let someone rescue her? Especially if that someone turned out to be a handsome cowboy. The idea appealed, a lot. Okay, so she wasn't exactly immune to his charms. He didn't have to know that. Besides, she had no experience with men, especially one as old and experienced as Blake. Better to stick to the real reason she was here—Justin.

Bud and Dee showed Justin up to his room. Gillian took the stairs at a much slower pace. "Maybe we can get you some fire truck sheets to match your backpack," she heard Dee suggest to Justin.

Then Gillian heard Justin jumping on the bed upstairs and chattering about it being the biggest one he'd ever seen. "I can't believe it's all mine."

Over her shoulder, she told Blake, "Justin shared my twin bed with me in the apartment once he outgrew his playpen."

"I don't know how you did it. You were just a kid."

"He was just a baby. It wasn't his fault his parents were useless drunks."

So matter-of-fact. So sad that's how she felt about her parents. "So you managed to go to school, and then home to him when he was a baby."

"Yes and no. I would take him to a sitter in the morning and go to school. Then I'd go to work, and then I'd pick him up. Our father couldn't be relied on to pay the bills or buy food, so I got the paperwork to set us up for some social services, and that helped with the rent and food. I had to pay him fifty dollars to sign the papers. Whatever was left from the state checks, he drank, smoked, or popped. The money I made I used to buy Justin clothes, food, and diapers. Without me, he'd have ended up in the system or dead. Our father wasn't capable of taking care of himself, let alone a baby. I wouldn't have been surprised if he dumped Justin with the first person who'd take him. For a price, of course."

She struggled to get up the stairs. Blake stayed two steps behind her, and even though he had her bags in his hands, he was ready to catch her if she fell.

"You've done a great job raising him. Most fourteen-year-old girls are worried about their hair and if a junior or senior will ask them to the prom."

"I wasn't a contender for an invitation to the dance, let alone a date."

"Why?" he asked, genuinely surprised. "You're beautiful. I can't imagine any guy passing up the chance to take you out on a date."

She ignored the compliment. In her condition, let's face it, he was just being nice. "Who wants to hang out with the girl who has a drunken drug dealer for a father and a baby to raise. I was a lot of fun on a Friday night. Poopie diapers, spit-up, and formula. It's real easy to lose a lot of friends when your excuse for not going to the movies is that you have a baby to put to bed."

"Do you regret it?"

She reached the top of the stairs and stared at Justin jumping on the bed in his room to the right. The smile on his face was enough to bring fresh tears to her eyes. "Not a single moment. Look at him. He's happy. I could have kept him and taken off and started over. It would have been hard, because I don't have anything. What little was left in the apartment I pawned or left. I brought him here because I want him to have a chance at a normal childhood. I want him to have that, and I will do anything to make that happen."

"What about you, what do you want, Gillian?"

The intensity in his gaze said her answer mattered.

For the life of her, she had no idea. Up to this point, she'd just been surviving and keeping Justin safe. She looked up at Blake, and although he was too close, she shrugged. She didn't step back and found that she didn't feel the need. That was something new.

Dee ran the water for Justin's bath in the bathroom across the hall. The smell of vanilla and peaches bubblebath floated out on the air. Dee came to the door, a soft smile on her face as sweet as the fruity smell.

"Your room is there. Go see if you like it. We'll fix Justin's room to suit him. I made up yours, but if there's something you need, just let me know."

Gillian walked into the room and stopped short. It looked like something from a magazine. The walls were a soft, pale green with white curtains across the tops of the windows. Pictures of antique water pitchers filled with spring flowers hung on the walls. French doors led out to a small deck area with a turquoise café table and chairs. A walkway connected with the apartment above the garage and served as a cover for the first-floor walkway that led to the garage and the stairs up to the second floor. She liked the design.

The room smelled of the lemon oil and beeswax Dee used to polish the wood dresser and night table. A cream bedspread with tiny pink roses embroidered into the material covered the queen-size bed. So very lovely, it looked soft and inviting. A green glass vase filled to overflowing with flowers from the garden sat on the bedside table. The flowers and the pretty bedspread that Dee had chosen touched Gillian's soul. No one had ever done something so nice for her in her whole life. No one had given her pretty things just to make her happy.

She put her hand to her mouth to stop the sob that squeezed her throat tight and threatened to escape.

Dee and Blake exchanged a concerned look. Blake raised his shoulders, letting Dee know he didn't know what was wrong.

"If you don't like the room, we can change whatever you don't like. I can put you in with Justin if you'd rather be with him."

Her grandfather walked in through the adjoining door. "Gillian, we can fix whatever's wrong. Just tell us," he coaxed.

She stood in the middle of the room, staring at the bed and night table, tears threatening to spill from her eyes. "Stop. Just stop. Stop being nice. I don't have any defenses for nice. It's too much," she said and looked from her grandfather to Dee. "Please stop." She turned to Blake and hoped he'd understand. Someone had to understand. "She polished the furniture. She put a pretty blanket on the bed. She put flowers in my room." She couldn't hide the misery in her voice. "Don't you see? You can't do this to me."

Justin snuck past their grandfather and came to her. He wrapped his arms around her leg and held tight. "Do we have to go now?"

Blake came forward and kneeled in front of Justin. "Your sister is very tired. She's in a lot of pain. She hasn't quite accepted that we want to be nice to her."

"Ron used to smile. It wasn't a nice smile. It usually meant that I had to hide, and then he'd yell at Gillian. Sometimes he hit her," he said as if Gillian wasn't standing right there.

Blake looked up at Gillian's devastated face, her eyes filled with anguish. Everyone had a breaking point. She'd reached hers. That she took a deep breath and pressed on made him all the more proud of her.

"Your sister is just now figuring out that not everyone wants to hurt her," Blake said as he looked up and met Gillian's steady gaze. No tears, just a sense of utter defeat. They'd overwhelmed her with kindness, and she didn't know how to deal with it. "Can you get yourself into that awesome bubble bath by yourself?"

"Yeah. I take a bath alone. She just checks on me to make sure I'm okay."

"Great, why don't you go get in, and I'll check on you in a minute. Okay?"

Justin went into the bathroom across the hall and closed the door, leaving it open a crack.

Dee stepped forward and stood beside Blake when he rose to his feet again. "Bud and I will go in the other room and turn down the bed for Justin. I'll find him a spare set of clothes. I'll put his things in the drawers. Would that be all right?"

At Gillian's nod, Dee and Bud left through the adjoining door, closing it behind them.

Blake remained only a couple feet from her, the closest she'd allowed him so far. "You're going to feel better in the morning."

Gillian let out a deep sigh and frowned. "I'm going to feel like an idiot in the morning. She did all this for me, and I was nothing but an ungrateful shrew."

"No, you weren't. You showed her that the effort she put into making you welcome here was worth it, because you appreciate that she made the room nice for you. You could have walked in and said, 'Yeah, it's fine.' Lots of people just look at the surface. You saw the details. You saw the love she put into this room for you, and it scared you half to death because for the first time you see that someone wants you. They want you here. I want you here. You may not want to hear that, but there it is."

He gave her a minute to absorb that, then he pointed

out the French doors. "I spend my evenings in the office above the garage. See that house over there." He pointed to his place across a field. "I've lived here the last five years. I've known your grandparents since I was a kid. They're friends with my parents and like a second set of parents to me. They're family. Dee feeds me." He shrugged and cocked up one side of his mouth in a half grin.

"I've got some leftover pain meds at my place from when I hurt my shoulder," he continued. "They won't cut the pain you're in by much, but they'll take the edge off. I'll take you into town tomorrow to the drugstore, and we'll get you a new prescription for whatever you need."

"Um, wait," she said, stopping him before he went out the door. "Ah, the cuts on my back . . . do you have any antibiotic ointment I can put on them?"

"Did your stuff go into the fire?"

"Yeah." She spoke to his boots.

He stared at the top of her head, fighting the urge to brush his hand down her hair and reassure her that everything was going to be fine. The set of her shoulders and the rigid way she held her body told him she wouldn't believe him. She was done. She needed to be in bed and get a solid three days' sleep before she felt better. Too bad she wouldn't be curled up next to him. It was a nice thought, but she had "Hands Off," "Stay Back, and "No Trespassing" stamped all over her.

"Just give me a minute. Okay?"

When she nodded, he left through the doors and walked across the deck to the office stairs to run over to his place. He was back in a matter of minutes with the pills and a bottle of water.

She glanced up. "Why are you doing all this? You could have gone home."

He made a show of looking out at his place not so far away. "I'm basically home."

"You know what I mean. You don't need to be here dealing with me."

"I don't do anything I don't want to do." It was the truth. He wanted to be here with her.

"Yes, poor Gillian. She's all beat up."

He should have known she wouldn't believe him. "No. That should be, *Poor Gillian, she's tired and hurt and deserves a break. If she'd stop being stubborn and accept a little help, she might feel better.*"

"Pity." Gillian spat the word out like it tasted as bad as the thought.

"No one could pity you, Gillian. You've got guts and strength and a will and determination anyone would admire. I do. When I look at you I see—"

"A dozen bruises, a broken arm, a sprained wrist and knee, and a baker's dozen stitched-up glass cuts," she said sarcastically.

"I see," he went on, ignoring her interruption, "a woman with enough guts to take on raising a newborn baby. I see a woman who worked her ass off to graduate high school and work a part-time job at whatever she had to in order to feed and clothe her brother. I see a woman who thinks about a little boy's welfare in exclusion to her own. I see a woman who is fearless and took on a drugged-out man with a gun in order to prevent him from hurting or killing a defenseless little boy. I see a woman who is fearless enough to put herself in the path of that man over and over again to spare her brother. I see a woman who is fearless enough to come to a new state, to a family member that she isn't sure will be decent to her, because she wants her brother to have a normal childhood, and she's hoping this is his shot. I see a woman who has enough guts to stick it out and see if it works, and who knows that if she has to turn around and leave, she'll do everything in her power to give that little boy that normal childhood even if it kills her. Pity," he said distastefully. "I don't pity you. I have an overabundance of respect and admiration for you."

She sat on the edge of the bed with her arms wrapped around her middle. He wanted to reach out and brush his hand over her hair and watch the colors change as the strands caught the light.

Offer up the comfort she didn't want, and he shouldn't give.

"I know you're tired and not strong enough right now to keep all your defenses up, so I'll forget that you could possibly think I pity you. I'll go check on Justin." Water splashed in the other room, and what sounded like bombs went off every few seconds. "It sounds like he's having a good time. Take the pills and unpack. You can take a shower and go to sleep. You'll feel better in the morning." Blake left her room.

She felt like a fool. She thought about what he'd said. It wasn't so much the words as the way he said them. He truly respected her and what she'd done to keep Justin safe and raise him the best she could. No one had ever acknowledged her in that way.

She'd never met a man like Blake. He had a way of getting past all her defenses and speaking right to her heart. He was dangerous in a whole new way. A very dangerous man, indeed.

CHAPTER 9

Two hours after he left the main house, Blake stared at the dark ceiling from the sofa in the office above the garage. He couldn't bring himself to go home. Too far away from Gillian her first night here. Some irrational part of his mind made him believe she might need him, despite the fact that she maintained a six-foot personal-space bubble around her. After the way she reacted to the room Dee made up for her, he didn't want anything else to upset her, but he wanted to be close if something did.

Like a nightmare about killing her father. How did she feel about killing the bastard? Did it haunt her?

The rage he'd been holding back since he'd seen her bruised and broken body wanted to surface and explode. He wanted to punch Ron and make him feel as bad as Gillian looked and felt. Ron was dead, but if he wasn't, Blake would hunt him down. He wouldn't stop until he found him and made him pay for what he'd done to her. Not just for her physical injuries but the torture he'd made her endure all her young life.

Blake couldn't conceive of how a person could hurt another like that. That Gillian had been physically and emotionally abused her whole life made him sick.

She could have turned out mean and bitter. She could have turned her back on Justin and the responsibility of taking care of him.

She could have, but she didn't have it in her to give up. The word "quit" wasn't in her vocabulary.

Under her strength and determination was an underlying kindness and love. It shined through every time she looked at Justin and cared for him with infinite patience and gentleness. Blake hoped one day soon she found an inner peace and learned to smile again. He'd really like to see her smile.

Blake kept his promise and checked on Justin in the bath. The fading bruises on his arms and back sickened Blake. Ron had gotten in a few licks before Gillian had stepped in and stopped him. Permanently.

Blake had watched Gillian with Justin. She adored the little boy. She'd given him some medicine to bring down his fever and tucked the sleepy child into his own bed, where she'd kissed him goodnight. Justin had hugged her tight and hadn't let go for a good long minute. Gillian had given him all the time he'd needed, despite how much it must have hurt her back to bend over like that.

Justin's piercing scream broke the quiet night. Blake jumped up from the couch barefoot and bare-chested, and he ran for the door.

The scream woke her with a jolt. Gillian should have known better than to let Justin sleep alone in a strange place. He wasn't feeling well, and suffered nightmares ever since the night of the attack.

She rolled to her side, planted her hand on the mattress, and pushed herself up sideways, ignoring the pain in her back and leg. She swung her braced leg off the bed and hobbled into Justin's room. He thrashed in the covers, trying to run, and whimpered. The sad sound broke her heart. She touched her hand to his cheek and called his name. "Justin." He woke with a start, eyes wide, and launched himself out of bed and into her arms. She caught him, but it cost her.

"That's it, now. You're fine. You're safe, baby."

Justin sobbed and held on tight around her neck. She rubbed his back with her fingertips and rocked side to side with her hips. Blake rushed toward her from her room, and her grandfather came in from the hall, letting the light spill into Justin's dark room.

"He's fine," she said to both worried men. "He's just fine. It was just a bad dream," she crooned softly and ran her fingers through Justin's sweaty hair. "Just a bad dream that's all over now."

"It was him. His eyes. He picked me up off the couch and threw me to the floor."

"Shh. Baby, you're okay. He can't hurt you anymore. No one is ever going to hurt you again."

Justin sobbed harder. "He punched you. You fell, and he kicked you in the stomach."

She fell back onto the bed and sat with Justin in her lap, with his legs wrapped around her. She pulled him back and held his face in her hands so his tear-filled eyes gazed into hers.

"I'm fine, honey. Look at me. I'm fine. He can't hurt us anymore."

Justin sobbed harder. "You aren't fine. You don't look fine." He put his hand to her swollen eye and touched it softly. Then he traced his fingers along the bruise on her jaw.

"They'll go away. They look better now than before. Right?"

The tears faded and he nodded. She brushed her fingers through the sides of his hair and wiped his tears from his red cheeks. Dee came in and gave her a warm washcloth. She took it and wiped his face and neck. His fever was back and most of the cause for the nightmare.

Dee handed over a tissue, and Gillian helped Justin blow his nose. Justin lay on her shoulder while she rubbed his back. His little body trembled against hers. Dee sat on the bed beside her and brushed her hand over Justin's head. Touched, Gillian smiled.

"I'll go get his medicine. He's on fire. We might need to call the fire department," she teased.

Justin's cheek scrunched on Gillian's shoulder when he smiled at Dee, and Gillian's heart felt lighter.

"Thank you." She glanced at her grandfather and Blake. "He's okay now." She couldn't help but take a second look at Blake, with his hair disheveled and his wide chest bare. The man looked rumpled and gorgeous. She felt like someone stuck her in the middle with a hot poker and the fire spread from there to encompass her whole body and throb low in her gut. He should register those biceps as a lethal weapon. All that strength, yet he stared down at Justin with such warmth and sympathy.

Did the man have to look so damn good in the middle of the night? More than the expanse of muscles rippling over his chest and belly, it was that damn hair of his that made her want to touch him. It looked like he'd run his fingers through it half a dozen times. She wanted to push her fingers through the thick mass and grab a handful and let the softness of it glide through her fingers.

She tore her focus from the half-naked man and tried to remember Justin needed her—she didn't need Blake.

"Justin. Look at me. You are safe here. Look,

Grandpa and Blake came running when they heard you needed help. They won't let anything happen to you."

Gillian caught the startled look on her grandfather's face when she called him "Grandpa." Maybe like her, he was settling into it. She hadn't quite made up her mind completely about him, this place, or the too-handsome-for-his-own-good Blake. She gave both men a stern look, making sure they understood they better not make a liar out of her. Both of them gave her a reassuring nod they understood her silent message.

Justin turned to Blake and his grandfather. "I'm sorry I woke you up."

"No trouble, buddy." Blake came closer and bent in front of him. "I'm glad you're okay now. Everyone has bad dreams once in a while."

"Do you have bad dreams?"

"Sometimes," he confirmed. Not tonight, though. He had a feeling his dreams would be filled with Gillian and her gorgeous, creamy skin, her long legs and silky hair. He'd dream about stripping her out of her pink tank top and flannel boxer shorts. She wasn't wearing a bra, and the thin tank top fabric didn't leave much to his overworked-since-the-moment-he-met-her imagination.

"I was once in a car accident." Bud came closer and bent on his knee so he could be at Justin's level, like Blake had done. "It's scary to relive bad things in our dreams, but I can tell you, they'll go away. I hardly ever think about that car crash, and I don't dream about it anymore. The same will happen for you."

"I don't want to think about him anymore."

"We're going to work real hard to make that happen. Tomorrow will be your first full day here with us, and you'll see that living here is much different than living with your father. I think you're going to like the ranch, and especially the horses."

Blake wanted to help reassure him, too. "That's right. Your grandpa and I will take you around the ranch, and maybe we'll even take you horseback riding."

"I can ride them." Justin pulled away from Gillian to look at Blake.

"Sure you can. I'll teach you how."

"Can I, Gillian? Can I ride them? Please. Say yes."

"If your grandpa says it's okay. You'll have to follow the rules and do what Blake says."

"Will you come, too?"

Blake answered for her. "Sure she will."

Dee handed Gillian Justin's medicine. "How about we all go back to sleep? Morning comes early on the ranch, and Justin can barely keep his eyes open."

Gillian poured the proper dose of medicine and handed the small cup to Justin to drink. He did so with a sour grimace at the end, but didn't complain. Gillian handed him the glass of water she'd left by his bed. He took a sip and laid back on her shoulder again.

"Thank you, Dee, for being so kind. I think we'll be fine now." She brushed her fingers through Justin's hair again. "You want to sleep with me?"

Blake wished she'd asked him that question.

"Yeah," Justin answered.

"Yeah." She pulled him onto her shoulder and stood. She smiled at her grandfather. "He'll probably sleep like a rock. Sorry to wake you all."

"It's no trouble," Bud assured her. "We'll see you in the morning." He stood with Dee as Gillian took a few steps to take Justin to her bed.

Blake moved back to let her pass. Dee gasped and

covered her mouth with her hand. Bud's eyes went wide with shock and his face paled with anguish. Blake followed their gazes to Gillian's backside. Blake had been right. She'd been hiding a lot more under her clothes.

A six-inch stitched cut ran down the back of her thigh. Another peeked out the bottom of her shorts on the same leg. The leg she had in the brace also had three or four smaller jagged cuts that were either sewn closed or scabbed over. Nasty-looking bruises spotted her creamy skin. Cuts and scrapes marred the backs of her arms and shoulders. He could only imagine what the rest of her back looked like.

The ominous quiet alerted Gillian. What did they expect? She'd gone through a window. Her back felt like one big bruise and looked much the same. She gently laid Justin in her bed and tucked him in, kissing his forehead. His eyes drooped as he fell into sleep again. "I'll be back in a second," she whispered. "I just have to get your blanket."

She limped back into Justin's room. Of course, everyone waited for her. She closed the connecting door and turned to face them. Dee's sad face almost did her in, but their sympathy sparked her anger, and she was only going to explain once. She didn't want their pity.

"Listen. The glass window cut me up pretty bad, but they sewed me up and the stitches come out in a week. As for the bruises . . ." She shrugged them away. "Some of them are from him hitting me and the rest are from hitting the car. The impact from the fall broke my arm and messed up my wrist and knee. Everything will heal in time and no one will ever know I was hurt. Justin will forget, but not if you keep gasping every time you see me. So, to get it out in the open and to assuage your curiosity, I'll only do this once."

She turned around, draped her long hair over her shoulder, and pulled the tank top up so they could see her back. Once she was sure they got a good look, she pulled her shirt back down.

"Any questions?" She faced them again but couldn't bring herself to look at Blake's face.

"Does that hurt? Are you in pain?" Dee asked the ridiculous question, unable to imagine herself in Gillian's shoes. Gillian wouldn't wish it on anyone.

Blake's steady gaze bore into her.

She gave them the truth. "The most colorful bruises go all the way into my muscles and make them spasm and cause excruciating pain. My broken arm aches all the time, and my knee at the moment feels like it wants to explode. I still get some nasty headaches, especially when I'm tired, like I am tonight."

"But you've been picking up Justin and carrying him. How can you do that?" Worry and concern filled Dee's soft voice.

"Because she doesn't want Justin to see that she's in pain," Blake answered for her. "And she wouldn't be in this much pain if I hadn't tossed her meds into the fireplace."

Bud stepped toward Blake. "Why the hell would you do that? She needs them."

Gillian stepped in between the two men. "He didn't know they were in my jacket pocket. Justin got upset. Even though I'd washed the coat, it still smelled like our dad. Justin didn't like me wearing it, and I happened to say that I'd like to burn the thing. Blake accommodated me."

Blake wondered if she realized she was standing not a foot in front of him, blocking him from her own grandfather, who wouldn't lay a hand on him no matter how angry he got. They were friends. They barked at each other once in a while, but they respected each other and didn't have any reason to come to blows.

Bud stared down at Gillian, with her hands planted on her hips, then looked up at Blake over Gillian's head. Blake gave him an, *I know, she's actually standing close to us* look.

"All right, Gillian. We'll get you some more pain medication tomorrow. We'll try not to make a fuss about your injuries in front of Justin," Bud qualified. "But if you aren't feeling well and need something, you have to let us know."

"I'll do my best. Asking for anything isn't my way."

Blake bent close to her ear. "Make it your way," he ordered. At her dirty look, he added, "We aren't asking you to surrender. We're asking that you bend. Just a little," he softened.

Gillian let out an exhausted sigh and let her hands drop to her sides, her shoulders slumping. In her condition, it hadn't taken much for them to wear her down.

"I can't thank you enough for putting a roof over our heads and giving Justin a chance at a normal life. Luck has never been on my side, but I hope it shines on Justin, and one day he forgets he ever knew our father.

"I know you aren't like him." She looked Bud right in the eye when she said it. "I knew it when you looked absolutely insulted that I would even consider you'd hurt that poor horse. That, and the fact that the both of you make a point to get down to Justin's level. You don't tower over him and try to intimidate him with your size."

"You don't miss anything," Blake said.

"I was trained from birth to watch people's behavior. Knowing when someone might turn on you was essential. Ron had a lot of *unsavory* friends."

She let that hang for a moment but didn't offer anything more. Blake's imagination conjured enough disturbing images and scenarios all on its own. He didn't need her to spell it out for him.

She grabbed Justin's old blanket from his bed and headed for her room. "I'll see you in the morning." She turned back to Dee. "Thank you for the flowers. For everything."

Gillian disappeared into her room. Blake gave Dee and Bud a nod goodnight and followed after her. He had a feeling he'd follow her anywhere.

"Nothing sweeter than a sleeping child," she said when he entered her room. She held one end of the blanket, flung the other end in the air, and let it settle over Justin.

He agreed. The boy's soft face made him look completely at peace. Gillian looked wiped out. He tried to control the urge to wrap his arms around her and kiss her shoulder. Her dark gold hair shined in the moonlight coming from the windows.

"The little guy is out like a light," he whispered.

"He'll sleep until morning now. He got the bad out of his system."

"What about you? Will you sleep in your condition?"

"I'll be . . ."

"If you tell me you'll be fine one more time, I'll throttle you." He regretted the impulsive words and expected her to retreat again. She didn't.

"It's hard to sleep with hardware on your leg and a cast on your arm. I'll either sleep miserably or just be miserable. Better?" she asked with an insincere smile.

"I'm sorry I asked."

"I thought you would be. Go to bed, Blake. Quit worrying about me."

"I can't seem to help myself." He pulled the blankets back and waited for her to carefully get her leg into bed and turn over onto her stomach so she wouldn't hurt her back. He covered her but never touched her. God, he wanted to.

"Thanks." She wiggled and settled when she found a comfortable position. Which meant she wasn't in agonizing pain. She closed her eyes and hoped he'd stop staring at her and go to bed. She didn't want to be the center of attention anymore. She didn't want him looking at her the way he did. Something odd came into his eyes sometimes and made her want to get closer and run away all at the same time.

She thought he brushed his fingertips over her hair, but it was soft, and gone before she could decide if he'd touched her at all. She opened her eyes but didn't see him. The soft click of the French door gave him away as he left.

She wanted to call him back. The quiet night settled around her, along with the loneliness she carried with her always. She shifted, trying to get more comfortable, and attempted to forget about the tall, handsome man with an eight-pack of abs and a smile that could send her to her knees.

She didn't need Blake, or anyone else.

A little voice inside called, *You're a liar.*

CHAPTER 10

The sun rose over the snowcapped Three Peaks. Blake stepped out on his porch. He stared up at the brightening sky and sucked in a deep breath of cold, crisp air, hoping it would help wake him. He stuffed his hands in his coat pockets and pulled the leather jacket close to ward off the chill in the air. He went down the stairs and followed the path to the gravel road and across to the meadow, heading over to Dee and Bud's place for coffee and breakfast. With a rush in his steps, he closed the distance between his house and Bud's, anxious to see Gillian again.

After making sure Justin and Gillian were tucked into bed last night, he'd gone home and fallen into a deep sleep only a few hours ago. He tossed and turned, with dreams of Gillian filling his mind. A mix of images of her bruised and cut-up backside, and others of her healthy and whole, burning in his arms and tangling up the sheets. He woke up hard and aching. Not even a cold shower and his hand dampened the hot need running through his veins. He couldn't remember a woman ever making him feel like this. The guilt poked at his gut. In her condition, he shouldn't be thinking about her this way. No matter what, he shouldn't be thinking about her this way. But being away from her tormented him with a tug and pull that he needed to answer. He didn't get it, but the compulsion to give in to the connection outweighed his common sense.

His head ordered him to go directly to the kitchen door like he always did. His heart took over for his brain yesterday, so he walked to the garage stairs and took them up two at a time, crossing the landing to Gillian's door and peeking in. Sound asleep, she lay on her stomach. Justin sat on the bed next to her, playing with a lock of her hair. He traced the ends across his cheek, back and forth.

Blake tapped his fingertip against the glass to get Justin's attention. He didn't want to scare the boy or wake Gillian. He opened the door quietly and stepped in. Gillian didn't stir from her deep sleep. Her breathing remained steady and even. Golden hair spread over her back and pillow like a field of wheat. Thick waves that begged him to grab a fistful and see how soft it felt sliding against his skin.

"Hey, buddy. What are you doing up so early?"

Justin leaned in closer to Gillian against a particularly bad cut with lots of stitches. His eyes filled with apprehension.

"Your sister could use some more sleep. Want to come with me and get something to eat?" Blake lifted his head and inhaled. "Smells like pancakes."

Justin's eyes narrowed on him. The boy swept his gaze over Blake's tall frame, assessing him. Blake stayed at the end of the bed, giving him a chance to make up his mind if he trusted Blake and thought he'd be safe. Blake couldn't remember being that guarded at six years old. Most kids at that age thought everyone was a friend.

"We'll only be downstairs. If you want to come back up to Gillian, you can." He gave Justin a reassuring smile.

Justin scooted to the edge of the bed. Blake turned his back, squatted to his level, and said over his shoulder, "Hop on. I'll give you a ride."

Justin hesitated. Blake waited patiently. With slow deliberation, Justin leaned on Blake's back and grabbed hold of his shoulders.

Blake stood, and Justin wrapped his legs around his waist. Blake put his arm under the boy's butt to hold him in place and turned back to Gillian. She slept soundly, although he didn't know how she could be comfortable with the brace on her leg. She'd pushed the pillow out from under her head and lay on the mattress with her purple casted arm by her head. Probably easier to sleep flat.

"She's pretty when she isn't hurt."

"She's beautiful no matter what," Blake said.

"You like her," Justin said from behind him.

"I like you both."

Justin leaned forward, put his chin on Blake's shoulder, and looked down at his sister. "If she hadn't come home in time, he would have taken me from Mrs. Wicks and done something bad. She hid me lots of times. She saved me."

"Yes, she did, buddy. She sure did." She'd saved Justin when he was a baby, and she'd been saving him ever since.

The sun shined through the window like a spotlight on her face. She peeked out one eye. Early, the sun wasn't very high. She should have pulled the roller shades down, but she'd loved staring out at all those stars. She could do without the sun, especially this morning, when her head pounded and the muscles in her back screamed in agony.

She pressed herself up on her elbows and hung her head between her shoulders, stretching the muscles. Then it hit her. Justin wasn't in bed with her. His sharp scream came from downstairs.

She rolled out of bed without any thought to her injuries and hobble-ran for the stairs. She hopped down them on her good leg, each step another painful lightning bolt to her back, rushed into the kitchen, and stopped dead in her tracks. Unable to speak, she stared. Justin lay across Blake's strong arms. Blake brought Justin's belly to his mouth and pretended to eat him, making silly chomping noises and blowing zerberts. Justin screamed and laughed with such joy that it brought tears to her eyes. She'd never seen him so carefree and happy.

Dee stepped in front of her, blocking her from Justin's view. "Good morning. How'd you sleep?" The false cheer in her voice didn't match the deep concern in her eyes. Under her breath she said, "He's fine. Take a breath. Blake's just playing with him."

Gillian's seized lungs let loose and filled with air. Her pounding heart stopped battering itself against her sore ribs and slowed. "I know. It's me. I overreacted. I heard him scream." She took a deep breath to try to calm herself.

"That's it, dear. Now, would you like a cup of coffee?"

"Desperately. Cream or milk if you have it."

"Sit down, and I'll get it. I'll bring you something to eat."

It took Gillian a minute to let the pain settle and for her to accept its pounding presence, then ignore it the best she could. She walked over to the table, where Blake had deposited Justin into his chair. Justin held a mug of hot chocolate with whipped cream on top, a spot of it on his nose and a mustache above his lip. The silly smile he gave her made the last of her fear disappear.

"Fever check." She leaned over and pressed her lips to his forehead.

"Blake already checked. He said I'm simmering."

Her gaze shot to Blake. Surprised, she asked, "Did you kiss this boy?"

"So what if I did," he said in defense.

"It's kind of sweet." She crossed her arms over her chest. Blake kept his eyes on hers, but something about the way he held still told her he saw a lot more than her face. She waited for his eyes to dip to her cleavage, but they never did. Huh. She didn't know if the glimmers of interest she'd sensed in him were real, or just imagined. Or wishful thinking. She didn't want to be interested in him.

Liar, liar, your pants are on fire. That inner voice stuck its tongue out at her.

"I'm a sweet guy. What can I say?"

"Oh, I don't think you're sweet at all."

Actually, she was right about that. Abigail, his long-ago ex, would agree. She had the scars from that fateful day when their fun had taken a turn toward disaster to prove it.

"Which makes you kissing him all the more sweet."

"Then let's just say it's you bringing something good out in me." Blake pushed thoughts of Abigail and that stupid dare out of his mind. He slid out a chair for her with his boot and waited for her to sit down with the coffee Dee handed her.

"Where's Grandpa?" The name kind of stuck on her tongue.

"He went down to check on the sick horse in the

pasture. He'll be back shortly," Dee explained, the soft smile on her face lighting her eyes. "Your grandfather is so happy to have you here. We both are."

Blake leaned in close. Too close, but she didn't move away, so he didn't back up. He whispered, "I'm sorry I scared you this morning."

"It's fine. What do you people do, have a contest with the sun to see who can get up first?" She yawned and tried to lean her head to the side, pressing her opposite shoulder down to work out a knot.

Blake laughed. "Not exactly. We have to get up early to feed the horses."

"Shouldn't you be out doing that?"

Still trying to get him to back off. Not going to happen. "I'm spending the day with you. Bud and I have several men working here. They can take care of things today."

She rolled her shoulders and made disgruntled faces, trying to stretch the muscles in her back. If she'd let him, and she wasn't so cut up, he'd get up and rub out the tight muscles. She wouldn't. And he didn't.

Hands off, man. Hands off.

Instead, he stood, walked into the kitchen, and took one of Dee's dish towels. He dampened it at the sink and popped it in the microwave. He set the time and waited for it to heat up. When the microwave dinged, he grabbed the warm, but not too hot, towel and carried it over to Gillian. She set down her mug. He leaned in close to her ear. She'd get used to him being close if he kept at it. "Lean over." Her eyes narrowed with skepticism. "Trust me."

He held back the smile when she cocked an eyebrow and met his gaze with a cold stare. She slowly leaned over, and he used one hand to pull up her shirt. He laid the warm towel on her back and pressed down on it to get the heat to work its way into her muscles. Her eyes closed, and she literally laid herself on the table. If she was a cat, she'd purr. Relief washed across her face and made her features go soft.

"A little trust goes a long way." He let the humor show in his voice. "I'll heat it again when it cools off. It should help loosen up some of your muscles."

"What do you want? Name your price," she said from the tabletop.

Blake shook his head. "You're easy," he teased.

She opened one eye and raised her eyebrow. "On second thought, you owe me. You burned my meds."

All humor gone, he let the smile fall into a frown.

She reached out to touch his hand but pulled back at the last second. Too familiar. Not her style. She raised her head. "I'm sorry. I was just teasing. Really."

"We'll get your meds today. Don't worry about it." For the first time, he touched her, reaching out with his big hand to the side of her face. She flinched at the initial contact but relaxed, her gaze locked with his. Watching. Waiting to see what he'd do next. He gently pushed, guiding her back down to the table. "Relax. Let the heat work on your back."

In an impossible attempt to distract himself from the woman studying him like an unidentified microbe under a microscope, he glanced over at Dee, who was watching them from the kitchen stove. She gave him a knowing smile that he refused to acknowledge in any way. She filled a plate for him, giving him extra bacon. Some kind of reward for taking care of Gillian. He didn't need a reward, he needed her to feel better. He hated seeing her in pain. It made his gut sour and his chest tight. Besides his family and the horses, no one had sparked this nurturing side in him. Gillian was good for him. She brought something out that no one else had seemed to find inside him. He liked feeling this way about her.

Does Gillian realize the kind of effect she has on me?

He shifted in his seat. She stiffened, then relaxed when he didn't do . . . whatever it was she thought he'd do to her. Nope. She still saw him as a possible threat. Well, he aimed to fix that. Immediately.

"Blake thinks you're beautiful," Justin announced over a mouthful of chocolate chip pancakes.

Gillian's eyes flew open at Justin's announcement. She stared at him as he watched her.

"He can't keep anything to himself, can he?" Blake asked.

"No," she confirmed. "He also repeats words he shouldn't, so watch your mouth."

"You have to eat extra vegetables for each bad word," Justin said.

"I found that out last night. She's tough," Blake eyed Justin.

"On Mondays, she takes me to the ice cream place, and I get to have two scoops."

"Tough and nice." Blake caught the haunted look in Gillian's sad eyes and leaned down close to her ear. "Let me guess," he whispered. "Ron was home on Monday nights, and you needed a place to hide out. Justin got ice cream, and you got a little peace."

She nodded, sat up, and shook the cold towel off her back. Blake took it off her chair and went to heat it again. He came back with her plate filled with eggs, bacon, and pancakes. He put the hot towel on her back again and went to get his plate, while Dee joined them at the table.

Justin chatted about everything under the sun with his normal six-year-old enthusiasm. Blake watched Gillian mindlessly eat her food and drink her coffee. He learned something about her this morning. She was slow to wake up and didn't mind sitting around half naked. One hell of a pretty picture. One that morphed into something completely inappropriate in his mind.

"Blake?"

Her voice brought him back to the here and now. The image of her naked in his bed slipped away, but not the heat pooling in his groin. He shifted to get more comfortable. Fantasizing about her was one thing, but doing something about it crossed the line. He owed Bud better than that and would keep his promise to watch over her.

He followed her gaze out the window to Bud, in the corral with the sick horse. Bud tried to coax the horse to go to his food and eat, but every time he got close to the animal, the horse shied away and ran around the corral.

"What's he doing?"

"Trying to get the horse used to him. Old Boots won't eat well, and he won't let anyone get near him. We'd like to take care of him, but he's making it hard. We don't want to push him, because he's been sorely mistreated. Bud thought it best if we take it slow."

Like I'm trying to remember to do with you, sweetheart.

"Blake, does your mother still make those nice quilts?" Dee asked.

"She made me one for Christmas. It's on my bed at the house. Why?"

"I thought I might give her a call and see if she could help me put something together for Justin's room. Maybe I'll invite your parents over for supper one night."

Blake didn't miss the wheels turning in Dee's sharp mind. She wanted to enlist his mother's help in setting him up with Gillian. The two of them liked to conspire to find him a wife. He'd be thirty in a couple of years, and maybe it was time to settle down. Well, he didn't need their help, or want it, but that wouldn't stop them from trying. The idea of Gillian meeting his parents didn't put him off in the least. In fact, he welcomed the idea. If Gillian saw him with his family, she might actually begin to trust him.

"Call her, you know she'd love it. Dad will love it, too. Anything to keep her busy."

"Dee, Grandma." The name stumbled off her lips. "You don't have to go to any trouble or contact Blake's mother."

Justin saw Dee's watery eyes and frowned. "Why is she sad now?"

Dee wiped the tears from her eyes and tried not to make Gillian uncomfortable. "Oh, I'm just being sentimental. Your sister was sweet enough to call me 'Grandma,' and it just made my heart so full it spilled out my eyes."

"Your heart's full of tears?"

"No, honey. My heart is full of love."

Gillian fidgeted, looking for an escape. This was getting to be too much for her. Blake sympathized, despite the fact this was good for her.

"Um, I'm going up to get dressed. Ah, Grandma, if you wouldn't mind doing my hair when I come back down, I'd appreciate it."

"Of course, dear. No problem. Then we'll go on our tour of the ranch. Maybe we'll let Justin feed some apples to the horses."

"Cool!" Justin yelled.

Blake waited for Gillian to leave the room before he looked back to a smiling Dee. "She's trying."

"You have to try," Justin confirmed, just like his sister taught him. He happily stuffed more pancake into his mouth and chewed. He'd settled into the family.

Blake hoped Gillian did the same. Soon. Maybe she needed it more than Justin. She'd suffered at her father's hands far longer and in a more brutal way. She needed to be surrounded by family and love. She deserved it and a hell of a lot more. Blake vowed she'd live a happy life from now on. He'd make sure of it.

CHAPTER 11

Gillian hobbled down the stairs after getting dressed and stood in the kitchen doorway, watching Blake play with Justin. Even when he wasn't trying, he got to her. She felt another brick in the wall around her heart fall and hit the others he'd already knocked loose with his quiet determination to get her to trust him. Well, she couldn't exactly say she did or didn't. So far, he hadn't earned it, but he hadn't done anything to make her not trust him either. The jury was still out.

The smile came easily when Blake held Justin's small hands in his large ones. Justin walked up Blake's legs and tumbled over backward, falling to his feet, then Blake let go of his hands when he landed safely. Each time, Justin laughed with such delight that her heart melted a little more. His laugh and smile got her through more days than she could count. Thrilled, Justin jumped up and yelled, "Again." Ever patient, Blake let him go again and again.

Dee wasn't in the kitchen. Judging by the dish towel slung over Blake's shoulder, he'd done the breakfast dishes. She appreciated a man who kept things clean and pitched in to help when needed. Her father's idea of helping out around the house had been to throw his garbage and beer bottles in the general direction of the trashcan. Too drunk and stoned, he missed by a yard, but still called out, "Swoosh," and laughed his ass off for no reason. She often felt more like a mother and a maid than a daughter who should have had no more worries than her next high school chemistry pop quiz and whether a particular boy liked her. She should have spent her days out with friends and her nights sneaking off with a boyfriend. Instead, she'd raised a boy to the age of six and tried her hardest to keep the evil that lived in their home at bay.

She'd done everything she could under the threat that her father would take Justin away from her if she tried to run away with her brother. Disappear. Then Justin would have been at his mercy. She'd wanted to take Justin away, but with her meager resources and the beating she'd suffered the one time she'd tried, she'd hesitated every time she'd thought to do it again. She'd feared that if it didn't go exactly to plan, she'd lose Justin, either to her father or the system. So she'd saved her pennies, every cent she could spare, and she'd planned, hoping one day she'd have the resources to take him and not end up living on the streets and in shelters, where social services was sure to take him from her.

But none of that mattered now. Look at him. Happy. Safe.

Blake smiled and laughed with Justin, and her heart tripped. This was what a man, a real man, looked like. This was what a father looked like. She'd told them last night to stop. She didn't have any defenses for kindness. Blake seemed to be the one who got past all her barricades the easiest. She wondered how he'd managed to do it in a matter of hours by being nothing more than himself.

She'd made it through her high school years without becoming another statistic of teen promiscuity and pregnancy. She'd managed to survive those tumultuous years without becoming like her mother. As she looked at Blake now, the muscles in his strong arms cording as he pulled Justin up for another flip, a door in her heart crept open. Part of a long-forgotten dream caught the first rays of light she'd let shine in since she was a little girl dreaming of being a princess in a faraway land. She wanted to slam it shut again, afraid he'd see those silly, girlish dreams, pat her on the head, and send her on her way so he could find a woman more his age and a lot less trouble and damaged than her. Someone further away from college than high school. Older, wiser, more experienced.

She'd dreamed a lot as a young girl, but she'd put silly things like that away the night her mother handed her Justin, bundled in his blanket, and left with her father, never to return. Yes, she'd put away silly things like dreaming that one day she'd find a good man who knew how to be kind and gentle, a man who knew how to smile and laugh without turning it into something ugly.

Blake made that door creak open, and she mentally put both hands on it and shoved it shut again. She had a brother to raise and enough baggage to fill the back of her pickup truck, pulling the added trailer full of garbage that went with it.

"Is Dee around? She said she'd wash my hair."

Blake glanced over, dismayed to see the sadness in her eyes before everything in her face went blank again. "She's on the phone with my mother, plotting a surprise for this one." He flipped Justin over again, not missing the way Gillian's eyes locked onto his arms as his muscles bunched to pull Justin up and flip him over. "Enough, buddy. Go upstairs and get dressed. Put on your shoes, and we'll go down to the stable to see my babies."

"What babies?"

"The horses." He took the towel from his shoulder and used it to swat at Justin's behind. Justin laughed and dodged the snap of the towel. "Go. Hurry up. The day's wastin' away."

Justin grabbed Gillian's leg and gave her a squeeze before heading upstairs.

She called after him, "I put your clothes out on your bed."

Blake walked toward her, trying to gauge how close she'd let him get this time before she backed away. He stopped three feet from her. She didn't move, but kept her wary gaze on him. Progress. "Ready to wash your hair?"

Undecided, Gillian eyed him and the sink and checked the other room over her shoulder. "Is Dee coming back?"

"She and my mother will probably be on the phone a while. There aren't a lot of women who work on the ranches, so once those two connect, it'll be a while for them to get their gossip all told. I'll wash your hair." He made the suggestion matter-of-fact, hoping she didn't run away. He was doing his best not to scare her off, when all he wanted to do was hug her and ease some of the pain and hurt she couldn't hide.

"You don't have to do that. I can wait. I can do it one-handed in the shower."

She bit her lip, still unsure about him. If she felt the pull half as much as he did, then her system had gone haywire along with his. Hard to tell if she kept her distance solely because of what she'd been through, or because of the attraction snapping between them like electricity across two live wires.

"I'm sure washing your hair that way is fine in a pinch, but I can do the job better. You'll feel better with your hair clean. I'll need you to show me where the stitches are so I don't hit them."

He gave her a minute to get used to the idea, then went to the cupboard and pulled down a large juice pitcher. He set it on the counter. She walked over and stood next to him at the big farmhouse sink. He didn't speak, just turned on the tap and waited for the water to warm up. He took the bottle of shampoo from her and set it on the counter beside him. She held her hair up. He helped her drape the towel around her back and shoulders.

"There're three lines of stitches. They should be pretty healed, so it won't matter if you touch them."

Blake shut off the tap. "Show me." He kept his tone casual. He didn't want her thinking they repulsed him. They wouldn't. He just wanted her to be comfortable with him. He wanted to rub his hand over her back and reassure her. He didn't understand his natural tendency and need to care for and tend her, but like every other strange feeling he'd had since he met her, he went with it.

She drew her hair away from her neck and the back of her head to show him the cut that disappeared into her hair. He helped her brush away some of the strands to see how far up her head it went. His finger brushed her hand, and she immediately jumped back and put both hands up to ward him off.

"Easy, now. I was just trying to see how long the cut is." He leaned back against the counter and crossed his legs at the ankle. He wanted her to see that he had all the time in the world. "Listen to me. Hear me on this. I will never, *ever* hurt you."

"I'm sorry. It's just . . ."

"No sorry needed. There's nothing to explain. It's no big deal, Gillian. Really."

He waited for her to come back to him. It took her a few seconds, testing him to see if he'd lose his patience. Not going to happen. Used to working with scared and wild horses, he'd learned to wait, because the payoff mattered. She came back to stand beside him and pulled her hair back again. This time, when his hands brushed her hair away, she jumped and caught her breath, but didn't back away.

He worked quickly and carefully to wash her amazing mass of hair. She didn't move or say anything, but her whole body trembled. He hoped from the effort it took her to bend over in her condition and not because he frightened her. He had to pile the long, thick strands on her head to wash it all without soaking her. The smell of flowers and citrus filled the kitchen and his senses.

It took several pitchers of water to rinse all the dark golden hair. When he was done, he took the towel from her shoulders and put it over her head. He gently rubbed her scalp dry and pulled the hair through the towel from her crown to the tips. Satisfied, he turned her toward him and used his fingers to comb the strands from her face.

His gaze met hers and held. Everything inside him went still. His heart pounded. He kept his hands on her neck, his fingers tangled in her wet hair. He let the moment stretch so they could both settle into the vibrations between them.

Gillian's eyes held a touch of fear. That was as natural for Gillian as breathing. Would she ever get past what her father did to her? Given time and her innate strength and perseverance, yes, she'd learn to be happy.

Here on the ranch, where he worked and lived and promised to take care of her—not date her.

Off limits, man. Get your head straight.

"Come on. I want to see the horses." Justin broke the strange tension.

Blake and Gillian shot apart from each other, like teenagers caught doing something they shouldn't. Dee stood behind Justin, smirking.

Gillian needed to get away from Blake. He did things to her system that shouldn't happen after only meeting him yesterday. Her fingers flexed, and she balled them up so that she wouldn't reach out and touch him. She had a real need to put her hands on his chest and see if it was as hard and strong as it looked. She wanted to slide her hands over it and around his big shoulders and feel his arms come around her and hold her. Only trouble with that, she feared if he did, she would break into a million tiny pieces. Better to keep her guard up and escape this strange pull that sucked her into him every time he was near.

"I'll just go up and brush out my hair. I'll meet you down at the barn."

"You sure you don't need any help?" Blake asked, all casual and kind.

He stayed in front of her, blocking her escape. They'd shared something elemental a moment ago. This was the closest she'd let him get to her, and he didn't seem inclined to give her any space. Not anymore. A dangerous man. Maybe more dangerous than her father, because he touched her heart, and it just wasn't up for another beating. This man had the power to break her, where her father never had.

"I can do it. You've done enough. Thank you." Yep, another dose of pride down her gullet. She appreciated the help but resented the need for it. She hated not being able to do for herself.

"You're welcome. No trouble at all. We can do it again tomorrow."

"I'm sure you have better things to do than wash my hair."

"Not really. I've got all kinds of time for you, Gillian. Get used to it." He grabbed Justin under the arms and hauled him up onto his massive shoulders. "Let's go, buddy. I'll introduce you to a horse. Have you ever seen a horse up close?"

"No. I've seen a sea lion at the wharf. Gillian took me. They bark like dogs. How come there isn't a dog here? There's lots of room, and you got lots of animals. Couldn't I have a dog?" Justin asked as Blake walked out the door with him.

"That boy has a one-track mind." Dee smiled.

"About the dog. This is your house and ranch, and if you and Grandpa don't want a dog here, I'll divert Justin's attention to something else. He'll probably get interested in the horses and forget all about the dog."

"Gillian, Bud and I would get Justin a dog today to make him happy and feel more at home here."

"You would?"

"Sure. This is your home, and a dog would be a great pet for Justin. But last night Bud and I also discussed the fact that you've been Justin's mother his whole life and it wouldn't be right for us to interfere in the way you raise him. You've done a fine job so far, and there's no reason for us to take over. That isn't to say we don't want to help you. We do. We'd just like you to know that we'll follow your lead with Justin. If you think it's time for him to have a dog, and you want to get him one, we'll help you get one for him. We want you to be at home here, Gillian."

Shocked, Gillian didn't know what to say. They'd discussed the best way to help her and Justin, not take over her life. After she'd arrived and they'd discovered they were taking on Justin as well as her, she'd expected them to discuss how to get rid of them, or how they'd take care of Justin without her.

"Although we weren't expecting him, we're so happy to have you both. Bud has spent a lot of years wishing things with Erin could have been different. He carries a lot of guilt, especially about the way Ron treated the two of you. He wants to make up for not helping you sooner."

Gillian's suspicions must have shown on her face, prompting Dee to go on. "He's not offering you a place to stay out of obligation. He wants you here. We want you here. You're family. You were right to hope this was a good place to bring Justin. He'll grow up with family, the ranch, the friends he'll make at school. There are good people in this place. People like Blake."

Gillian narrowed her eyes, trying not to give anything away about how she felt about Blake. Truth be told, she wasn't sure about him, or the strange way he made her feel.

"Oh, Blake might be a little rough around the edges, but he's got a good heart. You've seen it in the way he interacts with Justin. The man has turned into a big kid around that boy. It's nice to see."

So different than what she and Justin were used to with their father.

Dee patted her on the shoulder to reassure her. Gillian still didn't trust their kindness or generosity. Those two things had been missing from her life for too long.

Reading her mind, Dee said, "We'll never stop being nice to you and Justin. We do it because we love you.

No strings attached, sweetheart. Give yourself permission to accept it."

"I'll try. I really will."

"Justin is young. He'll find his place here and at school with ease. You'll find your place, too. Just give it time. In the meanwhile, give yourself a chance to heal. Don't rush things. When you're better, and you've had time to think about what you want to do with your life now that you have help and a home, we'll talk."

Gillian had never found her place, or dared to dream about what she'd like to do with her life beyond taking care of Justin. He needed to be here and deserved this chance to have a good and happy life. She would make sure he got it. As for herself, she couldn't hope for more than Justin's happiness.

She didn't dare think she could have some happiness of her own after she'd been denied so long. Could she? Now that they had a home, family who seemed to care, maybe some of those things she'd never allowed herself to think about could be a reality. College? A job she liked, rather than just something she did to earn money? There were so many choices open to her now that they overwhelmed her.

Blake popped into her mind, along with the crack in the door to her dreams in her heart. She couldn't seem to keep it shut around him. Damn if hope didn't shine a light on them again.

CHAPTER 12

Blake enjoyed spending time with Justin. Reminded him of playing and hanging out with his brothers when they were kids. Justin's enthusiasm sparked his own. Quiet in the stables this time of the morning, many of the horses were out being exercised or put through their paces in the training rings and on the track. Several stable hands worked in the empty stalls, cleaning them out, but otherwise Blake, Dee, Bud, and Justin had the stable and several horses to themselves.

"I want to give her another piece."

"Last one. This beauty is going to be a mama in a week or so. When she decides it's time to have her baby, maybe you can come and see him or her."

"Is that why she's so fat?" Justin took the slice of apple, held it in his flat palm, and offered it to Honey. She carefully plucked the treat from him, making him giggle when her fuzzy lips brushed against his hand. He wiped his hand on his jeans, a huge smile on his face.

"Don't listen to him, Honey. You're beautiful." He looked down at Justin. "She's not fat, she's full of horse."

Justin laughed, and every time he did, Blake became more and more attached to the kid.

"Justin, come see." The stall door stood open. Inside, Bud held a foal, his hands light on the animal's neck and back. The foal's mother waited patiently outside the outer door for her baby to be returned.

"Oh, my God, he's so little compared to the others."

"*She's* about two weeks old. She's going to be a champion. Her name's Dancer's Grace. We call her Grace. Her father was Dancer, and he was a champion racehorse. This little girl is going to run like the wind. Just like her father."

Justin pet her like Blake showed him, starting at the top of her neck and brushing his hand down over her back. "She's soft."

Blake watched from the stall door. Justin had adjusted to being here at the ranch with little fuss. Sure, his past haunted him while he slept, but while he was awake, he was a normal little boy. He seemed comfortable with them. Blake wished it came that easy for Gillian. Justin was young and resilient. Gillian had spent her whole life living with her guard up. He wished he knew how to get her to shut down her defenses.

Justin brushed his hand down the foal's neck. Maybe that's all it would take, a gentle hand.

"Grandpa, can I give Grace an apple, too?"

Blake handed over a small piece. "Be careful. Babies aren't as good about minding their manners. Keep your hand flat."

"Where's Gillian?" Justin asked for the fifth time. Although he enjoyed being with them, he still needed her.

"She's coming."

Ken walked up and slapped Blake on the back. Ken had been working at the ranch for about a year. Cocky, he didn't much like being the one on a lower rung. He'd made it clear that he wanted Blake's job. He didn't have

Blake's smarts or his training skills. Ken was good at putting the horses through their paces, but he didn't have the same heart and drive that made Bud choose Blake as a partner. Ken would either work the job he had for the rest of his years on this ranch, or he'd leave.

"Man, did you see the gorgeous blonde outside? Looks like she's been in a car accident. It didn't affect her fine ass. I can't wait to meet her."

Blake blocked the stall door and Ken's ability to see Justin and Bud. Justin backed away, snuck around his grandfather, and hid behind Bud's legs. His eyes lost their shine. Bud put a hand on his shoulder to reassure him.

Blake hated seeing the little boy frightened.

Here in the stables, guys were guys, and they talked and swapped tall tales. They used rough language and told crude jokes. Normal guy stuff. Exactly what Blake worried would bother someone like Gillian. Any woman, for that matter.

Anyone new on the ranch would draw attention, but the men would take special notice of a woman, especially one as beautiful as Gillian. Her injuries would spark even more curiosity. Ken's interest set off a wave of unfamiliar jealousy inside Blake.

Easy way to put a stop to it. "I see you met Miss Tucker. Bud's granddaughter."

If Ken was smart, he'd understand that any attention he paid to Gillian could draw the boss's attention, too.

Bud came forward out of the stall with Justin right beside him.

Ken's eyes went wide, but he covered his surprise. "Ah, sorry, sir. I had no idea. My tongue ran away with me, I guess. It was just talk, that's all."

"There'll be no talk about Gillian on this ranch," Bud warned. "I know single women are few and far between in these parts, but you even look at her sideways, it'll cost you dearly."

Bud's gaze shot from Ken to Blake and back. Blake got the message. That meant him, too.

Shit. If his interest in Gillian showed that much, he needed to rein it in.

"Gillian's been hurt." Blake didn't say in what way or how. He'd let Ken think he meant her physical injuries. "She requires a lot of space, so give it to her."

"Sure thing, boss." Ken touched the brim of his hat.

Ken's easy assurance didn't fool Blake. Ken only called him "boss" when he wanted to pacify him. Blake wasn't placated in the least. He sure as hell wasn't convinced Ken would give Gillian the space she needed. If not, fine. Blake would keep Ken too busy to pay attention to her.

Maybe Blake was being too sensitive. Under other circumstances, he might have joked along with Ken. All in fun, but he couldn't do it at Gillian's expense. She wasn't just some woman. She meant something to him. He respected her more than anyone else he'd ever known.

Before she arrived, he and Bud had discussed her coming to the ranch. They'd come to an agreement. Absolute zero tolerance for anyone making Gillian uncomfortable. This was her home, and she would live here without ever having to look over her shoulder. Blake assured Bud he'd take care of things. Before, it had simply been a chore added to his normal job. Now, it was his personal mission. Gillian was his responsibility, and he'd make damn sure no one made her want to leave. No one would ever hurt her again.

Ken glanced down at Justin, half hidden behind his grandfather. "Your mama sure is pretty."

"She's my sister."

"Even better." Ken's voice held a ring of interest.

Blake wanted to make Ken understand that Gillian belonged to him. Not exactly a lie, just not true. He'd never been a possessive man, but Gillian brought out so many emotions in him. Hell, he was still trying to figure out what the jumbled mess making his stomach tight meant.

Justin took his grandfather's hand. "I want Gillian now."

"Put Grace back out with her mother," Bud ordered Ken. He stepped closer. "Aren't you supposed to be up at the training ring working with Domino?"

"I'm headed up there now, sir." Ken went to put the foal out with her mother.

Bud took Justin's hand and led him to where Dee had one of the gentler mares saddled and ready to take Justin for a ride.

Blake dismissed Ken's interest in Gillian as nothing more than a novelty Ken couldn't resist. Now that he knew who Gillian was, he'd drop any notion of going after her.

Blake turned to get Gillian, hoping he was right. He released his fisted hands. He needed to relax before he saw her. He had no doubt she'd read any kind of tension or anger in him immediately. The last thing he wanted to do was make her think she had to be on guard with him. Well, more than she already was.

Gillian stopped to see the horse. Boots, Blake and her grandfather called him. Easy to see why, when the black at his hooves rose up his legs and turned to brown, covering the rest of him. That is, where he still had hair. His coat was a mess. He needed the thistles in his tail and mane combed out. The poor thing couldn't be comfortable. She hadn't been comfortable for days, when she'd been lying on her stomach in a hospital bed. She still wasn't comfortable with her leg in a brace and her arm in plaster.

She stood by the fence. Quiet. Still. Curious, the horse moved closer but kept his distance, standing several feet away. He hadn't gone near his food. Tired of hurting, he didn't care anymore. She understood the fatigue of dealing with the hurt and pain. What she couldn't understand was giving up. She wouldn't allow it.

Not an easy task, but she shimmied through the fence. Boots shied away. She walked toward him slowly until she stood about ten feet from him. She waited, mimicking what her grandfather had done this morning. He'd seemed to stand in that pasture forever, waiting on the horse.

Gillian had always been good with animals. They took to her like bees to flowers. Gillian seemed to have something that animals wanted, and she hoped the same would be true of this horse.

"I know how you feel. It hurts when someone is mean to you." She took a step closer and kept her voice soft and soothing. When the horse didn't back away or take off, she took a few more steps.

"That's it, sweetheart. I won't hurt you. You'd like everyone to just go away and leave you alone." She took another three steps. Still Boots stayed still, watching her.

"This is a good place. Look." She pointed to the hay and oats Blake left for him. "They gave you some nice food to eat. I bet if you let them, they'd clean you up nice."

She took a few more steps and stood only a few feet away from the large animal. She'd never been close to a horse. He hadn't seemed quite so large from twenty feet back. Now, standing in front of him, she could see that he was scrawny, but tall. His head was well above hers. If she spooked him, he could run her down.

"Blake washed my hair this morning. I bet he'd give you a nice bath and get those thistles out of your coat. He's real gentle."

Listen to you singing the praises of a man you barely know. So he's been nice to you. That doesn't mean anything. He could be a real jerk who has a string of women trailing after him. Could? He probably does.

Gorgeous. Tall, dark, and handsome. She understood why women fell hard for cowboys. Blake was quite the package. Quite a man.

And you're twenty to his nearly thirty and have a child to raise. Stop fantasizing about cowboys with hard muscles and a wide chest. There'll be no riding off into the sunset for you.

She held her hand out to Boots, and after a minute he leaned in to sniff her. His warm breath whispered over her palm. She smiled at the small triumph.

"That's a beautiful boy. I won't hurt you." Her gaze met the horse's sorrowful eyes. A kindred spirit. "Poor baby." She held out her arms. She didn't really expect him to come to her. When he moved forward, she almost stepped away. In the end, his sadness called to her and bolstered her courage. She wrapped her arms around his neck and held on. The big animal let out a heavy sigh that reverberated through her chest.

"That's a good boy. You're going to be okay." She ran her fingers gently down the sides of his neck, ignoring the stickers and patches of missing fur. She touched him to let him know she was there. She'd never hurt him.

"I'll be damned." Blake watched from the fence, unable to believe the sight before him. "She got him to come to her."

Dee and Bud came up behind him with Justin up on one of the horses, a huge smile on his face.

"Well, now, I spent the better part of three weeks trying to get close to that horse. Look at her. She just walked right up and hugged him." Bud could have forced it, but he wanted Boots to come to him and learn to trust again. Well, Boots certainly trusted Gillian.

"She just held out her arms, and he walked right into them. The damn horse wanted a hug," Blake said, amazed.

"Gillian hugs real good," Justin announced.

I'd love to find out. Blake wouldn't mind having her wrap her arms around him. Yes, sir, it would be a real pleasure.

"She's real good with animals. She saved a bird on the pier once. No one could get close to it. It had a fishing line stuck around its neck and foot. She talked real soft and touched it real slow. He let her untangle the line. She picked him up and took him to the end of the pier and threw him in the air. He flew away. She does stuff like that all the time. She doesn't like it when animals are hurt."

Blake understood why. Poor old Boots had been sorely mistreated. He came from champion stock, and his last owner had used him for stud. Then the owner got a better stud and left Boots to rot in a pasture with little food. When Boots turned uncooperative, he was whipped into submission. Blake didn't believe in the practice. No one on the ranch was permitted to resort to violence, no matter how ornery or mean the horse.

Blake called over the fence to Gillian just loud enough for her to hear him without spooking Boots. "Gillian. See if you can get him to go to his food. See if he'll eat with you there."

Gillian didn't stop stroking Boots when she looked over her shoulder. "What do you want me to do, get behind him and shove?"

Blake held back a laugh but couldn't hide his smile. Sassy woman. He liked her gumption. "No. Turn around, but keep your arm up around his neck, start walking, and see if he'll go with you."

She continued to stroke Boots. "You hungry? I bet you are. How about we get something to eat? I'll stay with you. I don't like to eat alone. I bet you don't either. Come on." She turned and held her arm up around his neck like Blake instructed. She took two steps, but Boots didn't move. He watched her every move. "It's all right. Come on." She used her arm to pull him.

Blake, along with everyone else, let out a sigh of relief when Boots took a step forward.

"That's it. Let's go over here."

Gillian walked Boots over to the food, but he didn't take any. He stood looking at her. She bent, picked up a handful, and put it up to his mouth. He sniffed at it and tentatively took a bite. It took him a minute to take the rest. She bent to get him more. He took that handful with more vigor. She bent to get him more. Anxious, he pushed his big head into her back. As she was off balance from her leg brace, he knocked her down. She landed on her casted arm and yelped out in pain.

Blake vaulted over the fence and rushed toward her. Gillian held up a hand to stop him.

"I'm fine." She turned back to the horse. "Go on now, eat." Boots chomped away on the pile of food in the trough. Gillian rolled over onto her butt and sat next to him. The muscles in her back spasmed into tight knots. Eyes closed, she breathed through the pain radiating up her spine and broken arm until she could think and relax again.

Blake stayed a good ten yards away, watching.

"You stubborn horse," she scolded.

Boots stuck his muzzle to her cheek and blew out a breath on her. She actually giggled, making Blake's heart melt.

"Sure, now you want to kiss and make up after you dumped me on my ass."

He blew on her hair and made her laugh again before returning to inhaling his food.

Stupefied, Blake stared. The damn horse had fallen in love at first sight with her. He was actually being affectionate. Blake could relate. He'd fallen for her, too.

"I think that horse just fell in love with you."

"He's like a giant dog."

"That big dog can stomp you to death."

Boots took a minute out of his meal to nuzzle her neck again. "Yeah. He's a real killer. He's going to kiss me to death."

"I'd like to do the same," Blake said under his breath.

"What'd you say?"

"He's playing a game," Blake covered lamely. "Justin's riding. Want to come and watch?"

"Okay." She awkwardly rose to her feet and put her arms around Boots again. "Be good. Finish your food."

Blake wanted to laugh at her treating Boots like she treated Justin. But how could he, when Boots finally ate after days and weeks of existing on little more than the grass he cropped in the field?

"Actually, could you lead him into that stall? It's just through there." He pointed to the open door. "I'll meet you on the inside. After you see Justin ride, maybe you could help me out by brushing Boots down. If you're up to it."

She held up her bandaged hand to show Blake that what he was asking wasn't an easy task. "I'll give it a shot."

Blake would bet she'd do anything to help Boots feel better. He'd do the same for her if she let him.

CHAPTER 13

It took some coaxing, but she finally got Boots to follow her into the stall after he inhaled his pile of hay and oats. She closed the outside gate and gave him another rub down his nose before she let herself out the stall door to the stables. She expected Blake to meet her and jumped when another man appeared.

"Hey there. I'm Ken. Damn." He reached for her face, but she backed away from his calloused hand. He smiled, but it didn't ease her mind. He took a step closer. She took two back. "No need to run away. You really got yourself banged up, didn't you? Look at that shiner."

"Where's Blake?" Gillian's heart pounded so hard against her chest that her ribs ached with every beat. Taller than her, he outweighed her by a good fifty pounds. Lean and wiry, dirty blonde hair, and a day's worth of golden beard shadowed his jaw. Cute, but not as handsome as Blake, with his corded muscles and ruggedly gorgeous face.

When did I start comparing all men to one?

Ken eyed her up and down, obviously liking what he saw, despite her injuries. She'd seen him staring at her when she'd been in the pasture with Boots. Ken seemed okay, but right now she wanted to be left alone. She didn't want to explain her injuries or how she got them.

"He's out with your little brother. If you need something, I'm happy to help."

Too close, he'd subtly closed the distance between them as she'd backed away. "Back off. Give a girl room to breathe." She tried to keep her tone casual and still get her point across. He didn't back off, just gave her another gentle smile. It didn't help dissipate the fear rising to her throat, warranted or not. He still didn't move out of her way, keeping her trapped with her back to the stall door.

"That's not what I call giving her space," Blake said from behind Ken.

Relieved to see him, Gillian breathed easier.

"Get away from her. Now." Blake didn't hide the steel in his words.

"Don't get all hot, Blake. I was just saying hi and getting a better look at her battered face. Looks like you were in some kind of fight."

Gillian flinched, despite her best effort to not show Ken he'd gotten things right.

Ken remained between Blake and Gillian, setting Blake's blood to boiling. Backed up to the stall door, Gillian remained wide-eyed and watchful, her whole body tensed for fight or flight.

Didn't she know she was safe now? Blake would never let anything happen to her.

"Back off, Ken," Blake warned again.

"What happened to you? Car accident or something?"

"Yeah. I hit a car," she said sarcastically. "If you'll excuse me, I need to find Justin."

Her vague answer amused Blake. She had hit the car, literally. Still, Ken barely gave Gillian enough room to brush past him. She never took her eyes off Ken, who clearly took Gillian's sharp gaze to mean she was interested. He gave her an appreciative grin as his eyes swept down her body without even the hint of subtlety.

Ken made his point. No way he gave up chasing after Gillian, especially when beautiful women like her were few and far between in these parts. Ken and some of the other guys drove up to some of the bars near the college campus in Bozeman to hit on coeds. Too old to be doing that, Blake always declined. He hoped Ken had another trip planned soon so he'd find someone else.

Gillian was off limits.

"I'll meet you outside, Gillian. Justin's there with your grandparents. He's having a blast. We're going into town soon."

She made a point to take a wide arc around Blake and Ken as she moved toward the stable doors. She kept her body slightly turned toward them to keep them in her peripheral vision while she made her way down the long aisle, her hands clasped, her fingers linked tight together. Nervous or scared? Blake wasn't sure which, or if it was both.

Ken rattled her. Damn.

"Gillian. Pretty name for a pretty girl."

"Don't forget Bud's warning from this morning. She's off limits. I told you to give her space. What do you do? You back her into a door."

"I just wanted to get a good look at her. The car accident banged her up, but damn, she's beautiful. The bruises just make her look more innocent." Ken didn't take his eyes off Gillian until she disappeared out the door. He put a hand to his chest over his heart, like it pained him to see Gillian go.

Blake didn't like it one bit. Rage boiled in his gut.

"No harm in saying hello and trying to get to know her."

"She's not here looking for a date. She's here to get better and raise her kid brother. She's had a rough time and needs a little breathing room. Give it to her. It's the last time I'm asking."

"Doesn't sound like you're asking at all, boss."

Back to the "boss" crap, which meant Ken wasn't going to do a damn thing Blake asked. "Let me put it to you this way. Bud has made it clear that your job and every other man's job on this ranch depends upon them leaving Gillian alone."

Ken closed the distance and stood toe-to-toe with him. Blake glared down at the shorter man. The height difference didn't bother the cocky asshole. Well, bring it on. Blake wasn't in the mood. If Ken wanted a fight, Blake was happy to oblige. He'd been in a few bar fights and his share of scuffles with his brothers. He could hold his own against the likes of Ken. Then he thought of Gillian and how it would make her feel if he decked Ken right in his smug mouth. She'd be afraid of him for sure, so Blake unclenched his hands and settled into a look of relaxed boredom.

"Then I guess that means you, too, boss."

Yes, it did, but it wouldn't stop Blake from doing what he'd promised—protect Gillian. He liked his job. It was the job he wanted for the rest of his life. He didn't want to lose it, but he'd never wanted a woman as much as he wanted Gillian. It went deeper than his desire to get his hands on her. He wanted to know everything about her.

"Don't look so down, boss. I guess if you stay away from the granddaughter, you'll get to keep your job, too."

"I'll be with her all the time."

That put a frown on Ken's smug face.

"I'll be sitting at the table taking my meals with

her and the family. I'll be the one watching out for her." Blake took a step closer, backing Ken up a step, making sure he got the message: Blake was the boss, and taking him on wasn't in Ken's best interest.

"Go after Gillian, and you'll find me in your path." Blake let those words settle in Ken's mind. "Now, you're supposed to be up at the training ring until two, and then you have two owners coming to ride today. Make sure their horses are ready when they get here. Slacking off on your job to make time to chase after Miss Tucker is only going to get you fired faster."

Blake walked away hoping that didn't go for him, too, because he was having a damn hard time remembering his job was to protect her, not chase after her.

CHAPTER 14

Blake found Gillian outside standing next to Bud with her good foot on the fence and her arms hanging over the top. Justin rode in circles, with Dee holding the lead rope on his mount. Justin called out for Gillian to watch every few seconds.

"I'm watching. You're doing great."

Blake stepped up beside her, closer than Bud on her other side. She didn't spook, so he didn't back away. To assure himself she was okay after her encounter with Ken, he ran his hand softly down her hair. He barely touched her. Just enough to feel the silky strands and unknot his gut. "You all right?"

Her head snapped to him at his light touch. Pain flashed in her eyes. She scrunched up her shoulders and cocked her head sideways to ease the ache from her abrupt movements.

"Oh God, sweetheart. I'm sorry. Take a breath."

"It's all right. I'm fine." But she did take a calming breath and gave him an annoyed glare.

Bud eyed him behind Gillian's back. Yep, Bud watched him, ready to step in and protect her.

"Did Ken introduce himself, or was it something

else?" Blake wanted her take on Ken and whether she was interested in the guy. He sure as hell wanted to know if Ken acted out of line.

"He might have gotten closer than I'd like, but that's probably more me than him. The other guys on the ranch stare at me. He's the first to ask about my injuries, that's all."

No, that wasn't all. If Gillian knew Ken's interest went deeper than her injuries, she didn't let on.

Bud closed the gap between them. "Was he bothering you?"

This time, Gillian read their intense interest and stepped off the rail, backing away a few steps. "Both of you stop. You're putting too much into something that's nothing. He's just interested because I'm new around here. Trust me, the shine will wear off. Everyone will get used to my presence."

Blake frowned, not buying her casual dismissal. No way Ken backed off. Not when he'd made it clear, at least to Blake, that he wanted Gillian. Still, she didn't show any interest in getting to know Ken. Blake tried to tamp down his worry. If she wouldn't let him and Bud close to her, not likely she'd let Ken anywhere near her either. Right? He hoped so.

Gillian changed the subject. "So, what job do you want me to do around here?"

"Nothing. You need to concentrate on getting better," Bud answered.

"I need to earn my keep. It's important that I contribute."

"Look around you, Gillian. It isn't as if you and Justin are a hardship on me. Take the time you need to heal."

Gillian had already figured out that her grandfather

had the finances to let her and Justin stay without any sort of blip on his checkbook. Still, she liked keeping busy, and it would soothe her conscience if she earned her way. A matter of pride. She'd eaten enough of it yesterday. She didn't want to eat any more of it.

She looked her grandfather in the eye. "I need you to give me a job. I realize that shoveling out stalls won't be my strong suit at the moment." She held up her purple cast. "But I can do other things. I'm a hard worker. If you show me what you want me to do, I'll do it."

"You grew up in the city," Blake stated the obvious. "I imagine you have no idea what working on a ranch is like."

Irritated, she frowned and narrowed her eyes. Blake had no idea how she lived or anything about her capabilities. "I've held a number of varied types of jobs. If you give me a chance, I'll prove myself."

"It's not about proving yourself," Blake assured her. "I wonder if you wouldn't rather have a job in town. You might find that you hate ranch life. It's dirty, messy, hard work. You might find you prefer city life." He said the words like they left a bad taste in his mouth.

"There's a lot of charm and advantages to living in a city like San Francisco. Everything and anything you want is at your fingertips. I miss the ocean," she went on. Hard to explain how the water became a part of your soul. "Right before I arrived at the ranch, I stopped out on the road. We'd been driving for a long time, and I wanted to collect myself before I got here. I can't tell you exactly what it was, but there's something here that I needed and never knew I wanted."

Blake's gaze narrowed on her. He sighed, like her wanting to be here came as a relief.

"I need to find my place here. Without that, I'll only

feel like I don't belong. You've given me and Justin so much," she said to her grandfather. "I'm not one to take without giving something back. I've had to work for everything in my life, and I can't turn that off now."

Few people had given her a break. Accepting one without paying back the favor went against the grain. Didn't they get how hard this was for her, to put herself out there like this to show them both she wanted to be a real part of this place?

Her grandfather's eyes softened with what she could only guess was admiration. He reached out and bushed a strand of hair behind her ear. She didn't back away but accepted the kind gesture without tensing for the expected blow. He'd never hit her. Over time, her learned responses would shift and change. She'd learn to relax. She'd settle into a new normal. God, how she wished that day would come soon.

"You're nothing like your mother and father. I don't know how you turned out so well, but you're an amazing woman. Stronger than anyone I know."

She cocked her head and studied him, acknowledging what they had in common. Not just blood but the qualities that made them who they were. "They would get the angriest when I'd harp on them about responsibility and doing the right thing. She always said I sounded just like her old man. I guess I take after you."

Stunned speechless, his mouth dropped open for a second before he recovered. "Can I hug you?" His words came out gruff and filled with emotion.

Gillian usually got hugs from close friends she'd been around long enough to trust. She should call the restaurant and garage and let them know she'd made it to Montana, and all was well.

Gillian mustered her courage. She gave in to the

overwhelming need in her heart to connect with her grandfather, her family, and walked right into his open arms. It took her a few seconds to settle in against his chest, but then she wrapped her arms around his middle. He felt nice. Strong. No vibe that he might turn on her at any second. His steady heartbeat against her cheek and his scent, something earthy tinged with spice, settled into her. For the first time, she thought, *This is my grandpa. He loves me.*

"This is your place, Gillian. You belong here. Never doubt that." He laid his cheek on top of her head. Dee stared at both of them, tears shimmering in her eyes.

The tension Blake carried with him since she arrived washed away. She wanted to stay. She felt like she belonged here.

Still, living on the ranch could be hard on some people. Forty-five miles from town, nothing to do out here but work and live a quiet life, care for the horses, and do an endless amount of chores. Mostly men worked the ranch. Women could feel isolated and lonely for company they could relate to. He didn't want to see that happen to Gillian. He wanted her to be happy here. He'd do anything and everything in his power to make that happen.

Bud set Gillian away and held her shoulders in his hands. "So, tell me what interests you about the ranch."

"I don't really know. I've never been around horses, so I don't know what jobs there are to do."

Blake tried to help her out. "What kind of work did you do in the city? Maybe we can apply something you did there to working here."

"Well, I was a waitress at a restaurant near the wharf. That was four nights a week. I washed dishes in Chinatown for cash and takeout. I unloaded fish from the boats at the dock for cash. Two days a week, I worked as a bookkeeper at a garage. I did oil changes and basic repairs on occasion. I did a lot of one-off jobs whenever I could get the work. Things like handing out flyers, selling tickets, filling in for vendors at the pier, babysitting, and pretty much anything that came my way. I took auto shop, woodshop, typing, and basic accounting in school. I can balance a checkbook, make small repairs, fix basic problems on engines . . ." She trailed off with a shrug. "None of which will help around here, I guess."

"How many hours a week did you work?" Blake couldn't believe she'd been going to school, working, and raising Justin pretty much on her own.

"As many as I could fit in. The waitressing and bookkeeping were on the books. You can only work so many hours when you're under eighteen. I had to supplement that with work off the books. Unloading fish at the docks is dirty and smelly, but it pays well and in cash. The same was true for many of the other odd jobs. I needed the cash for Justin. Sometimes my dad would shake me down or just steal what he could find. Mrs. Wicks watched Justin in exchange for my doing odd jobs for her like grocery shopping and cleaning house. Preschool was expensive, but I managed."

"You paid for Justin to go to preschool." Both Blake and Bud exchanged a look.

"It was important he learned to socialize with other kids before kindergarten. Spending the day with Mrs. Wicks, who's seventy-nine, isn't socializing. He needed more, and I made sure he got it."

"Of course you did," was all Blake could say. That she would think of Justin's needs like that at the age of seventeen or eighteen said a lot about the kind of mother she was. She didn't just make sure he had food in his belly and clothes on his back. No, she made sure his education and social skills were taken care of as well. She'd lived her whole life with next to nothing, and here she'd gone and made sure Justin got the best she could provide.

"Basically, nothing that I did before will help with the horses or the ranch."

"Not true," Blake put in. "You've got a lot going for you. The only thing against you at the moment is the fact that your hand is in a cast. You seem to have limited use of your other hand."

"It's getting better."

"Still, that's going to limit you for a while. Why don't we start with Boots? You're in charge of him. He loves you, and I'd like your help nursing him back to health. After that, we'll find you something to do. It will also get you involved with the ranch, and you might find something you like, or that likes you."

"Likes me?"

"You never know what you'll find you're good at. You didn't know you had a knack with wild, wounded horses. You do. We'll start with that and build on it. You said you know some basic accounting and kept the books for a garage. I have the horrible job of taking care of all the paperwork and accounting for the ranch. Maybe you could help me out there once you have your hands back."

"Okay, so Boots is my responsibility. He needs a bath. I can't do that." She bit her lip, defeat clouding her eyes. She failed before she started, or so she thought.

Not true. He'd prove it to her. "You can't get your cast wet, but you can hold him and keep him calm while I wash him down. We'll take care of it when we get back from town. We'll work together." He liked that.

"Which reminds me," Bud cut in. "I made an appointment for you at the school to get Justin registered. He'll start on Monday, like you wanted. I also made an appointment with the doctor at the clinic. Dr. Bell is an orthopedic surgeon who fills in at the clinic sometimes. She wants to check out your stitches and knee. According to your medical records, you should have had them checked by now."

"I didn't have time before I left."

"Then we'll do it today and get your meds. Dee wants to take Justin shopping for some school clothes and a few toys. He'll need some things to play with, and we don't have anything for him here."

"Books. He needs some books. There are a couple of boxes of things in the back of my truck, but I don't have much. I appreciate anything you do for him."

"She'd also like to get you some things. You'll need a new coat." He swept his gaze over Blake's jacket engulfing her tiny frame. "If you're going to work with the horses, you'll need some boots, warm sweaters, and jeans. It's dirty work, and you'll need the clothes for it."

She frowned, but accepted her grandfather and Dee's help and support. "Okay, but if that doctor comes at me with a needle, I won't be held responsible for what happens." She pointed a menacing finger at both of them, death in her eyes.

Blake laughed. "Don't worry, sweetheart, I'll protect you from the big, bad doctor."

She eyed him. "I have a feeling you'd be the first to hold me down if she said something was wrong with me."

So, she did feel the connection between them. He didn't expect her to acknowledge it outright so soon, but he'd take the small opening and go with it. "I want to make sure your body is as beautiful as your heart."

She rolled her eyes. "Ken's got nothing on you. That was smooth."

Blake glared. "Let's get something straight. I'm nothing like Ken. I'd think you'd recognize the difference."

She'd hidden behind her walls and defended herself against his kindness with sarcasm. He shouldn't let it bother him, but it did.

Blake walked over to Justin and Dee. He plucked Justin from the horse's back and put him up on his massive shoulders. Stunned, Gillian stared at Blake's retreating back. She'd never intended to anger him with her teasing.

"I've never seen Blake like this," her grandfather said. "Usually, he's all business. He's a hard worker. Got his heart broke once. He's had his share of relationships over the years. They're usually short-lived, but the women never seem angry with him in the end. He's different with you. I can only say that he cares about you, and it's taken him by surprise. He's a good man. He'd never hurt you intentionally, and if he did by accident, I think it would hurt him deeply."

"He just met me."

"Sometimes it's like that. It was for me with Dee. After my wife, your grandmother, died, I thought I'd spend the rest of my life alone. Then I saw Dee, and I knew right away that she was for me. I saw something in her that I recognized. Some might call it soul mates or destiny. I just call it right. When it's right, you know."

"And Blake looked at me and it was right."

"Could be? I can't speak for him. I think you like him. You seem to trust him."

"He had the same disgusted look on his face when I suggested you might have hurt Boots."

"You've only been here a day. You need time to adjust. When you said you liked being here and felt like you belonged, I can tell you that was a load off his mind. Mine, too. Ranch life can be lonely for a woman who'd rather be surrounded by people and stores and such. You might still find that you'd rather have that kind of life, but he's hoping you'd rather be here. I have to say, so am I."

They stood side by side watching Justin hold onto Blake's hair as they walked the horse back to the stable. Huge, his long strides carried him across the wide, open space in moments. She had to admit her brother and Blake looked good together.

"I guess we'll see," she replied. "Right now, my only concern is getting Justin settled. The ranch is good for him. I've seen such a huge change in him in the short time he's been here. He smiles. He laughs. He doesn't watch what he says or does around you two. He isn't scared. You, Grandma Dee, Blake, you're good for him."

"I can't tell you how it makes me feel to hear you call us 'Grandma' and 'Grandpa.' It's more than we expected and better than we deserve. Especially me. I could have helped you. Over the years, Ron called and asked for money. I never sent it, even though I knew you were with him."

"If you had, he'd have spent it on drugs and booze. He wasn't asking you to help with me, no matter what he said to you at the time." She caught the look in his eyes. He knew that, but appreciated the fact that she did, too. She didn't blame him. She'd done the best she could to make Ron come around, but the man hadn't wanted to be anything but what he was.

"I'm just glad you're willing to give us the benefit of the doubt."

"I'm trying to remember not to judge everyone based on my mother and father's example. They were two peas in a pod with friends to match. When I was little, I thought everyone was like them. I didn't know that other kids had parents who took care of them and loved them. When I started working odd jobs, I realized there were kind people in the world. I had a hard time finding work. No one wanted to hire a scrawny, under-age kid. A lady who owned a Chinese restaurant let me wash dishes for cash and food. Whatever day I showed up, as many days as I'd show up, she let me work. She made all the difference in the world sometimes. When Justin was a tiny baby, I'd bring him with me. She'd sing to him in Mandarin while I washed dishes and mopped the floor. She taught me how to take care of him properly. Later, she helped me get the job at the garage keeping books. Any time she heard of an odd job here or there, she'd send it my way. I met more nice people along the way."

She sighed. God, she was so tired. "Sometimes I go with my first instinct that people are generally bad. I'm sorry I did that with you. It wasn't meant to hurt you so much as it was to protect Justin and myself."

"Fair enough," Grandpa agreed. "You're smart and capable. I imagine your skill at sizing up a person's character comes in handy, living and working in the city."

"You mean in the neighborhoods most people avoid if they can help it."

"Right."

"So, you don't mind that someone who works for you is interested in me?"

"Blake is as good a man as I've ever known. I wish Ron had turned out to be even a quarter of what Blake is for my daughter's sake. For your sake."

"Well, that's saying something."

"I won't interfere if seeing him is what you want. But understand this, I've made it clear to every man on this ranch that this is your home. They are to keep their distance and act professional when you're around. If you want to get to know Blake, or one of the other men better, you hold the power and their job in your hands. If they make you unhappy, or look at you the wrong way, I'll oust them from this land. If God forbid one of them hurts you, they'll leave this place full of lead."

Wow, no one had ever been that protective of her. She kind of liked it. But she didn't like knowing that if she dated Blake and it didn't work out, he'd lose his job and his home. Her grandparents were like family to him. She didn't want to be responsible for him losing so much. She needed to process and think about her grandfather's words.

No matter what Blake was or wasn't to her, he wasn't her priority. She needed to get Justin settled in school. She needed to find her footing here. Grandma Dee had been right. Gillian needed time to figure out what she wanted to do with her life.

She wished she could think through the pain and breathe without suffocating on her past.

CHAPTER 15

Gillian hadn't really paid attention to the quaint town of Crystal Creek when they'd driven through the first time. She'd been focused on getting to her grandfather's place and finding the store to get Justin some medicine. Now, she looked around from the front seat of the truck, where she sat between her grandfather and Blake. Justin and Grandma Dee sat in back. No way for her to get back there with the brace on her leg. Both men took up a lot of space, but Blake seemed to invade hers just with his presence beside her. Hyperaware of him, she squirmed, pressing her legs together. She tried not to think of how good he smelled, or how his jeans stretched taught over his thigh muscles.

They drove past the post office and grocery store and turned down First Street. Cute shops lined both sides. People window-shopped and sat on benches next to pots overflowing with vibrant red, white, and blue flowers. Small-town Main Street was alive and well here. Her grandfather found a lucky parking spot outside the general store. Everyone got out. Blake helped her down. Actually, he grabbed her waist, plucked her from the seat, and set her on her feet beside him. He touched his hand to the small of her back and pushed her toward the door. She didn't mind the good manners, but having him that close did something strange to her insides.

She stepped up onto the sidewalk and stared down the street, drawn to the rumble of a motorcycle idling by the coffee shop.

A man sat with his tattooed arms stretched to the handlebars. The sun brightened his shaggy blonde hair. He turned and looked right at her. Time stopped along with her breath. She opened her mouth to scream, but nothing came out.

It can't be. I shot him. I killed him.

Fear swamped her body and every rational thought in her mind. That slideshow in her head played back: she shot her father, the blood spread across his chest, she crashed through the window. The motorcycle engine revved again. Instead of hitting the car, she jolted back to reality. The man took off down the road.

Blake cupped her face in his warm hands. She knocked them away and stepped back.

"Hey, what's wrong?"

"Nothing. I'm fine."

"No, you're not."

"Leave it alone." She left him at her back and stepped into the store, hoping no one else noticed she was losing her mind.

"Let's split up," her grandfather suggested. "We've got just over an hour before Gillian's doctor's appointment. Blake and I will take Justin. Dee, you help Gillian find what she needs. We'll meet at the register."

All for escaping Blake's intense stare, she followed her grandmother to the women's section. "Well, let's see, you'll need some jeans. Let's start there." Her grandmother stood before the wall of shelves stacked with jeans. "What size?"

"Four. Maybe?"

Grandma Dee grabbed several different pairs. "Try these on. Whichever fits the best and you like, we'll grab a couple extra pairs. Now, shirts." She followed Gillian through the racks and displays. Her grandmother picked out a couple of things, and Gillian added more to the growing pile in her arms.

"There now, let's hit the fitting room and try these on. We'll go from there."

"Grandma, I don't need this much." Gillian pointed her chin at the stack of clothes about to hide her face.

"Please let me do this for you. I don't have any children of my own to spoil. I'm so happy to help you with this."

What could Gillian say? She gave Grandma Dee a smile, accepting defeat gracefully. Grandma grabbed part of the stack and headed for the dressing room. Gillian tried everything on. That torture took half an hour in her condition, but she found several things she loved, including a couple of pairs of soft cotton leggings.

"I know you're getting tired, but let's stop by the lingerie section and get you some essentials." Grandma actually winked at her.

Gillian had gotten by on cotton panties and bras, though most were in sad shape. Grandma Dee headed straight for the pretty lace without even a smirk. She added a couple of pretty nightgowns in an ice blue and dark teal to the pile of clothes in Gillian's arms. "They'll make your hair glow and your skin look like it's been kissed by the sun. Every girl should have pretty things, Gillian. You deserve them."

Gillian's eyes glassed over. No one had ever given her pretty things or thought she deserved them.

Her grandfather, Blake, and Justin joined them at that moment, their arms filled with Justin's new wardrobe. Everything from new shoes, boots, socks, underwear, and a couple of sweatshirts, in addition to pants and shirts. Ready for school, by the looks of it.

Grandma Dee turned to her grandfather. "Take Justin to the register and start on his stuff, plus this." She handed over her pile, then took the things from Gillian's hands. "I'll leave you to pick out what you want," she said to Gillian. They all headed off to start paying for the new items.

Happy to be alone, Gillian walked through the racks and grabbed what she needed, including a short chenille robe. No way she spent another breakfast half naked next to a man who studied her every move and noticed every little detail about her. Like the way her nipples hardened when he gave her one of those cocky smiles. Or the way goose bumps ran up her arms when he touched her.

"Hey there, can I help you find something?" the salesgirl—Mandy, according to her tag—asked.

"I just need to pick out some essentials."

"What size?"

Blake walked up behind the salesgirl and cast a glance at the frilly panties and bras hanging on the rack next to Gillian.

"Do you mind?"

"Not at all," he shot back.

Mandy turned and sucked in a surprised breath. "Blake, what brings you by?"

"Shopping with Gillian."

"Is that right? Well now, you were never one to be alone long."

Blake's eyes fell away. Could the man actually be

embarrassed? Gillian did notice he didn't correct Mandy that they weren't together.

"So, Gillian, what size?" Mandy asked again.

Since he refused to leave her alone, she had no choice but to answer. Heat rose in her cheeks, so she swallowed another dose of pride and spit out, "Small panties and 34C."

Give the man credit, his gaze remained steady on her face and didn't dip to her chest once.

"I'll have to remember that," Blake teased, making her cheeks and ears flame.

Two could play this game. "I'd like to see you buy me underwear."

Damn the man. She should have known better than to dare him. He walked over to a pretty bra and panty set of cream satin with pink lace trim, found her size, and pulled it off the rack.

"Well, now, Blake's usually the one issuing dares," Mandy said.

Gillian didn't understand the shame and regret that filled Blake's eyes before he abruptly walked over to the cash register two over from her grandparents. He probably didn't want them to see what he was buying. Still, it didn't explain the look. Buying underwear wouldn't embarrass him.

"Never dare a cowboy," Mandy said, smirking like an idiot, completely oblivious to whatever bothered Blake.

"If you don't mind, I think I've got this."

"Sure thing." Mandy flitted away to help another customer in the shoe department.

Gillian grabbed what she wanted and needed and headed toward the cash register.

Blake walked over, carrying a white bag by the string handles. "For you."

"Why don't you wear it?"

"Not my color. Besides, it will look better on you."

"What will look better on you?" her grandfather asked.

The color drained from Blake's face. He opened his mouth to answer, but she chimed in. "The pretty scarf I saw on a mannequin. Blake bought it for me to welcome me to the ranch." She snatched the bag from Blake and held it to her belly. "Thank you." Her grandfather's earlier warning came back that Blake's job was on the line if he did something out of line. She didn't want to get him in trouble. She'd dared him. Her fault he'd had no choice but to take it.

"Well, okay." Her grandfather eyed Blake, who kept a neutral expression on his face. "Bring the rest of your things to the register and we'll settle up." He walked back to join Justin and her grandmother.

Gillian hung back a second when Blake stepped in front of her, blocking her path.

"Thanks for saving me from that awkward, potentially deadly, explanation. If there's anything else you want, it's yours."

Ah, that smile would be the death of her. Bold, the man had charm, a sense of humor, and knew just how to get past her defenses—and when to back off. She liked him. She really liked him.

"Thanks, but I'm good."

"Let me take those from you." He took the pile of lingerie from her hands.

"You just can't wait to get your hands on my panties." She'd never flirted with a man. Not like this. Maybe a smile. A look. But she found it so easy to joke and tease with Blake.

"I have all the time you need for that." No joke there. He meant it and made sure she knew it with a steady look before he turned and took everything to the register, where her grandfather handed over stuffed bags to Blake and Grandma Dee and paid the astronomical bill without so much as a gasp, or even a blink.

"Uh—"

Blake leaned in. "Just say thank you," he whispered.

She let out a heavy sigh. "Thank you. I really appreciate this. Justin, what do you say?"

"Thank you. Now I'll look just like Grandpa and Blake." Justin pulled on his dark brown cowboy boots and dumped his old battered tennis shoes into the box. He stood and rocked back and forth, testing out the boots. So cute. He smiled up at Blake, who ruffled his hair.

"Come on, partner, let's mosey." Blake walked past her toward the exit with his hands loaded down with bags.

Out on the street, Blake and Bud stuffed the bags in the back of the truck, and everyone except Blake piled in. She stood on the sidewalk, scanning the street, looking for a man she killed and couldn't be there. Just her imagination. Nothing more. Stress. Pain. They were taking a toll on her mind. She needed sleep. That was all.

She walked to the open truck door. Blake took her by the waist again and set her on the seat, carefully grabbing her ankle and helping her shift into the truck. He set her foot on the floorboards.

"Thanks."

"No problem. How's your pain level?"

"From one to agony? Take a guess."

"Let's go see the doc and get you some meds."

Her grandfather stopped outside the clinic. Blake helped her out of the truck again.

"We'll meet you back here in about half an hour," her grandfather said. "We'll take Justin to the bookstore and for some ice cream while you see the doctor."

"Okay." She hobbled to the front door.

Blake reached past her and opened it.

"You don't need to stay with me."

"Yes. I do. Come on." He held his hand out to indicate that she should walk inside. Since the people in the waiting area stared, she swallowed the sharp words she wanted to say to get him to leave her alone.

She walked up to the counter, but Blake spoke for her.

"Hey Tina, this is Gillian Tucker. She's got an appointment with Dr. Bell."

Tina beamed Blake a bright smile. Her eyes went soft on him. Gillian waited for the flirty giggle. Yep, there it was when Blake smiled back. Gillian waited for him to flirt back, but he laid his hand over hers on the counter. Tina caught the move and looked from Gillian to Blake and back.

Gillian slipped her hand free, understanding why the woman gave her a look that said she didn't get it. What the hell did a gorgeous man like Blake want with a beat-up nobody like her?

"Uh, take her into room four. Dr. Bell will be right in. There's a gown. Ties in back so she can check your injuries."

"Thanks." Blake took Gillian's hand and led her to the room down the short hall. "Here you go."

She walked in, and he closed the door. Good, she didn't need to ask him to leave and have yet another awkward conversation.

She pulled off her shirt. The crisscross stitches on her back made it impossible for her to wear a bra, so she'd opted for a tank top. She stripped that off, too. She unwrapped the bandage on her wrist and flexed her fingers. Her hand didn't really hurt anymore. She tore apart the straps on her leg brace and slid it down her leg. Pants piled with her other clothes, she pulled on the gown, left the back open, and sat on the table, waiting.

Blake knocked on the door, opened it a crack without looking in, and asked, "You decent?"

"Not really."

He walked in and found her with her hands braced on the table, one leg dangling off the edge, the other stretched out to avoid bending her knee. Her head hung between her shoulders, her gaze on her purple sock with the hole in the toe. Her favorite pair, but she'd have to toss them out now that she had new ones.

"Go away. Wait in the other room."

"Not a chance." He pulled up the chair and sat in front of her. He reached out to touch her swollen and bruised knee. She grabbed his wrist to stop him. Their eyes locked. "That looks bad."

His warm hand settled on her skin. Her hand remained locked on his wrist, but she didn't push him away.

"It all looks bad." She removed his hand, unable to bear the sweet touch. She wanted more, and wanting more was dangerous for both of them.

He set it on his corded thigh and leaned in close.

"Really, you don't need to be here for this. I can take care of myself."

"I promised. No way the doc comes near you with a needle when I'm around." He leaned back and settled into the squeaking chair.

She hated the doctor's office. The hospital stay had nearly driven her insane. Every five minutes someone jabbed a needle in her somewhere, or poked and prodded everything that hurt. She just wanted to grit her teeth and get this done without any witnesses.

"Gillian, are you okay?"

He must have read the fear she couldn't hide the longer she stayed here.

"No. I'm not okay. Get out. I'm practically naked." She didn't want him here. She didn't want him to see her like this.

"I can see that." He gave her an appreciative smile as he looked at her from the top of her head down to her purple socked feet. "I have to say it's making me a little nervous. I mean, we just met and all." He tried to tease her out of her fear. "Women have a tendency to lose their clothes around me, but I'm usually the one to help them out of them. For some reason, with you, I want to bundle you up and keep you safe. That's not to say that I don't want you naked. You understand?"

"Oh, I've got the picture. I don't sleep around. I'm nothing like my mother, so just get that out of your head."

"Whoa, I never said or thought anything of the sort. You're a beautiful woman, Gillian."

"Right." She swept her hands up and down her body to indicate the many injuries.

"Yes. Right. You've got more strength and persever-ance than anyone I've ever met. I admire you. I like you. And yes, I want you. But that's not why I'm here. In the truck, on the way here, you seemed fine, but the closer we got, the more you trembled. Look at you, holding your hands so tight together your fingers must ache. You don't want to be here. Your legs are shaking. You're terrified, so I'm going to sit here and distract you the best I can, because you need to see the doctor. I'll hold your hand through the whole thing, and then I'll take you out of this place. I promise."

He reached for her, placing both his big hands over hers. She gave in to his kindness and warmth and turned her hands to grip his. He turned her hand and examined her wrist. "Is it better?"

"Yeah, I think so."

"Good."

The doctor walked in with a tray filled with instruments. Gillian shifted to bolt. Blake squeezed her hands to still her and silently let her know with his eyes filled with sympathy that she wasn't alone.

"Hi, Gillian, I'm Dr. Bell. I've gone over your medical records, and your last doctor sent the MRI of your knee injury and the X-ray for your arm. How are you feeling today? Are the meds helping with your pain level?"

"Her meds got burned in a fire. She needs new prescriptions for everything," Blake answered for her. "She's in agony. You've got to do something."

"Okay, I'll take care of the prescriptions. How is your vision out of that left eye?"

"Back to normal. The swelling is gone. The bruises look nasty, but I can see."

"Great. Let's take a look at your knee first, then I'll check your back and arms."

Blake moved out of Gillian's way but never stopped holding her hands.

Dr. Bell gently touched her knee, testing her mobility, or lack thereof. Gillian hissed in pain when it bent too much. Blake brushed his fingers up her arm, trying to comfort her.

"This looks good, Gillian. Healing nicely. I've got a smaller brace you can use. It should make it easier for you to walk. That doesn't mean you shouldn't be careful and stay off it as much as possible." Dr. Bell gently put Gillian's leg back on the table. "Do you need help rolling over so I can see the stitches on your back and legs?"

Blake stood to help Gillian shift and turn over. He

pulled the gown down to cover her front, though her ass hung out the back. He hissed in a sharp breath when he got a good look at the cuts and gashes.

"It's been a while since I've seen someone with this many stitches. Any one cut bothering you more than another?" the doctor asked.

"The one down my thigh. I think it's just irritated because I have no choice but to sit on it. It itches."

"You're in luck. Most of these look good. We can take the stitches out. That should help. A couple on your back need to stay."

Dr. Bell got to work, quickly removing stitches from many of the cuts, including two of the lines up her scalp. Blake remained a gentleman and stayed by her head and held her hands, telling her to breathe when she held her breath to ward off the pain. He only peeked at her ass once when she winced at a particularly stubborn stitch that didn't want to come out.

"Okay, Gillian, you're doing great. The bruising is healing, though I bet your muscles ache."

"The spasms are the worst."

"The meds will help. We'll get you those before you leave. Let's have a look at your arms."

Gillian rolled over her good leg and Blake helped her sit up. The swelling in her broken arm had decreased considerably, leaving a huge gap between her arm and the cast.

"We'll need to cut the cast off and redo it. There's some swelling, but it looks like it's gone down quite a bit." Dr. Bell tested her other hand. "Any pain or tenderness when you flex it?"

"No."

"Looks good. You don't need the bandage, but be cautious using your hand. You don't want to strain it again. Go ahead and get dressed, then we'll get you a new cast. It will stabilize your wrist and help the bone heal and lessen the pain."

The doctor rummaged through the cabinet under the sink and pulled out the new, much smaller brace. Gillian would still have limited range of motion, but at least she'd be able to walk more normally.

Blake never left her side, but he did turn his back when she got dressed. He accompanied her into the other room to get her new cast and picked out the new color. Green. "It won't show the dirt and grass stains when you work with Boots." Steady, he silently let her know he was there for her, whatever she needed. It touched her deeply. No one had ever been there for her.

They left the clinic with her new meds and went to find her grandparents and Justin in the parking lot. He kept her fingers in his hand and slowed his pace to accommodate her hurt knee. She didn't say anything. She just went with him. It felt good to hold his hand and walk beside him. And damnit, she wanted to hold on to the light feeling she had when he touched her.

Gillian sat beside Blake in the truck, feeling closer to him than when they drove into town. Her grandparents and Blake waited outside the school while she and Justin went into the office and signed all the paperwork. Gillian walked Justin to his classroom and knocked on the door. His teacher stood at a table, setting out papers, brushes, and paints for an art project.

"Hello, Miss Crane. I'm Gillian Tucker. This is my brother, Justin. He'll be joining your class on Monday."

"Hello, Justin. Welcome."

"Hi. Can I look at all the toys?"

"Sure you can. I'll just have a few words with your sister."

Gillian smiled when Justin ran off and touched everything he could get his hands on.

"So, will this be his first school experience?"

"No. He attended school in San Francisco. I've given all the information to the office. I just stopped by so he could meet you and know where he needs to go on Monday."

"I'm glad you did. Looks like he's already settled in."

Yes, Justin settled in just fine. She was taking a bit longer.

"Are you okay? Were you in an accident?" Miss Crane asked.

"I'm fine. I hit a car."

Miss Crane's eyes narrowed on Gillian's beat-up face. Gillian didn't want to answer a bunch of questions, so she said, "Justin, come now. It's time to go. You'll get to play all you want on Monday."

"There's a green and yellow lizard in that tank and stick bugs in the other," he said, skipping over to her and wrapping his arm around her leg.

"Awesome."

"Well, I'll see you Monday, Justin. I'm glad you stopped by. We're going to have lots of fun learning this year. You'll like the other kids. We've got a bunch of boys for you to play with and a huge play set outside with two slides and swings and monkey bars."

"Way cool."

"Gillian, are you and Justin ready to go?" Blake asked, stepping up beside her.

"Blake, I never expected to see you here," Miss Crane said.

"Gillian and Justin are my boss's grandkids. I'm looking out for them."

"Let's hope you do a better job with them than you did

with my sister." Miss Crane looked Gillian up and down. "Though she already looks worse off than Abigail."

"Nice to see you, too," Blake bit out. He took Gillian's hand and gently tugged. "Let's go. Dee and Bud are waiting."

Gillian waited until they were back at the parking lot. "What was that about?"

Blake looked down at Justin. "Nothing. She's my ex's sister. Things didn't end well, and she's looking out for her family. That's all."

No, that wasn't all. "Does this have something to do with you daring someone, like Mandy said in the store?"

"Leave it alone, Gillian."

Blake dropped her hand, scooped up Justin, plunked him on his shoulders, and walked the last twenty feet to the truck. He'd stopped talking to her, but asked Justin, "Did you like your teacher?"

"She's nice. She's got a lizard and some bugs in tanks."

"Impressive."

Gillian didn't know what land mine she'd stepped on, but she'd try to avoid it in the future. They rehashed her past ad nauseam, but his remained off limits. His not sharing made her nervous. If his past relationships had turned out so badly, maybe considering something with him wasn't a good idea.

All the way home, Justin talked with Blake about his teacher and the cool stuff in his classroom. Blake kept his patience and listened even when Justin repeated himself.

Thanks to the pain meds and muscle relaxers, she dozed off in the truck on the ride home, her head propped against Blake's shoulder, thinking the trip to town turned out okay despite the visit to the doctor.

Blake hated to wake her, not when she looked so sweet cuddled up to his arm. Still, he couldn't sit in the truck with her all night. Dee and Bud had already unloaded and taken everything inside.

"Gillian, sweetheart, wake up." He touched his finger to her cheek. She came awake with a start and pulled away, hands up to defend herself, her eyes huge, but they softened on him.

"It's just me," he assured her.

"Hey. Sorry I fell asleep on you."

"You need it. I'll walk you up to the house before I tend the horses. Dinner's in an hour."

"But you said we'd give Boots a bath."

"We can do it tomorrow."

"No. He needs it. Besides, he's my responsibility now. I need to check on him and make sure he eats."

"Gillian, you're wiped out."

"It's just the meds. I feel better. The pain has sub-sided. Really. Come on." She waved her hand to get him to move out of her way so she could get out of the truck. "Where is Justin?"

"Inside. Dee's making him a snack, then he asked to watch TV."

"He loves TV."

"Who doesn't?" Blake took her by the waist and lifted her down from the truck seat. He took her hand again and walked with her to the stables and straight to Boots's door. The horse remained guarded, standing against the back wall, but when he spotted Gillian, he walked to the gate. She reached for him and gave him a pet down his long neck.

"There's my huge boy."

"I've been right here waiting for you," Ken said from behind them.

Blake turned and glared, putting himself between Gillian and Ken. "Take that horse out to its owner in the practice ring," Blake ordered.

"I'm on my way, boss. No harm saying hello to the pretty lady, now, is there?"

"Do your job."

"Doing it . . . even if you're not," Ken added under his breath, but Blake heard him, like Ken meant for him to hear it. Ken walked the horse out of the stables.

Blake turned back, but didn't see Gillian. He glanced over the gate and found her picking stickers and thistles from Boots's coat. He grabbed an empty bucket and two brushes and went into the stall with her. Boots shied and blocked Gillian from him.

"Hey now, you're okay. Blake won't hurt you," she cooed to the spooked horse.

Blake hoped someday soon she'd believe that statement. He moved in slowly, letting the horse see he wasn't going to hurt him. He and Gillian worked side by side, pulling every last sticker from his patchwork of hair, mane, and tail.

Blake slid a new halter over Boots's head. Ken poked his head over the stall door. The horse caught the movement and sidestepped, pushing Blake back two steps and nearly sending Gillian to the ground. Ken only had eyes for her. "Hey baby, you need to be careful with these big guys."

"I'll keep that in mind."

"Want some help?"

"Thanks, but I've got all the muscle I need," she said, stepping closer to Blake's side.

Blake had to admit he liked her style. She handled Ken with simple and vague answers, and now she'd gone and implied all she needed was Blake. He'd take it, even if she just wanted to get Ken to back off.

Gillian took Boots's halter and led him to the door. "Back up. He's shy."

"I'd love to take you to dinner tonight and get to know you better," Ken said.

Blake wanted to step in, but held his tongue.

"I already have plans."

"With who? Him?" Ken nodded his head in Blake's direction.

"With my family. Excuse me. I have work to do."

Ken smacked his palm against the gate. "Maybe another time." He walked away when she didn't say anything more.

"Thanks," she said.

"For what?" Blake asked.

"Letting me handle that. Maybe now he'll let it go."

He didn't think so. "You are having dinner with me, you know?"

"Yep. I know."

She unlatched the gate and led Boots down the aisle to the concrete pad they used to wash down the horses. Blake grabbed the hose.

"Hold his head. I'll wash him down. If he rears up, back out of the way as fast as you can."

Gillian snuggled her cheek against Boots's nose. "He's not going to do anything of the sort."

Blake made short work of washing down Boots, who stayed perfectly still as long as Gillian kept talking sweet to him. Blake grew more aroused by the minute as her hot gaze raked over every inch of his body as he worked. She liked his arms. Every time he flexed, her eyes zeroed in on them. He'd even caught her sweep the tip of her tongue across her bottom lip. The sexy as hell move nearly sent him to his knees to beg her to put him out of his misery. He'd never wash another horse

again without thinking about her in those tight jeans
and T-shirt with no bra to hide her tight nipples from
his view. Just watching him move made her aroused.
He desperately wanted to get his hands on her. God,
how he wanted her.

"Come on, let's put him back in his warm stall, and
I'll show you how to feed him," Blake said.

It took Gillian a full five seconds to tear her eyes off
his chest and meet his gaze. He smiled, and she sighed.
Yep, she was as lost as he was in this thing between the
two of them.

His desire for her grew more intense over the next
five days. He spent most of his days in her company.
Determined to do her part on the ranch, she cared for
Boots and shadowed him through his workday, helping
out wherever she could. Justin stayed with his grandfather after school, having a blast riding the tractor and
watching the men stack hay in one of the barns.

Unable to help himself, he studied her every move.
Smart, she learned things quickly and only had to be
told something once. When she tried to figure something out on her own, she squinted her eyes and
scrunched her lips. She ended every meal with one of
the chocolate chip cookies Dee made. Her laugh came
out soft and lilting when she allowed herself to give in
to it. The one thing that got to him more than anything
was her insatiable need to be with the horses. She loved
them. Everything about her calmed and relaxed when
she spent time with them.

She didn't back away from him every time he got
too close. If he accidentally brushed up against her,
or touched her shoulder to get her attention, she didn't

flinch. Spending time together, getting to know each other a little bit at a time while they worked, eased her guard around him. Progress. But the compulsion to touch her grew more and more each and every second he spent with her, which is why he'd resorted to hiding in the office today. He couldn't work beside her right now, or he'd give in to his compulsion to touch her beyond tapping her shoulder to get her attention.

Not an option. Hands off, man. Keep your mind on work and off her.

Someone knocked on the door. He growled out, "What!"

Gillian opened the door and peeked in. He didn't get up to greet her from where he sat behind his cluttered desk in the corner of the room; couldn't really, without revealing the bulge in his jeans. If he saw her, heard her voice, his damn dick snapped to attention, begging for him to bury it deep inside her soft body. God, how he wanted her.

Why wouldn't she go away and stop unknowingly torturing him for five minutes?

He hit save on the spreadsheet, narrowed his eyes, and scowled at her. He didn't really mean it. His own damn fault he couldn't control his thoughts and needs around her. Better to hide out with his numbers than lose everything by doing something stupid like grabbing her, crushing her to his aching body, and kissing her.

"Blake, your mom is downstairs. She'd like you to come down and see her."

He'd spent half the day avoiding Gillian and all day thinking about her. Now, she'd hunted him down, and all he wanted to do was take her in the other room and lay her out on the bed and cover her with his body and make love to her until morning.

On the other hand, he wanted her to go away. She made him ache. Thoughts of her kept him awake long into the night. He hadn't slept well knowing that she was only a short walk away and a million miles away emotionally. The bruises on her face had almost faded away. The last of the stitches on her back were probably ready to come out. Each and every day, she got stronger, more confident here on the ranch.

"Fine." He tried to ignore her, kept his focus on the computer screen, and entered another set of numbers into the machine from hell.

She walked up behind him and leaned over, distracting him with the soft touch of her hand on his shoulder, her sweet, flowery scent, and the silky strands of hair that tickled the back of his neck as they fell over her shoulder and lay down his back. She studied the screen without noticing he'd gone completely rigid beside her. Did she know she touched him more and more often without even thinking about it? Probably not. She was still ignoring the pull between them. She was still ignoring him. He smelled that damn shampoo with its flowers-and-citrus scent. He swore that smell lingered on the air for hours after she left the stable. He smelled it over the horses. He smelled it when he went to sleep.

"Why are you doing the calculations on the calculator and not having the computer do them for you?" Even her sweet voice tempted him.

He sucked in a breath and let it go more irritated, because he could smell her even better now that she had her hand next to his on the desk as she leaned down and stared at the screen. If he leaned back, her breast would press against his shoulder. He remained still. Very, very still.

"Because I need to do several calculations to get this

column here." He pointed to the numbers on the screen, then went back to tapping the keys on the calculator and ignoring his throbbing body, despite the fact he punched in half the numbers wrong.

"What are the calculations?"

Better to think about numbers than making love to her. "I have to add up these columns, take the total, and multiply it by twelve for the year. I take that total and multiply it by this row here, and that gives me the total for this column. Then I have to take that total and use it to do some calculations on another spreadsheet over here," he said and switched the screen to another complicated spreadsheet. He didn't know why he kept trying to get the thing in the computer when he could do it faster by hand.

"Why don't you add a column that has the total of all those columns? Use that to multiply by twelve to get this column. You can use that number to put on this spreadsheet if you have both open at the same time and link them. Do you need to use these figures for projections?" Gillian studied the columns and figures.

He made the mistake of turning his head to look at her and found himself inches from her mouth. He stared into her expectant eyes. Too bad she expected an answer and not a hot, searing kiss to ease the ache in his belly and between his legs.

Her eyes narrowed when he didn't say anything. "Are you mad at me? Did I do something?"

"No." *Yes. You stand here not knowing what brushing up so close does to me. I want you. I need you.* "Everything is fine. I do the projections over here on this paper. I don't have them in the computer. I hate this thing. It won't do what it's supposed to."

"Don't be silly. It'll do anything you tell it to do. Watch."

She took the mouse from his hand, her fingertips brushing his despite how hard she tried not to hit him with her cast. If she noticed the zap of electricity arcing between them, she ignored it. Like always, maddening him even more.

She added a column to his spreadsheet, dragged the mouse across the numbers he wanted to add, and, with a few clicks, told it to add up the numbers. With a few more clicks and drags, she had one spreadsheet linked to the total on the original spreadsheet.

"There. Now all you have to do is enter the information into the rows and the total on this spreadsheet, and the other will calculate for you."

"How do you know how to do that?"

"I told you. I took basic accounting in high school. I did the books for a garage. This is just a simple accounting spreadsheet. I can pretty much see what you're trying to figure out here. I can do the projections for you showing you what would happen in one year or five years, depending on the variables you want to use. Whatever you want. There're all kinds of things you can do with these spreadsheets." She looked at the folders on the desk and sorted through them, her concentration and focus on them, not him.

"For these salaries and benefits, I can set up another spreadsheet that will help you calculate pay increases, tell you how much you paid in salaries for the year, how much taxes are owed, all the deductions. You can total it for the year and use it for taxes next year."

She grabbed the other set of folders. "You know, you could take this spreadsheet that lists the amount of feed the horses consume and link it to this spreadsheet to determine the amount of feed you need to order and when. That way you only order what you need and the feed is fresh for the horses."

He watched her, studied the way she concentrated and mulled over her thoughts by biting the corner of her rosy lip. In less than five minutes, she'd gone through much of his paperwork and figured it out and told him how to do it faster and more efficiently. He knew she was smart, he'd just never thought she'd be interested in facts and figures. It seemed, given a chance and some teaching, she was good at everything she tried. Every task she took on, she put all her effort into it and did everything to the best of her ability. She didn't half-ass anything.

"Fine, you want to take a crack at it? Be my guest. Take all these folders, too. Figure them out. I'm going down to see my mom."

He needed to get away from her. Her smell, her hair brushing his shoulder, the fact that she was wearing her new jeans that fit her like a second skin, and the fact that he could see the strap of the pink and cream bra he'd bought her peeking out from under her shirt, driving him wild. His heart slammed into his chest. The hard-on pressed to his fly throbbed and kept time with his thrashing heart. He either needed to take a cold shower or bash his head into the wall. Maybe a little pain would take his mind off her and his aching dick.

He pushed back from the desk, letting the chair roll across the hardwood floor, accidentally ramming the chair arm right into her thigh. She cussed under her breath, bent, and rubbed her hand over her sore leg.

"What the hell?" She hissed in a sharp breath.

"Sweetheart, are you okay?" Shit. Bud would have his head for hurting her. "I didn't mean to hit you. I'm sorry." He leaned forward, grabbed her leg, and ran his hand over her thigh. She'd bruise. Again. His stomach went tight and burned like acid. Sick he'd put a mark on her, he dropped his head and pressed his forehead to her hip. "I'm so sorry."

He glanced up, ready for whatever wrath she wanted to spew at him. Instead, he found her steady gaze filled with concern and what he hoped was a longing that matched his own. Her eyes dipped to his hands wrapped around her thigh. He released her, jumped up, and stalked into the living room space. He kept his back to her as he collected himself, trying to forget that look in her eyes, the feel of her toned muscles under his palms, heaven at his fingertips. When she looked at him like that, her eyes soft, like she wanted him to touch her, she undid him. His heart reached out to her just the way he wanted to do with his hands.

He stood, hands on hips, shoulders rigid, and waited for whatever she said next.

"Blake, what's the matter? Did I do something wrong? You've been moody and avoiding me all day. If I did something to make you angry, I wish you'd tell me what it is. If you don't want me around you anymore, all you have to do is say so."

"How can you possibly think I don't want you around me?" That was the furthest thing from the truth. He wanted her as close as humanly possible.

Yeah, he was a little ticked. At himself. He felt so much for her that he didn't know what to do with himself, since he couldn't show her how much he wanted her. He tried to take his time. Go slow. But everything inside him wanted her. Right this minute. Now.

He needed the space and time to cool off, but she'd come to him this time. She'd sought him out. That meant something, right? He didn't know. Not for sure. If he made a wrong move, it could blow everything, so he stood there, trying his damnedest to keep his hands to himself.

"You barely spoke to me this morning. You stayed away from me all day. You haven't come into the house to get coffee like you normally do. Just tell me what I did. I'm a big girl. I can take it."

"What you did?" His anger simmered. Better to be angry than to yank her into his arms and devour her whole. She was completely clueless, and that drove him crazy, too. That, and the fact that she was standing there looking so damn beautiful. Her eyes pleaded with him to say something. How many times had her father blamed her for something she didn't do to make her believe that she caused his bad attitude? Okay, maybe in this case she played a small part, but it was him and his lack of control around her.

No, it was all him. The worst part, he'd made her feel that he didn't want her around him, when his goal from second one when he saw her was to make her want to be with him. His thoughts swirled. He couldn't keep up, so how could she?

"I'll tell you what you did." He forced the words out. "You showed up here a week ago and turned my whole world upside down. I took one look at you and my heart fell out of my chest and landed at your damn tiny feet. I can't sleep for thinking about you. Every time I'm near you all I want to do is grab you and kiss you. It's all I can do to keep my damn hands off you. And let me tell you this, I'm trying. I'm trying to stay the hell away from you because just being near you is making me crazy." He ran a hand over the side of his head and shoved both his hands deep into his pockets.

Stunned, she didn't react or say anything, then a soft smile spread across her face. One of those smiles that shows a woman knows something you missed.

"How old are you?"

"What does that have to do with anything?"

"How old are you?"

Exasperated, he said, "Twenty-eight."

"Does it bother you that I'm only twenty?"

"No. Why would it? You're more mature than half the women I know my own age. What does this have to do with anything?"

"I'm trying to figure out what made you mad. It isn't the age difference, so I guess you're angry, what, because you like me?"

"I *like* my mother."

The corners of her mouth curved up at that, but he wasn't finished being mad, at what, he had no idea anymore. "It's a hell of a lot more than liking you."

"So you're angry because you more than like me, and you've been thinking about me, and you can't sleep. You want to kiss me, so you're avoiding me. Is that about right?"

Her face and eyes remained serious, but on the inside she was laughing at him.

"You think this is funny? It's not. I can't concentrate on anything. I've been staring at that damn spreadsheet for over an hour."

"Oh, I'm taking you very seriously, because I think you really do have feelings for me, and you aren't quite sure what to do about that, so you're mad at me because I made you feel something. Since you're serious, and I'm serious, I have a question." She pointed her finger at him. "Lie to me, and I'll know it."

"What's the question?"

"What do you want? A quick toss in the hay to get me out of your system, or something more?"

The girl didn't mince words, shot from the hip, and took direct aim at his heart. Some of the tension went out of him. Unsure how to answer her without screwing this whole thing up, he took his time and thought about it.

He could keep things casual and give her a vague

answer, something in between the two she asked. Or, for the first time in his life, he could lay it on the line and tell her what he really wanted. Straightforward as always, she'd asked the bold question, so he figured he owed her the honest answer.

"You're the first person I ever thought about in terms of the future, and what that could mean." He wanted to tell her when he looked at her he thought of waking up with her every day, sleeping with her in his arms every night, rings, and babies. He'd never thought of having a wife and family, but when he looked at her, he wanted to make promises and spend the rest of his life keeping them.

Maybe that's how it happened to Gabe and Caleb. It explained the lengths Gabe went to protect Ella and win her heart, despite the obstacles of their very different lives.

"Nothing's going to happen. Your grandfather made himself clear," Blake said, silently reminding himself again that she was hands off.

"Yes, he did. If I want to get to know you better, the choice is mine. Not his."

"What?" Surprised, he didn't think he'd heard her quite right.

"You heard me."

Blake wanted to go to her and touch her, and still he held back. If he touched her now, he'd never stop. As much as he wanted her, he didn't want to screw this up. This was one of those moments when one decision could give him everything he wanted and screw everything up. He wanted her. He wanted his job and life here on the ranch. He wanted both, and choosing one meant losing the other. Or did it? Could he have both?

She took a step toward him. He took one back. They'd done this dance for days, but the other way around. Surprised by his move, she took another step, and he took one back. That secret smile touched her lips again. He liked it and hated it.

"Blake, don't you think that at the age of twenty-eight you should stop acting like a nervous fourteen-year-old boy and just come over here and kiss me."

She took another step toward him, and he took one back. Confused, he stopped dead in his tracks.

"What did you say?"

"Kiss me."

She took a step toward him, and he sidestepped the coffee table, making it an obstacle between them when he didn't even want a breath of air separating them.

"Stay still," he ordered, going against his mind screaming out, *Come here!*

"Kiss me." This time, the smile bloomed. She liked having him on the run.

"I can't." If he kissed her, he'd go nuts and drag her to the floor. He'd never stop kissing her until all her clothes were scattered across the hardwood and he kissed every square inch of her. That's not how he wanted things to be. Right now, he didn't have control of himself well enough to be gentle. She needed gentle. She'd had enough rough in her life.

"Why can't you kiss me? You said you want to." She pouted and took a step toward him. He took a step back and ended up in the exact place he'd started this strange dance around the room. The backs of his thighs pressed into the wood desk. Trapped.

She'd gone from computer wizard to siren in a matter of minutes. Damnit, he was trying to be a gentleman and keep his damn hands off her. Even her broken arm and sprained knee failed to make him stop wanting her.

"Because I don't think I'll stop at one kiss. I want you too much."

"That could be a problem, since your mother's downstairs waiting to see you."

"I really don't want to talk about my mom right now." He winced when her image came into his mind, replacing the one of a naked Gillian with her hair falling over her shoulders and breasts. He wanted that image back. Then he had a better idea. "On second thought, yeah, let's talk about my mom." That would definitely get his mind off getting Gillian naked and in his arms.

"Your mom's nice and all, but I want to talk about you kissing me."

"I'm not going to kiss you." Bud would kill him. Yes, think about that. A slow and painful death, not her full, soft lips. *Damnit.*

"Oh, you are going to kiss me." She walked right up to him and stood on tiptoe with her body pressed to his. His hands remained at his sides, wrapped around the edge of the desk. She ran her hands up his arms to his shoulders. "Kiss me, Blake. I want you to."

The devil inside him leaped. A man could only take so much. Having this beautiful woman pressed against his body drove him over the edge. He cupped her face in his hands and stared down into her beautiful hazel eyes. *Be gentle. Give her that much.* "I've wanted to do this since the moment I saw you."

Bad idea, his mind shouted.

She'd worn him down. He didn't care anymore. He had to kiss her.

His lips touched hers, soft, tender. That's when that door in Gillian's heart swung wide open and banged against the wall of her heart. Just that one light meeting of lips and mingling of breath and she wanted more. More than she'd ever wanted for herself. For the first time in her life, she wanted to love this man and be loved by him. She had a thousand dreams run through her mind, and all of them were filled with Blake. She should have known that she wouldn't ease into love. She hadn't eased into anything in her life. No, she fell hard.

She thought about flying through the window and landing on top of a car. In that moment, her life flashed before her eyes and the only person she'd thought about was Justin. Now, she could only think of Blake and the life they could build together with Justin.

Her fingers dug into his shoulders when his lips left hers. "You're so beautiful."

"Kiss me again, Blake. Kiss me like you've dreamed of kissing me."

He took her mouth, and she opened to him. His tongue slid against hers, tasting, tempting. He ran his fingers through her hair and pulled her head back so he could take the kiss deeper. His tongue slid over hers as he explored the depth of her mouth. His hands trailed down her back and cupped her bottom, pulling her hips to his. She pressed her aching breasts to his hard chest. His hand slid up over her bottom and under her blue sweater, his fingers tracing her spine and some of the scars that didn't stop him from exploring.

He filled her mind and her senses. His rough hands caressed her back, and his mouth never stopped kissing and nipping at her throat and back up to her mouth. Everywhere her fingers roamed over strong, taut muscles. She loved the feel of him. More, she loved the feel of his arms banded around her and the way he pulled her closer with gentle demand. She didn't think she could be any closer to him, and then his arms tightened, and he pressed her into the sturdy wall of his chest. Her thighs rubbed against his. The contact sent heat through her system in a tidal wave that washed over her, overwhelming her senses. Safe and protected in his strong arms, she never wanted to be without them wrapped around her.

Someone knocked, then pushed the door open. They broke apart in a start. Blake held her at arm's length with his hands on her hips. Both of them needed a moment to catch their breath. His gaze fell to her mouth. He wanted to kiss her again. She wanted him to do it again.

"Were you kissing?" Justin asked, staring from her to Blake and back again.

Gillian and Blake answered together.

"No," she said. "Yes," Blake said.

They looked at each other and she said, "Yes." Blake said, "No." They smiled at each other and laughed. It was just what they needed to break the coiling tension.

Gillian took over with Justin. He was her responsibility. "We kissed."

"So, you like him?"

"I do." Something weighed on his mind. He stared down at his feet and avoided looking at Blake. She went to him and kneeled on her good knee in front of him. "What's wrong?"

Justin leaned over to her ear and whispered, "Is he going to hurt you?"

Blake heard him and wanted to answer him immediately, but, like Justin, he waited for Gillian's answer. He needed to know that she knew he wouldn't hurt her. He wanted Justin to hear that she knew he wouldn't hurt her, because it would be more meaningful coming from her.

Getting involved with Gillian included Justin. A package deal. He'd never interfere in their relationship. He wanted to be included in it. Blake needed to prove himself to her and Justin. It wasn't one or the other, but both. Which added another layer, because if Justin wasn't on board with him seeing his sister and it caused problems, Blake had no doubt he'd not only lose Gillian but he could also lose his job and the home he'd built here.

Could he take care of Gillian and Justin? Be everything they needed? He sure as hell wanted to try.

Gillian wrapped Justin in her arms and held him tight. She looked him right in the eye and spoke the truth reflected in her steady gaze and voice. "Blake would never hurt me like that, Justin. He cares about me. He cares about you. He's a nice man. He'd never hit me. He'd never hit you." That was the underlying question Justin wanted to know. "Blake isn't like our father."

Blake kneeled in front of Justin, too, and looked him in the eye. The boy needed reassurances, and Blake needed to give them.

"I've never hit a woman or a child in my whole life, and I won't start now. You've seen me with the horses. I'd never hurt one of them. I don't believe in hurting others."

"You're nice to them," Justin confirmed.

"And I'll always be nice to your sister and you. That's not to say that we might not argue, or get upset with each other. That happens sometimes, even between friends. But I'd never hurt her. I'd never hurt you. I promise."

He held out his hand to shake on it. Justin glanced at Gillian to be sure she believed Blake, too. Then he put his little hand in Blake's big one and shook. Blake couldn't help himself. He pulled Justin into his arms and hugged him. So cute. So worried about his big sister. Blake stood with Justin in his arms and gave him a soft poke in the ribs to make him laugh.

"Justin, why did you come over here?" Gillian asked. She struggled to get up. Blake held out his hand, and she took it without hesitation. When they touched, their eyes met, and that strange energy that snapped between them came to life, crackling between them.

"Blake's mom wants to see him. She didn't think she should come up here."

"Your mom has your number, Blake. She said I'm as lovely as she'd heard. I wonder where she heard that?" Suspicion filled her narrowed eyes.

"I'm sure Dee had a lot of nice things to say about you the last time they talked."

"Dee, huh?"

"I might have mentioned you the last time I talked to her on the phone," he said vaguely.

"Go see your mother. I'll look through your paperwork." She took her seat at the desk and sorted through the files again. This time when he touched her hair, he made sure she knew it. Then, with Justin in his arms, he leaned over and kissed her on the top of her head.

He laughed when Justin made a disgusted noise.

"No way you're staying up here alone. Come with me." Blake held out his hand to her, but she didn't take it.

"But I need to go through all of this, input the data, complete the calculations, and—"

"Not tonight. Come on. I'll introduce you to my parents."

"I met them already."

"Gillian." The hint of a warning tinged her name as it passed his lips on an exasperated sigh.

She got the message and took his hand. He pulled her up, and the three of them left the office together.

CHAPTER 16

Blake led them down the stairs to the kitchen door. He held it open for Gillian and let her go into the house ahead of him. Justin sat on his arm, his hands at Blake's neck, happy to be carried into the house and not in the least afraid of Blake. He'd won the boy over. If the kiss he and Gillian had shared was any indication, they'd taken a giant step toward complete trust. Definitely a step in the right direction. When he'd touched her hair and kissed her on the head before they'd come down, she hadn't flinched. Progress. He'd build on it until he wasn't the one reaching for her, but she felt comfortable reaching for him from now on.

He needed to have a man-to-man talk with Bud. Since Gillian decided she wanted to be with him, Bud would listen, and hopefully give him a chance to make her happy.

They entered the living room together. Gillian stood beside him, Justin in his arms. His mother's eyes softened on them. She gave him one of those knowing looks that he ignored, trying not to make a big deal out of them standing together—almost like a family.

"So, you finally decided to come see us," his mother

said, giving him a soft smile and breaking the tension in the room.

Gillian fidgeted beside him, realizing they'd become the center of attention and everyone knew she was the reason he'd been delayed.

"I needed to finish some work upstairs," he covered, even if they wouldn't believe it.

"They were kissing," Justin announced.

Gillian's whole face flushed pink. She turned to him. "Justin."

Okay, no man-to-man talk with Bud. Blake would wait for the man to grab his shotgun, then do his damnedest to make Bud believe Blake intended to do right by her. Instead, Bud gave Gillian a questioning look. Blake couldn't see her face, but Bud looked back at Blake and gave him a nod that could only be construed as a go-ahead to see his granddaughter.

"Is that '57 Chevy C10 outside yours?" Blake's dad asked Gillian.

Blake gave his dad a look, silently thanking him for distracting Gillian from the embarrassment of being caught. Bad enough Justin walked in on them, but now everyone in the room stared and exchanged knowing looks. Especially his mother and Dee. Those two women were plotting happy-ever-after, but all Blake wanted right now was for Gillian to relax and get to know his parents. One step at a time. Though they'd taken a huge step forward, he didn't want to push too hard and end up five steps back, with Gillian retreating to neutral ground to keep him at bay, the way she'd done for days.

"Uh, yeah," she answered, her voice shy.

"Cool truck. My dad used to have one just like it when I was a kid. I miss that old truck," his father said, nostalgia filling his eyes.

"I, uh, bartered my way into it. When I got it, it didn't even run or have any tires and rims."

"Blake mentioned you worked at a garage. Did you do the work yourself?"

"Some of it," she confessed, warming up to the conversation and his dad.

"What did you barter to get it?"

"Well, it's a strange kind of circle. A woman down the street needed her fence repaired. She asked me to do it but didn't have the money to pay for the supplies, or for me to do the work. I needed some clothes for Justin, and she had a son who'd outgrown his things. So in exchange for the fence repair, she gave me the clothes. I knew a guy down at the pier who sold lawn ornaments and garden sculptures at the flea market. He worked as a landscaper during the week and had some extra fencing. He needed a babysitter for his four children for date nights with his wife. I traded him four Friday nights for the wood. I needed a way to get the wood, transport it, and transportation for myself, so I went to the guy who owned the truck. He wanted to impress his in-laws, who were coming into town for five days, so I offered to get the truck off the cinder blocks in his driveway in exchange for four fresh lobsters. I worked the docks for two days straight for them. I got a discount at the garage I worked at for the used tires and rims for the truck. The truck needed some minor engine work to get it running. I did that myself, picked up the wood, and built the fence."

His father, along with Bud, Dee, and Blake's mother, all stared at Gillian. No one spoke for several seconds.

"Very resourceful," his father said.

"In the neighborhoods I lived in, people didn't have a lot of money to pay for things, but I learned to figure out what they needed, how to get it, so I could get what

I wanted or needed. So, my friend got her fence fixed, and Justin got the clothes he needed. It just took some work and ingenuity to get it done."

Blake admired her even more for her cleverness. His father's eyes held a light of pride and admiration when he looked at her, then glanced at him. The slight nod told Blake his father approved. He didn't need to look at his mother to know she liked Gillian for him.

"I'd love a closer look. Mind showing me what you've done?" his father asked.

"You can take it for a drive if you'd like," she offered. "A trip down memory lane, so to speak."

His dad's whole face lit up with excitement. "I'd like that. My dad used to take me fishing. We'd cast off from the tailgate and spend the day on the edge of the river, telling tall tales."

"You took us boys all the time." Blake remembered the trips fondly. He loved spending time with his brothers and dad. The days when they all got together were few and far between now.

"Come on. I'll show you the truck." Gillian grabbed her keys from the table by the front door.

Justin wiggled down from his arms. "I want to go, too."

"Come on, young man." Blake's dad held out his hand. Justin grabbed it and walked out the door with him.

Gillian turned to Blake. "Did you see that?"

He smiled. "He didn't hesitate to go with him."

Her whole face beamed with happiness. "I can't believe it."

"I can. He doesn't need to be afraid anymore. He's got you, sweetheart. You were relaxed with my dad, so Justin was, too. You've kept your distance with me, so it took some coaxing to get Justin to hang with me in the beginning."

"Hang is right. He likes you because you're a giant jungle gym to him." Her gaze swept across his chest and landed on his biceps.

He didn't miss the heat in her gaze. Neither did Dee and his mother, so he didn't make a suggestive comment about her undressing him with her gorgeous hazel eyes.

"I like to play with him. He's fun. So serious when you arrived, but now he laughs and plays all the time."

Justin giggled outside at something Blake's father said or did. Gillian held up her casted hand and touched her fingertips to her bruised jaw and eye. Her gaze met Blake's, a silent conversation that Justin might have switched gears living here, but she still had so much of her past dictating her every move, thought, and decisions.

Blake closed the distance between them, but at the last second, Gillian took a step back, then caught herself. "I'm sorry."

"You don't need to apologize for what you need. Whatever that is to make you feel safe and comfortable. So, if it's space, take it. If it's time, it's yours. Justin's experiences are much more benign than yours, Gillian. You've lived a certain way your whole life, your guard up, every instinct on high alert. It will take time for you to change, settle, learn to live another way."

Her eyes went bright with unshed tears. She blinked them away. "I'm sorry." The words came out softer than a whisper, barely making it past her lips. She turned and fled through the door.

Lost in his thoughts, he didn't know his mother rose from the sofa to come and stand beside him until her hand touched his arm. He stared out the front door, watching Gillian with Justin and his father, standing by her truck. She opened the driver's door to show his dad the inside, then went and popped the hood. The whole time, she kept a discreet three-foot distance, even when Justin wrapped his arms around her leg as he always did when he sensed her guard up.

"You're very good with her," his mother praised. "She's beautiful and tragic all at the same time. She's smart and strong, nothing like I expected and so much more."

"Yes. She is." He didn't take his eyes off her.

"So, it's like that." His mother guessed all that he didn't say. "You really like her."

"I like you, Mom."

"What? You don't love me?" she teased.

"You know I love you. But her . . ." He shook his head, unable to put everything he felt into words. "I feel so much for her. I want to protect her. I want to rush her and give her all the time she needs. I want to kill every man who looks at her. I'd really like to kill her father all over again. Slowly. I want to wrap my arms around her and hold her and hope it's enough to make her feel safe. I want to make her happy and laugh and smile.

"It's strange, but everything she is, I am. If she's frightened, I feel it. If she's quiet and introspective, I calm and go inside, wondering how I can coax her back out. On the rare occasion she laughs with Justin, I feel so much joy inside for her because I know it's a triumph to allow herself to be happy and free to enjoy herself for even that small moment."

"Blake, she's getting better," Dee said. "It's only been a week."

"I know. I meant what I said. Anything she needs, it's hers. She deserves it and so much more. I want to give her everything, but sometimes it's hard to hold back when she needs me to."

"It's like that when you find someone special. You want to spend all your time with them," his mother said. "She may want to spend time with you, but her situation holds her back, when you want to leap."

"I want to hold on, but she won't let me close enough to even touch her most of the time. And I don't just mean in a physical way."

"I don't know about that," his mother said, watching Gillian, too. "You watch her. She watches you. Before she walked out, she hesitated for a second. I think she wanted to reach for you, but with me and Dee here, she didn't. If you'd been alone, she might have taken that step. She might not be like other women you've dated, Blake, but if what you two have is real and true, the time and effort you put into building your relationship will be stronger than anything others might have because she's got so much to overcome. For her to trust you, be close to you, you'll know it's real and true, because she wouldn't fight for it otherwise. The fact she's trying, despite the setbacks, both small and large, tells you she's not only interested in you but that she wants this to work as much as you do. Maybe more, because she needs to believe that some men can be good and kind. She believes that about you, so she tries. I bet she's scared to death that if she pushes you too hard, you'll give up on her. But she pushes, because she needs to know you won't give up. Remember that when things get tough, because they will. That's life.

"Look at all Gabe and Ella went through to be together. A relationship is work, Blake. It's never easy, but it's worth it if you love each other."

"She's worth it," he said to himself more than to his mother. She was right. For the first time in his life, he was building a relationship to last, not just seeing someone to have a good time.

"So, in addition to bringing Justin's quilt, I have something else for you. Gabe and Ella set a date. They're getting married in May at Wolf Ranch. It'll be an intimate affair, just family and a few of Ella's close friends from New York before she and Gabe go off to Bora Bora."

"The trip she planned to take with her sister before her uncle murdered Lela," he said.

His mother frowned. "Yes. She's still healing, too, from all the loss and betrayal that man put her through. Gabe wants to give his bride the closure she needs by taking the trip." His mother handed him the engraved invitation. "Dane told Gabe about Gillian after you talked to him the other day. He's put a plus one on the invitation if you'd like to bring her."

"But you said they only want family."

"That's what Gabe said."

Which meant that Gabe understood how important Gillian had become to Blake, even in such a short amount of time. Did he want to take that step and bring her to the family wedding? Yes. No hesitation. No worry that she wouldn't fit in. He wanted her there. But would she go?

She turned and stared at him across the yard. When he didn't smile or anything, she took a step in his direction, stopped, and smiled at him. His heart skipped. Then she waved for him to come out and join her. She wanted him to come to her. This time, his heart warmed and grew two sizes in his chest.

He stuffed the wedding invitation in his back pocket and walked out the door. He met Gillian in the drive. She didn't back away when he approached, but he still stopped two feet away from her. She closed the distance, stood beside him, and leaned against his side, looking up at him, smiling as they watched Bud and his dad going back and forth about the engine. His dad talked about working on his own father's truck when he was a boy of Justin's age.

When Gillian didn't pull away but stayed close, he wrapped his arm around her and held her to his side, feeling like he was ten feet tall and granted his greatest wish.

"They look good together," Dee said to Joan.

"Yes, they do, but she's wary of him. She hasn't let him in. Blake's nervous about Bud's reaction. Bud's keeping his eye on them. Blake's holding back, afraid to make a wrong move with him—and her.

"Blake's been so focused on work and just cruising through his life that it's nice to see him put on the brakes and actually think about his future. It started with Caleb and Gabe, but it was still more of a rolling stop—a passing thought that maybe he'd find someone to share his life. Now he's slammed on the brakes to pick her up and take her on the ride with him if she'll get in the car."

Dee laughed. "I have a feeling he'll idle beside her as long as it takes for her to decide to go along with him. Or knowing Gillian, she'll ask him to step out of his comfort zone and detour down the path she's on now."

"I know my son. He'll go anywhere she wants, because he's finally found someone who stopped him in his tracks."

"Let's hope they both find what they're looking for."

"I think they already have, now they just need to find a way to make it work and let it bloom into a lasting future."

Justin ran to both of them and threw his arms around Gillian and Blake's legs, holding onto both of them.

Joan's eyes softened on them. "They make a nice picture." Joan hoped the reality would be even better.

CHAPTER 17

Gillian accompanied Grandma Dee into town to do the grocery shopping. Justin wanted to come with them until Blake promised to take him riding again. Gillian couldn't blame Justin for staying behind. She found herself drawn to the horses, especially the wounded and sick ones.

"I've lost you," Grandma Dee said. She pulled the truck into a parking space outside the market and stared over at her.

"Sorry. I got lost in thought."

"Thinking about Blake?" The hint of a knowing smile and the glint in Dee's eyes made Gillian smile.

"No. The horses." And Blake, too. Always Blake.

"You're very good with them. Why, in just ten days Boots has improved remarkably. He eats regularly now. Even the vet said he's got more energy, and his blood work has improved."

"It's the feed mix Blake put together for him. High calories with lots of vitamins and minerals."

"You soothed Rocky after he hurt his leg on the track."

Gillian slid from the truck seat, closed the door, and walked around the truck to join Grandma Dee. They walked toward the grocery store.

"The vet said it's a mild sprain."

"You seemed very interested in what Dr. Potts did and had to say about Rocky."

"Once upon a time, I thought I might like to be a vet," she admitted.

"Why once upon a time? Why not now?"

"It always seemed a dream out of reach. I spent all my time scraping together the money my dad drank or smoked away instead of paying the bills. Although I had the grades to get into college, I didn't have the money."

"Why not a student loan?"

Gillian grabbed a cart inside the store and followed her grandmother. "Sure, that would help, but then I'd have to come up with living expenses and babysitting or daycare money for Justin. I saved some money, hoping one day I'd have enough to take Justin and set us up in our own place. I hoped once he was in first grade and in school for more than half the day I could maybe take some classes at a junior college. Get a start on becoming something more than a dishwasher, waitress, bookkeeper."

"Is that what you'd like to do? We could look into some of the colleges and see what is available to you. Your grandfather and I will help you."

"I'm not sure. I've never had the time to really think about what I want to do. Being a vet seemed a good choice. I love animals. They seem to like me."

"The horses sure do take to you."

"That's just it. I really like working with them. Especially the wounded and sick animals. I've enjoyed nursing Boots back to health. I'd like to keep at it. Right now, it's enough."

"I could talk to Dr. Potts about getting you some veterinary books. You could read up on horse illnesses and injuries and the proper way to care for them. You can see if it sparks your interest even more and whether you want to go to school for that. Even if you don't, it'll help you with taking care of the horses on the ranch. Talk to your grandfather. That man is an encyclopedia of horse knowledge."

"I'll do that. It'll be another way to break the ice and give us something to talk about."

"He lost your mother a long time ago. He's not used to talking to young ladies."

"Does he miss her?"

"He misses the little girl he raised. What about you? Do you miss her?"

Gillian selected two boxes of cereal. One healthy. One filled with sugar. She'd alternate them for Justin and balance out his need to be a kid with her need to feed him healthy food.

"I miss the idea of her, not the impatient, frustrated, drug-hazed woman who couldn't be bothered with me. When I was young, it wasn't as bad as things got a couple of years before Justin was born. She could be kind. She could be patient. She smiled. But those periods were brief and far between. I held on to those memories and hoped every day when I woke up that it would be a day that she smiled."

Grandma Dee added four cans of green beans and six cans of peaches to the cart. She turned from the shelves and touched her hand to Gillian's shoulder. "I wish there had been more days like that for you."

"Me, too."

"We better get some more ice cream, or Justin and Blake will both be grumbling tonight."

Gillian laughed. "Those two sure do like their ice cream."

"Like you love your cookies."

"It's the chocolate," she admitted. "I have a real thing for chocolate."

"Who doesn't? I keep a stash in the pantry all the time. I love to make brownies, but hardly ever do because up until recently it's just been your grandfather and I. Plus we have to fight off Blake to get any."

"I love brownies. Let's make some when we get back. We'll do it together. I'd like to learn to cook better. I'm good at a few simple things, like burgers, spaghetti, and fried chicken, but I'd like to cook like you."

Grandma Dee's eyes lit with pride and enthusiasm. "I'd like that. I'm happy to teach you everything I know. My mother taught me . . ." Her voice trailed off. "I'm sorry, Gillian. I wasn't thinking."

Gillian reached out and touched her arm. "It's okay. Come on, let's get what we need for the brownies and our other groceries."

"After we finish here, I want to take you to a little shop across the street. You need something."

"I do?"

"You'll see."

Gillian followed her grandmother, pushing the cart and grabbing what they needed off the shelves. They went through the checkout, and her grandmother paid. Funny, now that she felt closer to her grandparents, her pride didn't prick as much at them buying her food, clothes, everything she and Justin needed. They wanted to help. She had to admit, it was nice to have someone who genuinely cared.

They loaded the grocery bags into the truck, tucking the perishables into the cooler and covering it with the bag of ice they'd bought to get them home unspoiled. They locked the doors again.

"We'll have to hurry before that ice cream melts, but it's just right over here."

Gillian followed her grandmother into the cute little store across the way. Girly to the max. Accessory heaven. Scarves, hats, jewelry, and hair accessories filled the cases and racks. Colorful. Sparkly. Pretty.

Her grandmother stood before a tall display of head-bands in a variety of colors and sizes. Some plain, others with flowers or other decorations. Not little girl sweet, but grown-up chic.

"What do you think? Which ones do you like?"

"Oh, I don't need anything." The words didn't hold much conviction. She wanted to try on several. She'd seen women in San Francisco, their hair styled just so with pretty things like this to enhance their style.

"Gillian. You are constantly pushing that wild mass of hair from your face." Grandma Dee eyed her as she drew a wayward strand away from her cheek and tucked it behind her ear. "A headband will help keep the hair out of your face when you brush down the horses. Some hair ties will bind it when you go riding."

Gillian had thought the same thing, but figured a plain rubber band would do the trick. She'd never thought to buy something so frivolous. She'd never had the money to do so.

Her grandmother held up a set of three light brown bands. One plain, another with gold beads, and the last with blue crystals.

"These will look pretty and match your hair. You could tie it back in a ponytail and use the headbands for a bit of flare."

Gillian had to admit, she liked them, and they would look pretty. She took the bands and held them in her hand, tracing the pretty blue crystals.

"I really like them." She noted the price. Not bad at only three ninety-nine.

"Do you like more subtle colors, or would you like something brighter?"

"These are fine."

"Yes, for a start, but let's look at the others. What do you think? Something like this?" Her grandmother held up an ornate band decorated with a huge white flower, a fake gem the size of a quarter in the center of the bloom.

"That's a bit much. Maybe smaller. Subtle, but pretty."

"Okay." Her grandmother smiled and looked over the selection again. She helped Gillian try out several different ones. They laughed at some of the more ornate pieces and the ones that simply made her look ridiculous. In the end, they settled on the original brown headbands, a second set in navy blue with silver and light blue crystals, a pack of multicolored hair ties, a gold headband with white crystals in a swirling pattern for something dressier, and a pair of pretty copper butterfly clips with light green crystals. The copper color made the red in her hair stand out.

"You are going to look so pretty."

"Thank you, Grandma. I love all of them. I had such a good time picking them out."

"Me, too. I like having someone to shop with. We should do this again soon."

Gillian smiled. "I'd like that."

They stood at the counter together. Her grandmother dug her wallet out of her purse. Gillian checked out the display case. Her eyes fell on a pair of hair clips. Taken back to her time in San Francisco, she traced her finger over the glass and stared at the pair of silver birds with the tiny crystal blue eyes. They reminded her of the gulls soaring over the ocean.

The shopkeeper pulled them out and set them on the counter, ringing them up with their other purchases.

"No. We didn't choose those," Gillian pointed out.

"Yes, you did. You liked the others we chose," her grandmother said. "Those, you want. They're very pretty."

"They remind me of the birds flying over the ocean."

"I know you miss home."

"I like it here. It's different, and that's good. But sometimes I miss the water, the quiet solitude I found there. I have it here when I'm outside with the horses, but it's different. Not bad different."

"Just not the same," her grandmother said, understanding what Gillian couldn't put into words.

"Yes."

Her grandmother unlatched the clips from their holder and clipped one, and then the other, into Gillian's hair. "Very pretty."

Gillian reached up with an unsteady hand and touched her hair. "Really?"

"Oh yes."

"Thank you."

"You are very welcome, dear." Her grandmother took the receipt. "Come now. Let's get back before the ice cream is soup."

"Won't matter. Justin will still eat it."

"Blake, too," her grandmother added.

Gillian laughed and walked beside her grandmother back across the street to the grocery store lot. She wondered what Blake would think of her new hair accessories. Lost in thoughts of Blake and the wonderful outing she'd had with her grandmother, she stared off down a side street and caught a glimpse of movement at the auto repair place down the way. The man stood with his hands at his sides, his eyes narrowed on her.

Too far away to read his expression or see him clearly, she didn't need an up-close look. She'd recognize her father anywhere.

Her heart slammed into her ribs and stopped. Her breath caught in her throat, along with the scream pushing to escape. Everything inside her went cold. She turned from the threat and rushed to the truck, sliding in and slamming the door the moment her grandmother unlocked it. She turned back to see if her father was coming after her but found no threat at all.

Her grandmother slipped behind the wheel and started the truck. "Are you okay?"

"Fine."

Her grandmother narrowed her eyes at her too-quick reply.

"Really. I'm fine. It's nothing." Nothing but a ghost from her past haunting her. That was the second time her mind had played tricks on her. Why? Because she'd allowed herself to have fun with her grandmother: shopping, chatting, being normal. The guilt over what she'd done hung on like a barnacle. She'd never be rid of it, but she could ignore it for longer periods as the days passed and she embraced her new future. So why did she keep seeing her dead father?

I am not going crazy, she chanted in her mind, staring out the window as her grandmother drove them home.

"Gillian?"

"Huh?"

"We're home, sweetheart. You sure you're okay?"

"Yeah. Fine. Thank you so much for everything. I had fun today."

Her grandmother gave her a look that said, *Yeah right*.

Blake opened her door, and she jumped.

"Hey, sorry." Blake took a step back to give her some space. He hadn't meant to startle her. "You okay?"

"Why does everyone keep asking me that?"

"Uh, because you don't look okay."

"Would you please help take the groceries in?" she asked him. "I have something I need to do."

She slipped out of the truck, landing on her good leg in front of him. She darted around his side and took off for the barn.

He turned to Dee. "What was that all about?"

"I don't know. Everything seemed fine. We picked up the groceries and shopped at one of the stores. Kind of a girls' day."

"Sounds fun."

"Yes. But when we walked back to the truck, something happened."

"What?"

"I don't know."

Blake thought of the day they went shopping in town. "She got spooked, closed up, and went quiet on you."

"Yes. But there was no reason for her reaction."

"Killing her father is reason enough. She's fine most of the time, but when things really get to her, she takes off for the horses."

They both stared toward the barn doors Gillian disappeared through moments ago.

"Come on. Let's get this inside. I'll give her a few minutes to settle down with Boots and take her riding." Blake remembered the first time he'd gotten her up on a horse. The smile that brightened her face and eyes. She loved it. Every evening before dinner now, she asked him to take her for a ride. A quick study, she got better and better. She rode so well, she didn't really need his assistance anymore.

"I've never seen someone get up on a horse for the first time and make it look so easy."

"It's like she was born in a saddle. It's the only time I see her let everything else go and just be." He loved those short glimpses of the real Gillian. The girl who loved the outdoors, the horses, the quiet solitude of a ride. Spending time together alone.

Blake found Gillian in Boots's stall. Not surprising. She worked the brush over Boots's thickening coat. The horse looked better. So did Gillian. But not by much.

Boots noticed him first and huffed out a breath, alerting Gillian. Her head shot around, and she stared at him, eyes wide. Yep, still spooked.

"Come with me." He kept his voice soft. Calm. He wanted her to let her guard down, not reinforce her walls even more.

"Where are we going?"

"You'll see."

"Blake, I—"

"Need to come with me right now." She hesitated, so he added, "Please. You'll like it. I promise."

One eyebrow shot up, but he didn't add a teasing innuendo, even though she expected it. He kept things light.

He opened the stall door and let her out. Boots groaned at her, not wanting to let her go. He loved her visits as much as she loved being with him. She stopped and turned back. "I'll be back soon," she crooned. Boots nickered, letting her know he couldn't wait. They'd learned to communicate with each other. A must for working with the large animals. Gillian did it with little coaching from Blake.

"I'll bring her back," Blake told Boots.

Boots whinnied. A definite, *You better.*

"I think he's jealous," Gillian said.

"He'll get over it." Blake took her hand. She flinched. Not good, but he held on, hoping she'd relax. She did, but it took a minute.

He walked her outside. She stopped, stared at the saddled horses, and sighed.

"Let's ride, pretty girl."

"Pretty, huh?"

Blake took a chance and reached up to touch the bird-in-flight clip. He rested his hand against her head and stared down at her. "Beautiful." He let that sink in for a minute. "I like the birds."

She reached up to touch the clip, but her hand settled over his. Electricity snapped between them. The moment stretched, but he didn't make a move to kiss her, despite how desperately he wanted to. Right now, they both needed to feel that pulse and buzz between them. Whatever upset her earlier waned from her eyes. They softened and filled with a longing he hoped one day soon she'd allow herself to act on. Right now, he'd promised her time and space, and taking things slow. One step at a time. Today, they'd ride and spend time alone together. He told himself it was enough. But he wanted more.

"Remember everything I taught you on our last ride?"

"Yes."

Blake took her by the hips and lifted her into the saddle.

"That's not how you taught me to mount the horse."

Blake smiled but didn't say anything. He handed her the reins and mounted his own horse. No need to coax her; Gillian gave her mount a soft kick and took the path to the right and across the backside of the property. "Relax in the saddle, or your ass will be sore from all that bouncing."

Gillian caught herself. Tense. On edge. It took her a few minutes to let loose and settle into the ride.

They didn't speak for a good long time. The ranch buildings disappeared behind them. When they hit a long open space, Gillian kicked her horse into a gallop and took off. His mind took him back to another time he'd chased after a girl on a horse. His stomach tied in knots. Nervous, scared she might hurt herself, he let loose his reins, and his horse took off after hers. She slowed a ways up, and he walked beside her. She smiled and let out a huge sigh.

"That is so much fun."

Her happiness helped release the tension in his gut. "Yes, it is. I used to love to race my brothers."

"Is that what made you want to train racehorses?"

"My dad runs a cattle ranch. I hated working with the cattle. They're slow, unruly beasts. Horses have personality. My dad saw how much I liked the horses, so he put me in charge of them. I spent hours training them."

"You were born to ride."

"I love it. The faster the better."

"What else did you like to do with your brothers?"

"Everything. Fishing, riding, rodeoing, campouts. This one time, we scared the pants off Dane. He must have been about eight. It was his first time coming with us. Just us boys. Our parents stayed home. We pitched a couple of tents in the west pasture in the trees by the river. I'm sure my dad checked up on us, but we thought we were alone. We had a campfire and told ghost stories. Dane went to bed that night shaking in his boots. About an hour after lights out, we started making all kinds of noises. Gabe rattled one of the horse bridles. Caleb moaned and groaned like a ghost. I used a branch to poke at the outside of Dane's tent to make him think someone was outside."

"Not nice."

"He was the youngest, a tag-along. Call it an initiation. He spent every waking moment trying to be like us. It was our way of toughening him up."

Gillian shook her head with a slight smile on her lips. She got it.

"So we up the freaky noises and rattle his cage even more until he can't take it. He runs out of his tent screaming for Gabe, hoping big brother will save him. He runs into the three of us and gets us back good."

"What did he do?"

"Spewed hot dogs, soda, and s'mores all over our feet."

"Ah, yuck!" Gillian laughed. The sound made his heart melt. "You're joking."

"No joke. He fell to his knees, sick and frightened. Gabe picked him up and took him to the river's edge. We cleaned him up and our shoes. We all slept in Gabe's tent the rest of the night."

"You felt bad."

"We wanted to scare him, not make him sick. Tormenting our little brother is one thing. Hurting him is another. He never tattled on us. When our parents asked if we had a good time, he said he loved it and couldn't wait to go again."

"Did you take him with you the next time?"

"Always. We still picked on him. He's our little brother, but we never tortured him again. The thing is, he toughened up real quick. He gave as good as he got. In fact, he loved getting over on his big brothers."

"Did your parents ever find out what happened?"

"Dad never said anything, but everyone except Dane had extra chores that week."

"He was watching over you guys."

"Always."

"Did you guys ever fight?"

"Lots. But nothing that couldn't be fixed with an 'I'm sorry.'"

"Not even over a girl?"

"Unspoken rule. One of us liked a girl, she was hands-off for all the others. Not that we ever really liked the same girls. We're all two years apart, so there was enough separation in age and school grades to keep things easy."

"Did you play sports in high school?"

"Baseball."

"I can see that."

"Why?"

"You've got patience. While it's a physical sport, there's a lot of waiting for something to happen."

He had to admit she was right. "I guess so."

"Have you been in many serious relationships?" The words came out soft, shy.

"One really serious. The others committed but short-lived," he admitted.

"Why did the serious one end?"

"Not meant to be. We had a lot in common. Maybe too much. The two of us together spelled trouble with a capital T. We brought out our mutual competitiveness. We had to push the boundaries. Too bad neither of us remembered that we aren't invincible."

"What happened?"

"Disaster."

Sensing he didn't want to talk about what happened, she changed the subject. Kinda. "So, since then you've had several short-term relationships."

"I'm not a serial dater. I find someone I like, and

we see how it goes. When it gets too serious, I usually break it off."

"Why?"

"Because I didn't want serious. Not with them." *Hint. Hint.* Maybe he'd given too much away too soon, but he didn't want her to think she was like the other women who had come and gone in his life. She was different. Why? He didn't know. She just was.

They rode in silence back to the ranch. When the buildings drew closer, she asked in her shy way, "Is this something . . . Do you . . ."

"Gillian, you know it is, and I do. Go with your gut. It's never steered you wrong. What you see in me, whatever it is I make you feel, it's real."

Blake dismounted outside the stables, went to Gillian, took her by the waist, and carefully plucked her from the saddle to set her gently on her feet in front of him.

"I had a really good time," she said to his feet.

He touched his finger under her chin and made her look up at him. "I had a great time with you."

"You wouldn't rather—"

"I wouldn't rather do anything than spend time with you." He traced his finger along her jaw, up and over her cheek, and tucked a strand of her long hair, more gold today than brown and red, behind her ear.

He kept things easy. "Time to feed the horses. Boots is nickering for you." He led the saddled horses into the stables, Gillian following behind him. They'd made progress today. Whatever bothered her earlier had been erased from her mind and eyes with the long ride.

He liked making her happy. He liked sharing stories about his family with her. A good day. He wanted more. With her. Seemed whenever he was around her, or thought about her, he always wanted more.

CHAPTER 18

Gillian stood by Boots's corral, watching him prance around the small open space. After two weeks of eating regularly, he'd gained some weight and energy. The more time she spent with him, the more relaxed and outgoing he became, and the less he shied away from everyone and everything. Proud of him for coming out of his shell, she smiled and felt lighter. His accomplishment became her own. She'd done better the last few days, not looking over her shoulder every few seconds when she worked in the barn with Boots. She didn't try to hide from the others working in the barn, or time her entrance and exit for when there were the fewest men in there.

Things with Blake settled into a more normal friendship. She didn't back away when he approached. She didn't flinch when he brushed his hand down her long hair, his favorite thing to do any time she was near. The smile he gave her each morning when she came down to breakfast lit up her heart with such warmth that she couldn't help smiling back.

He kissed her goodnight before he left each night and gave her a look like it pained him to be away from her. The longing in his eyes matched what she felt in her heart. But they'd agreed to take things slow. Make sure the friendship they were building was the foundation for a future and didn't turn into the destruction of their lives at Three Peaks.

Today, he had some work to do training a couple of quarter horses, so she'd borrowed his MP3 player to pass the time while she waited for Justin's school bus to arrive. She worked her way through Blake's eclectic playlist.

Right now she didn't have anything more important to do than hang out by Boots's corral, watching him crop grass in the field and rest her aching arms and knee. She'd cut back on her pain meds. Each day she felt stronger.

With Jason Aldean's "Johnny Cash" blaring in her ears, she didn't hear anyone come up behind her. A hand settled on her shoulder and pulled her around. She expected Blake, but found herself staring up at a very tall, wide man looming over her. With her back pressed to the fence, she couldn't step away. He was saying something to her, but with the music blasting in her ears, she didn't hear him. She pulled one earbud out.

". . . Pain in My Ass. Have you seen him?"

All Gillian heard was "pain in my ass." The same thing her father said to her over and over again, day in and day out. The huge man's face faded and shifted into her father's. His heavy black coat turned to a white T-shirt. Blood bloomed across his chest. He reached out to her again, but she sank back against the fence, bent at the waist, and fell through the railing, her heart thrashing against her ribs.

He's back.

He'll hurt her again.

Fear washed over her and stole her breath. She tried to breathe but couldn't get any air.

She scrambled back as he leaned through the fence and reached for her again, grabbing her ankle. She screamed. Boots ran forward and reared up, but the horse didn't hold her attention—the man coming after her did. Boots's hooves landed inches from her leg. She scrambled backward on her hands, kicking with her feet to push herself back and her father away. Her broken arm hurt like hell, but she didn't care or stop. Everything inside her screamed, *Run!*

The man practically dove through the fence, stood tall over her, using one big hand to push Boots away. He took several steps toward her. She flipped over and tried to crawl and stand at the same time to run away, but she wrenched her knee and fell again, rolling over to her back, arms up to ward off the attack she knew was coming. Blake appeared out of nowhere and shoved the man in his chest, stopping him from coming forward. Relieved to see Blake, she stopped trying to get away.

Blake said something to the man, but she couldn't hear him over the thrashing guitars as the music blared in one ear and her heart pounded in the other. She pulled the earbud out and tried to take a breath, but still couldn't fill her lungs with the fear engulfing her. Everything in her wanted to jump up, flee, run as fast as she could, but she hurt so bad.

Blake stood with the man, his back to her. The guy explained, "I told her I was here to pick up my horse. I asked if she'd seen you, and then I don't know what happened. She scrambled to get away, but spooked the horse. He reared and almost trampled her to death."

Blake turned and stared at her, so much sadness and pity filling his tawny eyes. The same shade the man standing next to him had. In fact, they looked very similar to each other in height and build. Her brain stopped screaming for her to run and started processing the things around her again.

Blake took three steps to her but stopped five feet away and kneeled down, sitting back on his heels. "Gillian, sweetheart, please take a breath. Slow and easy," he pleaded.

Her gaze darted from him to the other man and back. She tried to breathe but couldn't.

"Sweetheart, look at me. No one is going to hurt you. I promise. Look at me."

She shifted her focus back to him.

"That's it, sweetheart. I won't let anyone hurt you. This is my brother Gabe. I should have told you he was coming today. I'm sorry."

Gabe moved to Blake's side and kneeled down, arms braced on his thighs.

Gillian put both hands up to stop him from coming closer, even though he made no move to do so.

"Hey there. I'm real sorry I scared you. I didn't see that you were listening to music and couldn't hear me. I never meant to scare you. I'll tell you, you took ten years off my life when that horse nearly stomped on you. That's all I was trying to do, get you out of the way of that horse."

Boots stood to her side, staring at Blake and Gabe.

"He'd never hurt you, would he, sweetheart? Boots loves you. He tried to protect you from Gabe. Like you, he didn't know Gabe wouldn't hurt a fly. I promise you, Gabe's no threat. He'd stand between you and danger the same way I would. I know telling you that doesn't really change your mind, but . . ."

She put her hand up to stop him. Her breathing slowed,

but her heart still pounded. For the first time, she realized tears tracked down her cheeks one after the other.

"I'm sorry," she said to Blake. She turned to his brother. "I'm sorry."

"Nothing to be sorry about. Totally my fault," Gabe said. "Blake told me about you. I should have known better than to come up behind you. He's right though, you've got the prettiest hair I've ever seen. What color is that?"

"All of them," she whispered.

Gabe laughed. "That's about right."

Blake stood and took two steps toward her. She put her hands up again to stop him, so he kneeled in front of her again. Gabe remained low behind him.

"Sweetheart, your hand is bleeding. After covering twenty feet of dirt and grass, your knee must be killing you. Come to me. I'll take you up to the house. We'll get you some pain meds, and you can rest."

She held her hand out in front of her. Sure enough, the plaster on her cast had scraped up the backs of her fingers as she'd scrambled away from Gabe.

"It hurts."

"I know. Let's go up to the house. I'll take care of you."

Justin ran down the driveway as the bus pulled out. Grandma Dee jogged from the house and intercepted him on the driveway, glancing over her shoulder at Gillian lying in the field, her eyes filled with concern.

Justin held up a colorful painted picture and said, "Gillian, come see."

"He can't see me like this," Gillian said to Blake and Gabe.

Grandma Dee distracted Justin, oohing and aahing over his picture while she led him to the house with a promise of fresh baked cookies.

"Gillian, can you get up and walk with me to the house?" Blake asked.

She sucked in a breath, tucked her good leg under her, planted her hands on the ground, and used her good leg to boost herself up to standing. She put her weight on her bad leg, testing out her aching knee. It hurt. Tired of being in pain, she glanced up and caught Blake's steady gaze, his whole body tensed to rush to her aid if she faltered. She wanted him to come to her, but her going to him would go a long way to easing his mind. With barely a glance at Gabe standing behind Blake, she limped to Blake and didn't stop until she reached him. He waited for her, not moving a muscle until she walked right into his chest, reached up around his neck, and held him close. He wrapped his arms around her, his fingers diving into her hair.

"Are you okay?"

"No, but I'm getting better by the second."

"You really scared me. I heard you scream, and I thought you were really in trouble."

"I thought I was, too. Something happened. My mind played tricks on me again. He didn't look like him anymore. He looked like my dad and reached for me. I heard the gunshot and smelled the gunpowder. I panicked. I needed to get away."

"You're safe here, sweetheart. I'll never let anything happen to you."

"I know. I saw you nearly knock your brother right off his feet."

"I'd kill anyone who touched you." Blake hugged her close.

"I believe that."

"But I don't scare you."

"No. Well, sometimes, but not in that way."

"You never have to be afraid of me for any reason."

"I'm trying, Blake. I know you're impatient for me to come around and be normal—"

"Stop. I don't think that at all. Today is nothing more than your mind still trying to process what happened. Maybe you need to talk to a professional."

She didn't want to, but she stepped back. He didn't let her completely out of his embrace but kept his hands banded at her back. She slid her hands down his shoulders and rested them on his huge biceps. So much strength, yet he held her in a gentle embrace she could break if she wanted to, though she didn't feel the need. His smile settled her. The warmth in his eyes eased her heart and erased the last of the fear running through her blood.

"No. I'm fine."

"Gillian, you're fine most of the time, but I know you think about it. I see it in your eyes sometimes. I bet you even dream about it."

"This happened before," she admitted.

"When we went shopping in town," Blake guessed. "And again when you went to town with Dee three days ago."

"I thought I saw him."

"He's dead and gone, sweetheart. He can't hurt you anymore."

"I don't want to dwell in the past. I'm moving forward. Yes, this is a step back, but I'm not going crazy. We don't need to call in the white coats and straightjacket."

"I never said anything like that. I want you to be happy and see this incident lift from your shoulders so that it's a real part of your past and not part of your every day."

"I'm getting there." She'd thought she was further

along in this process. Yes, it was a process. Some days she couldn't stop thinking about it, others she went hours without a thought, an image, a reminder. Blake's frown made her add, "It's only been a couple of weeks. If things get worse, I'll see someone."

"And you'll be honest with me. If you're having a bad day, tell me. Maybe I can help. The least I can do is be with you, distract you from your thoughts and make you smile."

"Like when we go riding together and you tell me stories about you and your brothers."

No one had ever cared enough about how she felt to offer to help her, let alone simply be there for her if she needed them.

"I don't know what to say," she said.

"Thank you," he suggested.

"Thank you."

"And you'll be honest about how you're feeling?"

"Yes. With you, but you can't tell Justin or my grandparents if I confide something I don't want them to know."

"As long as I agree there's no harm in keeping them in the dark."

She frowned, narrowing her eyes, but relented. "Okay. I need to go inside and reassure Justin everything is okay."

"You need to take care of yourself first. Come on." He coaxed her toward his waiting brother. "Gabe, this is Gillian. Gillian, my older brother, Gabe, who is deeply sorry for startling you."

"I truly am. It's nice to meet you. I came to pick up Pain in My Ass."

She flinched at the term. Blake squeezed her to his side. "He means his horse, not you. I've been training *Bo*."

"Sorry, but he is a pain in my ass."

"Not anymore," Blake assured him.

"So, you'll be at the wedding, right? Ella can't wait to meet you. I would have brought her with me today. She loves this one"—Gabe cocked his head toward Blake—"but she's in New York until Friday night."

"Uh, what wedding?" she asked.

"You didn't ask her?"

Blake frowned. "I haven't had the chance to bring it up." Blake stared down at her. "Gabe and Ella are getting married soon. I'd like you to come with me to the wedding at Wolf Ranch."

"That's a family thing." If he hadn't asked her already, maybe it was because he didn't want to take her. Then again, did she want to go, put herself in the position as his date, where others might think it was something more? *Is it something more?* Certainly seemed that way if he wanted her to go with him to a family wedding. Not just a cousin or distant relative's, but his brother's.

"Family and very close friends," Gabe clarified. "We'd love for you to come. Ella's friends are all in New York and all over the world. She doesn't know many people here. Neither do you, since you just moved here, so she thought you two might hit it off and she'd have a friend here, too. You'll like her. She's amazing."

"Says her love-struck fiancé," Gillian teased.

Gabe smiled, cocking up one side of his mouth in a half grin that matched Blake's familiar one, and nodded.

"Really, you'll like her. She's not much older than you. Even though she runs her own company, she's really down to earth. She's smart and kind and generous," Blake added.

"Sounds like love, all right," Gillian teased Blake.

Blake's mouth dropped open.

Gabe laughed and smacked Blake on the back. "Stay away from my woman."

"I . . . um . . . she's my sister."

"Nice cover," Gabe joked.

"Actually, that's kind of sweet you already think of her that way," Gillian commented.

"She's right," Gabe admitted. "Thanks, man. Let's get your girl up to the house. If she leans any further off her bad leg, she'll fall over."

Blake traced his finger over her forehead and tucked a strand of hair behind her ear. "Can you walk?"

"Yes," she said automatically. Blake's eyes narrowed with skepticism, and she remembered that not five minutes ago she'd promised to tell him the truth. "My knee really hurts."

Blake scooped her right off her feet and held her to his chest.

"My arm hurts, too. I need some pain meds."

"Let's go get them. You can lie on the couch and rest for a while."

"I have to feed Boots."

"I'll take care of him and you."

She wrapped her arms around Blake's neck and leaned her head on his shoulder, her face tucked at his neck. She inhaled his earthy, spicy scent along with the always-present leather and horses that clung to him. "Thank you." This time, asking for help didn't go down tasting like her pride—it settled in her gut as genuine relief and gratitude that he'd take care of her.

She hugged him close as he walked her back up to the house and his brother Gabe went off to the stables to get his horse.

Blake's arm supported her knees, his big hand on her thigh. He gave her a soft squeeze. "You'll be okay, sweetheart."

She placed her hand on his cheek and made him look at her. He stopped and stared, and she lost herself in his warm brown eyes. "I feel better already." After their first kiss, he'd always kissed her first. This time, she took the lead again and touched her lips to his for a soft, sweet kiss that washed away the last of her fear.

Blake took her through the front door, avoiding going through the kitchen, where Grandma Dee was probably distracting Justin with an after-school snack. He set her on the sofa and stared down at her. "Okay?"

"Can you get me some ice for my knee?"

"Anything you need. Wait there. I'll be right back."

Grandma Dee walked into the room, meeting Blake on his way to the kitchen. Blake leaned in close and whispered, telling her what happened without letting Justin overhear in the other room. Grandma Dee's eyes went wide, but her gaze settled softly on Gillian.

"I'm okay. It's no big deal," she assured her grandmother.

Grandma Dee glanced at Blake for confirmation.

"She's fine. She wrenched her knee and hurt her hands. I'll fix her up, and she can get some rest."

Blake walked into the kitchen, greeted Justin, and struck up a conversation about how Justin did at school today.

Grandma Dee came over and stared down at her. "Are you really okay?"

"I'm fine. Please don't make a big deal about it. I just want to forget it ever happened."

"Maybe working out in the stables and with the horses is too much for you."

"I need to do it. I can't hide away inside the house. I got scared. If I give in to the fear and close myself off, then what? How much of my life will I miss because I'm afraid to face it?"

"Maybe you need more time to settle in here."

"Trust me, Blake isn't going to leave me alone again until he's sure I'm comfortable." Funny how she knew that about him and counted on him to do it. "Gabe startled me, and I overreacted. It's happened a few times in the stables with the guys coming in and out." She thought of Ken. He tended to seek her out and show up unexpectedly when she thought she was alone with Boots. "I didn't sleep well last night. Well, most nights. I'm tired. It caught up with me today."

Blake walked in carrying a glass of water, several wet paper towels, and a bag of crushed ice. He handed her the glass, set the other items on the coffee table, and pulled her pill bottle from his pocket. He uncapped the childproof lid and poured out a single pill. She gave him a look, which he held, not wanting to give her more than she needed. Reading in her that she needed two pain pills, he shook out another and handed them over. She downed them with the water and set the glass on the table. Blake sat on the sofa beside her, grabbed her foot, and pulled off her shoe. He did the same with her other foot, then stood and made her swing her legs onto the couch. He propped her knee on a pillow, undid the knee brace, and dragged it down her leg. He set the bag of ice over her aching knee. Satisfied he'd settled her on the couch, he leaned down and kissed her on the forehead.

"I'll help Justin with his homework, and we'll watch a movie together while you rest. Those pills should knock you out soon." Blake kneeled beside her, took one of the wet towels, and dabbed at the scrapes on her hands, which rested on her stomach. "There, that's better."

Touched by the care and attention he showed her, she crooked her finger for him to lean in closer. She reached up, took his face in her hands, and pulled him down for a kiss. His lips met hers. With soft touches, he kissed her again and again, finally settling his lips against hers when she sighed. He took the kiss deeper, his tongue sliding over hers. She held him close with her hand on his shoulder. He ended the kiss far too soon and pressed his forehead to hers, his eyes closed. When they opened, she gazed into his tawny eyes, so filled with need and longing.

"You're killing me, sweetheart."

She smiled, her eyes drooping, the meds kicking in. "I don't know what to do with you when you're sweet."

"Kiss me all you want," he suggested.

"Kiss me now."

"My pleasure."

He kept the kiss soft, sweet, lingering, like he had all the time in the world. She wished things could be like this all the time, but had a feeling her relaxed, mellow mood had more to do with the pain meds smoothing out her rough edges than the fact that she'd truly settled into this new relationship with Blake. This was a good start though. She could definitely get used to kissing him and the warm feeling seeping into every cell of her body.

"Get some rest. I'll get Justin and be right back."

"Blake?"

"Yeah, sweetheart."

"Thanks for not making a big deal about what happened."

His warm palm settled on her cheek. "You're going to be okay."

She knew that, but hearing him say it helped.

His hand swept down her neck to her shoulder. He kissed her forehead and stood and left.

With her eyes closed, the knock on the front door made her jump, but when Gabe walked in, she didn't even flinch. She gave him a soft smile.

"Blake around?"

"Kitchen."

"Feeling better?"

"Pharmaceutically mellow."

Gabe smiled and laughed with her. Looking at him now, she wondered why she'd ever been afraid of him, when he looked so much like Blake. How could she have mistaken him for her father? Nothing but her mind playing tricks on her, and her subconscious letting her know she still needed time to deal with and overcome what happened to her—what she'd had to do to protect herself and Justin.

"Let's hope Blake's mellowed out, too."

"He's just looking out for me."

"As he should. I just got off the phone with Ella. Expect a package from her. She really can't wait to meet you. I hope you join us at the wedding. We want you there. I know Blake wants you there."

"What is Ella sending me?"

"A surprise. She does that sometimes for her friends."

Gillian didn't know what to say. She had yet to meet Ella, but the woman was treating her like a friend. Gillian had been on the ranch for a while. It might be nice to have a girlfriend her own age. Grandma Dee was great, but a friend to talk to and share things with would be nice.

"I need to get on the road, so I'll say goodbye to you and go find Blake."

"Again, I'm really sorry for the way I acted."

"Forget it. I have. Since you're staying here, we'll have plenty of time to get to know each other."

"I hope so."

Gabe left her. The meds made her comfortably numb and drowsy, but didn't stop her from watching the men say goodbye at the front door with a hearty hug and smack on the back. They smiled at each other, completely at ease in each other's company. Connected. More than brothers, they liked each other.

Walk me to my truck." Gabe opened the door and Blake followed him out, wondering what his big brother had to say in private.

Blake stopped next to the truck's open window after Gabe climbed in behind the wheel. "What?"

"You're robbing the cradle a bit there, bro. She's younger than Dane. She's younger than most of the women he dates."

"I know how old she is. And Dane doesn't date anyone. He sleeps with them. Gillian isn't like those women."

"No. She's broken." Blake opened his mouth to defend her, but Gabe held up a hand to stop him. "She's on the mend, but she's still got a long road ahead of her. You up for that?"

"Would you have let Ella handle her uncle alone?"

"No fucking way."

"I won't let Gillian go through this alone. Get to know her. All those things you love about Ella, her kindness, smarts, strength, resilience, determination,

Gillian has all those things and more times ten. I don't care how old she is, I care who she is."

Gabe pressed his lips together and nodded. "That's all that really matters. Mom and Dad really like her."

"You don't?"

"I do. I can't wait to get to know her better. I assume she'll still be around, and with you, when Ella and I get back from our honeymoon."

"Count on it."

"Great. I feel a family barbeque coming on."

"We're in."

"Catch you later. Thanks for training Pain in My Ass."

"Bo. His name is Bo."

Gabe laughed and took off down the driveway with a wave out the window.

Blake went back in the house, closed the door, and walked over to Gillian. "I thought you'd be asleep by now."

"Nearly there. Did your brother tell you to run away from me as fast as you can?"

"No. He thinks you're too young for me."

"Why? I thought all guys, no matter how old they are, want to date twenty-year-olds."

"That's what I told him." She frowned. "I told him I'm not interested in your age, I'm interested in you. He's just looking out for me, making sure you don't leave me for some younger guy. Like Ken," he added and wished he'd held his tongue about that concern.

Gillian huffed that away. "He's a chameleon. You never know who he really is."

"What am I?"

"Better than anyone I've ever met."

"Good answer." He leaned down and kissed her on the head. "Justin, come on. Let's get your homework done," Blake called into the kitchen. He sat on the floor beside Gillian, his back against the sofa. He looked over his shoulder and smiled. "Go to sleep. I got this."

With him inches away, making her whole being aware of him so close and his scent drawing her in, she hardly wanted to sleep.

Justin ran in, his backpack over one shoulder, a huge bowl of popcorn in his hands. Blake took the bowl before the boy dumped the contents all over the floor. Justin sat on the floor on the other side of Blake, closer to Gillian's feet, and pulled out his worksheets.

"Okay, let's practice writing the alphabet and work on your sight words."

Gillian listened to the two of them working through the homework. Blake's patience, the way he made the work fun for Justin and kept him engaged, warmed her heart and made her like him even more. It made her want to reach out and hold onto his goodness.

She scooted down on the sofa, draped her arm over his shoulder, and laid her hand on his chest. She rested her face against his other shoulder and settled into him and the sleep that pulled her under.

Blake reached up and over him to brush his fingers through her hair. He worked with Justin and kept up that hypnotic caress until she fell into a deep, dreamless sleep.

Gillian woke up two hours later to Blake and Justin laughing at one of Justin's favorite cartoon movies. Justin sat on Blake's lap, his back against Blake's chest, and held her hand. She leaned up. "I don't know what to do with you when you're sweet," she whispered to Blake. She kissed his cheek, settled her chin on his shoulder to watch the movie with them, and smiled when Blake kissed her on the head.

"Feel better?"

"Being with you always makes me feel better," she admitted, realizing how much she meant it. Still, she wondered if her crazy act today didn't put him off and make him wonder if he'd made a huge mistake getting involved with a head case like her.

CHAPTER 19

Gillian slammed the truck door and waited for Justin to come around to her side to join her. Upset, she held back her temper. She'd talk to him when she calmed down. Who knew how long that would take at this point.

"Go upstairs to your room. No TV tonight. No going down to see Honey and her baby." They'd become Justin's favorite horses. He went each afternoon to give her a slice of apple and a sugar cube. Gillian hated to keep him from the horses, but he needed time to think about what happened at school today.

He walked away with his head down and his backpack dragging on the ground behind him. He stomped up the steps and slammed the front door behind him. She remained by the truck. She needed the cold breeze to soothe the hot rage running through her veins.

Blake left a week ago. She wished he was here to talk and give her advice and perspective.

They'd spent every waking moment together for the last three weeks after that first kiss in the office. She'd spent much of that time redoing his computer work. She tried to tell him that her grandfather wouldn't approve of her taking over and that she didn't know the ranching business well enough to do the job. He balked at all her protests and told her she knew the paperwork better than he did.

Her grandfather surprised her and agreed with Blake, adding her as a signer to his bank account. Now she ran all the finances and payroll for the ranch. The first week she issued checks to the employees, she found one listed for her. She checked her new system and found that someone had entered her and given her a generous salary. She went to her grandfather and told him that she couldn't accept a paycheck as well as a place to live. He put his foot down and told her she was part of the family, therefore the ranch was her home, not a place to be earned but a place to be. It didn't upset her. In fact, she admired his tenacity. He was a lot like her, or she was a lot like him, she guessed.

Blake took her hand and kissed her palm and told her simply, "Stop fighting it. You're family."

How was she supposed to fight that? The job gave her a sense of purpose. Working with the horses fulfilled her in a way she couldn't explain.

She and Blake stole kisses in the stable and held hands as they walked. They went on long rides in the evening after they finished their work. Most times, Justin went with them. Blake never minded including Justin in their plans.

She'd gotten so used to having Blake nearby that when he left with her grandfather to take several horses to race in Nevada, she couldn't seem to turn around and not expect him to be there. As she stood in the driveway now, she missed him deeply. When had he become so important in her life that she counted on him to listen to her troubles?

"What happened?" Grandma Dee asked, walking up to stand beside her.

"The teacher asked the class to draw a picture of their hero and stand in front of the class and talk about who their hero is and why. He drew a picture of me."

"Well, that doesn't sound like it warrants a parent teacher conference."

"It does when the picture showed me with a gun in my hand and our father lying dead in a pool of blood on the floor. He told the children that I'm his hero because I killed our father."

She leaned back against the truck and looked up at the snow-topped Three Peaks looming over the ranch. "Apparently, he's drawn some other pictures the teacher passed off as his overactive imagination or too much violence on TV. When the teacher put together today's episode and picture with the others, she had a complete story. She said I willingly put him in harm's way, and I haven't provided him with the necessary counseling he obviously needs because of the traumatic event I inflicted on him. She said she wouldn't be surprised if he felt threatened by me."

She fell silent for a moment. Then her anger and frustration and hurt exploded. "Like I'd ever hurt that little boy. Traumatic event. His whole life has been a traumatic event! What the hell does she know about what happened to us? She wouldn't even let me explain. She called the sheriff to make sure I wasn't wanted in San Francisco for murder. She didn't even bother to let me take Justin out of the room when the sheriff showed up to question me."

"Did you explain what happened?"

"Hell no! I wouldn't give them the satisfaction. I gave the sheriff the name of the detective in San Francisco who cleared me. The detective was nice enough to be vague and tell the sheriff the shooting was self-defense."

Gillian pushed off from the car with her butt and took a few steps toward the house, then turned back to Grandma Dee. "I could see it in her eyes. She wasn't as concerned for Justin's welfare as she was about getting the dirt on what happened. I can just see what's going to happen now. All those children are going to go home and tell their parents Justin's sister is a killer. Their parents will talk to Miss Crane, and she'll tell them what happened in San Francisco. It'll spread like wildfire across town."

"Unfortunately, that's what happens in a small town."

"I don't want what I did to affect you and Grandpa. I don't want it to affect Justin. What will Blake think when the whole town starts talking about me? Us? Oh God, what will his parents think?"

"This will upset your grandfather and Blake. They won't like one bit that the teacher put you through this today. You didn't do anything wrong. He deserved what he got. I for one am glad you were there to protect Justin. Just think what might have happened if you hadn't shown up to stop Ron. I think about that. Your grandfather thinks about that. We know the truth. That's all that matters.

"Justin doesn't know how to express himself in a constructive way. You're his hero because you saved him. Yes, it was violent, and I'm sorry he had to live through something so terrible, but he did live. And so did you. His nightmares have tapered off over the last few weeks. He only got up once in the night this past week, and that's with your grandfather and Blake gone. I was afraid that he'd be scared while they're away. He sure does miss them. But he isn't scared, because he's got you. He knows you'll protect him with your life.

"You've been a good mother to him. He loves you. He's kind and caring. He befriends everyone he meets, and he trusts others. He's not a bully or disrespectful. That's a reflection of you, and the way you've raised him. Don't let his teacher take that away from you. That's something to be proud of."

Justin was a bright, energetic, loving boy. In a few years, he'd forget all about their life with their father. It had only been a short time since they'd come to the ranch, and Gillian already saw differences in him. He was happier, yes, but also more carefree and enthusiastic. Spontaneous, the caution that he usually used in speaking to someone or doing something subsided. He wasn't afraid to walk into a room without scoping out the situation to make sure it was safe.

Not like her. Still.

"You're right. I overreacted because she made me feel like I'd failed him. I've tried so hard to be what he needs. Even though it's difficult sometimes, I've done the best I can. To have someone say that Justin needed something that I didn't give him really hurt.

"I don't want other kids looking at him strangely or picking on him. I don't want parents to keep their children from playing with him because of what I did."

"If that happens, we'll deal with it. I bet this will all die down in a few days. Now, on a different subject, Blake called. He was disappointed he missed you."

"So am I." Over the last week, they'd used their long calls to get to know each other better. She let her guard down. He opened up about his family, his life. In the quiet evenings, the distance and phone a buffer, her past put aside, they connected on another level. Deeper than they had on the long rides they took together when he told her outrageous stories about the trouble he and his brothers used to get into when they were young. A bunch of rascals, they ran wild, played hard, and loved each other like family should.

"I want to tell him I got my cast off." She moved her wrist and wiggled her fingers. Nothing like having her hand free again. "Did he say when he'd be back? I thought he'd be here by now."

"He and your grandfather got stuck in a big storm, so they're staying an extra day at the Fairfield Ranch. They didn't want to risk driving in the storm with the horses in the trailers. They spook easily. They should be home late tomorrow night.

"I know it's not my place, but since you don't have a mother to talk to, I wanted to ask how things are going between you and Blake. You seem to have grown very close in the short time you've lived here."

"All I've wanted to do since I met him is get closer to him, even though it scares me. We agreed to take things slow. Though now all I want is for him to come home so I can get my hands on him." She said it without thinking, and the blush sparked at her breasts and spread up to her forehead like wildfire.

Dee laughed. "Don't worry, dear. You're a grown woman, and you know your own mind. Lord, that boy fell hard for you. Do you feel the same way about him?"

It wasn't obvious? Did she hide her feelings that well? If her grandmother had to ask, did Blake wonder how she truly felt? Didn't he know?

She knew her heart, but maybe she needed to share it with Blake. Scary, but necessary if she wanted this to work. "I love him. I don't know how it happened, but somehow he got inside my heart, and he won't let go. I don't want him to."

"Have you told him how you feel?"

"He knows I care for him. We like being together. Like I said, we're taking things slow. My feelings and his seem to be a force between us. I don't know how much longer I can hold off on letting them loose. Do you know what I mean? I've never felt this way."

Even now, just thinking about him made her stomach knot and her heart beat faster. If he was here, she'd go into his arms and kiss him. She knew exactly what he felt like pressed against her. She knew exactly the way his mouth fit over hers, and how he tasted of coffee and mint, tinged with his need for her. She knew his smell and the way he walked. She knew a thousand little things about him because she couldn't help but watch him when he was near or ask him everything about himself. She couldn't get enough of him. And she didn't think this feeling would ever go away. She hoped it never did.

"You look for him whenever you have something to say. You look for him at the table in the morning and at night."

"I miss him," she said miserably. "I don't think I've ever missed anyone in my whole life. I'm happy that I have him, and I'm terrified all at the same time."

"Sounds like you love him to me. I miss your grandfather something terrible when he's gone."

Things had been building before Blake left. She didn't want to wait for him anymore. She hoped he didn't want to wait for her. She loved him. She wanted to show him how much. She missed his kisses and the way he'd always run a hand down her hair. She missed the way he'd come up behind her in the stables and wrap his arms around her and kiss her neck. She missed the way his fingers gripped her hips and pulled her close when they got lost in a kiss.

She shook off thoughts of Blake. "I need to go up and talk to Justin. I punished him, and that was my mistake. He didn't do anything wrong."

"Talk to him about the reasons you did what you did. He'll understand."

Gillian hugged her grandmother. She'd become a real friend, and Gillian appreciated the easy way in which they talked. No judgment. No telling her what to do. "Thanks for the ear. Does Blake want me to call him back?"

"No. He and some of the guys are going out. He owed them a beer for all their hard work. I guess they've been going at it pretty hard since they left."

Gillian frowned, wishing she could talk to him.

"Does it bother you if he goes out with the guys for a drink?"

"No. Blake isn't a drunk. In fact, I haven't seen him drink at all."

"He usually has a beer or two in the evening. Since you've been here, he hasn't. I think he cares enough about you to respect that you might have a problem with him drinking."

She wrinkled up the side of her mouth. "Well, I don't know what to think. He should have a beer if he wants one. It isn't the same. I know he's not the same as my dad."

"He's being considerate."

"Seems to me that man has been too considerate and it's holding him back from being himself. I don't like that. The thing I like most about being with him is that I feel like I can be myself. If he can't do the same around me, then we have a problem."

"Sometimes you really surprise me. That was a very wise observation. You'll work it out when he gets back."

Gillian didn't know why it made her angry. It just did. She wanted him to stop holding back, thinking that's what she wanted. Her past made her different from other women. He didn't treat her like a woman he wanted, he treated her like someone he had to protect, even from himself. She didn't want just the parts of him he thought she wanted to see and experience; she wanted the whole man. She liked his manners and thoughtfulness, but not if it kept him from being himself. No, that would never do. Eventually, he'd resent her, when trying to be something that he wasn't wore on him.

"Oh, we'll work it out all right," she said to herself and walked up the stairs to see Justin.

Gillian found Justin lying on his bed. He loved the quilt Blake's mother made for him. Navy blue with a red fire truck on the top, with a yellow star on the door and a yellow ladder on the back. Legs bent at the knees, he swung his feet and pounded them down on the bed one at a time as he turned pages in his book, looking at the pictures.

"Justin, we need to talk."

"I didn't mean to get you into trouble with the police." His eyes glassed over, and his bottom lip trembled.

She rubbed her hand over his soft hair. "I'm not in trouble, honey. I owe you an apology. I punished you, and you didn't do anything wrong. I'm sorry I overreacted. You can watch TV tonight, and I'll take you down to see Honey."

"Really?" He bounced onto his knees on the bed.

She could leave things alone, and he'd be happy with his privileges back, but she owed him an explanation.

"It must be confusing why your teacher wouldn't let you talk about why you think I'm your hero."

"You are my hero. You stopped him from hurting me. He can't hurt you anymore either. He was going to kill you. He said so. The police said you didn't do anything wrong."

"I didn't. I protected myself. I protected you. I didn't have a choice." Their father took the choice out of her hands when he pulled the gun on her.

Justin's steady gaze met hers. "I wanted him to die. I didn't want him to hurt you ever again."

"Oh, honey. I can understand that, but it isn't right to want someone to die. He needed help. He was not himself when he took drugs and drank all the time."

"Taking drugs is bad," Justin confirmed.

Proud of him for remembering that lesson, she hoped it held through his teenage years, when he'd be at risk for starting a habit that could ruin his life, like it had ruined both their parents'. She worried about that and would remain diligent about reinforcing the lesson over the years.

"Miss Crane was concerned today because talking about how our dad died might scare the other kids. They don't know what it's like to live with someone like him. They didn't understand that he was trying to hurt us. Miss Crane didn't know what happened in San Francisco, and she wanted to make sure you were safe."

The pictures he'd drawn told Gillian that he still had a lot stored up inside him.

"Are you still scared? Do you think about it a lot?"

"Not really. Not anymore. I like it here with the horses and Blake."

"Is there something about what happened with Dad that you don't understand, or that you want to ask me about?"

"No. I'm glad he's gone, and we live here now. It's better."

"I like it here, too." So, he wasn't harboring anything inside him that should concern her. He'd drawn the pictures of what happened and wanted everyone to know that she'd helped him. Sometimes it was that simple. She hoped it was that simple in this case.

"Okay. I think it would be a good idea if you didn't tell the other kids or anyone about what happened anymore. You can always talk to me or Grandma and Grandpa, but other people might not understand what happened. Okay?"

"Okay." He sat up and hugged her. "When are they coming home? Blake said he'd take me fishing at the river."

"They should be home tomorrow night. About Blake, does it bother you that Blake and I are getting close?"

"He's your boyfriend."

She hadn't thought of it in those terms. Every day, they'd find as many moments as they could to be alone on the busy ranch. Blake was great at kissing her senseless. Boyfriend? Yeah, he was her boyfriend.

"We like being together. He's very nice to me."

"He watches you."

"He does?"

"All the time. When you aren't looking, he stares at you. He told me that he likes you a lot. He said he wouldn't take you away from me and that it would always be the three of us."

"He said that to you." News to her. Such a thoughtful thing to do, reassuring Justin he'd always have a place with them. It made her heart ache even more to see him. If she hadn't loved him before, she loved him just for that.

"He wanted to be sure I knew that I'm the most important person to you."

Her eyes filled with tears. Blake knew her so well. Justin was her child even if he was her brother. That Blake got her, understood her, made all the difference. When that man got home, she'd make sure he understood how important he was to her.

"You are and will always be the most important person to me, buddy. I love you. Let's go see Honey?"

"I promised Grandma Dee I'd pick the green beans and tomatoes in the garden."

She ran her hand over his hair and kissed his forehead. "I'll go down and check on Boots. We'll see Honey after you do your chores. Maybe one of the grooms will saddle a horse for us. We'll go for a short ride in the south pasture."

"Awesome!" Justin scrambled off the bed. He headed for the door but rushed back and hugged her. She held him tight.

Now, she needed Blake to come home so they could clear the air and she could get her hands on him.

CHAPTER 20

The horses in the stables kicked at the ground and at their gates, huffing and making strange, distressed whinnies. Gillian ran inside the huge doors. She stood for a second, letting her eyes adjust to the darker interior. One horse's upset agitated the other horses. She swept her gaze along the aisle and all the horses poking their heads over the gates. Ken stood in Boots's stall door, a rope in one hand and a whip in the other. The rope was looped around Boots's neck. Every time Ken pulled, the rope tightened. He tried to pull Boots out of the stall, but only succeeded in choking the immobile horse. Frustrated, he struck Boots on the shoulder with the whip. Boots tried to rear up and use his hooves to strike Ken. He pulled tighter on the rope around Boots's neck and kept him down on the ground. Boots's eyes went wide and wild as he struggled to back away.

Ken held the whip high to strike Boots again. "Stop!" Gillian ran between Ken and Boots. The stick whip caught her on the shoulder and sliced her skin. Blood ran down her arm, but she ignored the piercing sting. Adrenaline masked the pain. Her focus sharpened on Ken's surprised and irritated face.

He grabbed her forearm and tried to pull her out of the way. "Are you crazy? This horse could kill you. You can't get in front of him like that when he's trying to rear."

"Let him go." She stood her ground between him and Boots. She grabbed his hand and tried to pry his fingers from the rope, but he kept his grip tight. She gave up the futile attempt to free Boots and stepped closer to Ken, getting right in his face, despite being several inches shorter than him. Size never stopped her when it came to her father, and it wouldn't stop her with an arrogant asshole animal abuser.

"Boots is my responsibility. He doesn't like anyone handling him but me. Back off."

"No. This horse comes from champion stock. He used to race well before he was dumped in a pasture to rot. He's healthy now. You've got him working well on a lead. It's time he got back to racing. I'm putting a rider on him today. I'll work him back to the track."

"No, you won't. Boots is mine. He won't do anything for you, especially if you hit him into submission. Can you really be this stupid? Boots was abused. Do you really think hurting him more will make him cooperate? Idiot."

Darkness filled his eyes. They settled on her, but she didn't back down.

"It's not your call. I'm the trainer. He's a racehorse, and it's time he earned his keep. Back off, woman. You don't know anything about training and racing horses."

His hot, angry gaze swept over her and landed on her breasts for too long before he met her gaze again. The man didn't respect her. He just wanted her on her back, kowtowing to his every dirty need. Her stomach soured, but she held her ground, not giving an inch, because he'd take it and back her into a corner if given even a glimpse of weakness.

"I said no."

Ken pulled the rope from Boots's neck and walked out of the stall with Gillian on his heels. He turned, and she came up short. He reached over her shoulder and slammed the door closed at her back. She expected another argument about Boots. She never expected him to walk toward her and make her stumble back, smacking into the stall door. He loomed over her, only a few inches separating them. She planted her palm on his chest to keep him back and glared up at him, hoping her bravado lasted.

"I love it when your eyes flash fire."

Gillian's arm vibrated from the thrill that went through his body. Her gut burned and her heart raced.

"That's right, baby. I like seeing that heat in your eyes. I'll bet you're a hellcat in the sack. Does Blake have what it takes to make you burn? Tell me, baby, does he make you come until you scream." Her eyes shifted away, making him laugh. He leaned in and whispered in her ear. "No. He hasn't put his hands on your skin. I can feel you tremble. You want it, don't you? You want me. I can make you burn, baby."

"The only thing you make me want to do is throw up."

"Liar. Blake's not here. Stop pretending you don't want me, like you do when he's around."

Delusional, asshole.

She kept her eyes steady on his, hoping he saw her anger and not the fear rising from her gut to choke off her throat.

Jeff, the trainer who helped her with Boots, walked into the stables. Ken heard his footsteps and stilled. His eyes narrowed, and he scrunched his lips. "Too bad, time's up," he whispered. "Maybe another time." Disappointment and a promise filled his eyes, giving her the willies.

Jeff drew closer, his eyes narrowing on her legs, the only part of her he could see behind Ken's body while she peeked out at him from between Ken's arm and body. "Gillian, Blake's on the phone in the office. He wants to talk to you."

Gillian tried to sound normal. She hoped the fear she felt didn't come out in her voice. "I'm coming."

Ken kept his back to Jeff. She planted both hands on his chest and shoved. Surprisingly, he didn't budge. A knowing smile bloomed on his face. More feral than tame. His taunting chuckle made her blood boil.

He finally stepped back. His gaze dipped to her shoulder, and his eyes went wide. "Damn, baby, I didn't think I hit you that hard," he whispered, his voice hesitant. The first sign he might actually be nervous about what he'd done.

Gillian glanced at the blood running down the outside of her arm to her pinky and dripping on the concrete.

"I didn't mean to hit you. You know that." His initial apologetic tone turned to ice. "Say otherwise, and I'll make you regret it. Keep your damn mouth shut."

"What's going on here?" Jeff stood to the side of Ken, his gaze sweeping over her face and bloodied arm. He narrowed his eyes on Ken and the long stick in Ken's hand. "Where the hell did that come from? We do not use whips on this ranch."

Ken's bravado returned, and he faced off with Jeff. "It's mine. It's a tool for the way I train horses."

"Blake won't approve you using that on any of the horses." He made a point of looking at Gillian's bloody arm.

Her stomach tightened with dread. The last thing she wanted was for this to turn into a fight. Her grandfather would fire them both. She liked Jeff and wanted him to stay. Even though she disliked Ken, the last thing she wanted to do was make Ken an enemy.

"Blake hired me to do my job. He never specified how he wanted it done, so long as the horses win. I believe my horse, Kit, placed third. Blake and Bud will both be happy. That's what matters."

Jeff eyed Ken, making it obvious with a frown he didn't like the man. Gillian agreed. She'd given him the benefit of the doubt up until now. A little too cocky for his own good, Ken didn't take direction well and thought he could make others do his work for him. If the way he treated her was any indication, he had no respect for women.

"Blake's horses all placed first or second, and he never uses a whip or anything else that will harm the horses," Jeff pointed out.

"Yeah, well, Blake won't let anyone work with the best horses on the ranch. He gave me Kit, but it isn't like Kit is a top-of-the-line Thoroughbred. Third is better than anything he's ever done."

Jeff kept his mouth shut. All the horses on the ranch came from impeccable bloodlines. "What are you doing in here? You've got a rider waiting in one of the training rings."

"I came in to get Boots, but Gillian has a soft spot for the beast and had a hissy fit about me taking him."

"Boots belongs to her."

"Boots belongs to Three Peaks Ranch. He's a race-horse. He's only three and can be trained to race again. His bloodlines are some of the finest on the ranch. He should be racing and making this ranch money."

"You mean you want to train him. If he comes through and is as good as his lines, you want your share of the purse. You don't want Blake getting his hands on Boots and making him a champion while you're working with horses that only place third."

Ken closed the distance and got right in Jeff's face. "We both know who the better trainer is."

Jeff smiled and held his ground as Gillian had done with Ken. "Yes, we do." He turned to her, his eyes wide when he realized they'd blocked her in against the gate. "Gillian, go into the office and take your call. Blake's waiting and anxious to talk to you."

More than ready to bolt, Gillian held her hands tightly together in front of her and rushed past the two men, heading for the office door, thankful Jeff had come along when he had.

"That's a nasty cut. There's a first-aid kit in the office. Clean that up and put a bandage over it," Jeff called as she continued to walk away.

"What were you two doing?" Jeff asked.

Ken ignored Jeff's glare. "Nothing," he hedged, unwilling to explain himself.

"You better hope Blake doesn't hear about *nothing*. He'll fire you. He and Bud made it clear, Gillian is off limits."

Ken stabbed his finger into Jeff's chest. "You should keep your nose out of other people's business. You walked in on something, but you don't know what really happened. It's between Gillian and me, so leave it alone."

Ken stormed out of the stables.

Jeff walked into the office and stopped several feet away, staring at her cut arm.

"I thought you said Blake was on the phone." She staunched the blood with a tissue.

"You saw me walk in from outside. I only said that to get Ken to leave you alone. What's going on? Why are you bleeding?"

"Ken tried to take Boots out of his stall by force. I got in the way." Jeff's frown deepened. She shrugged his concern away now that she'd had time to calm down. "Blake will be back tonight, and Ken will mellow. He was just trying to take advantage of Blake's absence."

She thought about what Ken had said about Boots. Bloodlines meant a lot in horse racing. "Let me ask you something. Is Boots really capable of becoming a champion racehorse?"

"Sure. He raced when he was a one-year-old. I understand he did quite well before he was bought and used for stud. You've seen him run in the training ring. That's nothing. He wants to race. You can see it."

She could see it. She felt it every time she let him take the lead and go as fast as he wanted. A good horse, he minded her commands with little coaxing.

"Do you think Blake would let me work with him? Maybe I can get him saddled and put a rider on him." Jeff had taught her what she needed to do, and she'd spent weeks watching Blake.

"Boots is yours. At least, that's how Blake put it. Bud agrees. His only intention when he rescued Boots was to make him healthy. I don't see why you can't try. I'd say that you'd have a better chance of getting up on him than anyone. You're a good rider. Even the first time Blake got you in a saddle, you seemed to have been born to it. I saw you last night with Justin. You look like you could handle anything."

"I love to ride. Who knew a city girl like me could take to horseback riding so easily?"

"You're a country girl through and through. There's no city shine on you. Not when you've got dirt on your boots and hay in your hair." When she reached up to clean her hair, Jeff smiled. "Just kidding about the hay."

He leaned against the desk. Relaxed, her hands steadier, she didn't feel the need to back away.

"I don't like the way Ken had you backed up against the stall door."

"I didn't like it either. Trust me, it won't happen again." That was the second time he'd managed to back her into a corner. Next time, she'd come out fighting.

"Things looked pretty intense when I came in."

"Why did you come in?" She wanted to distract him from talking more about Ken.

"There's something wrong with one of the trucks. Blake mentioned you'd worked in a garage. I thought maybe you could take a look. You seem to be good at everything you do."

"I don't know about that." But she appreciated the compliment. "I'm not exactly a mechanic, but I'll see what I can do."

Jeff left her alone to finish cleaning up her arm and wrapping a bandage over the cut. Done and feeling her confidence return, she headed out to the truck Jeff left parked out back. She figured out the problem fairly quickly and found what she needed inside the toolshed. She spent an hour replacing the blown spark plug, adjusting the timing belt, and changing the oil.

She screwed the oil plug back on. Someone grabbed her feet and pulled her out from under the truck.

Ken dropped on her hips, grabbed her hands, and

pinned them on the ground by her head. He leaned over and blocked the sun from her eyes. She struggled, but the worst she could do was glare.

"Aw, there's that fire."

He leaned down and took her mouth in a hard, demanding kiss. When he pulled back and stared down at her with a smug smile on his face, she dipped her head and wiped her mouth on her shoulder.

"I knew you'd taste like honey."

She'd heard him spout off about his conquests. The man truly believed he was God's gift to women.

"Get the fuck off of me, you bastard!" She struggled to get him off her, but the more she moved her hips to buck him off, the more he laughed. With a supreme act of will to control her fear, she went limp and lay still, waiting to see what he would do. She could scream, but he was just the type to pop her in the mouth if she did.

Justin should be here any minute, his chores done, ready to go for another ride like they did last night after their talk. She didn't want him to find her screaming her head off. She didn't want Ken to remind him of their father.

"Get off, or I'll scream."

"Justin finished working in the garden and ran up to the house to wash his hands. He'll be here soon. You'll keep your mouth shut because you don't want him telling Blake how cozy the two of us look right now."

"Blake will break your face if he finds out about this. My grandfather will fire your ass."

"*If* they find out. You're going to keep that pretty mouth shut, because if you don't, I'll make sure you're sorry about it. In fact," he said and rubbed his hard dick against her pelvis, "I'll make you scream how sorry you are. No way I lose my job over a piece of ass like you—one who's nothing better than a murderous bitch."

She gasped. *Damn that nosy kindergarten teacher.*

"Everyone knows you killed your daddy. Is this how your arm got broken?" He pressed down harder on her wrists. "You like it rough, and he held you down."

"You've got a sick, twisted mind, asshole."

"Did he smack you when you let loose your sharp tongue?"

"Yes, then I shot him twice for being an asshole. Imagine what I'm going to do to you if you don't get off me right this second, you fucking bastard."

"Gillian," Justin called.

Ken let go of one of her hands and covered her mouth.

"You listen good. If you tell Blake I whipped that horse, or you, I'll make you pay. You keep your damn mouth shut, or the next time I catch you alone, I'll finish what I started and fuck you good."

Her heart thrashed in her chest. She tried to keep her head, think through the anger and fear. God, she wished Blake was here. Justin was coming. She needed to get Ken off her before Justin saw them.

She needed to teach him a lesson.

Stupid, single-minded man stared down at her breasts as she reached up with her free hand and grabbed at the tools she'd left out. Her fingers wrapped around a wrench. She swung it hard, connected with the side of his face, and split open a gash from his temple to his forehead. He fell off her, grabbing his head and moaning in pain.

She shoved him aside, scrambled up, and took three steps back. "Don't you ever fucking touch me again, or you'll wish the worst thing that happened to you is getting your ass kicked by Blake and losing your job."

Ken dragged himself up to his feet and wobbled, his hand pressed to the nasty, bleeding cut. "Fuck, that hurt."

"Stay the fuck away from me."

"You better keep your mouth shut." He stumbled away, walking off toward the bunkhouse.

The sense of triumph washed away the worst of the fear. She'd done it. She'd stood up for herself and made Ken understand he couldn't treat her that way ever again. If he tried, she'd defend herself. No one would ever hurt her again.

She rushed to meet Justin, but stopped at the side of the barn to catch her breath before she went around the corner to meet her brother. Funny, he looked like he'd just come out of the barn instead of coming toward it. She tucked the bloody wrench in her back pocket. Ken couldn't possibly be stupid enough to come after her again. But just in case, she'd keep the weapon.

"Justin. There you are. Do you want to go see Honey? I left an apple in the stables for you to feed her."

Justin's gaze never left his sneakers, even when he walked to her and handed her the cell phone. "Grandma said to give you this. Blake wants to talk to you. He's on his way home." Justin turned on his heel and walked toward the stables, dragging his feet in the dirt and kicking up dust.

Eager to talk to Blake, she dismissed his odd behavior and didn't scold him for getting his school shoes dirty. Gillian followed Justin inside with the phone to her ear. Desperate to hear his voice, she pleaded, "Blake, please tell me you'll be here soon."

CHAPTER 21

Every time Blake called home to talk to Gillian over the last eight days, he'd heard how anxious she'd been to talk to him, but not like this. He felt the same urgency growing inside him. He needed to hear her voice. He desperately wanted to kiss her.

"I'm on my way, sweetheart. It seems the storm we left behind in Nevada caught up to us again. It's slow going with the horse trailers. We won't make it back until late tonight. You'll probably be asleep."

"I don't care what time it is, you wake me up so I can see your face."

It did his heart good to hear how much she missed him. "I plan on it. I can't wait to see you. It's been too long. It seems like forever since I set eyes on you."

"It has been forever. I've missed you," she admitted, her words soft. "So much."

"I miss you, too." More than he thought he would. He'd never felt like this about anyone. He'd never felt closer to anyone. She pulled at him. The farther away he got from her, the more he felt the tug to return to her.

"I heard about what happened at Justin's school yesterday. I'm sorry I wasn't there to help you out. I can't believe they called the sheriff."

"Yeah, well, they thought I was a wanted murderer."

"It was self-defense," he spit out and slammed his palm on the truck's steering wheel. It pissed him off that Justin's teacher was trying to cause trouble for Gillian. He wondered if it had more to do with his past than hers. "He tried to kill you."

"His teacher thinks I'm a bad influence."

"Bullshit. You're everything he needs. You love him, and he loves you."

I love you, too. Probably not the best time to tell her. Better to do it face-to-face. He had a serious need to tell her. He didn't want to be without her ever again. This past week had shown him how much he wanted her to be a permanent part of his life. It had shown him how much a part of his life she was already. Without her, he wasn't whole.

"Hey, what do you think about me saddling Boots?"

Blake's gut went tight with dread. His mind conjured one image after another of her being thrown to the ground and breaking her bones. Still, he hated to tell her no. She loved riding and working with the horses. Her confidence with them and within herself grew each and every day.

He tried to be diplomatic. "You do not do anything of the sort without me there. He hasn't been saddled or ridden in a long time. He might take exception to you trying."

"I thought that's what you'd say."

The disappointment in her voice got to him. "I don't want you getting hurt, sweetheart."

"Speaking of, I got my cast off. I've got my hand back."

"I can think of a few things you can do with it." He had an entire eight days of stored-up dreams and fantasies about what she could do with her hands.

"Already taken care of. I fixed that truck that's been giving you trouble for the last few weeks. I've got all your spreadsheets updated and spewing out reports. This month's payroll is done."

The teasing tone didn't escape him. "That's not exactly what I had in mind."

"Oh, no. What exactly did you have in mind?" Her voice dropped a few octaves, sending a bolt of heat through his system. She liked teasing him. He had to admit, despite the need gnawing at him, her light-hearted game eased his heart. She felt safe enough with him to let her guard down, play, and have fun.

A slideshow of all the things he imagined raced through his mind. His blood heated just thinking about it, and his hands itched on the steering wheel. He needed to get his hands on her. "You're killing me."

"Killing you would be telling you that I can't wait to run my fingers through that thick mass of golden brown hair. I want to run my fingers over all your tight muscles and feel your skin under my hands. I want to feel your heart beat against my palm."

"Stop. I'm driving, for God's sake."

"It's very frustrating to be afraid to touch you because I might scratch you with plaster. Fingertips are okay, but I'll bet there's nothing like having my hands on you. I want that. I want that very much, Blake. I want you."

"Do you know how hard it is to drive in my condition?" He tried to stretch out his legs to accommodate his aching erection pressed up the length of his fly. "You know I won't be able to think in a minute, because there's no blood left in my brain." Her laugh made him smile. "I'll get you for this when I get home."

The laughing stopped, and she went dead silent.

Alarms went off immediately. The static on the phone got worse the last few miles, along with the rain. He listened, wondering if she'd hung up on him.

He talked fast, hoping to salvage this conversation. "Gillian? Gillian, I'm kidding. I'm sorry. I didn't mean it. It was a joke. I swear. I won't touch you if you don't want me to."

He didn't know how they'd gone from playful to silence in a split second. Stupid idiot. Her father probably issued threats all the time. He could just imagine that he'd do it with little malice in his voice, and then spring on her when she least expected it. Her father had been the kind of man who'd smile and then hit her. Even Justin had talked about the way their father's smile sent a chill up his spine.

Gillian had given Blake the wrong idea. She loved it that they were able to fool around on the phone and make them both want each other. It felt so normal, when her life had been anything but. Then her mind flashed on Ken telling her she'd better keep her mouth shut, or he'd make her sorry.

"Blake, I'm sorry. It wasn't you. I was just . . . it was only . . ." She took a deep breath to calm the foreboding feeling vibrating through her system. "I've had a really hard week, compounded by your absence. I want you here, Blake."

She should tell him what happened with Ken. Not over the phone though. He'd only be mad and frustrated he wasn't here. What could he do? She'd already taken care of Ken. She'd done what she had to do, what she needed to do for her own peace of mind.

"I'm on my way home to you. I'd be there already if it wasn't for this damn storm following me."

He didn't know how good that sounded to her. "I'm

impatient to see you. I'm sorry I made you think you'd said something wrong."

Ever intuitive when it came to her, he asked, "Why have you been avoiding the stables? You've only spent a limited amount of time with Boots."

"That's not true."

"Yes, it is. Dee told me that you've been acting strange. Jeff and a couple of the other guys said you only spend as much time as necessary to feed and work Boots. You've only taken Justin riding twice in the last week, when normally you go every day."

She ignored most of what he said. "I'm taking him riding again right now."

Done with subtlety, he asked her a direct question. "Is Ken giving you a hard time? Is that what this is about?"

"I handled it." She thought about the wrench in her back pocket. He'd think twice about cornering her again. She'd carry the wrench with her all the time. Just in case. You'd think that thought would tip her off to how much of a threat she found Ken, but she passed it off as nothing more than her past intruding on her present yet again.

"Which means he's giving you a hard time and you don't want to tell me about it."

"It's nothing for you to worry about."

"Like you'd tell me if it was." His temper tinged his deceptively calm words. "You know, Gillian, you don't always have to take care of everything yourself. Ken is an asshole who probably deserves a good ass kicking. He's a cocky SOB who thinks he's God's gift to women and horse training."

She heard his frustration loud and clear, despite the increasing static on the line. Thunder rumbled in the background. She prayed he'd be okay on the road.

Afraid they'd lose the connection soon, she tried to reassure him. "Blake, I'm fine."

"I know you well enough to know that when you say you're fine, you're really not."

"I don't want to fight with you. I don't want you coming home mad at me. I miss you. I'm looking forward to seeing you. Can't we leave it at that?"

"For now." What choice did he have? She was at the ranch without him and vulnerable to Ken. Blake would get to the bottom of this when he got back. Past time Gillian learned to trust him to take care of her. "I'm sorry, sweetheart. I want you to know and believe that you can count on me. If Ken is making a nuisance of himself, then let me know, and I'll take care of him."

She didn't get a chance to answer him. The phone went dead. With all the static on the line at his end, he couldn't be sure she'd even heard him.

Blake slammed the phone down on the dashboard and tried to concentrate on the road. He pounded his palm on the steering wheel and took a deep breath to try to calm down. Ken had better leave her alone, or he was going to wish he had. Blake wasn't going to put up with a guy who couldn't take no for an answer. Besides, everyone at the ranch knew Blake and Gillian were seeing each other. It wasn't a secret. Ken should know better than to go after another guy's girl.

Maybe it was a lesson Ken hadn't been taught. Blake would make sure he learned it well.

CHAPTER 22

Blake drove for hours with the rain following him home. The gray skies and icy wind matched his mood. The roads were treacherous, making the drive slow going with the horse trailers. Bud and the other ranch hands followed him. They used handheld radios to communicate between the three trucks. Everyone was exhausted, but no one wanted to stop somewhere for the night and ride out the storm.

An overwhelming sense of relief washed over him when he reached the turnoff and the Three Peaks Ranch sign. He passed the house and headed for the stables, but he couldn't help looking up at the second-story windows. A soft light glowed in her room, showing him the way home.

He'd never had someone waiting for him to come home. Not like this. Not someone who mattered more than anything else in his world.

It took him and the other men two hours to get the horses out of the trailers and into their stalls and settled for the night. He said goodnight to Bud and headed around the house with every intention of going to his place and taking a hot shower. The rain came down in sheets. Lightning flashed, and thunder rolled and rumbled. Mud caked his boots and left a trail up the garage stairs and the landing leading to Gillian's door. The shower could wait; his need to see her, kiss her, couldn't.

Soaked to the skin, he stopped outside her window and looked in. She'd left a night-light on near the door adjoining her room with Justin's. The door was left ajar in case Justin needed her. At the moment, it looked like Gillian needed him. Trapped in the midst of a nightmare, she tossed in her bed and rolled to her back. The sheet slid down her breasts and stopped at her waist as she kicked her feet. She threw her hands up to block her face, then they fell next to her head on the pillow.

He couldn't stand by and watch her struggle alone. Justin wasn't the only one suffering from nightmares. She had her own demons to fight in her sleep, and he hated that something ugly touched her when she was defenseless. He wanted to wipe all the bad memories clean. He wanted to be something good in her life that eclipsed all the bad.

He shook off most of the water droplets falling from his wet hair and pulled off his boots, leaving them on the deck before walking in through the French doors. Unable to stop himself, he went to her, planted his hands on both sides of her body, and leaned over. So beautiful. He took his time studying her in the soft light. Her hair—in a riot of different colors—glowed softly in the light and spread across her pillow and shoulders. Her soft, full mouth turned up just slightly at the corners, which made her always seem to have a slight, mysterious smile on her face, despite the somber look that clouded her eyes most days. Her long, dark lashes rested on her cheek. He wanted to lightly run his fingertips over her smooth, golden skin.

He swept his gaze down her body and landed on the bandage on her shoulder. He hated that she'd hurt herself. He didn't want her to hurt ever again.

The pale pink satin and lace nightgown hid nothing from his view. Her breasts swelled with each breath, threatening to spill over the lace top, her nipples a slightly darker pink shadow under the satin. His gaze slid down her body to her taut, flat stomach. He wanted to place his palm on her, spread his fingers wide and span her small waist. The rest of her was covered under the blankets and sheets he wanted to rip away so he could see those stunning legs.

He stilled when he found her watching him with her eyes half open. She didn't move. Her gaze met his, and he held his breath, wanting so badly to lie with her, love her with his body the way he did with his heart.

Standing on the edge of yesterday and everything he wanted for his future, he hoped she took the leap with him.

Like he'd done from the beginning, he waited, letting her take the lead.

"You're home." The words came out on a relieved exhale.

"Almost," he said a half second before his lips met hers.

Her lips were soft and warm and welcoming. She opened to him, meeting the slide of his tongue with hers. She combed her fingers through his wet hair and held on. Blake caught himself leaning down to press his wet body to hers. He ended the kiss with a soft nip to her lips and chin. He kissed his way down her neck, inhaling her sweet and tangy scent. Something Ella sent to her from her new cosmetics line. Thankfully, not the same one she sent his mother or that Ella wore.

Something soft and sweet, just for his Gillian. The joy in her eyes when the gift basket arrived stayed with him. He loved seeing her happy.

"God, I missed you."

Her warm hands cupped his face. "I missed you, too. You're freezing. You need to get out of those wet clothes."

He stood next to the bed, staring down at her lovely face. "I needed to see you before I went home to shower and change into something dry."

She rose and sat on her heels in front of him. "Don't go. Stay with me." Her gaze fell away from his for a second with her whispered, shy words.

Too much to hope she meant in her bed, he tried to read the look in her eyes. He wanted her so bad that he didn't trust himself to believe he saw the same gnawing need reflected in her eyes. He wanted her, to be sure. It would be miserably hard to leave her and go back to his place, but he'd do it if she needed more time.

"Stay with me," she said again, her voice definite.

They stood at a fork in the road, both of them coming from different directions. If they intended to follow a single path and not turn back to where they'd come from, she needed to know one thing. "I love you, Gillian." He whispered the words, but they held every ounce of love he had in his heart for this woman. She meant everything to him. If she felt the same about him, he'd love her tonight, and every day for the rest of his life. If she didn't, he'd walk away, because he couldn't sleep with her the way he had with others and walk away whole.

"Show me." Gillian felt full for the first time in her life. Every dark corner, every dream she'd ever dreamed and locked behind that door in her heart came alive with his words. He hadn't gotten into bed and said he loved her in the heat of the moment. No, Blake wanted her to know that he truly, deeply loved her by telling her before he'd even touched her. He meant it, and her heart, her soul, knew it for the truth.

"I need the words."

Point of no return. If this didn't work out, he'd lose everything he'd worked so hard to build here on the ranch, and Gillian would lose the only man she had ever trusted and opened her heart to love.

Yes, this meant something. This mattered. More than anything else they'd ever experienced in their past. This wasn't the next step in their relationship—it was the first step toward their future together.

"I've only ever said those words to Justin. He's the only one who ever deserved them—until I met you." She leaned up, cupped his face in her hands, looked him straight in the eye, and spoke the words he needed to hear and her heart needed to say. The words she hoped would make all those locked-away, never-to-be-believed dreams come true. "I love you, Blake."

His hands slid over her shoulders and up into her hair. His lips pressed to hers in a soft, languid kiss that held so much love tears stung the backs of her eyes.

He ended the kiss and stared down at her, his fingers toying with her hair. "You are so beautiful."

"Stay. Love me."

He shrugged his heavy, wet coat off. She helped him with his thermal shirt, mapping her fingers over his taut muscles. He sucked in a breath when her warm skin met his freezing body. She took her time looking at him. She'd seen him with his shirt off many times. Gorgeous, all hard planes and sculpted muscles, his skin tanned from the sun. His broad chest tapered to lean hips. The wet jeans molded to every contour of his corded thighs and outlined the long, thick length of his arousal.

He kissed her softly and left her only long enough to close the door and lock it. He stood beside the bed and stared down at her. She reached for the hem of her nightgown to pull it off over her head.

"Don't."

She let go, hoping he hadn't changed his mind, but the blazing heat in his eyes said he wanted her. Bad.

"I want to do it. I've been dreaming about this for a long time." He kissed her forehead, and then the tip of her nose before he stood before her again, undid the button on his jeans, slid the zipper down the rigid length of him, and peeled the wet material down his legs and off his feet. She couldn't take her eyes off all those lean muscles, nothing but his black boxer briefs covering him now. He hooked his thumbs in the band at his waist and slowly pushed them down his legs. Her gaze followed the journey down those lean muscles and came up and locked on his hard cock. She swallowed and met his steady gaze, saw the cocky half smile she'd grown to love so much and had missed these last days.

Her eyes went soft and seductive, and she tilted her head, giving him back an appreciative grin. His biceps were mouthwatering, his chest amazing, but the whole package put together was lethal.

He leaned in, planted his hands on the bed, and followed her down as she fell back onto the pillows again and stretched out her legs just as he lay beside her. His weight made her lean into him. She met him in the middle for a searing kiss and wrapped her leg over his and pressed her warm body to his freezing skin. She rubbed her hand up and down his back, warming him.

His hand slid up her thigh, over her hip, and covered her ass. He squeezed and pressed her closer, his thick length pressed to her belly.

With just his fingertips, Blake brushed the straps of her gown down her arms. First, the left side. Then, the right. He slid the bodice down over her breasts. Her arms came free, and he leaned down and took her hard nipple into his mouth. Her breath released on a soft sigh. The pleasure so sweet and warm it washed through her whole body in a wave of addictive heat.

She held his head to her breast and relished the feel of his thick hair sliding through her fingers. Cold and wet, such a contrast to his hot, wet tongue sweeping over her skin. She slid her hands down his neck and over his shoulders, the corded muscles bunching under her palms as he moved to her other breast, his big hand molding the other to his palm. She loved the feel of all that strength at her fingertips. His mouth left hot, wet kisses up her neck. He found her mouth again, and she turned to him and pressed her body to his.

Blake couldn't get enough of her. She tasted so sweet. That tongue of hers darted into his mouth to sweep along his. Sexy as hell. So giving, her body melted against his. Frustrated by the nightgown bunched around her waist, he grasped the material and dragged the whole thing down until his fingers met the top of her panties. He dipped his fingers inside and pulled them down her legs with the nightgown. He threw both over the side of the bed. He didn't want any barriers between them. He wanted her. All of her. Only her.

He smoothed his hand up her strong, smooth thigh and straight to heaven and her hot, wet center. She moaned, and he swept his fingers over her folds, dipped one finger deep into her slick, tight core just so he could hear her make that sexy sound again. She moved her hips against his palm as his finger worked in and out. He took her hard nipple into his mouth and sucked hard. She tightened around his finger, and he circled his thumb over her clit. She grinded her hips against his hand, grabbed a fistful of his hair, and held him to her breast, completely lost to the pleasure that was his to give.

"Blake."

Just his name on her lips nearly sent him over the edge.

He kissed his way down her belly to her hip, leaned over the side of the bed, and grabbed his jeans for the condom in his wallet. Her hands never stopped touching him, which worked to his advantage when he settled beside her and she swept her fingers down his chest and stomach, wrapping her fingers around his aching cock and stroking him from head to hilt again and again. Unable to take the sweet torture, he tore open the condom with his teeth, tossed the wrapper, sheathed himself, and settled between Gillian's thighs. Her hands wrapped around his waist and rubbed up his back, pulling him close, his heart pressed to hers.

Every fiber of his being wanted to rush, but he reined it in and joined his body with hers in a slow, focused glide that gave him time to feel every sensation of his body pressed to hers. Heaven. Home.

He pulled out and rocked forward. She rolled her hips back, then up to meet him. He kept the pace slow. He wanted to please her. He wanted to make this last.

His skin against hers was warm and soft and hard and intoxicating. He felt the tension building in her body as her hands moved up his back, her fingers digging into his taught muscles. Every long stroke into her fed that tension until she moaned, rocked against him, and grinded her hips to his.

So giving. So completely in sync with him.

She spread her legs wider, took him in deeper, and he craved more. Of her. Of this feeling she evoked deep inside him that wanted to burst free. Her hands slid down his back to his hips, gripped his ass, and pulled him closer. She dug her heels into the bed, raised her hips to meet his next hard, deep thrust. She tightened around him, the tension in him snapped, and he flew over the edge with her. Perfect.

He collapsed on top of her, his face buried in her long, silky hair, his breath sawing in and out just as fast as hers.

He tried to roll to his back, but Gillian held him close with her arms wrapped around his back. Her fingers made hypnotic circles on his shoulders. "I'm crushing you, sweetheart."

"Don't leave me, Blake. You feel so good."

"You're the one that feels good." He kissed her neck and shoulder. "God, you smell sweet." He buried his nose in her hair and inhaled deeply—flowers and citrus. Her scent would haunt him the rest of his days.

The thought made him smile when he thought of Gabe's obsession with Ella's perfume. Now he got it. He got a lot of things, like the protective streak that reared every time he thought Gillian needed him. He loved her.

She rubbed her feet up his calves, her hands down his back to cover his ass. They came back up to smooth over his arms and settle on his biceps. She squeezed, he flexed, and she sighed. He smiled. "You have a real thing for my arms."

"So much strength, yet you know how to be gentle."

He raised up on his forearms and stared down at her. "I'll be anything you want."

"I know that, Blake. I love that you try so hard to take care of me. But you have to stop tiptoeing around me, worrying about everything you say or do."

"What are you talking about?"

"The way you hold yourself back, giving me space when you want to be close. You used to have a beer or two after work. Since I got here, you don't."

"I don't need to have a beer after work."

"Exactly. So if you want one, have one. It doesn't bother me, because you don't need it to get through your day."

"And I'm with you all the time."

"Yes, but you're always so careful and polite about the way you approach and touch me. Look how long it's taken us to get here."

"I thought you needed time."

"I need you. The real you. The man who wants me desperately and shows me with every ounce of love and passion he can't contain when he touches me."

"I want to make you happy."

"How can I be happy if you're not?"

"I am. I'm with you."

She cupped his face and looked him in the eyes. "Please, Blake, I'm trying so hard to work on living a carefree life. Every accomplishment I make seems like I haven't actually taken a step forward if you keep treating me with kid gloves."

"Taking special care of you is not a bad thing."

"Being sweet to me is never a bad thing. Holding pieces of yourself back, changing who you are is not okay with me. If you want me to share the bad things with you, but you won't share all of yourself with me, how can this ever work? Eventually you'll get tired of it."

"Gillian."

"No, Blake. You want me to trust you, and I do, but how can that bond hold if we can't share everything with each other?"

He rolled to his side and kept her next to him. She put her hand over his heart, snuggled into the crook of his arm, and laid her head on his shoulder.

He kissed her on the head. "I want to give you everything."

She leaned up and kissed him softly. "I've never been happier than I am when I'm with you. You give me magic. You're amazing."

Something in her tone told him they were talking about the *amazing* way they made love together. "Amazing, huh?"

"Incredible. Stupendous. Fantastic." She nipped at his chin. "How do you like those adjectives?"

"I'll work on it. I'll do better next time," he teased, making her laugh.

He pulled the blankets over them, wrapped his arms around her, held her close to his side, and kissed her goodnight. He pressed his lips to hers, kissed her once, twice, and held the third for a long, lingering moment. "I love you." Now that he'd told her, he couldn't help saying it again. Until he met her, his life had seemed cold and lonely. She'd lit a fire in him that would burn the rest of his life.

CHAPTER 23

Gillian stared at her reflection in the mirror and ran a nervous hand down the skirt of her dress. Grandma Dee helped her pick out the pretty dress, and Gillian paid for it with the money she earned working for her grandfather. She turned to the side and studied the still pink scar lines over her shoulder and up her neck. She had a new one to add to her collection, thanks to Ken. She pushed thoughts of that nuisance out of her mind.

She hadn't told Blake what happened. Ken kept his distance. She'd made her point. To him and herself. She wouldn't be anyone's victim anymore.

The dress didn't cover everything. She liked the snug fit over her breasts and to her waist before its skirt gently flared and draped to her knees. The raspberry-colored roses with their deep green leaves made a lovely pattern against the white background. The color made the gold in her hair stand out.

"Gillian, get a move on, sweetheart," Blake called up the stairs.

The butterflies in her belly took flight again. Nervous, she bit her bottom lip, tucked a wayward strand of hair behind her ear, and turned from the reflection of the woman in the mirror she didn't quite feel attached to at the moment.

She walked down the stairs and stopped on the second to last tread. Gorgeous in dark gray slacks and a white dress shirt, Blake stared at her from the living room. Oh, but the look on Blake's face made her heart melt. Pure male appreciation. It made the extra half hour of makeup and hair worth it. She liked the side ponytail, her hair cascading down one side of her chest. His eyes blazed a trail from her head down to her pink-painted toenails encased in a pair of silver sandal high heels. Nothing like anything she'd ever worn, the pretty shoes made her feel sexy. And she knew how much Blake liked her legs. Bonus that her calves looked great, if she did say so herself. The look in his eyes when he stared at her legs told her he agreed.

"Uh, Gillian, you're beautiful."

"Thank you. Do you like the dress?"

"I love it. You look so . . ."

"Different?"

"Pretty."

She wondered if what he really meant was grown-up. The hair and makeup made her look a few years older. In jeans and a T-shirt, she could pass for a teenager. She often wondered if their age difference mattered to him. He'd said once that it didn't, but still, in a small town, little things like that mattered to some people.

"You two have a good night. We'll take care of Justin." Grandma Dee pressed her clasped hands to her breasts, not even trying to hide the huge, all-knowing smile on her face.

Her grandfather stood beside her, smiling. "You look lovely." The words came out gruff.

"Thank you."

"Why can't I come?" Justin asked.

"Next time," Blake said. "Tonight, I'm taking your sister out on a proper date."

"Why? You see her every day."

"Not like this." Blake never took his eyes off her.

She came down the last step and kissed Justin on the head, then ruffled his hair. "You be good for your grandparents. If you are, I heard something about roasting marshmallows in the fireplace."

"No way!"

"Yes way. Brush your teeth before bed. I'll see you in the morning."

Blake took her hand and led her out the door and down the porch steps. He stopped her next to his truck. "I have to do this before we go."

She didn't understand what he meant until he leaned down and kissed her softly, holding his lips pressed to hers, his fingers caressing her bare neck lightly. "God, you're beautiful."

"You said that already."

"I'll probably say it a dozen more times by the end of the night."

She touched her fingers to her cheek. "It's not too much? No one wears makeup on the wharf to work with the fishmongers. I'm not very good with the whole makeup thing."

"You're lovely. Ella knows her stuff. She picked out the perfect colors for you."

Her gaze fell away from his. Shy, she said, "I like all the stuff she sent me."

Blake helped her into the truck. "Tell her at the wedding. She'll probably send you more."

"No. That's not necessary."

Blake shrugged. "She likes doing stuff like that. She sent my mom a bunch of stuff."

He closed her door and walked around the truck to climb behind the wheel. They drove out of the ranch and headed down the main road to town. Blake took her hand and held it. So sweet.

"I'm nervous about the wedding."

"Why? You've met Gabe and my parents. They love you. Ella can't wait to meet you. Did you pick a dress?"

"She sent me three. Remind me to bring the other two to her so she can return them. I have no idea how much I owe her for the one I'll wear."

"Nothing. The dresses are yours to keep."

"What? No."

"Yes. One thing you need to know about Ella. She's obsessive about organization. She's driving Gabe crazy with the wedding plans. All the guys will be in black tuxes with dark blue ties and vests. Gabe's is a different shade of blue. All the ladies will be in different shades of blue dresses."

"Are you serious?"

"Yep. It's her favorite color, and that's what she wanted for the wedding. She and my mother went shopping in New York together to get Mom's dress. They picked out yours at the same time. Ella wanted you to come, but I told her you probably wouldn't want to leave Justin for four days."

"No. I mean, he loves being with all of you at the ranch, but . . ."

"He still looks for you to be with him all the time. Don't worry, he'll get there. He spends more and more time at my place during the day when I'm there."

"How come he's invited over, but I'm not?"

Blake turned his gaze from the road and stared at her. "Are you serious? You don't need an invitation to come see me. Besides, I spend most of my time up at the house with you."

She touched her fingers to his cheek to make him look back at the road.

"You're right. Sneaking in and out of my bedroom."

"I feel like a thief in the night," he admitted.

"Stealing kisses."

"That and little pieces of heaven."

"Aw, look at you, Mr. Romance."

"Just be thankful I walked you to the truck for dinner and not back upstairs to ravage you when I saw you in that dress."

"You're too used to sneaking in through the back door anyway."

"You know that's to keep Justin from knowing I'm sneaking into your bed. Your grandparents know we're sleeping together."

"No way." The blush washed up her breasts and flushed her cheeks.

"Bud gave me a very stern lecture about treating you right and protecting you."

"Are you telling me he gave you *the talk*?"

Blake chuckled. "It was like the same awkward conversation I had with my dad."

Gillian covered her face with both hands. "Oh God. This is not good. How can I ever look at them again?"

That made Blake laugh even more. "Don't worry about it. I told him exactly what I told you. It's fine. Though he made it clear—again—that my job and *life* depend on your happiness."

"Wait, what did you tell him?"

"I love you."

"That's kind of sweet."

He tugged her ponytail. "You know I love you."

"It's sweet that he cared enough to talk with you."

"Yes, the grandfather threatening to kill the boy-friend if he hurts his little girl is very sweet." Blake's words dripped with sarcasm.

"I don't think I've ever had a boyfriend."

"I can confirm you've had at least one," he grumbled.

She laughed. "That *one* had more to do with teenage hormones, movie night at a friend's place, and tequila. Pretty much one of the few times I acted out all my teenage angst and rebellion."

"Are you serious?"

"I thought we were doing this whole tell-the-truth-about-everything deal. If you want me to lie, I'm happy to tell you about Tom, Rick, Ja—"

"Shut up. I got it. Besides, I like being your first and *last* boyfriend."

"Is that right?"

Blake pulled into the parking lot outside the steak house and parked the truck. He leaned over, kissed her socks off, and leaned back with a stern look. "Yes." He kissed her again. "My life is on the line here, you know?"

He might be teasing, but the truth behind those words always stuck with her. "Blake, I'm sorry there's so much pressure on you for this to work out."

"Gillian, what does or doesn't happen between us is our business, and no one else's. If it doesn't work out, it's a big ranch. I'm sure we can stay out of each other's way. But, sweetheart, that's never going to happen unless we let it. I plan to make you happy every day of your life so you'll have no reason to want to leave me. To that end, let's go have dinner. I have a surprise for you."

"Really?" She couldn't help the giddy smile. No one ever did nice things for her the way Blake did for no reason.

"I love it when you smile."

She leaned in and kissed him softly. "You make me happy, Blake. I'm worrying over nothing."

"Yes. You are. You never had very many good things in your life. When you did, your father ruined them. That part of your life is over now. Nothing but happy and good things for you from now on."

One day, she'd stop waiting for something bad to ruin all the good. That's not the life she lived anymore. Right? She hoped. Still, she had yet to shake that sense of doom following her around everywhere. She couldn't outrun it or hide from it. It loomed.

She turned to get out of the truck, but he stopped her with a hand on her thigh that sent a shaft of heat right to her center. That always happened when he touched her. She hoped that good thing never stopped.

"Wait. Let me get the door for you."

She appreciated his manners and waited for him to come around, open her door, take her hand, and help her down from the truck. She turned to him and found him staring.

"You're so beautiful."

"I'm going to have to wear a dress more often if this is how you react."

"It's not the dress." He led her into the restaurant, her hand tucked through his and resting on his forearm.

"Blake, welcome," the hostess greeted them. "We have your table and order ready. Right this way."

Blake took her hand and escorted her through the crowded restaurant to a private table in the corner. People stared. A few called out hellos to Blake. He gave them a nod and a smile, but his focus remained on her beside him. He pulled out her chair and waited for her to take her seat. He kissed her shoulder and took the seat beside her, smiling.

"Amy will be your server. She'll have your drinks in just a moment." The hostess left them alone.

"What do you think?" he asked.

"I love it. It's cozy." She liked the white linen table-cloth, fresh flowers in the pretty blue vase, and taper candles, their flames dancing in the center of the table. Dim lights cast the room in shadows, lending a more private and intimate dinner setting. "She didn't give us menus."

"We don't need them. I ordered ahead."

"My surprise," she guessed.

That cocky smile might be the death of her. When he smiled like that, she wanted to sit in his lap and kiss him forever.

"You'll see. I planned the whole evening."

"To sweep me off my feet?"

"We both know all I have to do is kiss that spot on the side of your neck, and you're mine."

"Actually, all you have to do is look at me that way."

"Which way?" He swept his heated gaze over her face and down to her breasts. They went heavy, and her nipples tightened. She caught herself before she licked her lips, anticipating his touch.

"That way," she said, notching her voice down into a deep, seductive octave.

Blake swallowed, leaned forward, and clasped his hand to her thigh under the table. "Stop, or we'll never make it through this dinner."

She giggled and batted her eyelashes. "What? I didn't do anything," she said, all innocence in her voice.

His fingers squeezed her leg and swept up toward her hip. She sucked in a breath and let it out on a sigh when his thumb caressed the inside of her thigh inches from where she really wanted to be touched.

"Okay stop," she pleaded, though the words held little conviction. She laid her arm on the table, palm up. He pulled his hand from her thigh and gently ran his fingertips down her arm to her palm and settled his warm hand on hers.

"For now." The husky tone in his voice promised so much more. Later.

She loved the anticipation building in her stomach, like a colony of bats swirling at the entrance of a cave before they took flight into the night.

To distract herself, she reached for her purse to take out her phone. "Oh no. I left my purse in the car. I promised Justin he could call my new cell to say goodnight."

Blake pulled his keys from his pocket and rose. "I'll go get it."

She stood and grabbed his hand. "No. I'll get it. Sit. Relax. You've planned such a wonderful evening. I'll be right back."

He leaned in and kissed her. "Hurry up. I don't want to miss a minute of tonight with you."

Unable to resist his simple, yet lovely, request, she kissed him again and took off for the door to retrieve her clutch. Other guests stared at her abrupt departure, but she didn't care. As Blake had ordered, she hurried to get back to him. Right where she wanted to be.

She weaved her way through the cars in the parking lot, unlocked Blake's truck, and snagged her purse off the seat. She locked up, turned back to the restaurant, and took a few steps before a movement to her left caught her attention. A man stepped out between two cars, wearing a black leather jacket and black jeans. His face was in shadow, but his golden hair gleamed bright from the overhead light.

"Gillian."

That voice. Her father's voice. The fear swamped her from her toes up to her head. Suffocated, she opened her mouth to scream, but nothing came out. The man took a step toward her but stopped when she took three back. Afraid he was real, terrified he wasn't, she ran for the restaurant entrance. The hostess's eyes went wide when she rushed through the door and slammed it behind her.

"Are you okay?"

Gillian sucked in a ragged breath and tried to pull it together. "I'm fine." She cast her gaze to the floor and walked through the dining room toward her table with her purse clutched to her chest.

She stopped steps from the table when Blake said, "She's my girlfriend."

"Robbing the cradle these days, Blake?" a soft woman's voice asked.

Gillian looked up and noticed for the first time the beautiful blonde standing next to the table. Someone who obviously knew Blake very well.

He frowned. "She's an amazing woman. You'd like her. She's tough, like you."

Blake didn't mind running into Abigail. He hated the guilt that seeing her unleashed deep inside him, where he tried to bury it most days. The scar along her jaw would forever be a reminder of how being wild in his youth had almost cost her her life. Since that disastrous day, he'd played things straight. Reined in his reckless nature for a more cautious and thoughtful existence. Look at his relationship with Gillian and the way he tried to protect her, keep her safe, give her the time and space she needed to settle into their relationship. It worked. She trusted him now. He'd do anything to keep that bond.

"She's pretty. What's her name?"

Blake caught a glimpse of Gillian's dress behind Abigail. He leaned to the side and didn't like the scared, unsure look on her face. He rose to go to her before he consciously thought about it. Every instinct to protect her flared to life despite the fact that he didn't see any danger, or reason for her pale skin and wide, fearful eyes.

"Gillian, sweetheart, are you okay?" He wrapped his arm around her shoulders and pulled her to his side.

"Fine," she said too fast. Yeah, he knew that false "fine" all too well. He'd get the little white liar to fess up in a minute.

"Gillian, I'm so pleased to meet you. I'm Abigail. Blake and I go way back."

Blake dreaded the explanation ahead. He didn't want his past to intrude on his night with Gillian. He'd planned a romantic evening. Something special she'd never done with anyone else. A night for them to remember.

"Uh, hi." Gillian held out her hand to shake, but her gaze stayed on the scar on Abigail's face.

Abigail took her hand, turned Gillian's arm, and stared at the scars on Gillian's shoulder and neck. "Did he dare you to a race, too?"

Gillian pulled her hand free. "No. I hit a car," she said automatically.

"I hit a tree," Abigail said back. "Not Blake's fault, but he's going to tell you that it was." Abigail turned her focus to him. "I didn't listen to you. I didn't stop. I took the risk because I wanted to beat you."

Blake didn't know what to say. Everyone told him, including Abigail, that the accident wasn't his fault. He'd never believed them, but tonight he saw that fateful day more clearly and realized he owned part of the responsibility, but she had her part to bear, too.

Abigail glanced at Gillian and back to him. "Things happen for a reason. I'm here tonight with my husband."

"How is Gary?" Blake asked, happy she'd found someone special.

"Wonderful. We're celebrating. Two years married, and I'm pregnant."

"Congratulations. You deserve every happiness," Blake said, genuinely meaning those words.

"So do you, Blake. Gillian, so nice to meet you. I saw the smile you put on this one's face when you came in earlier. I've never seen him smile like that."

Gillian glanced up at him and back to Abigail. "Nice to meet you, too. I'm sorry I'm not myself right now. I hope to see you again."

"You will. Small town and all. Enjoy your evening."

Abigail squeezed his forearm as she passed and gave him a smile. Blake held Gillian's chair for her and took his seat beside her again. The other patrons went back to their meal now that Blake, Abigail, and Gillian weren't the center of attention.

Blake took Gillian's hand and squeezed to get her attention. "What happened?"

"Nothing," she said automatically. He waited her out. "I, um, saw someone."

"Who?"

Her gaze finally came up from her plate to meet his. "My father. It happened again. Like with Gabe. I got confused, or my mind played tricks on me . . . I don't know."

"Gillian, did someone come up to you outside? Did they touch you?"

"No. No. Nothing like that. I'm not even sure anymore if someone was really there. I'm sorry. It's nothing. Really. Let's not spoil the evening." She took a sip of her drink. Her eyes went wide on him. "Is this peach iced tea?"

"Your favorite."

"It's nice they serve it here."

"They don't. I got it for you." Blake picked up his beer—the first one he'd had in front of her—and took a deep swallow. She didn't even notice or comment.

"You got me my favorite tea?"

"Just wait. That's not all." Blake cocked his head toward the waiter, who held a huge platter of food balanced on his shoulder and hand. The other guests smelled the food and stared.

Blake and Gillian waited for the dishes to be served.

"Every diner in the place is going to be jealous of you two. Enjoy," the waiter said and left them to their meal.

Gillian stared at her plate. "It's like a seafood explosion."

"All your favorites, right? Lobster, crab, mussels."

"Who knew you could get seafood like this at a steak house in Montana?"

"Well, it's not impossible, but I had this flown in from San Francisco just for you." Tears glistened in her eyes. "I know how much you miss the city. I wanted to bring a piece of it here to you. You didn't even have to unload the fish off the boats to get it," he teased to make her smile.

"I can't believe you did this."

"Well, I had help," he admitted. "Ella owns a house in San Francisco. She was there about a month ago and raved about a restaurant. I told her what I wanted to do, and she put me in contact with the chef at Gerard's. He put the food together and shipped it overnight."

"Gerard's is one of the most exclusive restaurants in San Francisco. Blake, this must have cost you a fortune."

By far the most expensive thing he'd ever done for a woman. He'd never planned anything like this for anyone. "Do you like it?"

"I love it."

"Then I'm happy to do it for you."

Watching the way her eyes went soft with pleasure while she ate lobster dripping with butter made him wish they weren't in a crowded restaurant. Everything she did made him want her more.

She licked the sheen of butter from her lips, placed her elbow on the table, laid her chin in her cupped palm, and stared at him. "You're quiet, and you've barely touched your meal. You keep staring at me like that, I'll blush knowing you've undressed me in your mind."

Blake smiled. "Busted."

"I told you I freaked out in the parking lot, so spill it."

"What?"

"Tell me about Abigail and whatever wasn't your fault but you think it is."

"You saw the scar on her face. She's got a few others you couldn't see. We dated when we were seniors in high school. She loved to ride with me. She loved the speed but always wanted to beat me."

"Let me guess, no one ever beat you."

"A bunch of us used to get together and party in the fields. Bonfires and beers."

"Hook-ups and heartbreaks," Gillian said, understanding, even though she'd missed out on so much of her teenage years hanging out with friends, making stupid mistakes, and never worrying about the consequences of anything.

"It was dusk when Abigail showed up at my place so we could ride over to where everyone was meeting. I had the horses saddled and ready to go. She had a wild streak to match mine. Maybe the two of us together were a disaster waiting to happen. I don't know. I do remember I was the one who dared her to race me to the west pasture gate. A big storm came through two days before and knocked down a tree, blocking the road. When I saw it, I reined in and yelled for her to stop. She didn't. She thought she could jump it. I knew she couldn't, because the horse I gave her always shied at jumping anything. Ten feet from the tree, he slid to a stop and sent her flying over his head. She flipped in the air, hit her head on the trunk, and landed in a tangle of arms, legs, and tree limbs. A branch sliced open her face along her jaw. Several others cut up her arms and back. Not anything like what happened to you. Still, some nasty cuts.

"We weren't that far from where we were meeting our friends. They heard the horse scream when it stopped and threw Abigail. I whistled as loud as I could to make sure they came to help. I didn't want to move her. She was out cold. My buddies showed up in their pickup, and we used a two-by-six board he had in the back to slide under her, strap her on with our belts at her head, waist, and feet."

"Why didn't you call for an ambulance?"

"Too far out of town. It would have taken them an hour to get to her. Although she was knocked out, she was breathing on her own. We worried about her spine but played the odds that her head was the worst of the injuries. We drove her back to my house, picked up my dad, called the hospital to have them waiting for her and give us advice about what to do. An ambulance met us on the road in, and we transferred her to them. They got to the hospital. She remained in a coma for three days until the swelling in her brain went down."

"So, you were right, the head injury was the worst of it?"

"Yes. We got lucky. She woke up with her speech and thoughts slow, but over time she fully recovered."

"Yet you blame yourself that she didn't listen to you, when you knew the horse she was riding wouldn't make the jump, and you yelled for her to stop."

"I shouldn't have goaded her into the race in the first place."

Gillian shook her head and finished the last bite of her crab legs. "Not your fault. Once she got on that horse, it was her choice how fast she went and whether she should attempt the jump. Her choice not to stop when you warned her. It's admirable that you want to take responsibility for what happened, but you can only own your part. She has to own hers."

Blake had to admit she had a point. Seeing Abigail tonight put things into some perspective, too. She didn't blame him, so why did he continue to blame himself? He'd made a mistake and learned from it. He'd never been that reckless again.

Until he'd met a hazel-eyed beauty, who'd stolen his heart and put his job, his partnership with Bud, their friendship, and his livelihood on the line.

"Maybe you're right."

She narrowed her eyes on him, and one side of her mouth dipped into a half frown.

"Okay, you're right. Still, it was a stupid thing to do."

"Everyone does stupid things. We're human. We learn. We adapt. We hurt each other. Sometimes on purpose. Sometimes by accident. We say we're sorry. We make up. A few people go a step further and do something amazing to make someone else happy. This dinner was wonderful, Blake. You're a good man."

"I'm trying to be for you."

"You just are. It's your nature. You never set out to hurt Abigail. You'd never purposely hurt me or anyone else. Thank you for tonight."

"It's not a selfless act. I got to spend the night with a beautiful woman."

She smiled softly. "I hope this night doesn't end any time soon."

"We still have dessert."

"Well, we've had my favorite tea and a wonderful San Francisco seafood dinner. I guess you've ordered strawberry shortcake for dessert."

Blake panicked. "Uh, no."

Gillian laughed. "I'm kidding. I bet you got a chocolate silk pie with loads of fresh whipped cream."

He sighed out his relief. "Not cool."

"I'm sorry. I couldn't help myself. Listen, I'm stuffed. How about we take the pie home with us for a midnight snack," she suggested, with a hint of them needing the sustenance later. He liked her way of thinking.

"I don't know how you remember all these little details," she said.

"I pay attention to every little thing about you. Like although you got scared earlier, you're putting on a brave front and trying your best to enjoy dinner without looking at the door a hundred times, even though you know I'm watching it for you. Your right eye squints when you're nervous. You think I'm wondering if you're going nuts, but you know I don't think that at all. Besides, even if you are, I'm still taking you to bed tonight to do my best to wipe out all those thoughts and make you think of only one thing."

"You're all I want to think about."

"You'll get there. I'll keep working on it."

"You're doing a really good job."

When he walked her to the front of the restaurant and they stood before the door, she stopped and looked up at him. "I'm scared," she whispered.

That quiet admission tore at his heart and made it bleed. She no longer lived to survive every day. That desperate need had been slowly dialed down and turned off with each day she lived on the ranch and grew to love and trust in him and her grandparents. Living every day the way she wanted made it that much harder to rev up her strength to fight her past.

"I can go out and check the lot before I come back and get you."

"For who? My dead father?"

"Are you sure you didn't mistake someone else for him, like you did with Gabe?"

"He kind of looked like that biker dude I saw when we went shopping the first week I was here."

That got Blake's attention and raised the hairs on the back of his neck. "Have you seen him any other times?" He didn't want to frighten her more, but he needed to know if some guy was following her around. He needed to know if she wasn't seeing a real man but her dead father and might need professional help.

"I think I saw him when I went shopping with Grandma Dee and at Justin's school when I met with the sheriff. He was far away, but walking toward me. I rushed Justin into the truck and left."

"Gillian, why didn't you say anything?"

"Because I can't be sure it's real. The last thing I want is for you to think I'm crazy."

"It's never happened on the ranch, except that one time when Gabe surprised you?"

"No. Just in town. I get anxious when we leave the ranch."

"Why?"

"I don't really know my way around town or anyone here. I feel like I have to be on guard."

"Okay, we can fix that. I'm happy to come to town with you, show you around, and introduce you to the people I know. Then you'll feel more comfortable."

That didn't assuage the feeling in his gut that some guy was lurking in the shadows watching her. Who? Why?

He didn't like it and tried not to let it show. She'd asked him not to be so overprotective, but he couldn't help himself.

"Come on. You're safe with me." He wrapped his arm around her, and she snuggled close to his side. He walked her out of the restaurant to the truck and didn't say a word about the tremble that rocked her body against his. He scanned every corner of the lot, every parked car, and the street. Nothing out of the ordinary.

He helped Gillian into the truck and smiled when she slid to the middle and set the pie on the seat closest to the door. He went around to the driver's side and climbed in. She leaned into his side and rested her head against his shoulder, her arm tucked through his, her hand on his thigh.

Neither of them said a word until they were well on their way home and nothing but darkness, the stars putting on a show, and open land surrounded them.

"I had a really good time tonight. Thank you for everything. I loved it."

"I'm glad, sweetheart."

Her cell phone rang. She grabbed it out of her purse. "It's Justin."

"Take it. Tell him I said goodnight."

Gillian finished the short call and stared up at him. "When you were gone, he told me what you said about how he'd always come first."

"As it should be," Blake confirmed.

"I don't know what I did to deserve you in my life, but I am so grateful and happy you are. I love you, Blake. I really, really love you."

Blake wrapped his arm around her shoulders, held her close, and kissed her on the side of the head. He drove faster to get her home and into his bed. When they pulled up in the driveway that led to his house, she didn't say a thing.

He walked her up the porch steps and straight through the front door. He left her in the great room only long enough to put the pie in the refrigerator. She stood before the mantel, staring at the pictures of him and his family, until he came back, took her hand, and tugged her along with him down the hall and straight to his room. He'd left a soft light glowing. She stood beside him and stared at the massive bed strewn with red rose petals. Their sweet scent filled the room.

Nervous about what she thought of his corny attempt at romancing her, he stared down at her and waited. She didn't disappoint. Her face turned up to him, and a smile spread across her lips and lit her eyes.

"This isn't what I expected."

He'd tried to make the room nice for her. He'd even bought new sheets and a cover for the massive king-size platform bed. He liked the clean lines and chunky wood frame and headboard. He'd tried to make the simple bed more appealing with a navy blue and white patterned quilt, with navy-trimmed white pillow shams that looked like they belonged in some swanky hotel. Cost as much too, but he'd wanted her to feel comfortable here. He liked the effect and complement to his marblewood dressers and side tables. He tried to see the room through her eyes. It worked. Definitely nice, despite the sparse decorations, which consisted mostly of photographs of rocky streams and waterfalls with lots of green trees.

"You surprise me, Blake. I kind of expected nothing but cowboy country. This is country chic. I love it."

He let out a heavy sigh.

She smiled, turned into his arms, and gave him a sexy smile. "Now love me," she whispered a second before her lips met his.

He pressed her close and unzipped her dress. He trailed his fingers up her spine to her shoulders and pushed the dress down her arms to puddle at her feet. He stared down at her, standing in her white lace bra and panties. His mouth watered and his hands ached to get a hold of all that creamy skin.

"I liked the dress, but I love you naked even more."

She smiled, then giggled when he wrapped his arms around her waist, lifted her off her feet, took her mouth in a deep kiss, and walked her to the bed. He laid her down under him, crushing the rose petals at her back, and trailed kisses down her neck to her soft breast. He licked the top and slid his hand to the bra clasp in back, unlatched it, and pulled the pretty, but offending, barrier away. He took her tight nipple into his mouth and sucked hard, just the way she liked it. He loved the moan that escaped her lips. Her whole body went lax beneath his in a soft exhale of surrender.

He kissed his way down to her belly. She worked the buttons free on his dress shirt at his wrists. He hooked his fingers in the nothing of a strap at her hip and pulled her panties down her legs as she pulled his shirt off over his head. Somehow, her panties got tangled in his shirt. He let go, and she tossed both things away. He stood at the end of the bed, shook out his hair, and reached for his belt. She came up and kneeled in front of him, her hands sliding up his belly to his chest. She nipped his chin with her teeth and kissed her way along his neck and down to his nipple. She licked him. He nearly lost his patience for her wondering mouth and hands. He barely kicked off his shoes and the slacks he'd dropped to his ankles. Eager to be skin to skin with her, he playfully pushed her back on the bed. She landed with a bounce and a saucy smile on her lips. She wore only her slinky sandals. He took each foot, pulled the shoes off, and dropped them to the floor. He worked off his socks and stood before her in nothing but his boxer briefs. Her eyes slid down his chest to his hard length. He hooked his thumbs in the waistband and slowly slid the boxers down his legs. The heat in her eyes scorched him. His balls ached, his cock throbbed, he needed to be inside her. Now.

He grabbed the condom out of the bedside drawer and sheathed himself. He didn't lay down the length of her but reached for her, sweeping his wide hands down her thighs to her knees. He swept them back up, spreading her legs wide. Her eyes closed, and she gave herself over to him. Soft kisses along her thigh made her moan. He brushed his fingers over her soft folds up and down, then sank one finger deep into her slick core. She tilted her hips, begging for more, and he gave it to her, circling the wet nub with his thumb. He rested his chest on the bed between her legs and replaced his finger with his tongue, licking, tasting, tempting her to the edge.

"Blake."

He kissed his way up her supple stomach, as anxious for her as she was for him, detoured at her breasts to lick, taste, suck her hard, and make her want him even more. He slid his chest against her breasts, took her mouth in a deep kiss, sliding his tongue over hers, and settled between her widespread thighs. Her fingers dug into his back, she rolled her hips up to meet his, and took him in, surrounding him with her warmth and love.

She matched his every thrust. Every sigh and moan he brought out from her, she evoked the same response in him. He made her burn and followed her into the fire.

Gillian woke to the sound of Blake in the shower. The sun had barely peeked over the mountaintops. Its first rays brightened the darkness to murky gray. She stared around the unfamiliar room at the lovely photographs on the walls. She could almost hear the trickle of the streams. Of course, the sound of the shower helped.

The smell of coffee dragged her out of the big bed. Reluctant to put her dress back on just yet, she snagged Blake's white dress shirt off the floor and pulled it on over her head. She rolled up the sleeves and padded her way down the hall. She stopped outside one of the three spare rooms and stared at the Lego village under construction. Several unopened box sets sat on the floor. Someone had started a police cruiser. The tiny policeman stood, arm outstretched, with a gun in his hand pointed at a ninja holding a sword. She smiled and shook her head. A stuffed horse and puppy lay on the queen-size bed, along with Justin's collection of rocks. He liked to find the shiny ones down by the river.

She followed her nose to the coffeepot in the kitchen. He'd brought her here, so she didn't think twice about opening his cupboards to find a mug. By the coffeepot, of course. She found a plate in the cupboard next to the stove. A fork in the top drawer as well. She pulled the pie from the fridge and cut a big slice with a knife she took from the butcher block. She put the pie away and stood at the counter, staring into the great room, eating her pie and drinking her coffee. She spotted the bookshelf and the thick picture albums. She walked over, grabbed the first one, and paused to stare at the intricate Hot Wheels track on the four-foot-square coffee table.

"Not bad."

She sidestepped several metal cars and took the book back to the kitchen counter with her. She flipped through the pages filled with pictures from Blake's life, from the time he was a boy smaller than Justin to middle school. The pictures made her happy and sad all at the same time. What a wonderful family life he had growing up. He was never alone in any of the pictures. At least one, and usually all, of his brothers joined in his fun. Every picture, another smile.

Blake walked down the hall and stopped and stared at her in his kitchen. Bare feet, jeans unbuttoned, no shirt, washboard abs, solid pecs, biceps she wanted to lick, gorgeous face, and wet hair raked back. No man should look that good in the morning. Her man did.

"Do you have a kid I don't know about?" she asked and took another bite of the sinfully rich chocolate cream pie. His heated gaze watched the fork slide out of her mouth.

"No. Just yours."

"That's a nice racetrack."

"I love that thing. I don't know how he does it, but he beats me every time."

She laughed under her breath. "You've got a village going up in your spare room."

"We're working on it. The kid loves to build. He's smart. Reads the directions, follows every detail."

"Where did all that come from?"

"I got most of it on my trip to Nevada. We were busy during the days, but without you in my bed, the nights got boring."

"So you went shopping for toys for my brother."

Blake poured himself a cup of coffee and turned back to her. "Yes. I did. There's no children here for him to play with, so I play with him. Jeff came over a couple of times. We've got a whole racetrack competition going between the Camaro, the Corvette, and a Firebird."

That made her laugh even more. "I didn't think of it, but maybe I need to set up some play dates for him."

"Won't stop the racetrack fun. I plan on winning the trophy."

Gillian stared at the tinfoil goblet on the table. "Is that what that is?"

"Your brother is going down. That thing is mine."

His deadly serious tone made her laugh more. He leaned against her back, his hands planted on the counter on both sides of her. She forked up another bite of pie and fed him over her shoulder.

"I can make you a decent breakfast," he said around the mouthful.

She turned to him and ran her hand down every hard muscle, from his chest to his waistband. "Who wants decent when I have decadent."

Blake picked her up under the arms and set her on the counter, moving between her thighs. He pulled her close, his hard length pressed to her center. He dragged his dress shirt up and over her head, leaving her sitting naked on the counter.

"You are now my indecently decadent woman." He kissed her hard, his tongue sweeping along hers. He tasted of the chocolate pie, coffee, and mint toothpaste. She cupped his face, his freshly shaven skin pressed to her palms. His hands cupped her bottom and squeezed. She wrapped her arms around his neck and pressed her aching breasts to his hard chest.

The heat washed through her like water down a hose—fast and swift. "Blake."

Completely in sync with her, he swept his hand up her thigh, over her soft folds, and thrust two fingers deep into her slick core. She sighed out her relief, but it was short-lived when he pulled free and backed away.

He kissed her hard and quick to distract her and pulled a condom from his pocket.

"Aren't you prepared."

"I'm a fucking boy scout," he said, his teeth clenched on the wrapper as he tore it open.

She undid his jeans, pleasantly surprised to find his thick erection spring free. No underwear.

"Commando."

"Impatient."

He rolled the condom down the length of his dick. She cupped his balls and bit his shoulder at the base of his neck, licking the small hurt to soothe him. He growled something feral, clasped her thighs in his hands, and thrust into her, hard and deep. Neither of them wanted slow and sweet this morning. He took her hard and fast but made sure she found as much pleasure in the furious joining as he did.

She panted with her chin propped on his shoulder. His breath sawed in and out at her neck. His arms banded around her back held her close. She combed her fingers through his damp hair. Spent. Happy. "Good morning," she said with a smile.

"It is now." He leaned back and stared into her eyes. "I liked waking up with you in my bed."

She touched her hand to his face, the other she placed over his thumping heart. "Me, too." She loved being here with him. The quiet house surrounded them. They'd made love, but more, they'd strengthened the bond between them.

Blake picked her up with her legs wrapped around his waist.

"Where are we going?"

"I need another shower, and so do you. I'll wash your hair."

"You just can't wait to get your hands on my hair." The frizzed-out, tangled strands proved it. She hugged him close and looked back at her empty plate and coffee mug next to his on the counter. "I like your place."

"Want to stay?"

She leaned back and stared at him as he walked her through his bedroom to the bathroom. He stopped and kept his steady gaze on her.

"Just saying you do is enough for right now."

He got her. She wasn't ready to move in, make this her home. Their home. She wanted it, but it frightened her. Mostly because of how much she wanted it and feared something would happen, and she'd lose it. Him.

She whispered, "I do."

CHAPTER 24

Blake pulled into the gas station in Crystal Creek. "I'll just be a minute, sweetheart." He left her in the truck and stepped out to pump the gas.

It took some fast talking to get Gillian to agree to go to Wolf Ranch with him for Gabe's bachelor party/ Ella's bachelorette party. Ella already had a bash with her girlfriends in New York, but Gabe, who just wanted to get the deed done, hadn't wanted a party. Instead, they'd planned a quiet evening at home with just the brothers and the women in their lives. Caleb and Summer flew in yesterday and were staying with Blake's mom and dad. Summer was five months into her pregnancy. Blake couldn't wait to see her. Dane was helping out, staying at Wolf Ranch to oversee things while Gabe and Ella went on their honeymoon after the wedding tomorrow.

Blake knew that Gillian didn't want to interfere in the family occasion. He wished she believed with her whole heart that she was part of his family. He loved her. He wanted to marry her. But she still held part of herself back. It had to do with her seeing her dead father and whatever happened when he'd been away in

Nevada. She'd never said what happened between her and Ken, but something had. Every time he tried to coax her to tell him what it was, she shut him down and said she handled it. Well, as far as he could tell, the only way she was handling it was by avoiding the asshole. Fine by him. Still, Blake kept Ken busy and as far away from Gillian as he could.

Lost in thought, he didn't understand why Gillian had her back pressed to the driver's side door.

Gillian waited for Blake, her hands in her lap, nervous about being with all his brothers and Ella and Summer. She'd never been good in social situations. Spending a night with Blake's family seemed too close to their being something more serious than boyfriend and girlfriend. Of course it was. She knew it was. But this made it real. Which in her warped mind meant all this good could be taken away and she'd be right back where she used to be—miserable.

Plus, she was still embarrassed about the scene she made when she met Gabe. She didn't want something like that to happen again. They'd think her crazy and warn Blake away from her.

The rumble of a motorcycle engine drew her attention as the rider pulled into a parking spot by the gas station store entrance. She absently watched him stand and pull off his helmet. The sun lit his blonde hair to a golden gleam. He turned and looked at her, but didn't move. Her gaze met his hazel eyes and held. The world fell away. His eyes narrowed. She swore she heard her father's hysterical laugh. The one he couldn't stop the night she shot him.

The man walked toward her, and everything inside

her wanted to run. She couldn't go out her door. He'd be on her in a second. She scooted across the seat and tried to make herself as small as possible against the other door.

The man stood two feet from the door and called, "Gillian."

"Blake," she screamed.

He came out of nowhere and slammed both hands into the man's chest. Her father, but not. How did he know her name?

"Who the fuck are you? And what the hell do you want with my girlfriend?" Blake demanded, his words laced with steel. He stood between the man and the truck. Tensed to do battle, no way Blake let him anywhere near her.

"Most people I know call me Lumpy."

"What the hell kind of name is that?"

"Ask her. She gave it to me when she was four. Ever since then, the biker gang I belonged to called me by that name."

Gillian slid over to her side of the truck and stared out the open window. "Uncle Lumpy," she whispered.

"Hey, baby girl. You look good. Even more beautiful than I thought you'd be."

"Uncle?" Blake asked.

"Toby Tucker. Ron's older brother. I came back to town about a month before you arrived, baby girl. Got a call from the San Francisco coroner's office about Ron's death and taking care of his body."

"You live here now?" Blake asked.

"Dad died of liver failure near ten years ago. Meanest son of a bitch you ever met. I'm not saying it's an excuse for the way your father and I turned out, but it's an explanation. Bad men like us aren't born, we're made. You took care of your father. Jail and God took care of changing me. I've been living a good, clean, free life going on five years. I quit my old friends and went to mechanic's school. I work. I keep my nose clean. I've been sober going on eight years. Mom passed this last summer. I came back to sort out the family home.

"I tracked you down through the doctors, police, and social worker. Found out about your brother. Cute kid. I meant to go and get you, but they said you were coming here. I'm sorry I scared you those times you saw me. I was just trying to keep an eye on you. Make sure you're settled. Happy. Being treated well." Uncle Lumpy eyed Blake up and down. "So, you like this one?"

Her heart had settled into a normal rhythm again. Snippets of memories of this man teased the back of her mind.

"He's okay."

"Thanks, sweetheart. A real ringing endorsement."

"He's one of the best men I know. The other is my grandfather."

"An upstanding man. I checked him out. Not a single person in this town has a bad thing to say about him or the Bowden family. You're in good hands, baby girl."

Yes, she was.

"So, uh, where have you been? Besides jail?" she asked.

"California. Texas. Nevada. Arizona. Sometimes jail in one place or another. I've done some bad things in my life, but I never hurt anyone more than myself. Though there are a few crazy women out there who'd tell you different."

"Do you have any kids?"

"Never been that lucky. Maybe that was a good thing back in the day, but I sure do wish I'd gone the family route. Maybe if I had someone who needed me, counted on me, I'd have done better by them than I ever did for myself."

"You stole a doll for me."

"You remember that, huh?"

"You snatched it right off the shelf, pulled off the tag, and stuffed it inside your jacket. You walked out of the store like it was nothing."

"Not my finest moment."

"It's the only doll I ever had. My father took it from me, tore off her head, and burned her body. I kept that doll head for a long time."

"Why'd he do that, baby girl?"

"Because hurting me made him laugh. I thought you were him. I thought he came back, or I halluci-nated him. I thought I was going crazy," she admitted, making him frown and Blake come forward and put his hand over hers on the truck door frame.

"I'm sorry, baby girl. I thought maybe you remem-bered me, and all I did was bring back bad memories. Maybe that's exactly what I did, but you didn't remem-ber, did you?"

"Not until you said I named you Lumpy."

"Anyone want to explain that?" Blake asked.

"He came in and out of my life when I was real little. Every time he showed up, he had a bashed-up face. Swollen. Lumpy. I can't remember ever not call-ing him that."

"It became my biker name. I only wish I'd been more your Lumpy than the bar fighting Lumpy who showed up on your father's doorstep drunk and broken and miserable and looking in all the wrong places for something to make me feel better. You always did though, baby girl. I loved seeing you and that sweet smile of yours. I'm real sorry about your parents. Sorry you had to put that no-good brother of mine down."

Blake's fingers slid across her neck and into her hair. "That's over now."

Gillian grabbed Blake's hand, turned it, and checked the time on his watch. "Oh God, we're late. Uncle Lumpy, I'm sorry, we're supposed to be at Blake's brother's house for a family get-together. Um, do you know where Three Peaks Ranch is?"

"I've been out that way a few times. Seen you ride, baby girl. You're a natural. Like me on my bike, you love the wind in your face."

She smiled. "I'd like it if you came to see me again. Justin will want to meet you."

"I don't want to scare the boy."

"I'll talk to him. Tell him who you are."

"I'd like that. I'll let you get to your family thing. I hope when you see me again, you won't see him."

"I don't think I will anymore." She felt a weight lift, and she squeezed Blake's hand to let him know she was okay. His eyes softened when he read the relief that washed over her, knowing she wasn't crazy.

A car honked behind them. Someone waiting for the gas pump.

"Better get a move on. Nice to see you, baby girl. Blake, you treat her right, or I'll break your face."

Her uncle walked away without a backward glance.

"I think he meant that," Blake said.

"My father slapped me once when he was visiting. He beat my father bloody and knocked him out. He spit on him. They were both drunk and high. He left. We moved again. I never saw him again, but I wished all the time for him to come back. One day, I stopped wishing."

He cupped the back of her neck and leaned in for a soft kiss. "Do you want me to take you home?"

"No. I'm fine. Really. I want to meet your brothers and sisters."

Blake, Gabe, Caleb, and Dane sat around the living room waiting to get this show on the road. All the guests had gone down to where the wedding would be held in ten minutes. It was a last chance for the brothers to be together before Gabe married the woman of his dreams, the love of his life. Blake couldn't be happier for him.

"Was Gillian pissed you were hungover this morning?" Gabe asked.

"Good thing you had a designated driver," Dane chimed in.

"He wouldn't have needed one if you hadn't broken out the whiskey and called for shots."

"Hey, we needed a toast. Beer just doesn't cut it. Besides, Gabe's lady drank us under the table and won every damn poker hand once she started playing for him."

"Gillian and Summer were having a good time watching us. They really hit it off," Blake said.

"That's because they were the only two sober people in the room," Dane pointed out. "Summer's pregnant, and your girl's not old enough to drink."

"Like that ever stopped any of us," Caleb pointed out.

"When did she get her driver's license? Last month?" Dane teased.

Blake smacked him on the back of the head to shut him up. Their mother and father walked into the room, keeping him from laying into Dane.

"She's ready," his mother announced. "Let's go,

boys. We'll walk down first. Your father will escort Ella." His mother waved her hands to get them moving out the door. No one had to prod Gabe. He couldn't wait for this day to be over and for Ella to be his wife.

Blake wondered if Gabe suggested their father walk her down the aisle just to be sure Ella didn't run out on the ceremony like his first fiancée did. He dismissed the idea immediately. No way Ella backed out. She loved Gabe. The way she looked at him said it all.

He followed Gabe as they walked down the rose-petal-strewn path between the rows of family and friends waiting for the ceremony to begin. Gillian sat on the right. He caught her eye. Yep, that's exactly the way Ella stared at Gabe.

The brothers stood shoulder to shoulder at the front of the small crowd, the preacher next to Gabe, ready to start the ceremony.

"I was just messing with you, Blake. I like Gillian. She's nothing like the young girls who follow me around the rodeo circuit," Dane whispered.

"No, she didn't flash her boobs, despite how much you flirted with her."

"That was just to mess with you. Territorial much?"

"Leave my woman alone," Blake warned. Dane didn't mean the flirting. He did it with every woman he met, young or old. One day, Dane would find a woman who'd give him a run for his money and call him on all his bullshit.

"You two looked pretty serious last night," Gabe pointed out, talking out the side of his mouth in low tones, so no one overheard them.

"We are serious."

"How serious?" Caleb whispered, eying him.

"I'm going to marry her."

All of his brothers turned and stared at him, but he only had eyes for the beautiful woman sitting in the audience staring back at him with a pretty smile on her face. Lovely in her blue gown, she fit in with the rest of the female guests wearing similar shades of blue, as Ella requested.

None of his brothers got a chance to comment on his announcement. The music played, and Ella's bridesmaids, two friends from New York, walked down the aisle ahead of Summer, who served as the matron of honor. Her round belly filled out the front of her blue dress, which draped down to her knees. Beautiful in her pregnancy, she glowed.

Blake wondered what Gillian would look like round with his baby. He glanced at her, and she cocked her head, probably wondering why he stared so hard. He couldn't help it. Being at the wedding today made him even more anxious for the kind of life his parents shared for over thirty years, Caleb had with Summer, and Gabe was just beginning with Ella.

Their father stood with Ella at the end of the aisle. Her gaze found Gabe's, and she smiled so brightly that even Blake thought her the most beautiful bride he'd ever seen. The white beaded gown hugged her curves to her knees and draped down to cover her feet. The neckline dipped low. The sleeves encased her arms, one tucked into his father's, the other holding her bouquet of white roses and lilies.

Blake glanced at Gabe's face. Mesmerized by his bride, he never took his eyes off her as she walked down the aisle toward him.

"Breathe, man," Blake prompted.

When their father placed Ella's hand in Gabe's, his brother finally took a deep breath and smiled like a lunatic at Ella.

The ceremony was beautiful and sweet. When it came time to exchange rings, Gabe turned to him. An old gag, but Blake went with it anyway, patting his pockets, waiting for the look of panic to come over Gabe's face, thinking Blake had lost the ring. Blake pulled it out and smiled wickedly at his big brother.

Just the moment they needed to break the tension. Gabe's shoulders relaxed. Ella laughed and the rest of the ceremony flew by, ending with a steamy kiss.

The wedding party finished the photos and headed into the elegant tent that looked more like a ballroom, with a hanging chandelier, dark blue, cloth-draped tables covered in gleaming silver, crystal, white dishes, and overflowing blue vases with white flowers. Blake found Gillian talking to a few of Ella's friends.

"Hey pretty lady, come with me." Blake took her hand, smiled at the other ladies in apology for interrupting, and drew Gillian toward the dance floor.

"The wedding was beautiful. This place is amazing."

"You're beautiful. You're stunning in that dress."

"I'm so used to you in jeans, I can't get over how handsome you are in a tux."

"Only for my brothers—and you—would I wear one of these monkey suits."

He didn't know if she got the meaning of what he was trying to tell her, but he hoped she understood that unless it was their wedding, or one of his brothers', you wouldn't catch him dead in a tux again.

As instructed, Blake, Caleb, and Dane stood to one side with their ladies. One of Ella's bridesmaids stood beside Dane, since he didn't have anyone special in his life right now—or ever.

Someday, the right woman would show up and take him on the ride of his life.

Ella and Gabe walked in to a round of applause. The singer of the country cover band Ella hired announced, "Please welcome Mr. and Mrs. Gabe Bowden for their first dance as man and wife."

They stepped out onto the dance floor and lost themselves in each other's arms. Halfway through the slow song, Blake, Caleb, and Dane escorted their partners to the dance floor and joined the newlyweds. Over the next few songs, Blake, Caleb, and Dane took turns dancing with the bride—their new sister. Ella danced with their father, making him tear up, and Ella looked forlorn for her lost family. Gabe put the smile right back on her face when he pulled her close for yet another kiss as everyone tapped their spoons to their champagne glasses.

The rest of the night was a lot of food, fun, and more dancing until Gabe shot Ella's garter right into Dane's face with a "You're next, bro."

Dane shook his head no and swore, "Never going to happen."

Ella tossed her bouquet to five single ladies, including Gillian. Blake's mother had nearly dragged her to the dance floor to participate. She caught the bouquet.

"See, that makes more sense," Dane said and turned to him. "You're next, bro."

Gillian stared at him, the bouquet of roses up to her nose as she inhaled their sweet scent.

Yes, she'd make a beautiful bride. His bride.

CHAPTER 25

Gillian rode over to the track with Jeff beside her. They'd been working secretly with Boots for more than two weeks. The wind caressed her face. She turned her gaze up to the bright blue sky and let the heat of the sun warm her skin. She loved the warmer May temps and riding every day.

She spotted Blake by the rail, watching several horses speeding down the track. He held a stopwatch and a clipboard and wrote down the horses' times. She rode toward him. Jeff rode Daredevil beside her, an all-black colt that had a wild disposition. Boots was ready to run. He saw the track, and she worked hard to keep him from taking off from under her.

"Hey honey, taking Boots out for a ride?" Blake asked.

"Yes. I'm going to give him what he's been asking for, for weeks now."

Blake eyed her atop the horse and turned a penetrating gaze on Jeff. "You aren't seriously thinking about putting him inside the gates and racing him."

"Yes. I am."

"That wasn't a question. That was my way of saying, hell no. No way. Never going to happen."

"Blake, Boots is a racehorse. I nursed him back to health. He wants to run. He'll only let me ride him. He bites the other riders. I want to get him into the gates and race him once. I hope he likes it and lets another rider up on him."

Blake's scowl deepened.

"Jeff helped me," she said.

"Great. Get me killed, why don't you?" Jeff took a step back from Blake and his murderous glare.

She ignored Jeff and tried to make Blake understand. "He's ready. He needs a chance to prove himself."

Blake sucked in a breath, ready to talk her out of this. For her safety. But nothing he said would deter her.

"Gillian, I know how hard you've worked to get him to accept you as a rider. I figured you'd keep him as your own. Not race him."

"Blake, his bloodlines are some of the best on this ranch. He'll make a great stud, and his babies will grow up to be champions. He's finally feeling like his old self. He needs to race again."

"You don't know what he used to be like."

"He was a champion racehorse. I'm just asking you to give me a chance to prove to him that he still is. Do you know what it's like to be beaten down and have to drag yourself back up? He needs this."

No, Blake conceded, she needed this. She might think this was about Boots, but this had everything to do with her. Boots was healthy again. Gillian was healthy again. Gone were the nightmares that had haunted her nights for months. She didn't see her father in others anymore and had even started to get to know her uncle over the last couple weeks. A good man, even if he was protective of Gillian and gave Blake dirty looks, warning him all the time not to hurt his "baby girl."

Like Gillian, Blake imagined Boots had his own demons that haunted him. She saw that in him. She saw it in the other sick and injured horses. They responded to her. Boots wasn't the only horse she took care of now. She had an innate ability to get them to trust her.

He closed the distance between them and laid his hand on her thigh. "Sweetheart, is this about Boots, or you? If you think you need to prove something, you don't. You work hard on this ranch, and you've found your place. Aren't you happy here?"

He thought she had enough here on the ranch, but maybe he was wrong. Maybe she needed something more, and it wasn't here. The thought of her leaving the ranch to do something else terrified him. He loved working with the horses, couldn't imagine leaving. Could he leave to be with her? An easy yes came to mind. For her happiness, he'd make a life with her somewhere else, doing something else. He'd find a way to be happy as long as he had her.

"Blake, I'm happy here. I love the horses and the ranch. I delivered a foal yesterday. Do you know how amazing that is? Boots is in championship form, and I had a hand in that."

Gillian traced her fingertips along his jaw and watched the muscles bunch. No one had ever worried about her the way he did.

"Boots and I have a lot in common. We were both abused. We were both neglected. We were both rejected. I don't have anything to prove to anyone but myself. I know you don't understand, but it's a constant battle to remind myself every day that I'm worth something when there's a tape in my head playing my past. What he did to me. What he said to me. What he made me feel. It is still a part of me. I need to remember that

I'm stronger than he ever made me think or feel. I'm stronger than anything he ever did to me."

She looked out at the track and saw the reddish brown dirt, the white fences circling the inner field of grass. She imagined herself flying around that oval on Boots's back and feeling the wind whip past her as she and Boots flew. The freedom of it called to her.

"I need to do this, Blake. I need to know that I can. I need to know that I gave something back to him." She petted Boots from his head down his neck to his shoulder. He remained tense under her, like a spring ready to let loose. His anticipation became her own. He wanted to run.

"He needs to race and know that he's stronger than anything that man did to him. He needs to feel like a champion again."

"And what is it that you need to feel?"

She stared down into his warm eyes. "I already do. I'm loved, Blake. I'm loved by a great man who sees me inside and out and loves me for all that I am. The good and the bad."

"Ah, sweetheart. I have no words for that. I do love you, and I hope you feel that every second of every day. I hope I never make you feel anything less than what you are. Perfect."

"Not perfect, Blake. We both know I can't be that. But I am strong and capable. This is different. I need to do this. I don't know how to explain it to you, but I need to take him out on that track. He won't do it otherwise. If he doesn't race again, he'll always wonder. I want him to go out a champion. Not a horse that was abused and reduced to someone's pet. He's better than that. I know he is. Now he needs to remember he is."

"You do know how fast he's going to run around that

track. You aren't a professional rider. Have you even had him at a flat-out run?"

"Several times. I scared the hell out of Jeff the other day when we left him in the dust. I'm telling you, Blake, this horse can run."

Blake hesitated. His hand clamped onto her thigh so tightly that she knew he held himself back from snatching her right out of the saddle.

She leaned down and whispered, "I'm not Abigail. I know Boots. I know me. If at any moment I think it's too dangerous, I'll rein him in. I promise, being safe, being with you is more important than any race."

Blake sucked in a ragged breath and let it out. "You need a helmet and a vest. I'm not letting you on that track without proper gear." The words came out as if he'd torn them loose.

"Jeff's holding both behind you."

Blake turned to the other trainer. "You were in on this?"

Jeff gave Blake a wide berth and walked to Gillian to hand her the gear. "I gave her instructions on how to train him. She did the work. She's good. She retaught him everything, right down to saddling him and letting her up on his back." Jeff took three steps back before he admitted, "Boots threw her twice."

Blake's sharp gaze met hers. She hated making him this upset.

"What? Where did you think the bruises on my legs came from?"

"Damnit, Gillian. You could have gotten seriously injured or killed."

"And what about you? What were you doing this morning?"

Breaking in a new horse, that's what he'd been doing. Blake had gotten the horse saddled with no trouble, but the animal had been waiting for Blake to try to get on. When Blake leaned over the saddle and put his weight on the horse, he'd gone ballistic and bucked. Blake ended up dumped on his ass and damn near stepped on to boot.

He'd concede this one to her. He'd learned to pick his battles. Hardheaded woman.

"I should have stayed in bed with you this morning. Maybe we both could have stayed out of trouble," he grumbled.

Gillian's mouth dropped. "Jeff is right there, thank you very much."

"Don't mind me," Jeff said with a broad smile.

Blake narrowed his eyes. "Sweetheart, we're all anyone on this ranch talks about."

"Mostly it's that Blake is the luckiest son of a bitch on the ranch," Jeff said, a rush of red brightening his face.

Blake slapped him on the back. "Yes, I am. She's the most beautiful woman in these parts."

"Yeah, we're all wondering what she's doing with the likes of you," Jeff teased.

Blake ignored the jibe. "Kiss me before you do this and get yourself killed."

She leaned down and kissed him softly. He frowned at the chaste kiss she laid on him. He wanted more. With her, he always wanted more. She snagged his black cowboy hat, ran one hand through his hair, grabbed a handful, and pulled him to her to really kiss him. She ended the kiss tracing her tongue over his bottom lip. Sexy as hell. He fought the urge to drag her to the ground and have his way with her.

"Nobody's getting killed, cowboy. But I am going to show you what Boots can do. You're going to want to take him to the next race."

"We'll see about that." He reached for the reins. "I'll set you up in the gates, sweetheart. How about we put three other horses in with you to give old Boots here a run for his money."

Maybe when she lost the race, Gillian would give up and let Boots live out his days with the mares on the ranch.

Ken stood next to one of the horses he'd been training for months. Blake walked Gillian to the gates. She felt Ken's gaze following her, but she ignored him.

"Ken, bring Diamond Deuce over. Let's run him, too."

Gillian's stomach tied in knots. The fury in Ken's eyes frightened her. Angry men like Ken were a force unto themselves. He'd already proven that he'd resort to manhandling her to get what he wanted. She wasn't sure what he'd do if she showed him up in front of everyone.

Ken had kept his distance since she'd clocked him with the wrench and Blake had come home, but she caught him watching her all the time. Sometimes with purely sexual lust and other times tightly reined rage. One day soon, he'd make up his mind about which one of those he'd act on, and she'd have to defend herself against both. Unlikely to let things go and put the past behind them: no, men like Ken—like her father—had to win, no matter how wrong they were.

Well, she had a need to win, too. No way she let him beat her down and make her go running to Blake and her grandfather. She'd beat him once. She'd beat him again. Right now, she'd beat his horse to show him and Blake she had what it took to train Boots to be a champion again.

The other riders gave her a hard time about putting Boots up against their horses.

"It's like a tricycle against a ten speed."

"A Tonka truck against a bulldozer."

"Are you going to cry when you get my dust in your eyes?" Ken's horse's rider called. That one made her laugh.

She took the razzing in stride. She'd come to know everyone on the ranch. Like having an extended family, it made her feel good to be included.

Jeff helped her get situated in the gates as Boots made a valiant effort to stay out. Once inside, he tensed like lightning ready to flash. The anticipation built, and she tried to remember Jeff's coaching. Once the gate opened, Boots would take off like a rocket. All she had to do was hold on for the ride of her life.

Blake stood by the rail, eyes glued to the gates. Nervous. Anxious. Anything could happen to her. She could fall off Boots and be trampled by him or the other horses. He could take a fall and take her down with him and crush her. Every scenario in his mind ended with her lying dead on the track and him more alone in his life than he'd ever been.

Damn, but I love that woman. He needed to do something about making her a permanent part of his life. He didn't know what twisted his gut more, the thought of buying her a ring, asking her to marry him, and her potentially saying no, or the possibility of her getting herself killed.

The gate swung open and Boots sprang out with the other horses. Blake's heart pounded as fast and hard as the horses' hooves on the track. Gillian rode Boots like a pro. At the first curve, she had one horse beside her and two in front of her. She took Boots to the rail and gave him his head.

Boots was fast, faster than Blake had given him credit for.

Gillian rounded the second curve just as Boots reached his pace. His hooves thundered over the ground and echoed in her heart. She'd never felt more alive. They passed the lead horse so close that her leg brushed against the other rider's. She coaxed Boots on, the finish line in sight ahead. Boots seemed to know he was almost done. He lengthened out his neck and stride and picked up speed with a last effort that stunned her. They were flying.

They crossed the finish line, and Gillian screamed with glee. She reined in Boots and brought him down to a nice trot. The smile on her face hurt her cheeks. If she smiled any wider, she'd break her face.

She turned and found Blake in the distance with an astonished, but proud, look on his face.

She patted Boots's neck and leaned down to give him a big hug. "That's a boy. Outstanding," she cheered him as they trotted down the track. Boots practically danced on his hooves. Sweat glistened on his shiny brown coat. Proud of him. Proud of herself. She'd done it. She'd ridden him in a race and won.

Definitely a far cry from offloading fish at the docks for cash.

She stopped Boots down the track from Blake, and Jeff grabbed the reins. He'd cool down Boots for her.

"That was amazing, Gillian. I didn't think you'd win." Jeff tried to get Boots to stop dancing. He brushed a hand down Boots's nose and kept a tight hold on the reins.

"He wants to run. I told you. He wants to run like the wind. I can't tell you how that felt."

She jumped down from the saddle and didn't understand the strange look in Jeff's eyes until Ken spun her around and grabbed her shoulders to hold her in place.

Still riding a wave of adrenaline, she didn't notice right away the gleam of sheer rage in Ken's eyes. Excited for Boots, she didn't have her guard up.

"I'll train Boots from now on. I'm taking him to the next race."

Understanding dawned. "Get your hands off me. You are not training Boots."

"Like hell I'm not."

"He's mine. I decide who gets to train him."

Blake rushed in. Ken let her go and backed up a step. Blake positioned himself between her and Ken, then took two steps forward, forcing Ken to back away from her even more.

"Keep your damn hands off Gillian. I told you more than once to leave her alone. What the hell is your problem?"

"I'm taking Boots to the next race. I'm tired of you always getting the best horses on the ranch. I deserve a shot."

"You don't deserve shit. Boots is her horse." Blake backed Ken up another step. "So back off. I make the decisions on this ranch. I tell you which horses you train. You don't like it, quit."

"No way I'm quitting."

"Then go and cool down Diamond Deuce. He's your responsibility today. Not Boots. Do your fucking job. This is your last warning. Get in Gillian's way again, stand too close to her, and I'll fire you. Touch her again," he said menacingly, "and I will fuck you up."

Blake hoped every cold-as-steel word he spoke pierced Ken's small mind like a dagger. Something had to get through, right? The guy couldn't be this stupid. Just in case he was, Blake stood with his hands fisted, chest out, ready to fight.

Ken tried to stare him down. With three brothers and several dozen scuffles with each of them under his belt, Ken didn't even faze him.

Blake took another step forward. Surprisingly, Ken didn't back away this time. They stood a mere inch apart.

"You have something else you want to say to me?" Blake would like nothing better than for Ken to take a swing at him. That's all it would take for Blake to unleash the fury building inside him.

Gillian stood beside Jeff and Boots. The two men squared off like gunfighters. The intense anger in Blake surprised her. No one had ever stood up for her. She didn't know if she should be happy that he was taking her side or angry because he didn't think she could take care of Ken herself. No, Blake believed in her.

Gillian spotted her grandparents and Justin walking toward the track still too far away to hear the exchange. She hoped Blake ended this before Justin heard him arguing with Ken, who'd caused enough tension over the last several months.

"Blake, Justin is home from school." She walked up behind Blake and put her hand on his shoulder. "Enough." She spoke calmly, hoping to get their attention and not incite another round of arguing.

Both of them stared at her as she moved to Blake's side. "Let's be really clear. I will train Boots for the next race."

"Gillian, you can't be serious. You don't know anything about training a horse," Blake said.

He hadn't meant those words to make her feel incompetent, but she couldn't help but feel like he'd let her down in some way.

"I just raced Boots and won. I seem to know something about him." She turned on Ken. "As for you. You seem to think there's something between the two of us. Hear me on this. I don't like you. I don't want to be friends or have anything to do with you. Clear enough. You want to stay on this ranch, stay clear of me, because I guarantee you that you'll leave here before I do."

Ken took a menacing step toward her. Blake shoved her behind him and blocked her from Ken. Pissed off, she stepped around Blake and glared up at Ken. "You have something you want to say to me?"

Ken's gaze swept from Blake to her grandfather and down to her. "You won't always have them around to defend you."

"Then you'd do well to remember what happened the last time we met up alone."

Ken's whole face turned red with rage, but he turned on his heel and walked away.

Blake tried to go after him, but Gillian caught him by the wrist and pulled him back. Too angry to say anything, he took her hand and walked with her toward Justin and her grandparents.

"What the hell happened the last time you two got into it? I told you I'd take care of him if he messed with you."

She turned to face him and the cold glare in his eyes. She'd never had anyone who wanted to defend her and take care of her. Perhaps if she had, she'd have found it within her to be a little more accommodating. But taking care of herself, Justin, and Boots had become her only source of pride, and Blake had stomped all over it.

"Of course you'll take care of him."

"Yes, I'm going to fire his ass."

"Because I can't take care of him myself, right?"

"No, because he's an asshole."

"Now you want to take over Boots, too, because I can't possibly do that on my own either."

She pulled her arm free of Blake's grasp and headed for Justin, who ran for her, his brows drawn into a line of worry.

Blake caught up to her. "Damnit, Gillian, listen to me."

"You have to eat extra vegetables," Justin said, stopping beside both of them.

"I'll eat a whole crop if your sister will listen to reason."

"Reason. There's no reason. There is only you telling me that I can't take care of myself or Boots."

"That's bullshit, and you know it. You raced around that track like the hounds of hell were trailing you. The whole time I stood by terrified something would happen to you."

"I'm not Abigail," she shouted.

He grabbed her arms and held her tight so she'd listen. "No, you're the woman I love and can't live without. If something happened to you, that would be the end of me. Gillian, don't you see, I can't watch you risk your life like that again."

The sincerity of his words hit her heart. He meant it. He'd be devastated if something happened to her. She felt it all the way to her soul. He loved her beyond words or reason.

She didn't know what to do with that, or the overwhelming emotions swelling inside her, filling her eyes with tears and squeezing her heart. She couldn't stand there and feel all her emotions overwhelming her, crushing her. She ran.

Gillian bolted up the road. Blake tried to go after her, but Dee grabbed his arm and stopped him.

"Let her go."

His chest went tight and his jaw locked as he watched her jump into her truck and take off. "I made her cry." Every ounce of misery in his soul poured out with those words.

"She'll be fine. It just hit her that you love her."

"She knows I love her."

"Beyond you telling her you love her, you just showed her how much. You scared her. No one has ever loved her beyond everything. No one has ever been unreasonable about protecting her. No one has ever put her first. She doesn't know how to deal with that."

Blake stared at the empty road that Gillian disappeared down. "She ran away from me."

"She'll be back. Give her time to settle her heart. Once she sorts this out, she'll be ready to settle into compromise with you. She won't feel like she has to hold up the world on her own. She'll know that she has you to lean on."

"I want her to know that she can count on me. I want her to know that I'm here for her. She doesn't have to do everything herself."

"She knows that. Now. Give her time to get used to it."

"I didn't get to give her the card I made." Justin leaned against Blake's leg.

Blake automatically put his hand on Justin's shoulder. "What card, buddy?"

"Her birthday card. I made it at school today."

Blake stared at Bud and Dee, feeling the bottom drop out of his heart. "It's her birthday?"

Bud shrugged. "We didn't even realize."

Blake felt as disheartened as Bud looked.

"She always forgets," Justin said.

"How can she forget her own birthday?"

"Dad never did anything for our birthdays. Gillian takes me out for dinner. I get to have whatever dessert I want. Last year, I asked when her birthday was, and she told me. I made her a card at preschool and a clay fish. Today at school, when we were practicing the date and time, I remembered that her birthday is today. I asked my teacher if I could make her a card."

Blake felt like shit. He didn't know how to fix this. She'd done an amazing thing today. She'd brought Boots back from near death to racing and winning. She'd ridden him like a pro. Blake hadn't congratulated her, he'd fought with her. The problem with Ken overshadowed everything. That threat needed to be eliminated.

He didn't even have a gift for her. Hell, he didn't even know it was her birthday. He should have asked for the date by now. Pissed off at himself, he should have known.

"You know what, Justin? I don't think we should ever let her forget her birthday again. It's about time she realized that having people love her means they want the best for her and that she's important. I think Gillian needs a birthday party."

Dee's eyes lit up and Bud smiled. They hadn't had a party at the ranch in a long time.

"I think we should give Gillian a real surprise," Blake added. Gillian was already surprised by how much he loved her. She had no idea how deeply. He planned on showing her.

CHAPTER 26

Gillian turned down a long dirt road a few miles from the ranch, parked, got out, and climbed on the warm hood, her back to the windshield and her legs crossed. She sat for a long time staring at the rolling expanse of grass that gave way to the trees and mountains. Arms folded over her chest, her head resting on the glass, she simply took in the majestic scenery and thought about her life—and Blake.

Her thoughts settled, the way she'd settled onto the hood of the truck. The quiet of the land settled into her, and for a moment she thought of the hustle and bustle of the city and how far away San Francisco seemed from her life, from her thoughts.

If she'd been in San Francisco, she'd have gone to the wharf and let the rolling ocean soothe her mind. Now she didn't have the wind blowing off the sea or the fog to obscure the city and wrap itself around her in a misty blanket. Not here.

No, here she didn't have the ocean. She had something better. She had Blake. He loved her. She hadn't really thought about what that meant in her life.

He'd nearly lost his mind over Ken and her racing

Boots. Underlying it all, he wanted to protect her because he loved her.

She hadn't expected that. She hadn't been ready for that kind of depth of emotion from him. She couldn't expect him to love her and not be affected by the things she did or said. She couldn't expect him to be a passive participant in her life. She had to let him in and trust him to take care of her when she needed it. Even when she didn't ask for it. She'd handled Ken once. But even she had to admit this thing with Ken was getting out of hand. Maybe letting Blake handle him was the right thing to do.

The right thing to do. She didn't know what that was or how to go about doing it where Blake was concerned. She didn't have any experience with counting on someone to catch her when she fell. Usually, she just braced for the impact and picked herself up. Knowing Blake would throw himself down and give her a safe, soft place to fall was difficult to take in. It overwhelmed her heart and frightened her a little to think that if she lost it—him—she would lose something vital to her life.

Blake sat on the porch steps watching the road. She'd be back. When, was another matter.

Over dinner, they plotted and planned a birthday party she'd never forget. To pull it off, they'd have to deceive her, but he hoped in the end she'd be happy.

Right now, she wasn't very happy with him. But he'd fix that as soon as she came home, because his world tilted out of balance when she wasn't with him.

What if she didn't want to be a permanent part of his life? He couldn't lose her. He couldn't live without her. He'd just have to teach her to lean on him and trust him.

The only way to do that was to show her every day that he was hers to keep.

Underlying everything, she feared losing him, because in her tumultuous life nothing and no one had ever been a permanent part of her world. Nothing good ever happened to Gillian before she came to the ranch. Her body had healed, but her mind and her heart were still entrenched in the belief that she had only herself to rely on. No matter how close they got, she was always waiting for him to leave and for their relationship to fall apart. Not going to happen. But she didn't believe that. Well, he'd prove it to her every day for the rest of his life if she let him.

She sought him out during the day just to say hi. He often thought she wanted to make sure he was there, somewhere, and that he was real. So many times over the last several weeks, she made him feel like he was such a gift in her life. He tried to give her that feeling back, even by half, but today's events proved he'd done a piss-poor job. He'd spend the rest of his life doing it better.

Worried about her, his gut tightened with anticipation. She'd only been gone a few hours, and he missed her. He wanted to work things out.

He heard her truck before he saw it come around the bend. He waited for her to get out and make her way up the path. He didn't stand up to greet her. Man, she was a sight for sore eyes. Whatever they'd argued about earlier was so insignificant that it had blown away like sand in a windstorm. Every time he saw her, he was struck by her amazing beauty. Even in the night, her hair morphed from blonde to red to brown as it swayed at her back. He hated the worry lines on her forehead. She didn't stop at the bottom of the steps but barreled right up them and launched herself into his arms and buried her face in his neck.

Finally, he felt whole again.

Gillian couldn't help the tears or the catch in her voice. "I'm sorry, Blake."

His arms tightened around her. "Sweetheart, there's nothing to be sorry about. We disagreed. That's all. I just want to keep you safe. I can't help myself. I'm selfish. I want to keep you with me forever."

She pulled back and wiped her eyes, then stood on a lower step and tried for a compromise. "I'm not turning over Boots's training to you or Ken. He's mine. I've worked with him all this time. I'm not letting either of you take over—"

"Okay."

"—I realize there'll be other horses at the race that might be better, but I want—"

"Okay."

"—a chance to see what he and I can do." Blake smiled at her with that half grin she loved so much. "Did you say okay?"

"Yes. Boots is your horse. If you want to train him, I won't stop you or interfere. But . . ."

"No buts," she said, concerned.

"But someone else rides him. I can't watch you do that again. It damn near stopped my heart today. You came here hurt, sweetheart." His voice turned rough with emotion. "I can't stand to see you hurt again. You've proven you can train and ride Boots, and I'm proud of you. I really am. But I'm begging you, please, for my sanity and heart's sake, let someone else ride him."

The possibility of her getting hurt scared him. Yes, even Blake could be afraid. For her. Not so much for him to ask of her, she agreed to compromise. "Deal.

But that doesn't mean I'll stop riding him. I'll leave the racing to someone else."

"I'm just asking that you don't risk your life, because when you do, you risk mine, too. I can't even think of living my life without you."

She leaned forward and combed her fingers through his golden brown hair. He grabbed her wrist and pulled her to him. She went willingly. His lips met hers, and she melted into him. The kiss was soft and filled with love. He tasted of coffee and restrained impatience. He'd been waiting for her a long time. Not just tonight. Like her, he'd been waiting his whole life to find someone to love and be loved by.

She thought about turning on the heat and getting Blake riled enough to take her up to bed, but they still needed to talk about Ken. She wanted to feel Blake's hands and mouth on her body and know this dissension between them was over, but they'd never settle anything that way.

Blake pressed one long, soft kiss to her lips, tore his lips from hers, and stood up. Finding himself towering above her, he frowned and walked down the steps to the path. She stood on the second step to face him. Face-to-face. She appreciated his gesture. He understood her. Intimidating her with his size and height was an unfair advantage he never exploited with her.

"About Ken."

She sucked in a breath and opened her mouth to defend herself, but Blake touched his finger to her lips to stop her.

"Listen." He dropped his hand, and she closed her mouth. "Jeff told me today wasn't the first time Ken came after you. He found the two of you in the stable. Ken had backed you into a stall door. He said he came in just in time to save you before Ken did something suicidal."

Meaning Blake would kill him if he touched her.

She stepped down to the path and walked a few steps away, keeping her back to him.

She hated to think Ken was more than she could handle. She wanted to tell Blake, *It's fine. Nothing to worry about.* She'd keep her distance and avoid Ken at all costs.

Ken was a threat Blake wanted to eliminate. If some woman was causing Blake trouble, she'd want to protect him and get that person away from him at all costs. She couldn't blame him for wanting to do the same for her.

Ken was too aggressive, refusing to take a hint or even an outright snub. He didn't really have an interest in her outside the fact that he wanted to have sex with her. Ken's motivation for harassing her came from his underlying hatred of Blake. Ken wanted Blake's job, training the best horses and having the money that went with it.

"We managed to come to a compromise on Boots. Let's find a middle ground with Ken," Blake coaxed.

"There is no middle ground. He's an asshole. He'll always be an asshole. I want you to fire him." In over her head, she'd concede this one to Blake. Actually, she'd trust him to handle Ken for her. "The time in the stables isn't the only time he got too close."

"Now I'd really like to pound my fist into his face and make him bleed for touching you. Since that's useless, though it would be satisfying, I'll settle for the fact that Bud and I fired him today."

"What?"

"Your grandfather made it clear to everyone on this ranch. This is your home. Anyone who made it uncomfortable for you to be here, or did something that you didn't like, would be fired. No exceptions. No excuses. Ken's made a nuisance of himself with you. He's neglected his work. His primary job was to work with the horses that people board here. He's gotten into the habit of transitioning his work to others so he can spend time training the racehorses. I've warned him several times that he needed to do his job."

"I can't believe you guys actually fired him for me," she whispered, touched deeply.

"If someone had been making things difficult for Justin, you'd want them gone immediately. That's how your grandfather and I feel about you. As much as you want to take care of Justin and keep him safe, I want the same for you. You aren't alone anymore, Gillian. You don't have to take care of everything yourself."

"When I left, I didn't worry once about Justin. I knew I could count on you to take care of him." She closed the distance between them and stood on tiptoe to put her arms around his neck and look him in the eyes. "For the first time in my life, I let the worry slip away. I let someone else carry the burden. I didn't worry about Justin getting something to eat, that he got his bath and went to bed safe and sound. I didn't think about the problems with Ken. I sat and was quiet with myself, so I could hear what it is *I* want."

"What do you want, sweetheart?" He sat on the porch steps and drew her down onto his lap with her head on his shoulder.

"When I brought Justin here, I wanted him to have the childhood he deserved, a second chance to grow up like a normal kid. That was for him. I had no idea what I wanted for myself, but this place felt like the place I needed to be, too. Tonight, I realized I like helping run the ranch. I like working with the horses. I'd like to continue working with the sick and injured horses. Maybe take in more abused and neglected racehorses. I'll rehabilitate them. I'll help them find their way back to what they used to be, the way I did with Boots today."

"I think that's a great idea, sweetheart. You've done an amazing job with Boots. You're so diligent about learning everything you can from Dr. Potts and those books he gave you. I could probably learn a thing or two from you."

"I doubt that. But I love being with the horses. More than anything, Blake, I like being with you. I feel my best when I'm with you. I love you, Blake. I want to be here with you. This is my home, and I don't want anyone or anything to spoil it for us."

Blake scooped her off his lap and into his arms, stood, and walked into the house, kicking the door shut behind him with his boot. They'd talked enough for one night. He had a need for her that started somewhere deep inside him and flowed up to every part of him until his every breath was an ache of wanting her.

With determined strides, he took her up the stairs and into their room. He let loose her legs so she could slide down his body. He combed his fingers through the sides of her hair, held her head, and pulled her up to him. His mouth was a breath away when he whispered, "You're so beautiful." Out of words, from that moment on it was all heat and hands and mouths and sighs and pleasure.

Neither of them wanted to talk or think anymore tonight. They wanted to give in to their emotions and feel. So he pulled her shirt over her head and ran his rough palms down her soft arms and back up over her shoulders. She grabbed his sides. His muscles bunched.

She sighed and pulled him closer, her hands mapping the muscles in his back up to his shoulders.

He unclasped her bra and slid it down her shoulders, following its progress off her breasts and replacing the lace with his mouth. Hot, wet, openmouthed kisses made her skin heat and her nipples tighten. He traced soft circles on her other breast with his fingertips, making her sigh even more.

He wrapped his arms around her hips, lifted her off her feet, and laid her on the bed. He covered her with his body, cradled between her toned thighs. Her whole body eased into the mattress as she gave herself over to him. Not a surrender, but Gillian finally taking something for herself. He'd give everything in him to please and love her.

His fingers brushed, stroked, explored all the soft, wonderful places on her body that made her come alive with a sigh, a moan, and tug of his hair, demanding more. She lay beneath him, enjoying, taking.

He moved over her, pressing his chest to her hard-tipped breasts. She held his face in her hands and traced his bottom lip with her tongue before darting it inside to taste. He took the kiss deeper, and their tongues tangled as his hand slid down her side to her thigh. When he brought her leg up and pressed his hard cock to her core, she almost shattered right then.

Liquid fire in his arms. "Ah, God, Gillian, you make me burn."

He needed her completely naked. Now.

He trailed kisses down her neck, the underside of her breast, down her ribs to her hip. He undid her jeans, hooked his fingers into her lace panties, and dragged both barriers down her legs and right off her cute little feet.

He sat on the edge of the bed and found a condom in

the bedside table drawer. He removed his clothes, but that didn't stop her from caressing his back, kissing his shoulders and neck, sliding her hands around to grab his chest and hug him close. He sheathed himself and turned back, following her back down onto the bed. Cradled between her legs and in her arms, he thrust into her. Her hips rose to take him deep. Their slow pace gave them time to savor the feel of skin pressed to skin, and the intimacy of being joined so completely together in a way that transcended their bodies. He lowered his forehead to her hair and brushed a kiss on her ear. He thrust into her again, exhaled with pure pleasure, and whispered, "I love you."

Need overpowered their languid pace. He pressed her thighs wide, thrust deep, hard, and fast. They moved together and rose higher toward the peak that overtook them and sent them flying.

With his face buried in her hair, his lips pressed to her neck, and his thundering heart pressed to hers, he crushed her into the bed. He didn't think she minded too much, since her hands rested on his ass and one of her feet hooked over his calf. He'd poured everything he was into making love to her. He always did, but this time he hoped his love had finally filled all the empty places inside her.

She let out a gasp when he rolled over and dragged her across his chest, then wrapped his arms around her after pulling the blankets over them. He kissed the top of her head and brushed his hand over her hair and sighed, more content than he'd ever felt in his life. He felt the first tear touch his chest. She sighed and melted into him. He held her tighter with one arm and used the pad of his thumb to wipe her cheek as another tear slid down her pretty face.

"Ssshh, sweetheart. It's okay to let yourself be loved."

CHAPTER 27

The smell of roses and lilacs woke her. Lying on her stomach across the bed with her arms beside her head, she opened her eyes, expecting to see Blake lying beside her. Nothing but empty sheets and a single red rose lying on his pillow. A vase filled with roses and lilacs from the garden sat on the bedside table, along with a note. He'd picked her a bouquet. Lovely. Sweet. But the sun hadn't even come up, and he was gone. Why?

Sleep usually left her slowly, but waking up alone after making love to Blake in such spectacular fashion last night cleared her head quickly. She'd just woken up, and already she missed him.

She sat up and brought the rose to her nose, inhaled the heady scent, and closed her eyes. For a moment, she felt his lips on hers where the rose rested against her skin. She picked up the note and read it.

Gillian,
I've got a few things to do today in Bozeman. I'll be back later this evening. I miss you already.
                              Love, Blake

She threw back the covers and stood looking out the windows at the dawn of a new day. She couldn't spend the day in bed waiting for Blake to come home. A nice idea, but hardly productive. She showered and dressed and met the family in the kitchen at the breakfast table.

She leaned down and kissed Justin on the head. "Hey buddy, I'm sorry I left yesterday without talking to you."

"It's okay. Grandma made spaghetti for dinner. Blake ate his extra helpings of salad. He played battleships with me in the bath and read me a bunch of books before bed. We had a lot of fun."

It touched her heart to know that Blake took such good care of Justin in her absence.

She couldn't help but think for a moment what might have happened to Justin if her father had succeeded in killing her. Justin would have ended up in foster care. Maybe Justin would have come to live on the ranch anyway and have had Blake to look after him. If that had been the case, Blake would have been the father Justin deserved. Blake didn't play with Justin and watch over him just to score points with her. He did it because he genuinely cared.

"Gillian," her grandmother called, her voice sharp to get her attention.

"Hah. What?"

"Eat, dear. You're staring off into space. Don't worry. Blake will be home before you know it."

Her grandparents gave her patient smiles, and Justin smirked. If she didn't know better, she'd have thought something was going on with all of them. Justin bounced with energy this morning.

"I'd like you to take over training Diamond Deuce along with Boots," her grandfather said. "You and Jeff make a good team. I'd like the two of you to continue working together."

"Okay." She couldn't hide her excited smile. A great opportunity, she'd be responsible for the two horses and have a chance to prove herself to her grandfather and Blake.

That her grandfather showed such faith in her touched her deeply.

Jeff was a great source of information. He was good with the horses, but she connected with them in a way even Jeff couldn't figure out. When he couldn't get them to cooperate or respond, she managed to with little effort.

"Blake left a list of things for you to take care of today. If you could see to them, that would be great. Dee and I are taking Justin to school this morning, and then we have some errands. Is there anything you need from town?"

Odd. None of them left the ranch during the week. They usually ran errands on Saturday. She dismissed her concerns entirely when she saw the long list of things Blake wanted her to do. She'd be lucky to get lunch if she had any hope of completing the whole list.

"Blake wants all of this done today?"

"That's what he said." Her grandfather stood and took his coffee cup to the sink.

Blake put a lot of faith in her ability to accomplish everything on that list. Still, for him, she'd try to get it all done.

Her grandparents couldn't wait to get Justin out the door to school so they could run their errands. She worked nonstop through the day and barely had a minute to miss Blake or reflect on waking up to roses and lilacs. Every time she tried to get back to the house, someone distracted her and asked for her help in the stables or up at the track. As the sun set, she found herself beneath one of the tractors. One of the guys had accidentally snapped the oil line. By the time she was done fixing it, she was covered in grease and oil. Her hair was a tangled mess from lying in the dirt, and her muscles were sore from a long day tending the horses and working her way through Blake's list of chores.

Finally done, she lazily made her way to the house, thankful no one stopped her. That is, until she reached the porch and Grandma Dee greeted her on the steps.

"Gillian, you've got oil on your face, dear. Go on over to Blake's and get cleaned up." She handed Gillian a stack of clothes and a pair of sandals.

"Grandma, I'll just go upstairs and shower and be down for dinner."

"You can't, dear. There's a broken pipe. The water is off. Your grandfather is fixing it. I'm afraid you'll just have to use Blake's shower."

Too tired to argue, Gillian didn't fuss over the fact that her grandmother handed her a dress. She'd much rather put on her pajamas or slide into bed naked with Blake. Of course, she had no idea where he was, or when he'd be home. His phone went straight to voice mail every time she tried to call him.

"Go on, dear. Dinner will be ready soon."

"Okay. Um, have you heard from Blake?"

"He called a little while ago and said he'd be home shortly."

"That's good. I was getting worried."

"He's on his way. Go on, now. A nice shower will do you good. It'll put the glow back in your cheeks."

Blake could certainly put the glow back in her cheeks if he ever got his butt home. She could really use a kiss and a hug right about now. She'd like to curl up with him on the sofa and watch a movie and just relax in his arms.

Blake's house seemed too empty. She felt strange being here without him. His bed was perfectly made. Everything in the room was neat and clean. The only outward sign that this was his place was the hamper filled with his dirty clothes. He didn't spend any time in this room anymore. He slept with her in her bed. He only came back for his clothes and to shower. She wondered how long they'd continue to split their time between the two places. It seemed stupid for him to move his things into her bedroom. The man had his own house. Half of Justin's things were here, they spent so much time playing together.

How does a girl go about asking her boyfriend about moving in together?

She didn't know. They'd only been together for a couple months. Blake hadn't said anything about a permanent living arrangement. In fact, he seemed content with the way things were. Of course, they both wanted to be together, but she wasn't sure where Blake saw them in a year. Would they get married? Did he want to be married? Did he want to have children?

She wanted to be Blake's wife. She wanted that bond. She wanted to see him hold their child and love him the way he loved Justin. She put her hands over her belly and thought how wonderful it would be to have their baby growing inside her. They'd be a family. Oh, she wanted that very much.

Blake found her in his room. She walked out of the bathroom wearing a pretty dark pink dress, her hair still damp, hanging down her back. She stopped by the bed and stared down at it. Blake came up to her and wrapped his arms around her, then cupped her breasts in his hands and nuzzled her neck.

She sighed. "You're home." How much she missed him today infused those words.

"Thinking about me, sweetheart, and what we can do in that bed?"

"Would you rather be here?"

"I want to be where you are," he said without a second thought.

"You don't mind sleeping with me in the main house?"

"I don't mind sleeping with you anywhere." He ran his hands over her breasts and down her belly. He pulled her hips back and snuggled her bottom into his aching cock, groaning when she rubbed her hips against him.

She turned and wrapped her arms around his neck. "I'm serious. Do you miss having your own space, your own bed?"

Worried, he didn't think she was talking about sleeping in separate beds, but that's what it sounded like. "What's this about? Don't you want me with you at night?"

"I'm saying this wrong. This is your home, yet you barely spend any time here. You sleep with me every night at the big house because I need to be there in case Justin needs me. I wondered if it bothers you to be there with me, instead of here in your home?"

"I don't mind. We work so much, I enjoy the quiet time we share together in your room. It's not just the sex. I like that we talk and share our day."

He wasn't ready to talk to her about them living together permanently. Making her his wife took more planning than he'd expected. He could ask her now, but he wanted to surprise her. To distract her, he leaned down and kissed her until he was sure her mind had gone blank. Her soft lips and gentle demand for more made it easy for him to forget for a moment that he needed to get her back to her grandparents' house.

"Hungry?"

She smiled provocatively. "Oh, yeah."

He slid his hands down her hips and over her bottom. "That's not what I meant, but I like the way you think. Come on, I have a surprise for you."

He took her hand and walked her down the hall and out the front door.

"Who won the Hot Wheels trophy?"

"Championships are next week. Justin's second in the rankings behind Jeff."

"That makes you in third."

"Don't remind me." They walked across the field hand in hand. "You look so pretty tonight, sweetheart. I love that dress."

"Thanks, Grandma Dee picked it out, but I don't know why she gave it to me to wear tonight. Where did you go today?"

"You got my note, right?"

She stopped him outside the kitchen door. "Yes. And the flowers. They were beautiful, but I'd have rather woken up with you beside me."

He slipped his hand under the hair at her neck and drew her close. "Me, too. But I had to do something in Bozeman. It took longer than I thought." Three different jewelry stores to find exactly what he wanted, along with his other errands. "Come on. Justin is waiting."

He opened the door and she sighed.

"Oh God, that smells good. Grandma's been cooking up a storm. I'm starving."

"Your favorites. Vegetable beef stew, mashed potatoes, fresh bread."

"Let's eat."

"Come with me first." He kept her hand in his as he walked in front of her to the living room. He stopped and turned to her when they entered.

Her blank face made his gut clench. His heart stopped. Maybe he'd made a mistake. He glanced at Bud and Dee, Justin, his parents, and Gabe and Ella. All their smiles faltered at Gillian's silence.

The most beautiful sight Gillian had ever seen. Justin stood by her grandparents with a huge bouquet of pink roses. A "Happy Birthday" sign hung over the fireplace. Uncle Lumpy stood next to the mantel. She hadn't seen him since she and Justin had met him in town for lunch last week. Blake's parents stood beside her grandparents, smiling at her. Gabe and Ella, back from their honeymoon, sat together on the sofa, smiling at her.

Her grandmother had set the dining table in the other room with her fine china and silver. Crystal glasses sparkled in the chandelier's light around a centerpiece filled with flowers from the garden. A stack of presents covered the coffee table, beautifully wrapped with pretty, colorful bows.

She stared at Blake as the first tears fell from her eyes.

"I forgot . . . no one ever . . . I didn't expect . . ."

"Happy birthday, sweetheart. We know it was yesterday. Justin remembered. I thought about taking you out to dinner for another romantic evening."

She thought about the way they'd made love last night and how she'd woken up to roses and lilacs this morning. He'd been trying to make her birthday special. He'd succeeded in so many ways. She'd never felt more cherished or loved in her life.

"I thought you might like a family celebration."

She wrapped her arms around him. "It's perfect. It's the birthday party I always dreamed of having." She pressed her forehead to his chin and hugged him close. "It's better because I have you."

Justin came forward with his flowers and handed them to her. "Happy birthday, Gillian."

"Thank you, baby. The flowers are so pretty."

"Blake helped me pick them out."

"I love them." She turned to Blake's family. "I'm so happy you all came."

"Happy birthday, Gillian," Blake's mother said, a warm smile on her face.

"Thank you. Ella, how was the honeymoon?"

"Amazing."

"She says that about me all the time," Gabe teased, and received a friendly smack on the arm from his glowing bride.

The rest of the night was more fun and jokes, food and wine, presents and family. Gillian and Ella talked about her trip, clothes, New York, and horses. By the end of the night, Ella felt like a real friend. They'd even made plans to meet for lunch and go for a ride when Ella returned from a business trip to New York.

Blake had given her the perfect gift, aside from a gorgeous sparkling diamond heart necklace—a beautiful memory she'd never forget.

CHAPTER 28

Gillian stood outside the new mare's stall door, her arm outstretched to the spooked animal. The horse blew out her nostrils onto Gillian's hand and shied away again. Gillian would keep at it.

Dr. Potts had come by the ranch the day after her birthday party. With the support of Blake and Bud, she'd spoken to the doctor about what she'd like to implement here at the ranch. She was determined to see if she could do with another poor animal what she'd accomplished with Boots. Horse rehab. She wanted to rescue neglected and abused horses, get them well, retrain them, and find them good homes, maybe with a young child who'd adore them. Those she couldn't train and place would live out their lives pampered on the ranch with her.

Dr. Potts brought her Macey two days ago. In sorry shape, nearly starved to death, Macey had been rescued a week ago and taken to an animal shelter. Dr. Potts believed Gillian could do better. So far, she'd gotten the animal cleaned up, fed, and safely secured in the stall. Now, with a little time and patience, she'd teach Macey to trust her. She'd get her well again.

"Daydreaming about loverboy," Ken said from behind her.

Gillian stiffened. After two blissfully peaceful weeks without him on the ranch, she didn't want to see him. She didn't want him to spoil another day. "What are you doing here?"

He gave her a deceptively casual smile. "Just came to get my grooming box. It wasn't with my other stuff your boy toy left outside for me."

"Get it and go," she snapped.

Blake walked into the stable behind Ken. "Gillian, you ready to go?"

Gillian took her gaze from Ken long enough to catch Blake's ready-to-fight stance. His eyes remained locked on Ken. Her gaze shot back to the despicable man. Something sinister passed through his eyes before he turned away from her.

"Blake," Ken said snidely.

"Move on," Blake ordered.

"I was just saying hi to your girl and picking up my things."

"Leave *my girl* alone and get out."

"She's a pretty lady. Tastes like honey," he whispered as he passed Blake on his way out the door, laughing.

Blake felt the fire of rage rush through his system. He took a step to go after Ken to explain that last comment.

"Blake!" Gillian shook her head. "Don't give him the satisfaction. He's trying to pick a fight."

Blake checked Ken's progress out the doors over his shoulder.

"Is Justin ready to leave?" she asked to distract him from tearing Ken's head off.

Ken headed for his truck. Justin waited outside with the horses Blake had already saddled.

"Let it go, Blake. He's gone, and he's got no business coming back."

Gillian's eyes filled with worry as she waited for him to decide if they were going fishing at the river as Blake promised, or if he was going to kick Ken's ass.

"Justin's waiting," Blake finally said. "Are you ready to go?"

Relief washed away the worry, and so did her heavy sigh. "Yeah, let's go. He's been begging to go fishing for weeks."

"Well, I did promise that I'd take him, but time seems to have gotten away."

That was certainly true. May had been a busy month. They'd gone to Gabe and Ella's wedding and had her birthday, and last week they'd taken Boots to his first race since being rescued and brought to Three Peaks Ranch. He'd placed third. Not bad. He'd do better at the next race. Gillian had no doubt.

Blake had been a wreck leading up to that first race. Boots refused all riders except her. Blake had nearly made himself sick with worry that she'd actually ride in the race. Trying her best to live up to her promise not to do so again, she'd found a young kid who wanted a shot but hadn't been given a chance to prove himself. She'd put him up on Boots, and he'd taken him around the track at a breakneck speed that had stunned even Blake. Rider and horse had bonded over an apple. Adam rode Boots in the race to Blake's satisfaction.

Saddled up and ready to go, she followed behind Blake and Justin, her face raised to the bright sun. A perfect day for a short ride and dropping a hook in the river for an hour or so to get it out of Justin's system. He'd begged Blake nonstop for two days for this long-overdue outing.

Justin rode Spunk all by himself. "You're doing a great job, buddy," Blake praised.

"Grandpa said Spunk is just my speed."

"Grandpa was right. Spunk is real gentle. You're doing a great job riding him just like Blake taught you." Gillian smiled her encouragement. "Blake, what are those delivery trucks doing at your house?" she asked.

"I'm having something delivered." He kicked his horse into a trot. "Come on, Justin. The river is just up ahead."

Gillian frowned at Blake's vague answer but forgot about it completely when they reached the river and the beautiful rushing water, just past a pretty meadow of green grass and purple and white wildflowers.

Blake laid out the quilted blanket and picnic basket. They enjoyed the potato salad, cold fried chicken, fruit salad, and crusty French bread. Blake spoiled her with all her favorites. He did little things like that all the time. Every day, he found some small way to show her how much he loved her.

Justin remained overly excited and bounced on his butt the whole time he ate. He talked a mile a minute with Blake about fishing poles and casting, and he taunted Blake he'd catch the most fish. Blake was wonderfully playful and egged on Justin that he'd kick his butt and catch more. The smile on Justin's face said it all—he was happy. Exactly why she'd brought him to the ranch. Living here had given Justin so much more than a chance at a normal childhood. He had a father in Blake.

Unable to help the emotions filling her heart, she reached for Blake's neck and drew him to her for a long kiss. She poured all the love she had into it until the tenderness of the kiss sent tears to her eyes.

"Ah, yuck," Justin said from beside them.

Blake smiled against her lips and made her laugh with him. "What was that for, sweetheart?"

"For being you. I love you, Blake. You're a good man."

Without taking his eyes off Gillian, he asked Justin, "How about we get your fishing pole and see if you can't catch a fish, buddy."

"Yay! Finally."

Blake ran his hand through Gillian's hair. "Wait here. I'll set Justin up with his pole, and then I need to talk to you."

She nodded. Blake walked Justin the ten feet to the riverbank and up onto a flat-topped rock several boulders out into the rushing water.

Gillian packed up their picnic. Blake returned to the blanket and sat, plucking her from her spot beside him and settling her between his legs, her back braced against his chest. His arms wrapped around her. They stared off into the distance and Justin happily holding his fishing pole, calling the fish to come to him.

Blake's heart thundered in his chest. Could Gillian feel it? Alone with her finally, he grew nervous to talk to her. He took a deep breath and let it out.

"That was a big sigh. What's wrong?"

"Nothing." He brushed his fingers down her hair and leaned over her so he could see her face. "Gillian?"

"Yeah." She sat up and watched Justin jump to another rock, several feet from the really fast moving water. Blake had already warned him to stay near the shore and the slower current.

"You know I love you."

She shifted and studied his face, reaching up to place her palm against his cheek. "I love you, too."

"We only met a few short months ago, but I feel like

I've known you my whole life. We have a lot in common. We can talk about anything. You're my best friend."

"I feel the same way about you." She took her hand from his face and placed it on his chest over his heart. Her eyes filled with concern.

"Justin is a great kid. I love him. You're a great mother to him."

"I try to be. He has you to look after him, too."

Blake smiled. That was exactly his point. "Yes. I want to look after him. I want us to be a family together."

"We are, Blake. You are exactly the kind of man I want in his life."

"I want to be a permanent part of his life—and yours. I want to help you raise Justin and have children of our own."

Her eyes went wide with surprise. They'd been sleeping together for months, but they'd never discussed having children. She was on the pill, and except for letting him know that they were protected, they hadn't discussed it further.

"Blake, are you saying you want to have a baby?"

"Yes. Whenever you're ready, I'd like that very much. I never thought about having kids until I met you." He looked at Justin with his fishing pole and the smile on his face. His joy was Blake's.

He should tell Justin to move back closer to the shore, but lost the thought when an image of Gillian pregnant with their baby popped into his mind.

"I'd like to see you pregnant with my child. I'd like to see you with our baby pressed to your heart." He slid his hand up her side, leaned in, and kissed her softly. With his hand over her heart, hers over his, and his face an inch from hers, he looked into her eyes and asked, "Gillian, will you marry me?"

Her eyes got even wider and a beautiful smile bloomed on her lips a split second before she fisted her hand in his shirt and dragged him to her for a wildly urgent kiss.

He pulled her down on top of him; her body pressed the length of his. She pecked kisses on his mouth, his cheeks, his jaw. Happy and excited, she forgot to answer him.

"Is that a yes?"

"Yes, Blake. Oh, God, yes. I can't wait to marry you." She kissed him again.

This time, he cupped the back of her neck and slowed her excitement, making her concentrate on the passion between them. When she pulled back and smiled at him, he almost lost his breath. He'd never seen her this happy.

Her eyes narrowed with concern. "Tell me this isn't a dream, Blake. Tell me this is real."

"As real as my love for you. I can't live without you, sweetheart. I want you to be my wife, the mother to my kids, and my best friend for the rest of our days. We'll move into the house. The trucks were delivering Justin's new bedroom furniture. We'll spend our lives together raising Justin, our kids, and working here on the ranch. It's the life I never knew I wanted until I found you. Now it's all I think about." He held her tight, and she laid her forehead to his.

He gave her a mischievous grin. "Do you want your ring?"

"I want you, Blake. Only you. Always you."

Humbled beyond words, he hugged her close. She meant it. If she only had him, it would be enough.

He held up the ring in its case in front of her anyway. Her eyes lit with excitement and filled with tears.

"Forget what I said, I want the ring, too."

He laughed outright, leaned up, and gave her a smacking kiss. "I thought you might like it."

"What isn't to like? It's gorgeous."

He pulled the brightly sparkling, three-stone diamond ring from the black velvet box and slid it on her finger. The round stones sparkled in the light. "The past. Our present. Our future. You, me, and Justin, and the promise of a happy forever."

She pulled the hair away from her face as the wind whipped up. Tears slid from her eyes.

"Don't cry, sweetheart. It kills me when you cry."

"It's just the wind in my eyes," she lied sweetly to ease his discomfort.

He kissed away a tear, rolled her under him, and took her mouth in a passionate kiss. The world fell away, and he melted into her. He settled between her thighs, his aching cock pressed to her core. She rolled her hips and rubbed against him, sending a shudder of desire racing through his veins.

She tore her mouth from his, the bright smile returned to her lips. "Let's tell Justin."

"Aaahhh!"

The splash doused their happy moment with dread.

"Justin!" Gillian screamed.

Blake rolled off her and up to his feet, reaching down to take her hand and pull her up. They ran for the bank. Gillian sprinted along the shore until she reached a relatively deep part of the river. She jumped into the swirling, rushing water. Desperate to reach her brother, she swam hard, but the weight of her clothes and the bite of the ice-cold water made it hard to swim.

Justin flapped his arms, trying to keep his head above the water just up ahead. She used the quick current and her frantic strokes to get to him. She grabbed him around the waist and pulled him to her chest. She hoisted him as high as she could to keep his face out of the water.

Blake called to them, his voice filled with desperation. "Swim at an angle back to the shore!"

Debris hit her from all around. Wood and rocks seemed to jump up and hit her when she least expected. A set of really large boulders loomed in the distance. The water rushed around them in white-capped waves. No other choice; either the current carried her right into them, or she moved farther away from shore to avoid them. She needed to get Justin out of the water. His head bobbed back and forth, his whole body shook terribly, and his lips and eyelids had turned blue. Tired, her legs sluggish, she struggled with every ounce of energy she had left to keep Justin in her arms and above water.

The boulders grew larger. At the last possible moment, she turned her back and took the hit. Water pounded her against the boulders, holding her against them.

She caught a glimpse of Blake's face a second before he pulled Justin free and the water rushed over her head and pushed her down. Her feet hit the bottom, and she pushed as hard as she could at an angle and managed to come up and pound against another boulder before the current sucked her under again. Blake grabbed her hair and pulled. Once her head cleared the water, he reached down and grasped her arm.

He hated to handle her so harshly, but he had to grab her now or lose her to the rushing current. His muscles burned, but he ignored the ache.

"Come on, sweetheart. Help me. Try to use your feet to push up." He kept pulling, but the rushing water threatened to rip her out of his grasp. He couldn't let that happen. He couldn't lose her now. Not when they had their whole lives together ahead of them.

He nearly lost her, but she pushed, and he pulled her up the boulder and into his chest. He held her tight and pressed his face into her freezing hair.

"I've got you, sweetheart. I've got you." He thanked God he'd gotten her. Water poured out of her mouth. She shook uncontrollably, coughed and spit, trying to get her breath. If he hadn't reached her in time, she would have drowned. That thought stopped his heart and choked off his air.

Justin wasn't any better. He'd curled into a tight ball on the boulder beside them. In bad shape, he hadn't really opened his eyes. His teeth chattered, and his lips and fingers were blue.

Blake had no idea how he was going to get both of them back to the horses and home. He couldn't carry both of them.

"Take Jus-s-stin," Gillian stammered. "T-take him . . . get him h-help."

"I can't leave you here."

"Yes, you can. You have t-to. You can't t-take us b-both. He's freezing."

She had no idea she was in just as bad shape as Justin. She loved him so much that she wasn't thinking about herself. No changing her mind. Blake hated to do it, but he picked up Justin. Nothing but pure adrenaline and Justin's condition got Gillian up on her feet. She swayed, but managed to pull herself upright. He admired her strength and determination.

Gillian carefully walked from the boulders to the smaller rocks. She tried desperately not to show Blake how hard it was just to stay on her feet. Each step took all her focus and willpower. She trudged through knee-deep water to get to the shore. She faltered again and fell to her knees.

Blake held Justin in his arms, but managed to lean down, grip her arm, and haul her back up to her feet. "Wrap your arm around mine and lean on me. I'll get you back to the horses."

She did what he asked, but no way could she ride. Her body wanted to give out. She shook so bad her bones ached. Her teeth chattered so much she was surprised she didn't chip a tooth.

She hadn't realized how far downriver they'd gone. Once she was warm and had her wits about her, she'd realize just how lucky she and Justin were to be alive. At the moment, her mind wanted to shut off. All she could do was put one foot in front of the other and follow Blake where he led.

Feet from their picnic, unable to hold on any longer, she slid down Blake's arm and body. He couldn't grab her with Justin in his arms. She hit the ground hard and struggled to put her hands down to push herself back up. No use. Energy zapped, she lay in the soft grass, exhausted.

"Grab the blanket. Take Justin's coat and shirt off. Wrap him in the blanket and take him home," she pleaded.

Blake laid Justin beside her in the sun. "Sweetheart, you're shaking so hard. I need to get you warm."

"Justin," she said weakly. "Please, Blake."

He tore Justin's wet clothes off him, grabbed the blanket, and dragged it out from under their picnic. The basket and food tumbled to the ground in a heaping mess. He wrapped Justin, hoping the little guy woke up.

Justin's eyes fluttered open. "I'm so cold, Blake."

"I know, buddy." Blake scooped him up and held

him in his arms, rubbing his hands over his back to try to warm him up and get his blood flowing.

"Take him, Blake."

Blake leaned over with Justin in his arms and kissed Gillian's forehead. "God, sweetheart, I'm sorry. I don't want to leave you."

"Go." Her eyelids fell closed.

He considered laying her over the saddle and tying her on, but he couldn't take the chance that she'd fall off and get trampled. He wished he'd brought one of the two-way radios. His cell phone didn't work out here. Damn. No other options, he took Justin. He'd get him home and rush back to get Gillian. No way he lost her now.

CHAPTER 29

Gillian heard the horse coming, its snort and hooves walking across the meadow from the direction of the trees. Anxious for Blake to rescue her, she opened her eyes, wondering why he'd come from the wrong direction. Her hopes sank to dread when Ken dismounted beside her.

A jolt of adrenaline hit her. Trouble haunted her life and had come calling again. Ken smiled without a hint of kindness, his eyes filled with fury. She'd avoided that something stupid he was bound to do until now.

"I thought those two would never leave, though I thought Blake would be the one to jump in after the kid and they'd both wash away."

"You pushed Justin in?"

"You got me fired, you fucking bitch. Blake's made sure I can't get a job anywhere. You owe me, and I came to collect."

"I thought you left." She tried to get up but fell back to the ground. She scooted away, but he took a menacing step closer. No way she'd get away this time. Ever since he'd left weeks ago, she'd stopped carrying the wrench around. Not that it would do her any good now, when she had the strength of a baby in her condition.

"I followed you out here. A touching moment, really. That's a big-ass fucking ring. You, on the other hand, look like a drowned cat. That river is colder than a witch's tit. The wind blows any harder, you'll freeze to death before Blake gets Justin back to the ranch. Guess it's up to me to warm you up right."

The relentless wind felt like razor blades slicing against her skin.

Ken leaned down, grabbed her arms, and pulled her up and over his shoulder. She dangled down his back as he walked to his horse and swung up in the saddle. He had to rein in the dancing mount as it shied from their combined weight and Ken's awkward rise into the saddle. Mostly dead weight, she lay over his shoulder limp as a rag doll. He brought her down in front of him with a grunt, settling her in front of him. He wrapped his arms around her to hold the reins and set out across the meadow toward the tree line with the horse going at a fast trot.

"Where are you taking me?"

"My out-of-the-way place. Someplace no one will hear you scream for me."

Those ominous words sent a chill through her frozen body. So cold, she couldn't even hold onto the saddle pommel to keep herself steady. Her blue fingers refused to move. She tried not to lean into him or scoot her bottom further into his groin. No use, her body wouldn't do what her brain told it to do. She slumped against him, barely able to stay upright at all. It only took a minute to realize exactly what was pressed against her bottom. He rubbed against her backside. He moved in the saddle far more than the horse's gait made necessary.

She cringed and shoved her elbow into his belly. He

ignored her. "Stop," she yelled, panicked this had gone too far.

"You are one fine piece of ass. I'm going to fuck you good. You'll be warm and hot in no time, baby." He nibbled on her neck and bit hard enough to get her to settle down, making her scream in pain.

"Stop," she begged. He didn't. Last resort—if she couldn't stop him, she'd stop the horse. She grabbed the reins and tugged hard, hurting the poor animal. She hated to be aggressive with the horse, but she had to get away from Ken.

The horse skidded to a jarring stop. She swung her leg over the horse's neck, breaking Ken's hold, and fell hard to the ground. Lightning shot up her feet and legs when she landed. She let her shoulder take the brunt of her fall as she tipped over like a felled tree onto the dirt and grass. She tried to keep her face from skidding in the dirt, but it was just no use. She could barely move anymore. The shaking and the cold went down to her bones. She might just shatter into a million pieces. She wondered if she'd ever be warm again.

Ken dismounted a few feet away, closed the distance, rolled her over, and sat on her hips. He ripped open her shirt, buttons popping as he spread it wide.

Blake, her mind screamed. She didn't have the energy to scream herself.

Ken leaned down and kissed her. She tried to turn away, so he grabbed her jaw and held her in place. "You cost me my job. Time to pay up." He smashed his mouth to hers again, and then he licked her cheek, her jaw locked tightly in his grasp.

"Yeah, you taste like honey."

No way she let this asshole defile her.

No way she let another man tear her down when she had a man who wanted to lift her up.

The fury gave her strength. She reached between them and grabbed his balls, squeezing as hard as she could. He bellowed and grabbed her wrist, pulling her hand away, but she held on as long as she could. His whole face flushed red with rage.

She threw a right cross and hit him in the eye. He fell back but came forward. She used the last of her energy to rear up and head-butt him in the cheek. She fell back, exhaustion stealing the last of her energy. Her head hurt like hell. Ken's fist rushed toward her face, until a flash of brown leather crossed her blurry vision and Blake's boot connected with Ken's jaw. The bastard fell off her and landed in the dirt.

Ken rolled to his knees, spit blood, swiped the back of his hand across his mouth, and jumped to his feet to take on Blake.

Blake saw red. A kick in the face was just the beginning. Blake stalked Ken. Not finished with the fight, out for blood, he'd bury the bastard.

In a mindless rage, Blake went after Ken and punched him in the mouth. He ignored the sting in his knuckles, cocked his arm back, and swung again, clipping Ken in the eye Gillian had already made swell. Ken fell back but came out swinging, nailing a shot into Blake's gut. Blake pushed Ken back by the shoulder and returned the favor. Ken stayed on his feet, but Blake swung again and got him in the jaw, sending his head snapping to the side before he caught his balance and swung back at Blake. Blake feinted out of the way and punched Ken in the face again.

Ken stumbled back into Uncle Lumpy's chest. The

big man grabbed Ken by the shoulders and spun him around to face him.

"He's gone crazy. Stop him," Ken pleaded.

"You know what they do to rapists in jail? You're going to find out, asshole." Uncle Lumpy cracked him in the jaw with a meaty fist.

Ken fell to his knees, swayed, and fell back onto the dirt.

Blake leaned down, grabbed him by the shirt, and hauled him up. "I told you, touch her, and I'll fuck you up." Blake punched him in his fucking face again.

"Blake. Enough. Stop."

Gillian's soft voice penetrated his rage-induced haze. She leaned against his back and slid down. He shoved Ken away, turned, and caught Gillian before she hit the ground again.

"Gillian? Gillian, baby. Can you hear me?"

"Stop," she said weakly. "Please stop."

Ken tried to get up. Uncle Lumpy grabbed him by the collar and dragged him ten feet away, then tossed him back to the ground. Ken tried to get up again, and Uncle Lumpy slammed his biker-booted foot into Ken's chest and held him down.

"Don't move, fucker, or I'll make sure you never move again."

A couple of the other men rode in from the ranch. Blake left them to help Uncle Lumpy get Ken back to the ranch. He touched his fingers to Gillian's too-pale face, and the rage slid away. His focus shifted from killing Ken to taking care of the woman he loved. He gently picked her up. So cold, her eyelids and lips were purplish blue. She looked like a ghost.

Three guys from the ranch waited beside his horse.

"Jeff, can you help me up." Jeff and two other guys

supported Blake's back. He put his foot in the stirrup, and they helped him into the saddle without him having to let go of Gillian.

"You guys bring Ken back to the ranch. I'll have Bud call the sheriff to arrest his ass for assaulting Gillian."

Jeff's gaze went to Blake's bloody knuckles. "You okay, man?"

"Fine. Gillian needs the help."

"We'll see you back at the ranch," Jeff said.

Marty and Tim dragged Ken toward the waiting horses. Blood ran from Ken's nose, mouth, and the cut on his cheek where Gillian nailed him.

Blake didn't give a shit if the guy's face rotted off in prison.

He settled Gillian in his lap, then pressed his lips softly to her forehead. "I love you, Gillian. I'm so sorry." He held her limp body close. "I'm taking you home now. You're safe. I'll take care of you."

When she didn't respond or even blink, he kicked his horse and sent the animal flying over the field. He held onto Gillian and went as fast as his horse could safely carry them. Gillian had been in her cold, wet clothes for far too long. Shock had set in. She wasn't shaking or trembling anymore. A very bad sign.

He held her tighter and rode hard to the house, praying she'd wake up and be okay.

CHAPTER 30

Bud and Dee met Blake on the porch when he got to the house. Blake swung his leg over the horse's neck, slid off the saddle, and landed hard on his feet with Gillian's lifeless body in his arms.

"Bud, call the sheriff. Ken attacked Gillian." That's all he could say. If he said anymore, he'd get angrier and do something stupid. Gillian was all that was important right now. Bud would take care of Ken.

Bud beat him to the door and opened it for him. He took Gillian inside. Bud went to the gun cabinet, unlocked it, and pulled out a rifle and bullets. "He's not leaving this ranch until the sheriff arrives. If he tries, he won't leave here alive."

Bud grabbed the phone, and Blake took the stairs up two at a time.

Dee kept at his heels. "I made a warm bath for her."

"How's Justin?" he asked over his shoulder and took Gillian into the bathroom.

He laid her out on the floor and cupped her face in his trembling hands. She was everything to him. He couldn't stand thinking about what she'd been through over the last half hour. She deserved so much better.

She looked out for everyone else and always put herself last. She'd made him leave her behind for Justin's sake, but it didn't soothe his conscience.

"He's better. He soaked in the tub for about ten minutes. I got some hot broth into him, and we tucked him into bed. He was too tired to keep his eyes open once I got the liquids into him. I'll check on him again in a minute."

"That's good. He'll get a good night's sleep, and he should be fine."

Unconcerned with Gillian's modesty, especially with her shirt open and her bra-covered breasts showing, he stripped off all her clothes. She'd hit her shoulder hard. A large bruise darkened under her milky white skin. The bruise on her forehead looked worse. The lump had swollen to the size of a golf ball. He hoped she didn't have a concussion. He went back and forth asking himself if he should take her to the hospital. At the moment, he didn't want to let her out of his sight or his reach. Touching her and seeing her was the only thing keeping him sane at the moment. And it was a tenuous hold at best. Especially when her hair slipped to the floor, revealing the bite mark on her neck.

Set on his task to get her warm, he undid her jeans and pulled them down her legs. She tried to curl into a ball to stop him. He put his hands on her thighs and held her legs down.

"No more. Stop," she begged.

"Gillian, sweetheart, it's me." He leaned over and pressed his forehead to her cheek, then whispered in her ear, "It's me. Blake. You're okay. You're home. I'm going to get you into a warm bath."

"Blake?"

"Yeah, sweetheart. It's me."

"I'm tired. So cold." She tried to curl up again, but he held her, and her strength gave out again.

Blake had to stay close to her to even hear her. He looked up at Dee.

"She'll be okay. Get her in the bath. I'll get some broth. Something warm in her stomach will go a long way to making her feel better."

"I shouldn't have left her." He gently laid her in the tub still wearing her bra and panties. She squirmed and moaned in pain, her skin extrasensitive to the warmth of the water. In another minute, the heat would work its way into her body and ease her discomfort.

Once she relaxed into the water's warmth, he sat back on his heels and took off his own wet coat and shirt. He'd get out of the rest of his wet clothes when he settled Gillian in bed.

Dee came back in with a mug of warm broth. He held it to Gillian's lips and coaxed her to drink it down. He got half into her before he let her rest. He turned the hot tap on and warmed up the bath even more. Her pale skin finally warmed to a healthy glow, and her blue lips turned back to a dusky pink.

He took a washcloth and washed her face. He rinsed out her hair. She opened her eyes a slit and watched him. The first tears spilled down her cheeks.

He cupped her face in his palm. "It's okay. You're safe. I swear he'll never touch you again. I'll take care of you."

"I know you will." She shuddered with sheer relief. Still, her chin trembled and the tears silently fell. Traumatized, she needed time to settle her emotions. Once he got her out of the tub, he'd hold her close and let her sleep.

"Are you okay? I should take you to the hospital, or at least the clinic and have Dr. Bell check you out."

"I'm fine. Warmer. Need to stay . . . with you."

"You're sure? If something happened to you . . ."

"Mmm, I'm fine. Tired . . . that's all."

"Your grandparents got Justin warm and settled into bed. He's okay. I promise."

"I knew you'd take care of him." The words were slurred, but she got them out.

"Ah, sweetheart, I shouldn't have left you behind. I had no idea Ken was still on the property. I never thought he'd try anything with you again. I'm so damn sorry I left you."

"He just wanted to get back at me. And you." She took his right hand and the washcloth. As she lay nearly naked in the tub, she gently washed the cuts on his bruised and swollen knuckles. When he hissed in pain, she took his fingers and brought them to her lips and kissed them, one after the other. No one had ever stood up for her. No one had ever come to her rescue. She had no doubt Blake had meant to kill Ken for laying a hand on her. Glad she'd stopped him, she didn't want Blake to suffer any consequences for saving her.

"Thank you for saving me."

"Sweetheart, that was pure selfishness. I just can't live without you. Justin can't live without you." He pulled his hand from her grasp and touched her face. He just needed to keep touching her to reassure himself that she was alive and safe.

He helped her out of the tub. She stood on wobbly legs. After stripping off her wet panties and bra, he wrapped a towel around her, sat her on the toilet cover, and used another towel to gently dry her. He didn't want to take her to bed with her hair wet, so he snagged the hair dryer and kept working his fingers through the thick, dark mass until the strands were fairly dry and the gold, red, and brown tones changed with each pass of the dryer.

Her head slowly fell forward. Her eyes were closed when he picked her up and carried her into her room, completely tapped out. He set her on her feet just long enough to take the damp towel off her and pull the bed-covers back.

"Get in, sweetheart. You need to sleep." She slipped into bed, and he tucked her in. She grabbed his hand and held tight.

"Stay with me, Blake. I don't want to be alone."

He leaned over and kissed her softly on the lips. "I need to go downstairs and make sure Bud, Uncle Lumpy, and the sheriff took care of Ken."

"Don't go, please."

Her nails dug into his hand. He felt, in the tremble that rocked her whole body, her frantic need for him to stay. He brushed his other hand through her hair. He couldn't leave her. Not when she was too scared to let him go.

"Okay, honey. I'll stay with you." He'd left her once already. He wouldn't do it again. She had never let her-self need someone, and he wasn't going to let her think it was a mistake to need and trust him now.

He slipped out of the rest of his wet clothes and boots and into bed beside her. He brushed a soft kiss against the lump on her head and wrapped her in his arms, tight against his chest. She pressed her palm to his heart. He looked down. The diamond ring he'd placed on her finger not more than an hour ago twinkled in the soft light. He sighed and held her closer, so damn happy to have her here with him, safe and sound.

The soft knock drew his attention to the door, and Gillian jumped, even in her sleep. He held her close, tucked under his chin, her head on his chest, to let her know she was okay.

"Yeah," he called softly.

Dee opened the door. "I see she's got everything she needs."

"Everything all right downstairs?"

"The sheriff took Ken a few minutes ago. In addition to the charges for hurting Gillian, he's wanted in Texas for sexual assault and battery. Bud is downstairs in the library having a drink with Uncle Lumpy." Dee rolled her eyes at the man's name. It's all he'd answer to, so they all went with it. "The sheriff wants to talk to Gillian tomorrow. He needs to know what happened to her while she was alone with Ken. He needs to know if . . ."

"He didn't rape her." Blake hadn't meant to raise his voice. Gillian stirred next to him and wrapped her arms around his back and pulled him to her tighter. He didn't deserve to have her love him so much. He couldn't shake the feeling that he'd failed her. He'd promised to protect her, whether he'd spoken the promise or made it in silence. He and Bud had both promised that this was her home, and she'd be safe here. She and Justin. Today, he hadn't kept that promise. They had hired a rapist and put Gillian in harm's way every day that she'd been here with Ken.

Dee read his turmoil. "You couldn't have known. The background check Bud ran was before the charges were filed. She won't blame you for what happened, so don't blame yourself."

"I promised her she'd be safe here."

"She is safe here. Ken was a problem waiting to happen. Whatever happened with her and Ken, she handled it. You got to her in time."

"She shouldn't have had to handle it!" Blake reined in his rage, brushing his hand down Gillian's hair to calm her, too.

"You can't be everywhere. Ken is in jail, where he belongs. He won't be coming back here to cause trouble."

"I should have fired him the first day, before he had a chance to fixate on her. He was causing trouble from day one."

"Shoulda. Coulda. Woulda. We could do that all night. The fact of the matter is Gillian is going to be fine. Give her some credit. She'll wake up tomorrow morning, talk to the sheriff, and put this all behind her."

"I brought this all on her."

"No. You didn't. Besides, look what she's gotten from being here. She has a family. She has you." She waited until Blake looked at her. "She's wrapped around you like you're a part of her. She's wearing your ring. You love each other. She's happy. You're going to have a happy life together. You belong together.

"If you want to take credit for the rest, you've got to take some credit for the good things that have happened to her. She's blossomed here. And Justin is a vibrant, happy little boy."

The words began to sink into Blake's thick skull.

"You'll see tomorrow. Gillian won't blame you. She's a fighter. If I know my girl, had she been able to fight against Ken, she'd have kicked his ass."

"Amen to that." He leaned down and kissed the top of Gillian's head as her breath lightly whispered over the skin at his throat as she slept. Even in her weakened condition, she'd gotten in her licks. The door closed softly. Dee was right. Gillian wouldn't blame him for what happened. She loved him.

CHAPTER 31

Gillian woke him in the predawn hour with hot, open-mouthed kisses up his chest and neck to his waiting mouth. She pressed against him and pushed him to his back. She kissed his jaw and lay on top of him. His hands settled on her hips, and she whispered in his ear, "I need you wrapped around me."

He felt the exact same way. They both needed this closeness and connection. It told him more than any reassurance she gave him last night that she was okay.

Her breasts pressed to his chest and her legs slid against his. Her soft skin felt so good against him. He ran his hands up her back and down again. His splayed fingers cupped her bottom, and he pressed her down snug against his erection. She kissed his neck, then leaned up, grabbed the condom from the side table, and tore it open. In one quick motion, she sheathed him. He slid his hands up her ribs to cover her breasts and she slid forward, then pressed down and took him into her warmth. She kept her body tightly pressed to him and rocked back and forth. That shimmer of desire he'd felt upon waking to her kissing him exploded into an all-consuming need. He liked her as the aggressor, leading him where she wanted him to go. He gripped her hips and held on for the journey.

Gillian had to be close to him. She pressed her body to his and rubbed her breasts against his chest as she moved slowly over him. His jaw was rough against her lips. She flicked her tongue out to taste his neck and pressed her lips to the pounding pulse in his throat. He groaned deeply and dug his fingers into her hips, pressing into her deep. She rolled her hips, and that sparkle inside her glimmered and glowed.

His hands slid over her back, down over her bottom and thighs, until they came back to grip her hips. The lazy pace she'd woken him up to was overcome by need that drove them ever faster to the final crest. He thrust, one last deep push, and emptied himself in her as her body tightened around his. Her breath exploded from her lungs on a satisfied moan.

He dug his hand into her hair and held her head to his chest. His other hand rested on the curve of her hip. When she snuggled into him, he relaxed.

"Good morning, love," he whispered.

"Mmm, it is when I wake up with you."

She went downstairs an hour later to meet Blake and everyone else for breakfast. A hot shower had loosened the muscles that making love to Blake hadn't after her ordeal yesterday. Blake, Justin, and Grandma Dee sat at the kitchen table. Their concerned gazes locked on her when she entered. Grandpa spoke quietly with the sheriff in the living room. When the two men saw her, their eyes clouded with worry.

"Good morning, Sheriff. I believe I owe you my statement about what happened yesterday. How about we use the library?"

"That'll be fine." He nodded.

She went to her grandfather and wrapped her arms around him. "Thank you for taking care of Justin yesterday. I knew he could count on you, just like I can." She held him tight for a moment. She didn't miss the shine in his eyes when she stepped back.

A half hour later, she found them all sitting at the table in the kitchen. Justin was happily stealing whipped cream from his mug of hot chocolate and licking it off his finger. She went up behind him and kissed him on the head before going to Blake and sitting in his lap. She wrapped her arms around his neck and held him close as his arms wrapped around her.

"You okay, sweetheart?"

"I am now," she said and kissed him softly.

They watched and waited to see if she'd fall apart or blame them for what happened.

"The sheriff will charge Ken with attempted murder and assault," she said instead.

"Wait. What?" Blake asked. "Attempted murder?"

"He pushed Justin into the river, hoping Blake would go in after him and they'd both die so he could have me."

"Justin, buddy, why didn't you say anything?" Blake asked.

Justin stared at his hands in his lap.

"It's okay, honey. You were scared, and that's okay," Gillian said.

"I thought I'd get to talk to the sheriff, too. Too bad you didn't have your wrench with you. You could have hit him again to keep him from hurting you."

"What do you mean, Justin?" Grandpa looked at Blake, puzzled. Blake turned his angry gaze on her.

"Ken was sitting on top of her behind the barn by one of the trucks. She grabbed a wrench and hit him and bloodied his face."

They all looked at Gillian with anger and accusation in their eyes that she'd kept that to herself.

"What? He didn't want Blake to find out that he'd hit me with a riding crop and cut my arm. Or that he'd made several passes at me. I let him know I wasn't going to take his shit."

"You have to eat extra vegetables," Justin chimed in.

"She gets that one for free," Blake said to Justin. "She deserves it after having to deal with Ken alone."

"I'm never alone. I have all of you. Blake, I know it makes you angry that I tried to take care of the matter on my own. It wasn't because I didn't think you'd help me or couldn't take care of it for me. I needed to know that I could take care of myself. I couldn't let him take that from me. Not after everything that's happened."

He wasn't quite ready to stop blaming himself.

"Besides, you saved me when I couldn't save myself. I knew you were coming back. I knew you'd help me. I knew that you guys," she looked at her grandparents, "would take care of Justin for me. I knew I could count on my family."

The weight of guilt that they hadn't done more to protect her faded from them.

Gillian held her arms out to her brother, and he came to her and crawled onto her lap. They sat together on Blake, and he wrapped his arms around the both of them.

Gillian held her hand out to Justin and showed him her diamond ring. He held her hand and turned her finger and watched the light sparkle in the diamonds.

"Justin, Blake asked me to marry him. I'm going to be his wife, and we're going to live in his house on the other side of the property. You'll live with us."

She looked at her grandparents and hoped they

weren't too disappointed. Their smiles told her they weren't. They were happy. They'd all still see each other every day.

"Blake asked me if he could marry you. I told him it was okay," Justin said.

Gillian stared at Blake, tears shimmering in her eyes. So sweet he'd ask for her brother's permission.

"So, Blake will be my dad?"

"No, honey. He's going to be your brother. But he'll be like a father to you. We'll raise you. You'll always have the both of us. Soon, Blake and I will have children of our own. You'll be an uncle to them."

"I'll show them how to pet the horses and feed them apples."

"That'll be great, buddy. They'll have to learn the rules of the ranch, and you're just the man to show them." Blake ruffled Justin's hair and kissed him on the head.

"So, I can tell people you're my big brother?"

Blake smiled and held the boy close. "You sure can."

"Cool! And Gabe, and Caleb, and Dane, too."

"Yes," Blake said on a laugh. "All of them. Though I don't know why you'd want them, when you've got me."

"I'm glad I got you. I'm glad we came here and didn't have to leave."

Since Justin was happy with the situation, she looked to her grandparents.

"Grandpa, Grandma, if it's okay with you, I'd like to be married here at the ranch." Their eyes lit up and their smiles broadened. "Grandpa, if you'll give me away, I'd be honored."

"Ah, Gillian, I love you. It would be my honor to give you away."

They spent the rest of the morning sitting around

the breakfast table talking about wedding plans. Gillian finally had everything she'd ever wanted. A safe and loving home for Justin. A family who cared about them. And she had Blake, a good and decent man who loved her above all else. He would spend the rest of his life making her happy.

EPILOGUE

Eager to start the rest of their lives together, they were married two weeks later, the second Saturday in June. She wore a white gown that she and her grandmother picked out together. She carried a bouquet of red roses and lilacs, like the flowers Blake had left for her the morning of her birthday party. He looked so handsome in his tux, with Justin standing beside him in his own little tux as Blake's best man. Justin's new brothers, Gabe, Caleb, and Dane, stood beside them as well. Her new sisters, Ella and Summer, stood beside her in pretty purple gowns they picked out to complement each other. Summer had grown even rounder and more beautiful with her pregnancy. In a few short months, they'd welcome their little girl.

Gillian's grandfather walked her down the stairs to Blake. They were married by candlelight and firelight in the living room. Blake's parents looked so proud of their son and his bride. Her grandmother cried as the vows were said. Gillian even caught a glimpse of her grandfather wiping a tear away. Justin proudly handed over the rings he'd kept guard over all morning. When Blake slid her diamond wedding band onto her finger, he sealed it in place with a kiss. When the preacher pronounced them man and wife, everyone cheered, and Blake cupped her face in his hands and kissed her so achingly tenderly that the tears she'd tried to keep from shedding all morning slid down her cheeks.

Justin was excited about moving into Blake's house with them. They wanted him to have something special, so after the ceremony and a lovely dinner, Justin got the surprise he'd been wanting for a long time. Blake disappeared and came back and met Justin in the living room, a chocolate lab puppy biting at his heels. Justin went nuts. The two were inseparable from that day forward. Wherever Justin went, Charlie chased after him.

The first weekend in October, Boots won the first of several races. A champion again. As Gillian and Blake celebrated with everyone in the winner's circle, he picked her up and kissed her soundly to congratulate her.

"Hey, you're squishing us," she said playfully and kissed him again.

Blake held her close with her feet off the ground. He stared up at her as she smiled like a maniac down at him. "Us?"

"Us," she confirmed.

He boosted her up higher and kissed her belly and laid his forehead against her as she held onto his head with her fingers in his hair. He let her slide down his body until they were eye to eye. "You're sure? We're going to have a baby?"

"I'm sure. You'll have your baby in about eight months."

"But you never said . . ."

"When you asked me to marry you, you said you

wanted to have a baby whenever I was ready. I wanted it to be a surprise."

"It is," he said and smiled hugely. "This is the best surprise. I can't wait to tell the family."

"We'll tell them all together. We'll save Dane for when we see him ride in the Las Vegas bull riding championships in a couple of weeks."

He kissed her until Justin came to them and hugged both their legs together. They had so much to celebrate today.

Gillian bent to Justin's ear and whispered her good news. He smiled and jumped, pumping his fist in the air. "I'm going to be an uncle!"

Everyone in the winner's circle cheered and shouted congratulations.

Blake laughed, staring at his beautiful wife. She looked radiant. She looked happy. So far from the woman he'd seen get out of a truck more than six months ago. Life changes so fast. Gillian's was full of love and family now. And his was even better having her and Justin in it.

Gillian leaned up and kissed him. She settled into him, into her happiness, into her new life with such ease that she smiled.

A hawk flew above them, drifting on the wind, just like when she'd stopped the truck that first day before reaching her grandfather's ranch and the unknown. She finally felt as free as that bird. She had her family and Blake to thank for that.

Love had set her free and allowed her to soar.

Keep reading for a special sneak peek at the next book in *New York Times* bestselling author Jennifer Ryan's Montana Men series

HER LUCKY COWBOY

Everything's bigger in Big Sky country Including the hearts of the Montana Men

Champion rodeo rider Dane Bowden is eight seconds from winning under the Vegas lights. One last hurrah before reluctantly returning to his family's Montana ranch. But his bull has other plans. When Dane wakes up, he's sure he's died and gone to heaven . . . because the doctor who comes to his aid is the same girl who saved his life and disappeared years ago.

Bell would do anything for Dane. He's the fantasy that always kept her going. A child genius hidden away by her family, Bell was the secret no one talked about, the girl no one wanted. Despite finding success as a young surgeon, she's still the awkward girl who's never had a boyfriend. So why does Dane, a notorious play-boy and sizzling-hot cowboy, insist on taking her on a real date?

Bell is the only woman in Dane's heart. When a rodeo rivalry turns deadly, it's his turn to save Bell's life—because he sure as hell won't lose his guardian angel again.

COMING AUGUST 2015

PROLOGUE

Bowden Ranch, Montana – Eleven years ago

Dane was flying.

One moment he'd been riding his horse across the far reaches of his family's land, the next his horse reared up and kicked his massive hooves in the air, spooked by some unseen threat. Dane let loose the reins and fell sideways, hoping the horse didn't trample him. Dane's left foot hit the ground first, his ankle twisting painfully as his body slammed into the packed dirt and weeds. His shoulder hit next, breaking most of his upper body's fall, but his head smashed into a jagged rock. Pain exploded through his head.

Hombre galloped away. Alone now, Dane rolled and lay flat on his back, staring up at the canopy of tree branches overhead. The sound of the rushing river next to him added to his thrashing heartbeat in his ears. He rubbed his hands over his eyes, hoping that cleared his spotty double vision. His left hand came away wet and sticky with blood from the gash swelling on his head.

He closed his eyes tight, his hands falling limp on his stomach. When he opened them moments later, he stared into a pair of dazzling blue eyes. The young girl's dark hair hung down covering most of her pale face as she stared at him. The most beautiful girl he'd ever seen.

"Are you okay?"

Such a soft, sweet voice. Where had she come from? No one lived out here. He liked the peace and quiet. The solitude.

"I must be dead. You're an angel."

Those ethereal eyes went wide with surprise. "Trust me, I'm no angel." She filled those soft words with as much shock and disbelief as showed on her pretty face.

Calling her a liar probably wouldn't make her like him.

She crouched, opened her hand, and set a long blue feather on his chest before touching her fingers to his aching head. The sting made him hiss in pain. Definitely not dead. Which meant she was real. Despite his prone body and inability to think clearly, one thing came through loud and clear. He wanted to know this girl.

"I need to stop this bleeding."

He must have torn his T-shirt when he hit the ground. She ripped a piece free and walked to the edge of the river and dipped it in the icy water. His vision blurred. He closed his eyes and moaned when she pressed the cold cloth to his head.

"There now. You'll be okay."

At fifteen, the last thing he wanted to do was ask for help, but his head swam and his ankle throbbed in time to his heart and the headache pounding in his head. No way he got home on his own. "My ankle hurts. Please, you have to get my dad. Find one of my brothers."

Her soft hand settled on his chest over his heart. "You'll be okay." She snatched it back, like touching him burned her. He missed the sweet contact.

She reached for his foot and carefully pulled off his boot. He tried to bite back the groan, but it burst from his tight lips when the pain shot up his leg. Not cool to look like a wuss in front of a pretty girl, but with his head busted open, he was in bad shape.

She ripped his shirt again and used the long strip to bind his ankle. It actually felt better.

She sat beside him, her hands clenched in her lap. "I shouldn't be here. I shouldn't have touched you. I'm sorry."

He didn't understand her distress. He tried to sit up and comfort her, but fell back to the ground, his eyes closing as the blackness swamped his dizzy mind.

A hand settled on his shoulder and shook him. He groggily moaned and tried to open his eyes. The bright sun blinded him until his father leaned over and blocked the light as he stared down at Dane.

"Dad?"

"Are you okay, son? Is anything broken?"

"My head hurts. Ankle too, but nothing is broken but my pride. I fell off my damn horse."

"Okay, now. I'll get you home. Can you get up?"

"I think so." Dane pressed his hands down at his sides and rose to sitting. The wet piece of fabric fell from his head and landed on his bare belly along with the blue feather that fluttered into his lap. "Where is she?"

"Who?"

"The girl."

"Dane, no one is here."

"She helped me. She's got to be around here somewhere."

"There's no one for miles."

"How did you find me?"

"Your horse came home without you. I know you like to ride along the river, so I followed your trail." His dad cocked his head, his eyes taking on a thoughtful gleam. "I did think I heard you whistle for me."

"I passed out."

"Must have been the wind in the trees."

Dane didn't think so. He pinched the end of the feather between his thumb and index finger and stared at it. He scanned the riverbank and out toward the hills. He didn't see her anywhere. He didn't understand the way his chest went tight and the sadness that overtook him. Nothing but his regret that he didn't get to thank her, or say goodbye. He never got her name.

His dad held out his hand. Dane took it. His father pulled him up, and he stood on his good leg. He tested out his twisted ankle. The slight pressure sent a bolt of pain up his leg.

"How's your vision?"

"Better."

"You did a good job using your shirt to bind that ankle and staunch the bleeding on your head."

"I didn't. She did."

His father eyed him, shaking his head side to side. "Dane—"

"I'm telling you, Dad, there was a girl. She helped me."

"Okay, son. I believe you, but I didn't see anyone out here with you. I don't know where she could have gone. We're in the middle of nowhere."

Which was the reason Dane liked it out here so much. Still, how did she get out here, and where did she go?

He lifted himself up into the saddle and grabbed the reins on the horse his father brought back for him to ride. He kept his eyes trained, searching the entire area the whole way back home, but saw nothing, no one.

Dane went back to the spot beside the river more than a dozen times looking for his dark-haired, blue-eyed angel. He never found her, but he'd never forget her either.

CHAPTER 1

Bell loved everything about her first rodeo. The cowboys in their Wranglers and chaps. The beautiful horses. The excitement that built with every second of the ride. The lights in the arena, and the roar of the crowd as they cheered for each competitor. She'd never seen such a spectacle.

She'd thought the same thing when her plane flew over the Las Vegas strip the other day.

Her half-sister Katherine grabbed her arm when another bull burst out of the chute. The crowd's cheers turned to an ominous *oh* as the rider flew off the massive animal and landed on unsteady legs, making a run for the fences when the bull turned and rushed his way. Katherine's husband Tony waved his arms along with the other rodeo clowns to distract the beast from going after the retreating bull rider.

"He's so sexy," her sister said about Tony, finally letting go the death grip she had on Bell's arm.

Bell smiled at her vibrant sister, wondering how the hell they got here. Bell had tried to get out of this trip to Las Vegas and of all things, the Pro Bull Riders World Finals. She might be from Montana, but she'd never been a ranch girl.

Two years ago, Katherine showed up at her grandmother's house—Bell's purgatory—and discovered the family secret—a half-sister from an affair her father had years ago. The look on Katherine's face changed from shock to dawning understanding about all those snippets of whispered conversations between their father and her mother. For Katherine, it finally all made sense. Angry about being kept in the dark, she'd apparently contacted their father in California demanding answers. Only one was given. Bell may be Katherine's half-sister, but she was not family. Flabbergasted by their father's response, Katherine went against their father's dictates and continued to contact Bell.

While Katherine knew nothing of Bell, their grandmother rejoiced in sharing all the details of Katherine's blessed life, torturing Bell with the fact she was nothing more than an unwanted burden. Katherine had been the chosen one. Bell the whisper behind one's hand. The skeleton locked in the family closet. Never to be seen again.

Somehow Bell ended up here, sitting beside the woman who had the life Bell had once dreamed about. Katherine grew up in a beautiful home surrounded by love from both her parents. She'd been the golden, spoiled child.

Bell's life had been anything but charmed. Her whole family hated her, including the grandmother who raised her. A religious zealot, she'd told Bell every day that she was nothing but a sin, a spawn of evil, something to be hidden away from civilized, God-fearing people. Even her own parents recognized the evil in her and cast her out. She should be grateful her grandmother took pity on her and raised her, trying every day through prayer to convince God to save her from her wicked ways.

She'd lived in hell, under her grandmother's rigid dictates, enduring her sharp, bitter tongue. Because once she'd known kindness.

Before her grandfather died, he'd taken a keen interest in educating her and sparking her interest in gardening and raising chickens. She'd never forget the day he brought her outside to the new coop and asked her to hold out her hands and close her eyes. She cupped them in front of her, closed her eyes, and thrilled at the anticipation rising inside of her. He set something fuzzy in her hands. When she opened them, she squealed with delight at the bright yellow chick he'd given her and the ten others flitting about her feet.

She remembered his kind smile and the playful way he'd tug her hair when she did something well. She wished she remembered him better. For him, she continued to take care of her grandmother. One good deed deserved another. Though some kindnesses were harder to repay than others. And her grandmother made it extremely difficult to this day.

Why the hell did Bell agree to come here? They had nothing in common. Polar opposites, Katherine's optimism clashed with Bell's realistic outlook on life. Their awkward conversations and interaction proved the divide between them might never be bridged. Still, Katherine plugged on, trying and trying to connect with Bell, despite Bell's reluctance to open up. No one in the family ever wanted her. She didn't understand why Katherine cared, so she kept things polite but distant. Until Katherine begged her to take this trip with her and Tony. Bell gave in to that nagging voice in her heart, telling her to stop pushing Katherine away, let her in, and try to forge a relationship with her one and only sister.

So she'd flown in with Katherine and met Tony at the hotel after he drove his bulls in for the competition. She planned to make the most out of her short vacation and try to get to know Katherine better.

The crowd cheered again and Bell silently admitted she had another secret reason for coming. A chance to see *him* again.

"Our last rider of the night," the announcer began. "A man who needs no introduction. Dane Bowden!"

The crowd went wild, rising to their feet, fists pumping in the air, cheering, "Great Dane. Great Dane. Great Dane."

Bell sat on the edge of her seat, heart in her throat, eyes locked on the man she hadn't seen since that day his horse threw him by the river. He climbed up onto the gates of the chute, pulled off his black Stetson, and gave a single wave to the crowd, flashing that devilish grin she remembered from her childhood. Everything in her went still, the crowd and noise fell away, and all she could see was the man she could never forget.

Geared up in his safety vest, chaps, spurs, and signature black Stetson, Dane climbed over the rails and into the bucking chute and took his position on the beast's black back. Twelve hundred pounds of pent-up raging bull beneath him, he slipped his hand beneath the flat braided cord, pulled the rope over his hand, secured his grip, and held on for dear life. Eight seconds to decide where he'd land between victory and death.

It sucked that he had a tear along the thumb in his favorite pair of deerskin gloves, but he tried not to let it throw him off his game. Someone had been messing with him, his gear, and his truck for the last two weeks but nothing could stop Dane today. He'd always been able to put everything aside, focus, and reach for that thrill and the win. This was his last championship ride, and he meant to go out a winner. He'd promised his parents and brothers he'd come home, run the family ranch, give up his wandering ways and settle down to a normal—boring—life.

Yeah, right after this ride.

He'd tame this black beast tonight, then deal with the one within when he settled back home in Montana. Tonight, he'd ride under the Las Vegas lights.

Dane nodded, the chute door opened, and the bull bucked and reared. Dane held tight, one arm in the air as the bull twisted and the crowd went wild. He sank his spurs into the bull's side, held tight with his knees, and moved with Black Cloud. The bull kicked, reared, and spun around. Blake held tight for another round. Time to get off this ride, collect his winnings, and go out number one. The spot he'd been chasing these last years, but always seemed one place out of his grasp. With three big brothers, first always seemed out of reach. He'd been second this whole year. Might as well be last. Tonight, he'd finish first. A champion.

The buzzer sounded eight seconds. Done. Victory. Dane smiled as the crowd cheered.

There are two great athletes in every ride. The two-legged one won this time.

Dane tried to dismount, but the bull spun at the last second and caught him in the side before his feet hit the ground. The rodeo clowns moved forward in his peripheral vision, but not in time. Black Cloud turned, rammed his head into Dane's chest, and sent him flying again. The impact pushed the air and his mouth guard out of his mouth. He bit the side of his lip and tasted blood. Sideways in the air, his left foot touched the ground first, then his body slammed into the dirt. His head bounced with the impact, making his vision spark and blur, but not before he saw the bull's body swing over the top of him in slow motion, his massive hooves coming down at Dane's legs, snapping his left leg bones like twigs. The flesh tore along with his jeans. White-hot pain shot through every nerve like lightning. Dane's heart jack-hammered in his chest and ears. The bull rammed him again with his huge head, sliding Dane several feet along the dirt. The fierce pain shot through him, stealing his breath. His heart slammed into his ribs.

Shit. This can't be it. I can't go out like this.

So many things he wanted to do with his life. Instead of the past coming back to him, flashes of all he'd never do ran through his mind. He'd never run his own ranch. Never get married. Never have children. Never know the kind of love and happiness the rest of his family had found.

Damn if fate hadn't swung the rope, lassoed his life, and yanked him from victory toward death.

Overwhelmed with pain, his body went numb, a collective gasp went up from the crowd, and the lights went out.

At Avon Books, we know your passion for romance—once you finish one of our novels, you find yourself wanting more.

May we tempt you with . . .

- **Excerpts** from our upcoming releases.

- Entertaining **extras**, including authors' personal photo albums and book lists.

- Behind-the-scenes **scoop** on your favorite characters and series.

- **Sweepstakes** for the chance to win free books, romantic getaways, and other fun prizes.

- Writing **tips** from our authors and editors.

- **Blog** with our authors and find out why they love to write romance.

- **Exclusive content** that's not contained within the pages of our novels.

Join us at
www.avonbooks.com

AVON

An Imprint of HarperCollins*Publishers*
www.avonromance.com

Available wherever books are sold or please call 1-800-331-3761 to order.

FTH 1013